A sweeping novel of two powerful families bound together by greed, obsession and revenge . . .

To a passing stranger, the exquisite, high-born Angie Wyatt seems perfectly in control of herself and her surroundings. But that is only a skillful facade. . . .

When her husband suddenly dies, Angie decides to go back home to London, where her father, the austere Sir Jarman, owns one of the biggest publishing empires in the world.

After years of working and living in Manhattan, Angie believes that the past no longer has the power to hurt her. She's wrong. The intricate lives of the people around her are about to unravel—and Angie is the catalyst. For her icily patrician parents, her return is an unwelcome intrusion to their well-ordered lives. For her brother Oliver, she is one more reason to drink himself into oblivion. For Paul Angelou, the powerful, charismatic entrepreneur, she is the first real threat he has ever faced. He becomes totally obsessed by her—even as he realizes he can never possess her.

And Angie, who has spent most of her life running away, now finds herself fighting for survival in a complex world of ambition and corruption—a world where the ultimate abuse of power leads to the ultimate crime. . . .

RELATIVE STRANGERS

Maureen Rissik

BALLANTINE BOOKS • NEW YORK

Library of Congress Catalog Card Number: 86-21749

ISBN 0-345-35238-6

This edition published by arrangement with William Morrow and Company, Inc.

Manufactured in the United States of America

First Ballantine Books Edition: March 1988

For my mother and father

I would like to thank my family and friends for their unstinting support and encouragement, especially Jenny Howson for all her practical and cheerful help; Fanny Blake and Antonia Till for their skill and patience, and June Hall for putting up with yet another neurotic first novelist. But most of all, my grateful thanks to Moris, Nina, and Rachel Farhi for their love and generosity. It's only real because the Turk said so.

Part
One

1

☐ The sound of the rain drumming on the flat roof woke her up for the second time in an hour. Disoriented, Angie stretched out her arm, then pulled it back. Lou wasn't there. She turned quickly and lifted her head to look at the illuminated face of a tiny digital clock. Three hours into the first anniversary of his death, and she still awoke to find herself on the other side of the bed, where she'd moved to find him.

The air in the vast room was tepid, but Angie was conscious that her hands and feet felt icy, her breasts chilled. She switched on the bedside lamp, slid out of bed, and pulled a flimsy cotton dressing gown over her nakedness. Her mouth felt dry, and her limbs heavy with exhaustion. She went to the fridge and stared for a moment at a carton of orange juice; then she shut the door again, picked up a large tumbler, and found the bottle of Black Horse whiskey where she'd left it: on the floor beside Lou's favorite piece of furniture—a grotesquely uncomfortable sofa with rickety legs and stuffing that oozed like brain matter through a faded gray covering. "It looks like a botched vivisection," she'd commented the first time she'd walked into the room. He hadn't disagreed.

Angie had arrived back in New York from New Orleans earlier that afternoon. She'd gone straight from the airport to the office and, under the concerned eye of Maxwell Reith, worked through the next few hours. The ABA, where publishers presold their forthcoming books to the country's booksellers, had accounted for four days of frenzied activity. The trip had been successful, she knew. There was no need to prove it to herself by laboriously tying up every loose end. At eight-thirty Maxwell had taken the dictaphone from her hand, picked up her suitcase, and steered her out of the Bennett-Poore Building. He had fed her and talked into the silences, and it was past midnight before he took her home.

Lou's best friend did everything but press the button for the seventh floor in the juddering old commercial elevator.

Lou had occupied the top floor of the converted warehouse on Broome Street for more than twelve years; Greenwich Village was around the corner; to the south was Little Italy and, farther down, Chinatown. Soon after their marriage he'd confided his early fear that she would want to move uptown, where her money would have ensured both status and more comfort. By that time he'd known her well enough not to be surprised when she told him that the idea had actually never occurred to her. She loved the high-ceilinged room with its utilitarian finishes. Old wood barn siding covered the brickwork, squat radiators ran along the skirting boards, and thick Aztec-patterned rugs were scattered over the hardwood floor. Two of the four wide windows faced north and dazzled them with light. They'd spoken from time to time about getting more bookshelves built; it had bothered Lou more than Angie that books leaned against the base of their bed and stood in piles around the screen that sectioned off a tiny kitchen.

Angie pushed away the image of Lou on his knees, peering short-sightedly at the faint lettering on a spine. This space was still so unmistakably his. His clothes hung in the cupboards; his typewriter, jam jars spiked with pencils, reams of paper, and lined yellow writing pads were where he'd left them. . . .

The room was suddenly stifling. Angie lit a cigarette and was splashing whiskey into the tumbler when the telephone began to ring. At three o'clock in the morning it could only be Oliver. Or Cissy. And she had no intention of speaking to either her brother or his wife. She downed the whiskey in a quick gulp; then, trying to shut out the sound of the telephone by letting in the sound of the rain, she attempted to raise one of the heavy sash windows one-handed. The effort brought a sheen of perspiration to her face. The panel stuck halfway up but let in enough air to dampen a flare of nausea.

Clutching the bottle and glass to her chest, she eased herself over the sill and out onto the fire escape. Within seconds her hair was plastered down over her head and the dressing gown clung where it touched. The sound that escaped from her lips was half shock, half pleasure as she slid down onto the studded surface of the platform. She came to rest with her shoulders against one of the massive cast-iron girders that ran up either side of the open window behind her. The metal felt cool through the material of her gown, and the whiskey was beginning to coax some sort of symmetry into the night. The lights of midtown Manhattan winked at her. The city had hunkered down around her like a warm, steamy animal; another two hours would pass before it stirred and yawned up into the unseasonal humidity of this late May weather.

The telephone had stopped ringing, but that didn't mean that they had given up. "You can't stay there forever," Cissy shouted at Angie each time Oliver, frustrated by his sister's transatlantic silences, handed the phone over. "It's not even as if you're holding down a proper job. At least come back for a few weeks."

Angie had not attempted to explain. She couldn't have, even if she'd tried. The past year had simply been a year of her life without Lou, nothing more. She'd worked occasionally on special publishing assignments; the people she saw were mostly Lou's friends, who still missed his amiable presence. And she had no doubt at all that their unruffled tolerance of her these last few months had everything to do with their clear memory of him. She had done nothing herself to earn their company or their kindnesses. Without their friendship and patience the city would have been a desperately lonely place.

A flash of lightning scarred the horizon over the East River. Angie listened for the sound of thunder, which was unexpectedly close when it came. Rainwater diluted the whiskey in her glass. She brought her knees up and hugged them to her chest. Oliver wasn't responsible for her; neither was his wife. They never had been. She could not get this through to her brother. Three years ago he had entrusted her to Lou, handed over his imagined responsibility like a relieved father marrying off a spinster daughter. Now, with Lou gone, he wanted her back in London again, somewhere close where he could keep an eye on her. It was absurd, particularly as she had not lived in England for any length of time over the past fifteen years.

Going back to England was something she and Lou had planned to do together. They would do it when the time was right, he said, and that would be up to Angie. She would know when she was ready. Lou had made it sound so *simple* for her. . . . Angie shivered and shook water out of her eyes. Why was she sitting out in the rain? This wasn't the fine, misty wetness of a shower in Sussex; there was no one to call

her in out of this lusty, sheeting downpour. Sussex . . . elm,
oak, birch. She searched her memory, rummaging carefully
through the silt of twenty years but couldn't make a connection between then and now. But there had to be something.
"Bring it out, dust if off, and let's take a look." Who'd said
that? It sounded like Lou, but she could not remember. Not
Oliver. Cissy perhaps? *Benn!* Puzzled, Angie put the glass
down and covered her ears with her hands, trying to concentrate. Benn. She hadn't thought of him in a long time. The
butler went with Calvert Hall; the two were inextricable. . . .

She would not let her mind play tricks on her, but the
sound of the rain was having an isolating, womblike effect.
Angie winced as a clap of thunder exploded directly overhead. Her hands came away from her ears, and she saw herself looping the cord of her dressing gown about her wrist.
And she saw Benn unraveling it, pulling at it crossly. "These
are reins, not ribbons. What will happen if you fall off?" He
never told her what would happen if she fell off Oliver's pony.
Oliver did. "You'll be dragged, and your arm will come off."
She'd gone on doing it because it sounded risky and because
she felt brave even when no one was there to notice.

She tugged at the cord, pulling it tight around her wrist.
She knew where her thoughts were taking her: back to Calvert
Hall, back to Sussex, and back nearly twenty years. Lou had
been no part of it, but it was his voice that echoed eerily in
her head. "It happened, there's nothing you can do about
that. I'll be with you when we find out, and we *will* find out,
I promise you that."

"You lied," she whispered. "You lied, and you left me."
She turned and lifted her face up to the rain, her mind exploding with loathing and fear and the pain of inducing oblivion. . . .

The year Oliver brought Andrew Colquhoun and George
McFee home for the Christmas vacation, Angie was seventeen. The three men arrived unannounced, to the obvious
displeasure of Belinda Jarman.

"I expect you to keep your rooms in order, young man."
She addressed Oliver as though he were ten, not twenty. "You
will be fed if you arrive at the table on time, and I expect
you to be civil to the staff and appear at Mass on Sunday
morning."

They were all in the drawing room. It was an appropriate

setting, Angie thought, watching her mother. As she was faced with the unexpected, Belinda Jarman's high-cheek-boned aristocratic features looked set to quiver with annoyance. Her eyebrows swooped down, echoing with eloquence the tightening of her beautiful lips. Without doubt, the dignity and grandeur of the drawing room at Calvert Hall suited the present Lady Jarman exactly. Richly paneled and decorated with voluptuous limewood carvings, the room had an ambience nonetheless austere; a functional elegance overlapped any suggestion of softness, just as it did the woman who stood at its center. Calvert Hall was Belinda Jarman's domain, and she controlled it and everyone in it with a glance that weakened the knees and brought instinctive apologies to the lips.

Angie could see that her tone surprised Oliver's friends. Well, if they were going to spend two or three weeks at the Hall, it was just as well that they accept her mother's rules sooner rather than later. It was all too easy to be fooled by that delicate beauty, to mistake the touch of color in those cheeks for something other than asperity.

Angie could not hide her delight. She grinned at the three men, despite the look of dull moodiness on her brother's face. He was taller than the other two and gauntly handsome, with light brown hair and his mother's gray eyes. He was the most casually dressed, in sweater and flannels, and he held a cigarette between thumb and forefinger, rolling it back and forth with short, nervous movements. Andrew Colquhoun was ginger-haired, with a small ginger mustache which served to elongate his freckled, mousy features. George McFee looked like a boxer, bulky and muscled, with a slightly flattened nose and vivid blue eyes.

"Who would this be then?" George grinned back at Angie.

Oliver turned toward her as if she'd just come into the room. "My sister, Angie. Andrew . . . George. See the dragon, George?" He nodded in the direction of the door his mother had just shut behind her. They all laughed, and Angie blushed, feeling suddenly silly in jodhpurs and riding boots. She turned to leave.

"Don't go." George stepped forward, took the riding crop from her hand, and tested its sting against his open palm. He grimaced. "Effective. Do you have to use it much?"

Before she could answer, he had leaned over and was slashing the tip of the crop against Andrew's shoes. Andrew yelped and leaped backward, catapulting over the back of a settee. There was a moment of guilty silence before Oliver's bellow of laughter rang out.

"So that's how you make a horse jump a fence." George placed his arm companionably across Angie's shoulders and felt her tremble with suppressed amusement as Andrew's astonished face peered out over the top of the settee. "Maybe I could try it out on the real thing sometime?"

"Of course," Angie said. "I'm sure Oliver—"

"Ollie's no horseman, he's told us." George winked at Oliver. "Right?"

Oliver glanced at her without expression and said, "Right." It sounded grudging. She was about to contradict him when he snatched the riding crop from George's hand and held it out to her. He was asking her to leave. Angie shrugged out from beneath George's weighty arm and walked out of the room with as much nonchalance as she could muster. By the time she reached her bedroom, a sharp, familiar sense of loneliness had colored her joy at having Oliver home for the holidays. She had been foolish to imagine that anything had changed.

If someone had asked her to pinpoint the time when it had all begun to shift, she would have said the summer of three years before. It had to do with so many things that she could no longer distinguish one from another. Oliver had been the focus of all her years until then, the buffer between her and the world of her parents. How, then, had that mocking gentleness with which he teased, questioned, and supported her disappeared so suddenly? Where had the carelessness, the vast lack of interest in the minutiae of her life come from? Oliver had always been ready to join in her games, but then, as now, she recognized a movement away.

Angie went to the window and drew the curtains, shutting out the gray afternoon light. She sat down on the bed and began to pull off her boots. She told herself loftily that she didn't care, that she understood his behavior. He was, after all, a sophisticated man. At twenty he was being groomed to take over Jarman's, one of the largest and most distinguished publishing houses in the country. She was an adolescent, leggy, gauche, given to sudden passions, aching to break out of the confines of school, uniforms, and gym classes. They lived on different planes. It was as simple as that.

Angie scarcely set eyes on the three men during the following weeks. When she did bump into Oliver, he was silent and morose. The other two, particularly George McFee, were like boisterous puppies. Twice she saw them trying to force Oliver into something he didn't want to do; on both occasions George delivered what looked like painful punches to Oliver's upper arms, and Andrew made him squirm by digging his fingers into Oliver's ribs. It was embarrassing but successful. Without giving it much thought, Angie assumed that they were spending their days in London with friends. She knew they were drinking a lot, and she knew that Oliver was drinking more than either of the other two. When they appeared at breakfast, she kept her glance averted and ate quickly. They drank orange juice and black coffee and remained sheepishly silent.

On the morning of New Year's Eve she awoke early and had coffee in the kitchen with Benn, the butler, who crouched over the table, both hands clasped around a hot mug. The air outside was biting, and Angie knew how the cold seeped into his arthritic fingers.

"You're going to ask why I'm not wearing the mittens you gave me," he said. "Please don't."

"I wasn't going to."

"Good."

She left him sitting at the table and went outside. The cold took her breath away. She retreated to the back steps and surveyed the singular brightness of this winter morning. The area between the hall and the greenhouses had begun to take on that tattered look the wind brought. Leaves, shriveled and mixed with feathers, skated across the frozen ground. The wind dipped and dragged. Today it came without the smell of hay and horses, and this somehow made it an intruder, even less friendly.

Oliver was breakfasting alone on black coffee, as usual. He didn't hear her come into the room, and the sound of her voice startled him. "Angie?" He passed his hand over his eyes, as though he were having trouble focusing.

"Oliver, what's going on?"

"Not you, too. . . ."

"What do you mean?" She saw his features draw into a stubborn line. "All I was going to say was—"

"Well, don't! I feel like hell."

"I'm not sure I like your friends, Oliver," she said honestly. "I don't like what you're doing."

"And what do you think we're doing? Do you think they care whether you like them or not? That *I* care? Grow up, there's a good girl."

"Don't you dare patronize me!" Angie hissed.

Benn came in with a pot of fresh coffee. They waited in silence until he'd left, and then Oliver said, "I'm sorry, I didn't mean—"

"Can we talk? Just the two of us, before you leave next week?"

"Yes." Oliver made a small, uneasy movement with his hand. "Of course."

"When?" she asked insistently.

"How the hell should I know?" he flared, crashing the cup down onto its saucer. "Tomorrow . . . next week. How the hell should I know?"

She heard him thudding up the stairs, and a few minutes later the three of them roared off in the Land-Rover and did not reappear until early evening.

Her mother had had for once no choice but to join her husband in London. The servants had been given the night off for their own celebrations.

At eleven-thirty Oliver knocked briefly and shuffled into her room. He looked wild and disheveled and maniacally happy. He fell onto her bed and draped his arm over her. "I've come to talk," he said sonorously.

Angie sat up and pushed him away. "You're drunk."

"OK, I'm drunk and I want to talk."

"Go away, Oliver, please. I'm going to bed."

"No, look, you're dressed. Come downstairs and have a drink. My friends like you very much, d'you know that?"

Angie remembered the first time Oliver had offered her a drink from his hip flask. It had seemed wicked, adult. She'd tipped the neck of the flask into her mouth and exploded in a fit of coughing as the undiluted gin hit the back of her throat. He'd laughed. When she stopped coughing, she'd laughed, too. And sipped some more because it had been such a long time since they'd shared anything.

"You're bleeding," Angie said. There was a scratch high up on his forehead, near the hairline.

Oliver dabbed one finger on it and sighed. "Do you remember all those extravagant designs for liberation and equality we planned in the cellar, Angie?"

Angie smiled despite herself. "You never allowed me to

be a real freedom fighter. You were always bandaging the baddies even before I got around to planting the dynamite.''

"If I let you, you'd have blown up half the country. Who were we trying to liberate anyway?''

"Benn. Mostly Benn.''

"What would he have done with his freedom, d'you think?''

"I don't know. Hated it probably. What would we have done without him? Not you so much . . . me?''

Oliver sighed again. "It was a good game, though.''

Angie said nothing. A radio was on somewhere downstairs, but the sound was so distant that it seemed to add to the silence.

"Ollie?'' George called from the doorway. "We've been looking for you. Bring Angie and come downstairs.'' He looked enormous in the doorway.

"You go, Oliver,'' Angie said.

"Come on, Angie,'' George cajoled. "We'll be going in a few days, and . . . come on down for a drink. Let's see the new year in together.''

"No, thank you,'' Angie said tightly.

George, obviously drunk as well, said, "Methinks the lady protesteth too mucheth. Ollie?''

Oliver smiled at her ingenuously, paused, and seemed to be weighing his words. "All right, Angie. I just wanted to— I just wanted—''

"You coming, Ollie?''

"Where?'' Oliver hiccuped, easing himself off the bed.

"For a drive, why not? Let's drive somewhere and have a drink, see the new year in. What do you say?''

"Good idea, George.''

"Drive?'' Dread enveloped Angie like a billow of smoke. "You're drunk, both of you. You can't drive, for God's sake.''

Oliver took her face between his hands. "Then you'll drive us, won't you, Angie? Please? We'll get a taxi back. . . .''

What happened to you? She wanted to hit him, to punch him into sensibility. He was smiling at her crookedly, pointing at his forehead. "Look, I'm wounded.''

That made her smile. "All right, but only because . . . you're hurt. Where to?'' She took up a thick woolen cardigan and followed them downstairs.

Tonbridge, they said, hooting and shouting and stumbling about. George snaked a massive arm around her waist when

Oliver wasn't looking. She pulled away and aimed a good-natured slap at him. They all seemed to find that hilarious. Angie felt like a reproving grandmother as she accepted some sherry from Andrew. They toasted each other, and Oliver leaned over to whisper something into her ear. She didn't catch it but was happy enough to assume that it was complimentary.

George clambered into the front seat of the Land-Rover with two full bottles of wine in his pockets. Angie turned the ignition key. It was unbelievably cold, and her head had begun to ache.

She drove in silence, listening to George and Andrew trying to outdo each other's schoolboy cracks. The gist was unmistakable but also inoffensive. She even smiled to herself, aloofly, in the darkness. Oliver was snoring on the back seat; perhaps he would have sobered up by the time they reached Tonbridge.

Two miles from Calvert Hall George suddenly clutched at himself with one hand and put the other on her knee and squeezed. "Turn off here, darling."

Angie pushed his hand away. "Why? There's nothing down there."

"Oh, yes, there is: the river. Going for a swim, are we, George?" Andrew sounded excited. Oliver was slumped against him, breathing heavily.

"Swim?" George guffawed. "No, I've got to have a pee."

Angie sighed. She slowed down and drew up near a patch of dense shrubbery. George slid out of the car, whistling with relief. In the back seat Andrew was trying to wake Oliver.

Angie looked around. Trees, sodden leaves, blackness beyond the beams of the headlights. It wasn't a good night for driving; a thin sheeting of ice cracked under the tires, and there'd been seconds when she'd had no control at all over the car's movements.

Andrew gave up trying to wake Oliver. "Hey, I think he's fallen into the river," he said.

"George? I don't think so. It's more than half a mile away."

Ten minutes later there was still no sign of George. The interior of the Land-Rover had become uncomfortably stuffy, condensation streaking down the side windows.

"I think I'd better go and look for him," Andrew said. "Damn fool, he's probably passed out somewhere. You'll have to come with me, in case."

Angie hesitated. Andrew was right. If George had passed out, he'd need help to get him back to the car. "Oliver." She turned, hoping to see Oliver sitting up and grinning at her. All she heard was a rasping snore. "I think we should all go back to the hall when we've found George," she said.

"All right by me," Andrew grunted as they got out of the car and crossed a grassy embankment glittering with frost. "You follow me."

They walked unsteadily in the darkness, Andrew calling out his friend's name. They'd gone no more than a hundred yards when George leaped out between them. Andrew spun away but managed to keep his feet. Angie caught hold of George's jacket for support. "Where have you been?"

"Reconnoitering the layout of the territory." He slurred the words. "Couldn't find the river, though. Do you know where it is?"

Angie turned away. "I know, but not tonight, George. Come on, we're going back to the Hall."

George caught her arm. "No, wait. You're very pretty, do you know that?"

"Thank you. Shall we go now?"

"Pretty but uppity. Don't you like me?"

"I like you," Angie countered lightly. "I like you both, but I'm freezing to death here."

Before she could move, George had his arms around her. Crushed against his chest, Angie tried to ignore the first stirrings of fear. As she turned to find Andrew, George enclosed her chin and mouth in his palm and wrenched her face to the front. "Let's you and me go for a walk," he whispered.

"No," she snapped, trying to free herself. "Andrew!"

"Forget Andrew, just you and me . . ."

"Hey, George," Andrew called out. "Hey, maybe we . . ."

"Piss off, Andrew. George gets his on New Year's Eve. You go screw yourself."

"I'm not going anywhere with you, George," Angie panted, trying to dig her heels into the soft earth as he pulled her behind him. "What are you doing?" He ignored her, and she turned, reaching up to rake her nails across his face, to shock him into releasing her.

He didn't bother to take her much farther. With the stumbling, erratic movements of a drunk, he tore at the zipper of her jeans. She kicked out at him, coldly furious and humiliated.

"Do that again," he said quietly, "and I'll break your arm, understand?"

Angie lashed out at his face, and immediately his fist buried itself under her ribs. All the life in her body exploded out from her lungs, and the world went from black to red. He released her and watched as she doubled over in agony, mouth wide open and gasping for air. Everything else receded; only the intolerable pain of trying to breathe remained. She was still on her knees when Andrew appeared. For a wild moment she thought he was going to help her. Using what little breath she had left, she cried, "Help me! For God's sake, help me, Andrew!"

Maybe he didn't hear. Together they pushed her down onto the wet leaves and straightened her body. She tried to curl up again, fighting her fear and the pain that was tearing her apart. Andrew, encouraged by the silence, yanked her hands away from her midriff and up over her head. Angie became minutely aware of what was happening, the sound of material as her jeans were jerked down, her cardigan opened, and her T-shirt pushed up. She felt her hands and wrists sink into the mud as Andrew knelt on them. Above her the sky was clear, the stars bright and cold. Hands pulled, tugged, kneaded, spread. An icy chill touched her nipples briefly, then a warm alien sensation as lips closed on first one and then the other.

She fought silently, twisting, trying to bring her knees up to gain leverage. A mouth leaned over, impersonal, unattached, and fixed itself over hers. It crossed her mind that being kissed while being raped was more obscene than anything else. She gagged. The mouth clung like a limpet, taking her cries, swallowing her pain. Then her head was free, the mouth was gone, and she could breathe. The first thing she did was cry out, but because they were hurting her, no longer because she was afraid. A hand chafed between her thighs, rubbing at the dryness. She lurched away in fury as they touched her, burning with the hurt and indignity of it. Fingers invaded her, then another impossible pain. She could do nothing, held, spread-eagled, impaled in the wet undergrowth. George bore down again and again, urged on by the watching Andrew. Then he spasmed briefly, withdrew, and it began again. Neither held her now. The stars spun overhead in the cold sky as they drew grunts of pain from her at will.

Then it was over.

* * *

The telephone exploding into life again brought her to her feet on the fire escape. In the drowning blackness she conjured up Benn's face, his light blue eyes shocking into her system. He'd cleaned her up that night, swabbed away the mud in a shallow bath, and bound her bruised ribs, all the time talking to her, softly, as one would to a startled colt. . . .

Momentarily blinded by the rain, she leaned over and fumbled for the whiskey bottle with her left hand while trying to pull the cord of her dressing gown from the other wrist. She cursed, shivering in the darkness, as the bottle slipped from her fingers and shattered around her bare feet. Every muscle in her body was now cramped with cold.

She turned toward the half-open window, groping onehanded for the sill even as both feet started to slip on the smooth studs. Twisting to keep her balance, she was unnerved by the realization that she felt no fear, only scorn at her own stupidity, as she went down into the broken glass. There was a brief sensation of pain as the base of what remained of the bottle tore into her lower forearm and the corner stanchion of the platform caught the side of her head. A warm gout of blood ran down her wrist and over her hand. Dazed, she got to her feet again. Her right hand had freed itself in the fall; she patted her shoulder and hip, feeling for other wounds, but it was just her arm dripping blood onto the broken glass.

"What do you make of this, old man?" she growled into the rain, edging carefully back toward the window. He had seen the end of what had been started that night; he'd been with her until the last moments before her daughter was born. Do you know where she is? He knew. There was no way he couldn't. . . .

She clambered back into the room and turned to close the window, immediately shocked to see herself covered with blood. The telephone was still ringing. First things first. She lifted the hem of her gown and pulled the material over her arm. To her inexperienced eye the sheer volume of blood was alarming; but the gash was long and straight, and she'd somehow managed to avoid severing an artery.

She peeled off the sodden gown and found Lou's heavy terry-cloth robe. With fingers clumsy with cold, she knotted a kitchen towel over the wound as tightly as she could, staunching the worst of the bleeding. Then she sat down on Lou's gray sofa and picked up the phone.

2

☐ The British Airways terminal at Kennedy Airport was unusually crowded for the time of night. There seemed to be a lot of children running around in circles, playing tag among the suitcases. As Paul Angelou walked in, the hubbub suddenly died down as the tannoy crackled, twice. When no message came through, the level of noise rose once more and settled at its former pitch.

Paul gestured brusquely in the direction of the first-class check-in desk and followed the porter wheeling his luggage. The man moved purposefully, scything through the crowd, missing shins and buttocks by millimeters. Paul was grateful for his silence and his speed. The sooner he got out of the crush and into the executive lounge, the better. Everything to do with Arion—even a phone call from the old man, innocuous as it had turned out—made him feel harried.

Paul had accepted the call from his father because Arion had never before telephoned him in his Wall Street office. When the telephonist had ignored an earlier instruction and put the call through, Paul had been surprised enough to lift the receiver. He'd experienced a slight start of apprehension as Arion's voice reached him. Arion would call from London only if something had happened to Ani. Or to Susan or Benjamin. He would take it upon himself to call Paul in those circumstances. The fact that the conversation had in the end had nothing to do with his mother's health or that of his wife and son had annoyed Paul instantly.

He listened because he had no choice. Had he been alone, he would simply have refused Arion's idiotic request. As it was, he sat through an unsolicited report on his mother's activities and tried to ignore the amused glances from his three codirectors. This sort of thing happened to other people, never to Paul Angelou. He was on the third and last day of his monthly visit to New York. As usual, the schedule he had imposed on himself and the three other men in the room had been a strenuous one. At ten-thirty in the morning a working breakfast was behind him and he was fifteen minutes into his second meeting of the day.

He was just about to interrupt Arion's monologue when his father said, "Frank Sheldon. You know Frank?"

"Of course I know him," Paul replied flatly. And you know I'd cross the road to avoid him, he added to himself. He loathed everything about Sheldon, from the way he spoke to the casual way he dressed, and it had nothing to do with the long-standing friendship between Arion and the younger man.

"Do you remember the mantilla Frank brought back for your mother the first time he went to New York?"

"Mantilla? You're calling me about . . ." Paul stopped. Arion was being deliberately slow and provocative, which meant that he was enjoying himself. He knew exactly how inconvenient this call was, that there were other people in the room. Paul felt a throb of fury pulse through his body. "Wait!" he snapped into the receiver, and turned to the other men. "This shouldn't take long, gentlemen, but we might as well break for coffee now. Kindly adjourn, and I'll join you in a moment."

He waited until they had filed out of his office and then lifted his hand from the mouthpiece. Before he could say anything, Arion was talking again. "Ani has said nothing but yesterday I saw that the lace has many holes—"

The gently teasing note in his father's voice infuriated Paul. "I would prefer to call you back later," he interrupted, with no intention of doing so.

"No, no, listen. I know you have important people with you. Your girl, the one who answers the telephone, said so. But this is important to me, you understand? Your mother wears the mantilla for church every day . . . you will do this for me?"

At least he had the grace to make it sound like a question, not a demand, Paul thought. And he had yet to say exactly what it was he wanted Paul to do: replace the worn mantilla Frank Sheldon had given Ani more than ten years ago.

Paul had promised nothing, scribbling down the name of a shop in Little Italy that probably no longer existed. It was just what he needed after three exhausting days in New York. Apart from the nuisance value, he had no desire to involve

himself with anything even remotely connected with Frank
Sheldon. . . .

There was only one couple ahead of him at the check-in
desk. As he took his place behind them, Paul made a conscious effort to quell his irritation. Arion would never change.
He mostly feigned ignorance of the distance Paul had imposed on their relationship, although he realized full well that
his son had deliberately constructed his life in such a way
that contact between them would be minimal. He applauded
Paul's success while pretending that the world of the commodity broker was far too complicated for an old man with
no formal education. Paul knew differently. His father had a
keen knowledge and understanding of the stock market in all
its guises. It hadn't been simply luck and hard work that had
brought Arion Angelou his fortune.

A shabby gray bear, that was how he saw his father, someone who took an almost obsessive pride in concealing his
wealth. Paul had long since decided that the old man's behavior was an elaborate game, a masterly disguise he adopted
to enhance his own power and mystique. Why else would a
man who could have afforded a fleet of cars still ride a deliv-
ery boy's bicycle—at least until two years ago, when Ani had
put a stop to it? Paul's mother had confiscated the bicycle,
not because it was unseemly for Arion to be seen riding it
but because the narrow streets of Soho had become too con-
gested with cars. Paul knew that his father saw nothing incongruous in sitting on a Soho doorstep in cardigan and
sandals, sharing koulourakia and coffee with an old crony,
when he owned one of the best restaurants in London. The
old man combined the role of peasant with the role of benefactor. Like a village elder, he dispensed wisdom and largess.
Yet Paul knew for certain that Arion now bore no more resemblance to the penniless Greek immigrant of the 1940s
than the Soho of the 1980s did to the village it had once been.

The girl behind the desk slipped his boarding card in between the leaves of his ticket and held both out to him with
a quick, professional smile. Paul returned the smile and was
rewarded with "Have a good flight, sir."

That was precisely his intention, the reason why he had
decided against Concorde, to give himself more time. He was
looking forward to the next few hours and the luxury of running through his plan in uninterrupted detail once more. Now
that he had decided to go ahead, he found a curious exhila-

ration in probing those areas of the plan over which he would eventually have little control. He was not a gambler. He seldom took chances and never allowed himself to rely on other people. For the first time in his life he was about to break all his own rules.

Beaumont Gracie had, on his instructions, investigated no fewer than nine potential recruits without being specifically aware of what Paul was looking for. The aging investigator was good and Paul had, in the past, been cautious enough to use him sparingly; but in this instance he had simply bought a year of Gracie's time.

Gracie's instructions were, as always, essentially the same. When Paul Angelou called for a rundown, he meant a complete picture. Occasionally he would specify an area, ask Gracie for a report on a client's financial status alone or his business methods. But more often than not Gracie would be left to his own devices and produce a comprehensive document which covered not only the subject's own life but the lives of those closest to him—whether they were colleagues, friends, or family. No detail was too small to be included. *That* was what he was being paid for. How Paul Angelou used the information was none of his business.

Whichever way Paul examined his final choice, it came out right. He'd known from the start that out of the nine men investigated, Harry Baird was the one he wanted. The merchant banker was thirty-two, confident and ambitious, a man shrewd enough not to discount an obvious solution simply because it was obvious. The established hierarchy looked askance at Baird's working-class background, his youth and relative inexperience. It wasn't that they didn't take him seriously, just that they weren't prepared to take him seriously enough. Yet. And this was an advantage; it allowed Baird, as a junior partner, the freedom to use the plush corridors of one of the City of London's largest merchant bankers to brilliant effect. Most important of all, as far as Paul Angelou was concerned, Harry Baird played to win. Up till now he had never been asked to risk anything of himself in the game, and Paul guessed that this was one of the factors in his proposition that would appeal to Baird: that and the prospect of a sizable deposit in a numbered Swiss bank account.

Each time Paul thought about the risks involved in his plan, the more certain he became that they were acceptable. What Sir Richard Jarman was on the verge of offering him was an opportunity to strike out in a different direction. The accumulation of money was no longer Paul's sole preoccupation. At the age of forty-two he was a rich man, but until eighteen months ago it would not have occurred to him that his professional life would not end as it had begun, in the City.

He harbored no illusions about Sir Richard or the reasons why he and his committee had approached him. In suggesting that they put Paul Angelou's name forward in a midterm by-election, they knew exactly what they were doing. The seat, held with a marginal majority by a Tory, encompassed one of the most multi-ethnic boroughs in London. The very foreignness of Angelou's name would help him retain that seat. They were using him. Paul knew it, and he also knew what was expected of him: gratitude, acquiescence. Outsiders were seldom, if ever, invited into the club. He was to be given a glimpse of that exclusive inner sanctum. What the coldly aristocratic Sir Richard and his friends did not know was that once Paul had accepted the invitation, he would then—and only then—decide what dues he was ready to pay.

As he strode through the crowded terminal, skirting groups of people, Paul's fist closed reflexively over the handle of his briefcase. Only one man could jeopardize his nomination: Arion. The old man could play havoc with his ambitions; all it would take would be one dogged researcher digging into the past. Some tabloid would pay handsomely for the details of Arion's business ventures. In his mind's eye Paul could see the name of Doric Video, in particular, spread over the top of a page, with his own photograph inset beneath it. It didn't matter whether he had any connection with Doric Video or not. The name was the same: Angelou.

He had consciously dismissed his irritation about the telephone call by the time he walked into the executive lounge. There were perhaps fifteen other people present, and apart from a woman sitting awkwardly upright in one of the armchairs, all were men. Only two were in conversation with each other.

Paul collected a large whiskey and soda and chose a chair near one of the windows. As he took the first sip of his drink, the tannoy came to life again, and out of the corner of his eye he saw a jerky movement of surprise from the woman. "Mrs. Wyatt, traveling to London, please call   he inquiry desk for a telephone message." Wyatt. The name sounded familiar. He turned toward her idly and noticed that her wrist and lower forearm were bandaged. She remained where she was, staring down at a newspaper spread out over her lap, a glass in her right hand. The message had obviously been for her, and she was just as obviously ignoring it. Why? he wondered. Oddly intrigued, he nonetheless glanced down at his briefcase and considered reading through Baird's file once more before the interview took place tomorrow. Then he decided against it. He had studied Beaumont Gracie's report so often and so closely that he felt he knew Baird better than the man knew himself.

There was something distinctly unapproachable about the woman, he thought, staring at her, trying to pinpoint just what it was. Her dark brown hair was cut in a shoulder-length feathery style which, as her head bent over the paper, curled down over her cheeks and chin, accentuating the almost bloodless pallor of her partially hidden face. He couldn't make out exactly what she was wearing, but the fabric was wildly striped and patterned, creating an effect that was exotic in the extreme. She looked like a moneyed gypsy, an image which actually made him smile. His wife did not dress to amuse herself, as this woman obviously did. If he'd thought about it, he would have acknowledged that Susan chose her clothes according to his tastes, which meant elegant tailoring rather than flamboyant designs. He could not picture Susan in such a crazed combination of colors, deep orange and gold, tan and black, with everything wrapped and layered and falling in soft folds.

The realization that he was enjoying his speculations about a total stranger made him slightly uneasy. That and the fact that he couldn't place the familiar name served to bring back some of his earlier irritation. He felt both drawn and repelled by the notion that when she finally looked up, he'd see a cross-eyed, disappointing face, features that would put an end to his thoughts and take him out of the room without a backward glance. Cross-eyed or not, she gave the impression of being capable enough, sitting there, withdrawn and uninviting. He knew instinctively that she was alone because she wanted to be. If she needed help, she'd ask for it.

Angie was aware of the scrutiny and unamused by her response to it. She'd seen him come in, check the occupants of the lounge with a sweeping, confident glance, then dismiss them. As he moved across the room, away from her, she'd registered a quickening of her pulse and immediately short-circuited an intense desire to catch his eye by concentrating on the conversation she'd had with Cissy in the small hours of that morning. Dazed and with blood plopping down onto a patch of bare floorboards, Angie had found herself wondering at the shock of relief in her sister-in-law's voice. "You're coming back? Really? When? Are you properly awake, Angie?" As though the staccato conversation had not been bizarre enough, Cissy had reacted with fury and disbelief to Angie's brief account of the mishap on the fire escape.

"A broken bottle?" Cissy repeated suspiciously.

"It was raining. I slipped."

"What in God's name were you doing on the fire escape in the middle of the night? Do you know what would have happened if you'd hit your head and been out for an hour? You'd have bled to death!"

"It isn't an artery," Angie said calmly.

"How do you know!"

"Because blood isn't hitting the ceiling—"

"You sound very strange," Cissy interrupted, suspicion once again thickening her voice.

"That's probably because I am *very slowly* bleeding to death here. Now get off the line, Cissy. It *is* four o'clock in the morning. Where's Oliver?"

"Asleep."

"Good, you go to bed, too. I'll see you tomorrow."

"I'll collect you at the airport—"

"There's no need."

"I'll meet you!"

Angie had hung up, oddly comforted by Cissy's impatient anger. But the feeling that Cissy hadn't come even close to saying what was on her mind persisted. That sort of reticence was so unlike Oliver's wife that Angie had, despite the fact that she would be in London the following day, begun to fret. The telephone message on the tannoy a few minutes ago—that, too, had to be Cissy. She was either afraid that Angie had changed her mind about coming back or, having thought about it, had decided that she had indeed tried to slit her wrists, or one of them at any rate. But that still didn't account for the almost despairing urgency that had crept into Cissy's urgings to return home over the past few weeks. Something was wrong, and Cissy hadn't the heart to tell her.

Paul finished his whiskey and glanced at his watch. It was almost time for their flight to be called. He was debating whether to have another drink when the Wyatt woman began to fold the newspaper in front of her. She did this carefully, keeping her good arm well away from the glass balanced on the armrest of the chair. That done, she picked up the glass again and seemed surprised to find it empty. Then she, too, glanced at her watch as though considering whether she had time for another drink.

Paul picked up his briefcase and walked over to her. "If you would tell me what you're drinking, Mrs. Wyatt, I'd be happy to get you another."

Angie had been staring at the newspaper for so long that the sound of his voice made her start. She was less surprised by his use of her name than the fact that he'd anticipated her need for a refill. She looked up, smiling, and handed him her glass. "Vodka on the rocks. Thank you."

Soft hair, short, almost black, and beautifully cut. She watched him move across the room, and a painful, overlapping image of Lou suddenly made her wince. Lou's thick fair hair, curling untidily around his ears and down over his collar, his angular body and irresistible energy . . .

Paul came back with her drink and a bottle of tonic water. He gave her the glass and when she waved the tonic aside, he said, "You shouldn't drink that straight."

"I don't normally."

He remained standing where he was, and Angie felt an agitated shiver raise goosepimples on her arms. Despite the conservative gray suit, this man looked like a gangster, slick, dark, veneered. His voice was deep and pleasant, impersonal. A solicitous stranger, that was all, she told herself sharply. The bandage, innocuous as it was, seemed to bring out solicitous strangers by the handful. Her jacket, with wide, full sleeves, was slung over the back of her chair. She reminded herself to put that on before boarding the plane. Sleep, not sympathy, was what she needed.

She looked up again and said, "Cheers," hoping he would take his whiskey and go back to his seat. Instead, he reached over and pulled an adjacent chair closer.

For the second time that day Paul Angelou had been taken totally by surprise. He told himself later that he had remained in the lounge because he, too, had needed another drink. The truth was that curiosity had overcome him; he wanted to know who this woman was, why her name was so familiar, and why she looked as though she were afraid of him. His own uncharacteristic behavior in approaching her in this way was something he would have to work out later.

"Does that hurt?" he asked, indicating her wrist.

"The stitches pull a bit, but that's all."

"You should be wearing a sling."

"A sling?" He was serious, looking at her so intently that she had to resist an urge to glance away. "It's a gash, six or seven stitches, not an amputation." Her sharp tone brought not a hint of reaction. To prove her point, she opened her handbag, brought out a packet of cigarettes, and extracted one with her left hand.

"That's something else you shouldn't do," he said softly.

"Do you mind if I breathe?"

Paul was scarcely aware of the sarcasm. Her wide amber brown eyes looked as though they'd been ringed with a light dusting of soot; small, impatient frowns gathered between her brows and then cleared, quickly, as though dispersed by sheer force of will. The eyes, and lips devoid of color, gave him the sense of a woman depleted; that high-cheekboned face was too pale, the body too thin. Yet he saw a vibrancy, dormant but still stubbornly visible in her gestures. . . . What had happened to her? He guessed her to be in her mid-thirties, a very beautiful woman who was clearly used to money. He was bemused by the reality of that fact alone and couldn't understand why he should be. Most of the women he came into contact with wore outrageously expensive designer clothes and jewelry. Klein, Lauren, Missoni, Versace—he was familiar with the names because he had sat through more than one fashion show with his wife. It mattered little to him whether Susan spent ten thousand or fifty thousand pounds on additions to her wardrobe. Why, then, was he so surprised to recognize an Ebel watch on this woman's wrist?

She lit her cigarette with a disposable lighter, and Paul noticed a large square-cut wedding ring on her finger, also that the ashtray on the table beside her was filled with half-smoked stubs.

"Don't you want to know how I knew your name?"

Angie shrugged lightly. "You were standing behind me at the check-in?"

Paul shook his head and glanced down at her bandaged arm. She'd reacted so defensively to the injury; could it have been self-inflicted? Knowing it would shock her, he said, "Was that telephone message from someone who doesn't quite trust you to get back to London under your own steam?"

There. Not only surprise, but an instant anger jerked her forward. Her eyes darkened with a rich, almost burnt-orange glow. More, much more than tiredness took over just then.

"What are you talking about?" she demanded. "Who are you?"

"My name is Paul Angelou," he replied softly.

Angie sat back and forced herself to look at Angelou. He seemed to relax, too, deliberately, to give her time. It was a face that should have had more mobility, she thought; everything seemed to be tensed around the dark, watchful eyes. Slightly curved brows, an unlined forehead, strong square jaw and a mouth—oppressive was the word that came to mind, but it wasn't that. Inflexible, autocratic. She couldn't envisage him laughing. Handsome was not a word she would have applied to him just then, although he was handsome by anyone's standards, including her own.

Paul swirled the whiskey around in his glass. His earlier question had brushed against an exposed nerve. He decided to try again. "I wouldn't have thought you needed your hand held, Mrs. Wyatt. Unless of course there's the possibility of a repeat performance of that." He nodded at her bandaged arm.

Angie glanced down, too, confused. Did that mean what she thought it meant? His words sounded playful but she could see nothing soft in Angelou's expression. He was beginning to make her feel uncomfortable. "Repeat performance?" she echoed.

"How did it happen?"

"An accident," she said before she could stop herself. She was stirred and angered by his casual questions, aroused by his sheer persistence. Like Cissy, he had simply jumped to the wrong conclusion: had the wound been anywhere else, the notion of suicide would not have occurred to either of them. At a loss, and feeling like an irresponsible teenager up before the headmaster, she muttered, "Cissy and probably Oliver . . . now you."

Oliver. She hadn't meant him to hear it. Oliver Jarman, of course! That was where he'd seen her name—Angela Wyatt, née Jarman, in Beaumont Gracie's report. Paul did a quick calculation. His business association with Sir Richard Jarman had begun in 1979, seven years ago. He remembered Gracie's original report quite well, but less well the update two years ago. Granted, he'd asked Gracie to concentrate on Jarman himself on that occasion, but still, not recognizing the name of the old man's daughter was a definite oversight. With the nomination in the offing, it wasn't only Sir Richard's financial status that was important any longer. Paul's mind leaped ahead. He and Susan had been invited for the first time to Calvert Hall the following weekend. Would Angela Wyatt be there?

"Did you?" Paul leaned toward her, resting his glass on his knee.

"Try to kill myself? It's none of your business but if I had, don't you imagine I'd have found an easier way than slowly bleeding to death from *one* cut wrist?" The bitterness in her voice was undisguised. Damn them all for their fantasies and interference . . . she put the cold glass to her forehead and sighed. Angelou was enjoying himself. She turned away just as the announcer began to call their flight and, with a mixture of relief and reluctance, reached over her shoulder for her jacket.

"There's no hurry, Mrs. Wyatt."

"I realize that," Angie murmured. She wanted to stay and escape at the same time. "I don't know who you are, but I'm in no shape to join in whatever game you're playing. Please understand, I caught this night flight so that I wouldn't have to—"

"Talk to anyone? So did I." He took the jacket from her, registered the Montana label, and said, "I'll let you know when it's time to go. Stay there."

Angie laughed in astonishment at the command but remained seated. Leave it, she told herself, light-headed with exhaustion and a curious growing elation. She was momentarily grateful that Cissy would be waiting for her at Heathrow. Would the idea of suicide have occurred to Cissy had she known her reason for returning to England? Probably not, she thought perversely. Oliver would oppose her; Cissy, too, although Cissy was more likely to keep her reservations to herself. In his logical, protective way Oliver would be horrified, for the sake of the child as much as for any other consideration. Except that the girl was nineteen, not a child any longer. Just thinking about it brought a flush of apprehension to her cheeks. Maybe she wouldn't tell Oliver at all, or anyone. . . .

Paul saw her shake her head and reach for another cigarette. He wanted to ask her directly what she'd been thinking about, what had taken her so completely away. For a moment the wide, full mouth had softened, the hard light gone out of her eyes.

They sat facing each other in silence as the lounge emptied around them. Lou would have found this amusing, Angie decided; certainly he would have been baffled by her obedience. She lit her cigarette without taking her eyes off Paul Angelou. The air of concentration about him was so complete, his attention so minutely focused, that the lingering edge of excitement grew again.

"This could become embarrassing," she said at length. "Who are you?"

He ignored her question. "Tell me why you're returning to England."

"You're either deaf or you have the social graces of an armadillo," Angie said easily. "Don't you think you're carrying this a bit far?"

Her words brought a half smile to his lips. "You haven't answered my question."

"I'd lay odds that you somehow know the answer, Mr. Angelou. My husband was killed in a car smash some . . . a year ago, and just now there doesn't seem to be much point in staying on in New York."

A faint stain of color showed in her cheeks. She was becoming angry again, and Paul wondered why. He said, "I'm sorry."

"Why?"

"Why am I sorry? Because you loved him very much."

The two women who were clearing the tables stopped working at Angie's mirthless shout of laughter. "Well, I'll be damned. You say that as if you know. We might have been on the verge of a divorce."

"But you weren't." His words were flat and final. Decisive.

Did he *really* know? And if he did, did it matter? He was a stranger; they shared nothing, not even a cursory knowledge of each other. Yet this man could harm her. Angie understood that with a stunning clarity just then. A tiny part of her was shocked by the admission and the flicker of heat that accompanied it.

Now wary, trying to think ahead of him, she said, "Why do I get the feeling you're holding something in reserve . . . about me, I mean?"

Her jacket was a splash of color over his knees. Paul hesitated. The tone was bland enough, but there was an intolerant, warning gleam in her eyes, as though she were daring him to nudge her again. He did, picking up the challenge neatly. It was the only way he could keep her from walking away. "I was thinking how little I do actually know about you. But even that—" he paused and ran his palm in a light, dusting movement over her jacket—"even that is more than whoever it was whose message you ignored."

"What do you mean?" She was honestly curious.

"Just that I would have known you'd never take such an easy way out."

Angie made an almost imperceptible motion of assent, as if she'd been expecting him to say just that. "By committing suicide? Then I can only assume you have no imagination. That, in addition to your natural arrogance makes you a dangerous man, Mr. Angelou!" Her voice had dropped to a husky rasp.

Paul appeared to be undisturbed but was in fact taken aback by her vehemence. And he could see that she was mystified by her own aggression. It was time to break up the encounter. He made that decision with reluctance and only because she was reaching him in a way he did not understand. His response was instinctive: to retreat until he knew more about her, until he felt less exposed and unsure of himself.

"You're overwrought," he said calmly.

Angie wanted to lash out at his complacency but found herself nodding in agreement. Whoever he was, none of this was his fault. He was not to blame for the raw state of her nerves, for the mixture of exhilaration and dread that coursed through her veins at the thought of being in London in a few hours' time. And he wasn't responsible for the fact that she was being swamped by a sensation she had no choice but to identify. Her glance dropped from the stony expression on his face to his hands. She expected to see small tufts of hair growing on his knuckles but the joints were hairless, splayed over the exotic colors of her jacket. . . . My God, she thought, shifting uncomfortably, I fancy you. She almost said

the word aloud. Fancy. A nice English word, comically inadequate for what she felt. She couldn't remember wanting a
man since Lou's death. She had no idea why Paul Angelou
or why at this moment. . . .

He rose to his feet. "Come on, it's time to go."

For no reason other than overwhelming desire to stay where
she was, alone, a prickle of tears stung at her eyes. She turned
her back on Paul Angelou and felt him ease the sleeve of her
jacket carefully over her bandaged arm. By the time she faced
him again with a murmured "Thank you," her eyes were dry
and clear and she was moving without having to draw on all
her willpower.

He walked slightly ahead of her. In contrast with his earlier
concentration, he now seemed to have dismissed her, given
up on whatever game he'd been playing. She was grateful for
that and slowed her own step to put more distance between
them. He was a complication she could do without.

Three hours later, in the flickering light thrown by the in-
flight film, Paul paused beside her seat. She was sleeping,
but he could see a clear frown drawing her eyebrows together.
Her right hand lay protectively over her bandaged forearm
where the sleeve of her jacket had ridden up, and everything
about her looked uneasy, tensed. She gave herself no peace,
not even in sleep. He had an impulse to wake her by putting
his hands on either side of her face, to draw into himself each
separate day of her past life. The fanciful desire was so strong
that only a hissed "Sit down, for God's sake!" kept him from
reaching out.

Back in his own seat, he removed his jacket and tie and
switched off the reading light. This was not how he had
planned to use his time on the flight. His briefcase lay un-
opened under the seat in front of him. In the darkened cabin
he shut his eyes and tried to concentrate on Harry Baird and
his interview with the man in a few hours' time. Nothing
came: not Baird, nor Arion, nor Sir Richard Jarman. He'd
caught more than a glimpse of her father in Angela Wyatt,
mostly in the bearing, the way she held herself, so effortlessly
confident. Now her face was all he could see. By sheer force
of will he conjured up the delicate beauty of his wife's features . . . but they paled and receded even as he sought to
define them more clearly.

3

☐ Arion Angelou counted himself blessed many times over. True, his pleasures were not the same as they had once been, but life had treated him well, better than many of those he had left behind in Mandraki all those years ago. Some of it had to do with luck, but mostly it had been hard work, especially during their first years, a daily grind to make enough money to feed his wife and baby son, to keep them warm in the accursed English winters. Even now the first fall of snow each year brought a tightness to his lips, a shortness of temper that lasted until the bitter memories eased.

Arion allowed the breath to whistle out from between his teeth as he bent to slip his sandals on. Age had, quite suddenly, been visited upon him. Overnight his joints had stiffened, his step had slowed, and his memory had begun to mix up times that recently had been as clear as the waters of the Aegean.

"Ari." He heard Anya calling him from downstairs. The sweet, heavy smell of freshly ground coffee beans seeped up through the old house. In this was he blessed most of all, in his wife, Ani, his miraculous bride of forty-six years.

"Eh, *attesa*, Ani," he murmured, using her father's language. "I am coming." Behind him the curtains moved. They were seldom drawn, the windows thrown open except in the harshest cold. Today the chill was offset by the brightness of the early-summer day.

Arion straightened and pulled on a cardigan and, seeing himself in the wardrobe mirror, automatically straightened his shoulders. He was a tall man, bulky now, with heavy shoulders and a thickened midriff. He smiled at himself, a sharp, wolflike grimace.

"If they knew, if they only knew." Ani would laugh at his vanity in the old days, unable to understand why men of authority feared her husband. "Powerful and imposing,"

some journalist had once described him. Arion Angelou knew
how to use his smile and his power. It got him what he
wanted.

On the landing he paused to listen at Cory's door. The boy
slept noisily, like a young boar, snuffling and grunting through
his dreams, twisting the sheets into damp rags. Arion heard
him now and was satisfied. This boy, the grandson of his
long-dead brother, brought him much pleasure and not a little
pain. Like the others of his generation, he wanted everything,
and he wanted it now. Arion feared for him and loved him
fiercely and protectively.

In the large stone-flagged kitchen Ani stood with her back
to him, hunched slightly over the bright red Aga. He stood
for a moment and listened to her murmur encouraging words
to the pot that held his coffee. Since the doctor had ordered
him to cut down on his intake of coffee, the two cups a day
he was allowed were made to a ritualized perfection.

Ani turned to see her husband standing in the doorway.
"Ari." She said his name almost shyly.

"Let us drink our coffee outside this morning. Look, the
sun is already shining."

"It is not yet seven o'clock," she said doubtfully. "Are
you sure it is not too cold?"

"I am sure. Come and see." Arion led the way through to
the back door and out onto the porch. A small wooden table
covered with green baize stood in one corner. On a low wall
was a jumble of plant pots, hibernating bulbs and freshly
uprooted globes of garlic. He took a deep breath and turned
to his wife. "See?"

Ani nodded. "I see. Come inside, it is too cold."

"You are right." He shrugged. "Maybe tomorrow . . ."

Nevertheless, he paused to look out over the garden. The
house and the patch of land it stood on were something of
an anachronism in Soho. Set in the curve of a bulb-shaped
cul-de-sac, the eighteenth-century house was one of the few
private dwellings that had survived, intact, the commercial-
ization of Soho. Although the house was now flanked by the
offices of a small film production company and a newly registered advertising agency, its location and the uniformity
of the other houses gave it an air of seclusion. In the early
years, because Ani loved the bright, light greens of a tem-
perate climate, they had planted a flowering cherry tree and
blanketed the small front garden with shrubs. The original

spear-tipped railings still stood, no more than fifteen feet away from the front door.

The front garden Ani tended with care but without the love she lavished on the larger area that lay beyond the back porch. That, too, was small, but in a curiously undeliberate way she had managed to re-create a part of their Greek village there. The greenery was lush and bright, but without the hardiness that resulted from a parched Greek soil. Still, a vine thrived in the shadow of a fig tree; simple stone urns held a wild array of flowers, mostly yellow; two haphazardly organized patches were already sprouting spring onions, dillweed, garlic, and mint. Tomatoes, peppers, lettuce, and artichokes were grown in a ramshackle corner greenhouse. Even to a stranger's eye there was an erratic beauty about the place.

For forty-four years they had lived here. It was an inconvenient house in many ways, and Arion would have liked to make Ani's life easier; but at her insistence, they stayed.

"Ari, come inside now. What does Cory do today?"

Arion took the first sip of rich, syrupy black coffee. "If you can tell me what he did yesterday, then maybe I can tell you what he will do today."

"That boy . . . three o'clock this morning I hear him come in."

"You were awake at this time?" Arion spoke sharply, fearful that she had been ill without telling him.

"No, no. I heard him drop something, his keys . . ."

Arion took a slice of her homemade bread and nodded. "I will talk to him. Tonight . . ."

"Tonight Paul and Susan are here. You have forgotten?"

He had not told her about his telephone call to Paul in New York the previous day or about their son's predictable reaction. "Yes, I have forgotten, but it is only age, my love. Do not concern yourself. What time will they come?"

"Eight o'clock."

"And our son will be on the dot, as they say. Ask Cory to check the wine. If we need more, I will tell Scotia."

"Ari . . ." He wasn't fooling her. She stood up and walked behind his chair, and he felt her hands on his shoulders. Like the sturdy body under the shapeless black dress, they were strong and capable, seldom still. He leaned back into her, angular and clean and majestically familiar.

"I will be what I am, Ani, a loving father to my only son. Do not concern yourself."

"I know it, but you—you two do fight so."

"Argue, Ani, not fight. He is my son, and I love him, but a man is permitted to argue with his son, no?"

She kneaded his shoulders, pulling him closer. "A little, Ari. Not too much, please. Promise me, please."

"We have not seen this son of ours for three months. We will have a lot of other things to talk about. Angel Publications is not the only thing, yes? And it will be good to see Suzy again. A good girl, a good wife . . . Maybe Benjamin will come, too?"

"Paulie did not say. If Benjamin is here, Cory will perhaps stay at home." Ani cuffed the back of his head gently. "*Caro*, how much I would have loved a girl child."

"Then we will make one for you, *koukla mou*, tonight when there is no one here."

Now she slapped him hard and hissed a spate of Italian into his ear. She used her father's language more frequently of late. He did not understand everything she said. Without looking he raised both hands above his head and felt her lips touch each in turn. "*Basta!*" She shooed him out of the house.

Where Berwick and D'Arblay streets intersected, a narrow sliver of Angel House was visible, eight stories of high-rent office space, built to blend into the face of Soho. Arion was ashamed of it. In the boom years of the late 1960s he had allowed himself to be persuaded by those whose language derived from balance sheets, investments, capital appreciation, and all the legitimate ways of minimizing the burden of taxes. Arion had refused to consider any of the plentiful offshore deals on offer and had shunned the suggestion of dummy companies into which he could have diverted his money. Instead, he'd agreed to the office block. But in the event, Angel House and all the other redevelopments had changed, for the worse, what was still to him a village, no less intimate than the one in which he'd grown up.

The stalls in the Berwick Street market were being stocked up, and already a few early-morning shoppers strolled by. Later, empty wooden crates would litter the spaces between the stalls, and the cobbles would become slippery with crushed vegetable leaves and discarded overripe fruit.

Soho was deceptive to strangers. They saw sex for sale, some of the best restaurants in London, but little else. For

Arion it was a place of attics and basements, cramped places where journeymen tailors had cut and stitched the clothes that later bore Savile Row labels. He knew the clockmakers and goldsmiths, a saddler, the women who salted herrings, and those who taught at the one remaining primary school. Like a softhearted whore, Soho lay open and inviting for those who knew her; the others were made to pay for their pleasures and saw only what they were meant to see.

Old Compton Street was still relatively free of traffic at this hour. As he turned into it, two swarthy schoolboys split from each other, brushing past him on either side. He seldom saw children these days, certainly not playing on the pavements under some parent's watchful eye. The children of Italians, Greeks, Chinese, Cypriots, Poles, and Germans—they had all found a way of communicating with each other. Arion had learned to speak English with them in those postwar years, taking words back to Ani, the strangeness of it made easier because there was always a newcomer who understood even less than they did. The array of forms to be filled in, signatures to be placed was bewildering. Fear of deportation, of something wrong was contagious. Alarm would spread like a dark shadow, sparked at random by gossip and greed. In Soho, as in that other community of immigrants in the East End of London, there was money to be made from innocence and the promise of betterment.

Scotia was waiting for him outside Ani's restaurant. "Boris," Arion called from ten yards away. No one else dared call Scotia that to his face. Arion's cousin was a dark, fierce-looking man whose long face was molded with sunken hollows and sharp edges. He resembled Boris Karloff to an uncanny degree until he smiled, and then the "dark one" lit up with all the uncomplicated happiness of a baby.

In spite of his formidable looks, Scotia was an endearing man, softly spoken and slow to anger. He had managed the restaurant now for more than twenty years. Arion ensured that he and his wife and children lived well but could not persuade Scotia to accept any part of the profits from the restaurant he had made famous throughout London.

The two men embraced each other, and Scotia put the door on the latch once they were inside. Their ritual was simple: while Arion lit his first cigar of the day, enjoying the sounds that came from the kitchen, he would eye the young women who prepared the tables, wiping and polishing them before placing cloths, napkins, cutlery, ashtrays, and the slender glass vases which would each later hold one of Ani's beloved yellow blooms. Everything was muted yet not dark. Polished wood and glass, mirror-bright strips of brass, plants richly lit, it was at once opulent and unintimidating, created precisely as Scotia had intended, down to the last fluted glass.

Once they were seated, Scotia would begin to relate the previous day's events as if they were all somehow secrets to be relished. Over the years these conversations had become much shorter now that Ani's was a way of life to many of its patrons, with new faces appearing only rarely.

If Scotia had one fault, it was his disapproval of unaccompanied women. Nothing Arion said could persuade him that times had indeed changed so much that not only was it acceptable for women to lunch or dine alone but it was not an insult to present them with the bill.

Arion pulled at his cigar. He still found pleasure in this place. With the money he had made by selling the magazines and comic books sent over as ballast on American ships during the war, he had signed a short-term lease for what had been no more than an empty, dilapidated room. Not a chair or a table had matched in those days, but Ani's food brought in first their friends and then others. When the outdated magazines and comics stopped coming in, he began to import small quantities of other publications. The worldwide shortage of paper after the war ensured high profits, and Arion accepted and sold everything offered, from magazines to books and newspapers. When the demand began to drop off, he turned to pulping his excess stocks. One business fed the other until neither could expand any further. He bought his first warehouse and then the freehold on the tiny café. Years later he bought the property next to it and watched Ani's alarm falter into unabashed pleasure as her name went up outside. She continued to make her special dishes long after there was any need for her to work. Arion did not object because it pleased her. It also gave him a chance to observe her during the day. He could tell how she felt by the care and speed with which she handled her tools. The only thing that could take the transparency out of her eyes was their son. When Paul sapped her energy and her joy, she replenished both by laboring with infinite patience over her food.

Arion's next call was at the delicatessen, managed with ease and dedication by Scotia's younger daughter. It always surprised him to see this diminutive child. She was thirty-five now but had changed little and grown less. In his eyes she was still the girl in a pleated gym slip, always running, talking, fetching. He never understood how she found the time to oversee both the delicatessen and the patisserie across the street, cope with her two small children, and still brighten visibly at every piece of gossip.

He had to bend almost double to touch her cheeks with his lips. "My father is well?" she asked.

"Boris is Boris," he replied, as was their custom. It was just after nine-thirty, and already there was a queue at the cold meat and cheese counter.

"Ani will telephone you for tonight," he said, relishing the pungent odors of his childhood. "Paul is visiting us. Your children are well?"

"Too well. They are like two baby goats; they eat everything but each other. . . ."

Arion laughed at the description of her two demure little boys. He could see Scotia in both of them; of her English husband, nothing.

"You will bring your family for lunch one day soon. Sunday perhaps . . ."

"Thank you." Olga smiled her acceptance. "I'll talk to Ani." She moved through to the back of the shop and began rearranging small bottles of olive oil. She knew what Arion's next question would be and did not know how to answer it. Hoping to deflect the question, she dipped a wooden spoon into a large vat of black olives and brought one out. "This is new, Ari. Taste."

Arion swirled the olive around in his mouth before biting into it. The taste of oil was minimal, the salt tangy, the flesh soft but firm. "Perfect."

"And cheaper. I'll make up a bottle for you."

"Thank you, Olga. Now tell me, how is the boy? Is he of help to you?" He saw her glance away quickly toward the door, as though to escape the question. "What is it you do not wish to tell me?"

"There is nothing. . . . I tell you always that Cory is a lovely boy. My girls here are all in love with him, and he helps me, yes."

There was too much haste in what she said. It wasn't what he wanted to hear. "Does he come in every day, Olga? Was Cory here with you yesterday?"

Olga made a fuss of wiping the rim of the bottle she had just filled with olives and brine. "Yesterday? Yesterday, no. But a lot of other days—"

"A lot?" Arion broke in. "Not each day?"

"Ach, you know what boys are like. . . . So he does not come in every single day. I do not *need* him every single day."

"What does he do when he is not here?"

Olga shrugged gracefully, still trying to make light of it. "When he arrives later, I will ask him and tell you. He is a good boy, Ari, but he is young."

Arion patted her shoulder, took the bottle of olives, and turned to leave. "I remember what it is like to be so young. What I do not remember is . . . disappearing, not coming home every night. This I do not understand. Say nothing, *cara*."

She watched him from the doorway. In her heart she felt a thread of dislike for Cory. How could he behave in such a fashion? Who else could bring such tiredness to the old man's face? She heard things. It was impossible not to hear from people who wanted to tell you. Cory was either very clever or very innocent, because there was nothing she could confront him with. Or Arion. Just absences. He came and went and spent time with people none of them knew, in places they weren't aware existed. Olga did not *know* this. It was what she felt. In some ways Cory was like another son, but unlike her own, he never flinched at her rare frown or felt obliged to involve her in his life. Instead, he used Arion's words and his own persuasive charm. Please God, he didn't break Arion's heart.

4

☐ For the fourth time in three weeks Frank Sheldon read the words "Sold by Lisa Barrett." It was becoming standard *Bookseller* copy, he thought, and wondered why his usual pleasure at seeing her name in print was now tinged with annoyance. After all, her success could do nothing but enhance the reputation of the Sheldon Literary Agency.

Frank shoved his chair back and swung his feet up onto the corner of his desk, easing his compact body into a comfortable position. From the day he'd hired her, and for not entirely unselfish reasons, he'd seen to it that as many doors as possible were opened to her, and now that she was opening them for herself, it was beginning to rankle.

It was twelve-thirty and the traffic noises filtering up from the Strand had evened out into a low, almost pleasant growl. From his third-floor office, which overlooked a small courtyard at the rear of the building, Frank registered the gradual disappearance of individual sounds.

"You'll be aware of one of the busiest thoroughfares in London only during the noon hours and early evening." That had been the estate agent's way of explaining away the continuous rumble. Frank had found out by himself later that "noon" had meant from eleven o'clock until three-thirty, and "early evening," from four o'clock until seven.

Feeling oddly unsettled, Frank reached for his diary. The entry for that evening read: "Farley Esterhuys, Connaught, 9 o'c." He grimaced. Getting old, he thought resignedly. The American literary agent's twice-yearly visits to London seemed to be occurring at least once a month. They had the usual reciprocal arrangement: Frank sold the British rights to Farley's books, and Farley sold the American rights to the Sheldon Agency's books. The arrangement worked so well that Farley did not need to visit London so frequently, but then they both knew that business was not uppermost in Farley's mind when he did come over.

"Lisa," Frank yelled. In the outer office Ruby and Lilian had stopped typing and were opening up their sandwiches. He could see their outlines through the glass paneling in his door. Lisa, located in the smallest office, usually worked with her door open; not using the internal line had somehow become a habit with them, to the annoyance of Lilian, Lisa's fussy secretary.

The buzzer on the telephone sounded almost immediately. He depressed the speak button. "Yes!"

It was Lisa. "I'm on the other line. Wait a sec."

Her irritable response didn't surprise him. He was becoming resigned to being told to wait by a girl who had walked in off the street eighteen months ago, and to spending endless evenings with Farley Esterhuys, drinking pseudomartinis in Soho and seeing to it that the American wasn't ripped off in some sleazy joint.

He took a mouthful of well-watered whiskey and glanced around the room. Everything about this particular room pleased him: its one wall of floor-to-ceiling bookshelves; the worn leather of the studded captain's chair in the corner, flanked on one side by a monstrously healthy cheese plant and on the other by two four-foot piles of typescripts listing drunkenly together.

The light on the telephone extension came on a split second before the instrument rang. Frank snatched up the receiver and held it to his ear.

"Frank? Frank, Sidney Niklas. C'mon, you bastard, I know you're there."

"I'm here. What can I do for you, Sidney?"

"Been a long morning, buy you a drink?"

"Uh-uh, got things to do. But thanks anyway."

"Too bad. I heard about the Piedowski deal you did with Meredith's. They're paying over the top these days, but it wasn't bad, not bad at all. I hear it was one of the lady Lisa's. . . ."

Frank didn't know what he was talking about. God, how he hated that false American twang Sidney affected. How the hell did Oliver Jarman put up with him? "You heard right, Sidney. I can tell you, hand over heart, that I haven't read a word of the novel."

He heard a low, appreciative whistle at the other end. He didn't like Sidney Niklas. He particularly didn't like the other man's tone whenever he referred to Lisa. It seemed to suggest that he and Frank shared some secret about her.

"A cool one, Frank. Cool. But I bet she loses her cool in bed, eh?" Sidney said it as though he had read Frank's thoughts.

"I don't know what you mean," Frank said stiffly.

"C'mon, Frank, this is Sidney, remember?"

"I know who it is. Go away, Sidney."

Frank slammed the phone down and half expected it to ring again. Instead, Lisa Barrett came through the door, smiling. She always looked as though she'd just stepped out of a shower, clean and cool. Cool; at least Sidney had been right about that. The sight of her did nothing to improve Frank's humor.

"Sit down and tell me about Piedowski," he said abruptly.

Lisa stopped midway across the room, startled by the irascible tone. He was loosely sprawled in his chair, but there was, unusually, something forbiddingly tense about him.

"Piedowski, Lisa. I've just been told that Meredith's bought it."

She moved then, taking the chair directly in front of him. She looked ridiculously young and appealing, a fall of blond hair framing her oval face. Sometimes she tied her hair back, but strands would inevitably escape, giving her a distracted air. She had a small, straight nose and a resolute dimple in her chin. There was a gravity about her, a seriousness which sometimes took him aback, yet she also had a quirky sense of humor that often surprised him. Altogether, he didn't know much about her, although he suspected that this evasiveness wasn't deliberate. In some respects they were very alike. He understood instinctively her sudden and inexplicable need for prolonged stretches of silence; when it seemed to her that he'd had enough of people and telephone calls, she behaved with similar sensitivity by withdrawing into her office and rerouting all his calls through to her.

"You'd left before the auction closed yesterday, and this morning neither of us has had much time to talk. To cut a long story short, you heard right. Thirty-seven thousand pounds, with a good paperback split built in. What else do you want to know?"

Frank lit his fifth Gauloise of the day. A good sale, without any doubt. From the description of the novel she'd given him a few weeks ago, he would have put the top price at around ten thousand pounds.

It all came so easily to her. It wasn't that she didn't put the work in, just that she made it appear simple. For someone who hadn't had any publishing experience before, her swift grasp of contracts alone was astonishing. Frank couldn't quite explain it to himself. Was he angry because she didn't appear to need him any longer? There was no logical way she could, but she knew as much as he did about the agency. She baffled him by predicting advances with uncanny accuracy, stating without hesitation which books were likely to be placed with publishers and which weren't. Mostly she was right. When challenged, she was prepared to explain; if the explanation was not accepted, she seemed unruffled.

"Has it occurred to you that I might like to know *when*

you're auctioning a book *before* you auction it and to which publishers you're submitting it?''

"Shall I go out and come in again? Is this a new rule, or are you making it up as you go along? I know what I'm doing, Frank.''

"That's not the issue here. *I* want to know what you're doing.''

Lisa was surprised by his persistence. He didn't appear to be genuinely annoyed, just . . . scratchy. He'd loosened the knot in his tie, a sure sign of irritability. Right now she was not going to let him get to her. "Forget Piedowski, will you? Finished and done with. Sold. Frank, do you remember Elliot Stone?''

"Stone? No. Should I?''

"Three or four years ago he wrote a novel about a hijack, old hat even then but not badly done—''

"Four years? How do you remember? You've only been here for eighteen months.''

"He didn't collect his typescript,'' she said patiently. "I found it when I was clearing out some shelf space soon after I arrived.''

Frank eyed her speculatively. "Want a drink?''

"Thanks, no. I'm due at Joe Allen's in twenty minutes. I'm really excited about this book.'' She was sitting forward, her blue eyes alight.

"So, tell me.''

"I had him in a few months ago, talked to him, told him what was good and what was bad about the book. Then I advised him to put it aside . . . did you meet him? He's young, thirty-threeish, a bit pompous, lives in Northumbria—''

"Good thumbnail sketch, but get to the point, will you? I take it there *is* a point to all this?''

Lisa laughed with enjoyment. "He's written another novel, and it's *brilliant.* I could hardly believe it.''

"What makes you think so?''

"That it's brilliant? Read it yourself. I've had some copies made. Take one home tonight and read it. Tell me I'm wrong.''

Frank swung his feet off the desk and stood up, stretching. He didn't recognize his own voice when he said, "Me? Tell Lisa Barrett she's wrong? God forbid, woman. What would the *Bookseller* say?'' He saw her blink as he stood over her for a moment, his body blocking the light from the window behind his desk.

It took Lisa a few seconds to digest the sarcasm. She couldn't see any humor in the dark eyes. His chunky five-foot-ten frame filled her vision. "It isn't just Piedowski, is it?" she asked quietly. She felt not a twinge of guilt about the circumstances of the Piedowski sale. In fact, she felt scarcely anything apart from a mild confusion. She liked Frank Sheldon; she liked his easy manner and square good looks, his sports jackets and ill-chosen ties. And she enjoyed working at the Sheldon Agency. By an unspoken and hitherto unbroken agreement, they stood at arm's length from each other. It suited Lisa to stifle her amiable curiosity about Frank Sheldon. When it became necessary or desirable, she would find out about him. For the moment the job took all her time, and she felt no more than an occasional spark of interest in her employer's outside life.

Frank turned away quickly to stare down at the courtyard below. Trying to analyze her sense of disappointment, Lisa felt cornered by the sudden knowledge that she needed this man's approval—for all her certainty about Elliot Stone's novel. He really had seemed to take for granted everything she had achieved over the past few months. She was honest enough to admit that his lack of acknowledgment might have had something to do with her growing independence. Was it that he felt he'd come off second best? He certainly wasn't a man to accept second best lightly. . . .

"Since you ask, I'll tell you exactly what it is, Miss Barrett," Frank said. His pompous tone annoyed him, but he persisted. "Am I correct in stating that you work *for* me, that I do in fact pay you a not inconsiderable monthly salary? Don't speak, just nod."

Lisa nodded, feeling foolish, wondering if he could see her reflection in the glass.

"Is it not our arrangement that books which come into this office addressed to the Sheldon Agency earn a commission for me, which goes into paying your salary and other little incidentals, like rent, rates, equipment, et cetera? And did we not agree that anything you brought in, like Piedowski, would carry a clear five percent commission to you and five percent to me? Am I right so far?"

Lisa nodded once more. It was beginning to sound like an inquisition. "I know what the arrangement is—"

"And did we not further agree that books addressed to the Sheldon Agency which you took under your wing would bring you, personally, a two and a half percent commission only?" He turned to see a slow flush of anger redden her cheeks. Perversely this pleased him. "Well?"

"Well what? For God's sake, Frank, can't we talk about this some other time? I'm late as it is."

"What I want to know is . . ." He paused. It was the last thing on earth he wanted to know, but he couldn't stop. "What I want to know is why you're getting so excited about . . . what's his name, Elliot Stone. How big can the novel be that it would make your two and a half percent commission worth jumping up and down about?" Good Christ, had he really said that?

"That sounds as though you suspect me of something," she said, her blue eyes chilled. "Well, the answer is simple. I think the book is good. I think the author has potential, and damn it, I enjoyed working on it with him. Besides, the agency could do with something other than the smut your Mr. Esterhuys ships over by the yard."

Frank sat down and eyed her with reluctant admiration. Her composure was impressive, but she could not disguise the fury gathering in her eyes. "I see," he said. "In the name of literature you're now going to suggest that we sack Farley Esterhuys and say good-bye to twenty thousand pounds a year in commission? That's what his books bring in."

Lisa gritted her teeth and tried to guess what was going on inside Frank's head. He must know what he was doing. It was as though he wanted her to admit some betrayal. "I'm not suggesting anything of the kind. If you can stand it, keep him! All I'm saying is that it's the quality of our own writers that will attract other authors to the agency, not the likes of"—she glanced at the bookshelves to the left of his desk—"*The Story of O to Z.*"

He wanted to go back to the beginning, to tell her that all *he* wanted was to be briefed on her activities, not to have to rely on information from outsiders. But all he found himself saying was "It also seems to me that you have recently become more concerned with seeing your own name in print than in promoting the agency's."

He saw her draw back for the first time. Strands of hair fell across her forehead, and she had gone a little pale. Although she remained seated, hands folded in her lap, when she did speak, her voice was distinctly edged with anger. "Are you serious?"

He went on compulsively. "Do you know what Sidney Niklas just said on the telephone?"

"I don't want to know." Sidney Niklas made her skin crawl.

"He asked me if you lost your cool in bed."

That brought her to her feet. She got up and automatically smoothed the material of her skirt over her hips. Frank rarely did anything without a purpose. What purpose could he have in trying to humiliate her? And why this way? She felt a cold flutter of uncertainty as she turned away.

"Lisa . . ."

She didn't stop or look back. From behind the desk Frank watched her helplessly. A slate blue tunic hung loosely to her hips; from the way she held her shoulders, he guessed she was holding her breath. There was something unyielding about her just then.

He remained where he was until he heard the outer door slam behind her. Partly in defiance of her, partly in disgust at himself, he downed the whiskey in his glass and rose to pour another. He understood quite clearly that the victory was hers.

Balancing the telephone deftly between his neck and shoulder, he dialed Arion Angelou's private number. The old man answered immediately. "Frank, *ti kaneis.*"

"I'm well, Ari. Well. I would . . ." He hesitated. "Are you free for lunch?"

"Ah, yes. I am shortly to be faced with a sour English apple and a goat's milk yogurt. It will give me much pleasure to call Scotia. Frank . . ."

He had never been able to hide anything from Arion; it was as though the Greek were able to call on some sort of sixth sense as far as Frank was concerned. For nearly twenty years Arion had been friend, mentor and surrogate father.

"It's all right, Ari. I've just made a complete ass of myself, that's all. I'll be with you in ten minutes. *Kherete.*"

Frank replaced the receiver. The prospect of seeing Arion cheered him. They each filled a vital space in the other—one born in a fishing village in Greece, the other in a dingy terraced house in the East End of London—and their ever-present need to participate in each other's life was no longer incongruous to outsiders.

As Frank crossed Frith Street into Old Compton Street, it struck him that Soho wasn't Lisa's territory at all. What did she do when she left the office? He knew she lived in a flat in Camden Town, had a small garden, presumably, because she often brought flowers to the office. She was twenty-three, a graduate from Bristol, with parents who lived in Worcestershire. Maybe she read typescripts every night. The idea pleased him. He comforted himself with the thought that it must be her professionalism which stopped her from discussing her private life or talking about her rare holidays. Who did she go with—a lover? She never spoke of boyfriends—could she be gay? The image of another woman arousing that slender body made him fumble uncharacteristically for a cigarette. Or another man! As he thumbed the lighter into flame, he was astonished to see that his hands were trembling.

5

☐ Oliver Jarman flinched as he splashed icy water onto his face. His head thudded with pain. The pain was so bad that even his teeth felt swollen. It was ten o'clock in the morning, and he was alone in the office washroom. As he straightened, he caught sight of himself in the mirror above the basin: straight brown hair fell untidily over his forehead, and his gauntly handsome face was seamed with tiredness. He made an effort to square his shoulders, noting through reddened eyes that the once-solid bulk now looked wasted, even fragile. The mouthful of neat whiskey he'd swallowed at home had done nothing except blur his vision for a while, making it difficult to get out of the house without alarming Cissy.

He grimaced and went through to his office. Everything was as it should be: papers and files aligned on his desk; pencils sharpened; ballpoints capped. He caught a faint whiff of furniture polish, which brought a rush of bile; walking unsteadily, he crossed the room and, without drawing the vertical blinds aside, reached behind them and fumbled for

the window catch. After a few moments the chilly air began
to clear his head. He looked down at the Mayfair traffic and
thought with longing of the penthouse flat on the floor above
him. Aspirin, cool sheets, relief from the constricting pressure of his collar. It was on days like this, unaccountably
worse than others, that he felt himself drained dry of the will
to survive the next ten minutes. The day spread itself before
him like a wasted year, not to be contemplated.

He went back to his desk and lit a cigarette, inhaling deeply.
Angie's plane would have landed by now; she and Cissy would
be driving home. He hoped Cissy had been able to persuade
his sister to spend what remained of the day at their house in
Kensington Square. He knew Angie would want to be taken
straight to her own flat in Chelsea, and although Cissy had
seen to it that the flat had been aired and dusted and that
there were groceries in the cupboards, he still didn't like the
idea of Angie going there straight off. . . .

There was a light tap on his door, then a brief pause before
it opened. Jane Bullivant, his father's secretary, put her head
round. "Good morning, Oliver."

"Hullo, Jane, come in."

"Can't stop. I've just come to tell you that Sir Richard will
be out all day. Seeing the moneymen." She made a wry face
at him.

Oliver hesitated. You'd have thought the old man would
want to see his daughter after five years. "Thank you, Jane."

"Oh, and he also asked if you'd be good enough to stand
in for him at lunch with Jason Corbett today."

"Jason? Any particular reason?"

"I don't think so. Just their regular once-a-month date.
There wasn't enough time to cancel it."

"Fine." Oliver made up his mind quickly. "Incidentally,
I'll be out all afternoon as well. You can get me at home if
necessary."

"Will do, Oliver. Angie's back today, isn't she? Please give
her my love."

Oliver nodded as Jane Bullivant shut the door. *Your father
is at an all-day meeting, but his secretary sends you her love.
Well, we have to take what we can get, don't we?*

Don't fuss, Oliver. He could hear Angie's sigh of exasperation. *Does it matter? Does it* really *matter?* It was always
that way. And his stock answer was *"Of course, it doesn't.
Not* really.*"*

At least lunch with Jason Corbett would be a pleasant affair. Apart from being a good businessman, the northerner had a blunt honesty that had always appealed to him. Jason, a handsome, laconic man who viewed the world with a disenchanted eye, was a few years older than Oliver. He was practical and somewhat mysterious; Oliver could not imagine what his first wife had been like to produce a son like the glum, wispy-haired Martin. There was nothing at all of Jason Corbett in his son.

The telephone buzzer sounded, and his secretary announced, "Martin's on the line for you." Talk of the devil, Oliver thought, and had a quick image of Martin Corbett slouching in his chair, one arm slung over the backrest. His habitual pose was one of boredom. At the age of twenty-five Martin had only one asset: he was the son of Jason Corbett, who owned and ran the Corbett printing empire. Jarman Publishing kept the Corbett presses rolling, and Jason Corbett kept the Jarman printing and binding costs down. The arrangement was extremely profitable for both companies, but the price was high: Oliver had to endure the presence of Martin Corbett on his editorial team.

"We lost the Piedowski novel," Martin said without preamble.

The news didn't come as a surprise to Oliver. He could not remember when they'd last won a book at auction. "I'm sorry to hear that. Do you know who bought it?"

"Meredith."

"Have you got any idea what they paid for it?" Oliver asked patiently.

"I saw Peter Meredith at a party last night, and he wasn't exactly forthcoming."

You're not exactly forthcoming this morning either, Oliver thought waspishly. Martin hoarded nuggets of information as if they were gold he would get rich on someday. Just listening to that surly voice was an exercise in restraint.

"But then I saw Lisa Barrett," Martin went on slyly.

"Lisa? I thought it was Frank Sheldon's book." Lisa Barrett. She was either in the middle of an incredibly good run or the brightest new literary agent in London. And she was nice. The first time Oliver had seen her had been at Luigi's, where she'd been lunching with a paperback editor. She had been relaxed and smiling, unaware of his scrutiny. He saw a slender, fair-haired girl with serious blue eyes and a noticeable dimple in her chin. The dimple deepened when she smiled and drew his attention to her mouth. Oliver almost laughed now, recalling Cissy's reaction when he'd described Lisa to her. She'd listened without comment until he'd finished, then said flatly, "As long as she doesn't find anything remotely beautiful about you." Still, Lisa was the one fresh element in a world which had grown intolerably stale for him. . . .

"They *are* at the same agency, you know," Martin interrupted his reverie. "Anyway, Lisa said it went for thirty-seven thousand pounds."

Oliver frowned and repeated the figure. In commercial terms the novel had not been worth anything close to that. "What did we go up to?"

"Twelve thousand, *your* top figure, remember?"

"Well, I'm sure Peter Meredith knows what he's doing. It's a pity, though. The book would have been good for our list."

Oliver rummaged in his desk drawer, looking for one of the menthol cigarettes he occasionally smoked. He was about to cut the conversation short when Martin said, "Sidney's here with me. He wants a word."

"Not now, Martin—"

"Right. Ten minutes, he says."

Oliver hung up and glanced down at the memo on the top of a two-inch stack of papers in front of him. He knew what it was; he'd read it no fewer than four times over the last few days. Three suggestions for the autumn sales conference venue: a hotel in London, one in the Lake District, and the other in Majorca. He knew which one both the academic and trade sales forces would prefer. He also knew which one his father had already selected. The only question was whether or not he himself objected to the choice of the London hotel on behalf of the Jarman trade salesmen. But how could he? The trade list was weak, so weak that he would have a problem selecting which titles to treat as "major." Jarman academic made the money, and Sir Richard Jarman controlled the academic list and professed to know what the academic salesmen wanted. If he said London, it was London. Oliver knew that raising any objections on behalf of his trade division would be a waste of time.

He slotted a fresh tape into the small recorder he used to keep notes to himself. Before he decided what to do, he'd have a word with the overall sales director, see how strongly he felt about being cooped up in a London hotel for the fifth year running.

Oliver had just set the tape rolling when Sidney Niklas walked into the office. Oliver looked up at the glowering features of the editor with distaste and wondered just then who he despised more: himself for being there at all or the people he worked with—in particular Sidney Niklas and Martin Corbett. Between the two of them they exacted an atrocious price.

Dunne Morrissey, the publicity manager, followed Sidney in. From the way Dunne walked, hunched down into his baggy tweeds, Oliver knew that Sidney had all but dragged him here. Sidney was a bully, and Dunne had no ammunition against his tactics.

"What can I do for you?" Oliver asked.

Dunne sat down on the couch, perching in one corner, head down, as though willing himself to disappear. Sidney remained standing, arms folded. "Do you know what our whiz kid publicity manager here has just done?" he demanded.

"I'm neither a schoolmaster nor a mind reader," Oliver replied sharply.

Dunne, clutching his own elbows, cleared his throat. "Mervyn Hart's astrology book—I've fixed up an extract on *Woman's Hour*, and Mervyn will be a guest on Craig's phone-in program."

Oliver looked from one to the other. "What's wrong with that?"

"Small potatoes." Sidney leaned forward, placing both his fists on Oliver's desk. "Small fucking potatoes. Now tell us what you *didn't* do, Dunne!"

A faded burgundy bow tie lurched at Dunne's neck, emphasizing the pathetic plucked-chicken look about him. "We— I missed a deadline for first serial rights in the *Daily*—"

"Five thousand fucking pounds' worth of first serial!"

"Calm down, Sidney," Oliver rasped. The sound of his own voice sent a livid slash of pain through his temples. "Who's Mervyn's literary agent?"

"No agent," Sidney said. "Mervyn's an old school chum, came to me first with the book. What do I tell him now? That our witless friend here just chucked away four and a half thousand pounds of his money? Christ, talk about the great fucking unearned. We paid Mervyn a seventy-five-hundred-pound advance. We'd have been home and dry."

"No chance of getting the newspaper to change its mind, Dunne?" At least Mervyn Hart didn't have a literary agent to discover the mistake. If he had, there would have been an almighty rumpus. "No? Well, I don't see that there's anything useful to be gained by discussing it any further. Thank you, Dunne."

Sidney lurched back, his heavily bearded face pinched with fury. OJ looked like death, he thought savagely. Served the bastard right, didn't even have the sense to wear dark glasses and pretend to have an eye infection. There was no point in trying to get through to him when he was in this state. Sidney turned and strode across the room, reaching the door before Dunne. "What a bloody way to run a publishing company," Dunne heard him mutter and looked quickly to see if Oliver had heard. If he had, there was no indication of it.

Oliver blinked rapidly as the door shut behind the two men. The light tortured his eyes. From the top drawer of his desk he took half a bottle of Bell's whiskey and thought briefly about pouring the liquid into a glass. Why? Appearances. His mother's word. It covered every conceivable eventuality and at that moment suggested hidden and observant eyes . . . everywhere, watching with scorn as he raised the bottle to his lips. He still marveled at the awesome simplicity and brevity of most of his mother's precepts, and he cursed himself for still being bound by them. Only Cissy's gruff laughter stopped him from passing them on to his daughter, Pamela. Cissy . . . He took momentary refuge in the thought that she was not far away, that he could actually leave here now and be with her in less than thirty minutes. . . .

He had not handled that well. He'd done nothing to bolster Dunne's crippled self-confidence, and he'd failed to react to Sidney's last comment, which he knew he'd been meant to hear. God, how he loathed them all, the foulmouthed, ambitious, ineffectual lot of them. He could expect a visit from Deborah Anderson soon, he knew. She made sure she saw him at least once a day. Deborah was forty-two, small, neat, and inconspicuous, and she had been with Jarman's for precisely half her life. For fifteen of those twenty-one years she had been in love with Oliver. She monitored his life from the sidelines and defended him with dogged devotion. Graying brown hair, mottled gray-brown twin-sets—more than any of the others, even Sidney and Martin, Deborah exhausted him.

Oliver took another large mouthful of whiskey before cap-ping the bottle and locking it back in the drawer. The pain ringing his temples had eased somewhat. Perhaps he'd been wrong in persuading Angie to return. But then he comforted himself with the knowledge that neither he nor anyone else had ever been able to persuade her to do anything she didn't want to do. He hoped to God Cissy hadn't written to tell her about the results of his medical tests. He felt himself flush. *That* would have brought her home, and he didn't want her back for that reason. He'd realized long ago that Angie expected people to earn her loyalty and her love, commitments she did not undertake lightly. She'd given them to him, and she'd given them to Lou and professed scorn at Oliver's fears she had invested too much in Lou. Oliver had wanted to pull the two of them apart a bit. He and Cissy had met Lou on three occasions, twice for only a day or two; the third time they'd spent a holiday week together in a rented house in Sag Harbor. Oliver had recognized the flawless bond between his sister and the astonishingly placid man at her side. It seemed as if they breathed through each other's skins, and he wanted to shout words of caution. His fear was obscurely rooted in that other time, when his protection was all that had been left to her. . . .

No, she wasn't coming home because of some quack's doom-laden prognosis. He would tell her next week about the reports or maybe not at all. Or perhaps when she'd settled down and his father had taken himself off on his yearly trip to southern Africa. Next week . . . Now he wanted to lie down.

He told his secretary that he was going to the penthouse to make some private calls. He had a direct line, one which did not go through the switchboard, on his desk. She did not remind him of it.

He used his key to the private lift and unlocked the door of the flat with clumsy fingers. Halfway across the living room he stumbled and caught himself angrily. Peripheral neuritis they called it, the shooting pains in his hands and feet. He placed both hands against the small of his back and stretched, bringing on a stab of pain that caught at his breath. Then it was better, easing off as he lowered himself onto the bed. Alone. Quiet.

The light overhead was encased in an ornate silver and white shade. He looked at it for a moment. Had he seen it before? Puzzled, he continued to focus on it until his eyes closed. He never knew exactly when the idea came to him, but as he lay there, it became very clear that not *being* there would not be such a bad thing after all.

6

☐   The wheels slammed against the tarmac, and the woman sitting next to Angie crossed herself surreptitiously. The plane lifted and came down more gently, a great lumbering cocoon of noise and juddering movement.

A feeling akin to claustrophobia centered itself in Angie's chest, making it difficult for her to breathe. She concentrated on the woman who was now clutching at the armrest between them. Angie envied her that basic fear of death and also the relief that sent her into a giggling fit the moment all the wheels were safely on the ground. The irony of a crash landing at Heathrow after all that had happened was something Angie could almost have wished for. As the memory homed in, she drew a ragged breath and pulled her injured arm into her body, dragging it deliberately across the metal buckle of her seat belt, feeling a welcome wash of pain. This was the second time she'd flown since Lou's death, and she'd known it would be like this again: coming down, landing, no matter how hard she tried, there would be a dreamlike certainty that Lou would be waiting for her. He had been killed driving to meet her at Kennedy Airport, and he would now be at the end of every flight. . . .

The jolt of the reverse thrust of the engines sickened her as much as the pain in her arm, but the sensation of arriving here, in London, continued to elude her until the plane came to a full stop. And then only because of the spreading crimson on the bandage. She looked at the stain in dismay and tugged the sleeve of her jacket down impatiently. The blood made her think of Angelou. Good God, why? She hadn't seen him once during the flight and could do without his hectoring advice now.

By the time she reached the baggage hall, the flow of blood and the throbbing had eased, but she was grateful nonetheless that she had brought no luggage. She walked quickly, now eager to be out of the terminal and into the fresh air. When she saw Paul Angelou waiting at the entrance to customs, she found a smile. He looked immaculate, shaven and rested, completely at ease. He stood without moving until she reached him, and she was aware once more of that lapping warmth . . . and also a contradictory chill that lodged a warning in her brain. It struck her just then that for all he knew—or guessed—about her, all *she* knew about him was his name.

"I'm safely in London, see?" she said with a laugh. "I'm sorry if I was less than courteous at Kennedy, but you caught me on the hop with all that nonsense about suicide."

"I'm glad it was nonsense," he replied carefully. "I take it someone's meeting you?"

"My sister-in-law."

In the harsh fluorescent lighting he could see dark gold specks of color splinter around her dilated pupils. He said, "Good. Give my regards to Sir Richard when you see him."

He was doing it again. Angie ran the tip of her tongue between dry lips and waited for him to continue. When it became obvious that he was not about to elaborate on his statement, she said, unnecessarily, "You know my father?" And then: "You're not a doctor by any chance, are you?"

"Arm giving you trouble?"

"Don't you ever answer a question!"

"Sometimes, Mrs. Wyatt," he said calmly. "No, I'm not a doctor, and yes, I've known your father for some years."

Standing there, Angie experienced the novelty of embarrassment. Her face felt like a mask, eyes gritty and inflamed. What was the matter with her? "I'm sorry."

"There's no need to apologize."

She could have sworn it was said almost speculatively, but before she could react, he'd left her. In a quick, compact movement he'd turned on his heel and was striding back into the hall to collect his luggage.

Angie opened her mouth to call him back. Tired and confused, she resented him hugely at that moment. She imagined what he must be thinking: that she was a spoiled and vain woman, used to demanding and getting her own way. Her outburst had been petty. He had provoked it, but that was no excuse. As she swung around and began to walk through the green customs passage, she made herself face an unpalatable truth: she actually cared what he thought of her; she was excited by the somber, secretive aura about him and the fact that he frightened her.

Stupidly her step faltered, and every thought of Paul Angelou was driven out of her head by the stunning impact of not seeing Lou's face among all those ringing the exit doors. Her arm came up, as though to ward off a blow. She saw Cissy edging forward through the crowd toward her. She wasn't smiling. Maxwell Reith hadn't been smiling either that day at Kennedy Airport. . . .

"Unless you're waiting to fly out somewhere, Max," she said, in greeting him, "Lou's blackmailed you into meeting me." Maxwell had recently been appointed publisher of the Bennett-Poore trade division. He and Lou had worked together on the thirty-fourth floor of the Bennett-Poore building for seven years. "Where is he?"

"Lou couldn't make it," Maxwell told her. He took her suitcase and steered her toward the exit. "Christ, Angie, I don't know how to tell you this."

"You've sent him to the Ozarks to shack up with Willard, haven't you? I know the deadline's next week, but couldn't it have waited one more day?" They were outside, being jostled by cabhunters. He took her arm again.

"Angie, you must be brave."

And she knew Lou was dead. She knew it as her suitcase slipped from his fingers; she could tell by the hard held-in feel of him. "What happened?"

"He was on his way to meet you." Maxwell pressed her into the back seat of a waiting police car, then climbed in beside her. She stared out of the window as he spoke. A furniture van crossing the central reservation, unavoidable, head-on . . . instant. Instant?

Her mind split away. The police driver chose a route into the city that took forever. She made no comment, concentrating on turning a deaf ear to Maxwell's pleas. "They won't let you see him, not yet. For God's sake, Angie, give them a chance to—to clean him up."

They didn't want to take her past the scene of the accident, and now they didn't want her to see him. A dazed kind of anger made her push Maxwell away. "I'll wait."

"Morgue?" The driver glanced back at them.

"Angie . . ."

"The morgue, yes. Do his parents know? Has anyone told them? His brother?"

"I guess so, by now," Maxwell sighed.

They sat in silence in the icy corridor for nearly four hours. She thought it looked and sounded more like a hospital than a mortuary. Maxwell ran out of words, and it was all she could do to stop herself from screaming at him to leave her alone. He must have made some telephone calls because people kept turning up, weeping. She hardly recognized them, relieved when they turned to go.

She was expecting a refrigerated drawer to be pulled out of a vast filing cabinet of a wall. Instead, he lay on a gleaming chrome table. She was expecting crisp white cotton as a covering but found a plastic sheet. Was he still bleeding? The thought shocked and comforted her. It suggested life. One of the two men in the room lifted the plastic sheet away from his face. Angie frowned and half turned to tell Maxwell, who hadn't come in with her, that this was how she'd left Lou, sleeping. They had brushed some hair down over his forehead to hide a livid bruise. He'd allowed his hair to grow longer because of her "English-poncy-public-school" preference, then admitted that it suited his long, clean-shaven "English" face. She pushed the hair back and was aware of both men moving simultaneously as she leaned over to place her cheek over his mouth and nose. No breath . . .

"Take the sheet away," she said softly.

"That's not advisable, miss. No."

Angie turned to the second man. "Can he refuse?"

"I'm a doctor, and no, he can't, but he's right."

"Then take the sheet away."

The blood looked fresh, the bones of his crushed chest bleached white, incredibly fragile. His hips and legs were pale and unmutilated. It wasn't truly real, the pulp and splintered bone. Less than four days ago that stopped heart had been thudding against her breasts. . . .

"Angie!" Cissy was shaking her. "Hey!"

"Stop it," Angie whispered, feeling herself jolted back into the present. She focused with difficulty on the tall woman who was clutching her shoulders. "Cissy . . . let go, I'm all right. Listen, I'm . . . happy to see you."

Cissy studied her closely for a moment, then said, "Rub-

bish, you're not, and neither would I be in your shoes.
Where's your luggage?''

"I didn't bring any."

"Fine. Let's go, I'm double-parked."

The hurting sounds in Angie's throat turned into a hiccup
of relief. Lou had loved this quiet, eccentrically down-to-
earth woman. There was no one, not even Oliver, who could
so effectively have drained her welling panic.

Outside, the early-morning air smelled damp. She followed
Cissy to a red, low-slung Citroën, which was not so much
parked as abandoned, the driver's door left wide open.

"Always works," Cissy said smugly. "See?"

Angie watched as Cissy smiled at an advancing policeman,
as if daring him to admonish her. She saw the man hesitate,
take in the beige Burberry, buttoned up to the neck, the silk
headscarf, and what must have been a glint of warning in
Cissy's eyes. "See?" Cissy said again. "Makes them think
of emergencies, sick children, *guilt.*"

Oliver was ferociously law-abiding, but even he had become inured to Cissy's vendetta against traffic wardens and
strolling policemen. She'd bought the Citroën as part of the
vendetta. Whenever she parked, she moved the suspension
lever into its low position, ensuring that the chassis settled
down, half obscuring the wheels; it was the one saloon car
which could not be immobilized by a wheel clamp.

As they slipped into the traffic on the M4, Angie broke
into Cissy's nervous chatter; there was a brittle, disquieting
defensiveness about her that Angie could not remember having encountered before. She also looked worn-out. "How's
Oliver?"

"He promised to be home early . . . threeish. What are
you going to do now that you're back, Angie? How long are
you staying?"

The questions came too quickly. Angie said, "I don't
know."

That at least was partly true. She already felt displaced by
the familiar sights and sounds of London. Everything seemed
less possible here. She said warily, "Publishing, and American publishing at that, is just about all I know. How is Jarman's doing?"

"Well enough," Cissy replied, but without conviction. "If
Oliver hasn't been able to kill it off after all these years, it's

obviously bigger than all of us." The response was mechanical, but the strain in Cissy's face told a different story.

"He still hates it so much?" It wasn't really a question.

"More than ever. I've always thought how odd that must sound to you, being with Lou and sharing so much of what you did, together."

"Lou wanted to be an editor the way some children want to drive fire engines or be nurses. It was like some kind of religion to him."

Cissy seemed scarcely to be listening. Like her earlier inconsequential observations about the weather, the price of petrol, and the general intransigence of Margaret Thatcher, this abstraction worried Angie. She said, changing the subject deliberately, "Did you leave a message for me at Kennedy?"

"You got that? I actually thought I might be able to speak to you there."

"You amaze me." Angie sighed. "I can't imagine what it must be like to believe that all things are possible—even getting *through* to the airport. Do you know what Paul Angelou does for a living?"

"Who?" Cissy took her eyes off the road to glance quickly at Angie.

"Angelou—he was on the same plane. He said he knew my father."

Cissy tapped her forefinger against the lower rim of the steering wheel. "Come to think of it, the name *is* familiar. He's something in the City, I seem to recall, but we've never met. Why do you ask?"

"Because you and he . . . and probably Oliver, too . . . jumped to the same conclusion about this." Angie raised her arm slightly.

"Oh. I'm sorry . . . I was anxious about you. You can't blame me for that, can you?"

"I suppose not, but please remember, if I ever decide to do away with myself, you and Oliver will be the first to know. And by that I mean I'll address the suicide note to you. All right?"

Cissy reacted sharply. "That's not funny, Angie."

"It wasn't intended to be. Incidentally, I need to get this dressing changed sometime today. No, don't pull over now, for God's sake!"

Cissy pulled over onto the hard shoulder and made Angie lift the sleeve of her jacket. No fresh blood was evident on

the bandage. "Not too bad," she muttered, and Angie had
to laugh at the reproachful tone. "Hammersmith Hospital has
an outpatients department. We'll stop there."

For the first time that morning Cissy sounded like herself,
assured and decisive. Getting the bandage changed was
something to *do*. Angie sat back as the Citroën began to pick
up speed again. "Come on, Cissy. I want to know more
about what's been happening here." She hadn't meant the
words to come out sounding so dispassionate and demanding,
but the instinctive feeling that something was amiss still
nagged at her.

"Not now. Give yourself some time—"

"Don't, we know each other too well. What aren't you
telling me? And incidentally, why aren't you at the school
today?"

Cissy made a show of grinning sheepishly. "Teachers'
strike. School's closed. Very convenient."

"Nice try. I'm too tired to go about this gently, so you
might as well tell me about those bloody great circles under
your eyes."

"Don't bully me, Angie. Don't you have nights when you
just can't sleep?"

"Often," Angie said dryly. "But you don't. That was one
of the first things Oliver told me about you. He said you slept
like a dead rhino."

"And don't make me laugh, my head hurts."

Angie lit a cigarette. The first inhalation tasted like the
regurgitated air on the plane. She watched Cissy's hands
clench on the steering wheel as she pulled out into the fast
lane. "It's Oliver, isn't it?"

"Why do you say that?"

"Because he looked gray and ill the last time I saw him."

"Nonsense," Cissy said thickly.

"Is it nonsense, too, that he was getting through the best
part of two bottles of whiskey a day, even then? That he could
scarcely focus before noon?"

"You know he drinks. You've always known. Everybody
knows."

"Cissy, please, don't make me work for this. I'm coming
apart. . . ."

"Yes, and you don't need this right now. Light a cigarette
for me, too, would you?"

"You're crying!" Angie was amazed. Her sister-in-law

coped and cared and solved. Self-pity was no part of her makeup. The sight of tears purling out of her eyes was something Angie thought she'd never see. "Is it Pamela? Is she ill?"

"Shhh, no." Cissy accepted the cigarette with shaking fingers. "Oliver had some tests done a few weeks ago, and he has to . . . go away."

"What do you mean? What tests?"

Cissy swiped angrily at a wet cheek. "This is ridiculous. I can't see properly. I haven't cried for—they say that unless he stops drinking altogether and immediately, he won't live the year out. His heart muscles are almost irreversibly weakened."

Angie's mouth went dry. Her tongue fastened to her palate, and Cissy's words came to her as if from a great distance.

"It's his last chance, and I'm frightened, Angie. He won't check into a clinic; he says he can't leave Jarman's for a year, but it's really that he can't face life without drinking. He tells me he feels fine, all doctors are quacks anyway, but you saw . . . you'll see . . ."

"Don't cry. Please stop crying. Does my father know?"

Cissy nodded vehemently, tears tracking straight lines down to her chin. "I called him the moment I found out, but he—he—"

"He wouldn't discuss it," Angie interrupted flatly.

"He was annoyed, angry. He thanked me for telling him and put the phone down."

"Why haven't you told *me* all this before? Poor Cissy, how terrible it must have been for you."

"I was going to write to tell you that Oliver was going in for the tests; but you'd lost Lou, and I couldn't burden you with another crisis." She recalled the strange, wary tension that had hung over them all for the past twenty-four hours, ever since Angie's decision to return. Even Pamela, who hardly knew her, speculated about the suddenness of her decision.

"I expect it won't be for long" had been Richard Jarman's comment.

"Benn will see to it that Angela's rooms are prepared" was Belinda's.

Now Angie tipped her head back and closed her eyes. "You should have told me, Cissy. Shut your window, please, I'm freezing." Her jaw was clenched to keep her teeth from chattering, but it wasn't the cold. It was a sudden shock of desolation that gripped her. This was what Lou would have called the penultimate straw, the one that ensured that the last one broke your back. She had come back for one reason and only one reason: to find her daughter. Everything else she'd seen as a distraction, a maze that Lou would have been there to guide her through. Now this. Lou was gone, and Cissy was warning her of a life without Oliver.

"Thank God Pamela's at school," Cissy was saying. "I don't want her to see me like this."

"Does she know?"

"Not yet, but I'll have to say something soon. It's just that she's coming up to A-levels . . . seventeen should be such a wonderful age."

"It wasn't for me."

"Oh, God, I'm sorry, I didn't mean . . . I think I'm going crazy. I wouldn't blame you if you took the next plane out."

Angie found herself laughing. "You're the sanest person I know, and the last thing I'm going to do is walk away."

"All right, but hysteria is not what you need right now."

"You needed to weep as much as I need to sleep for a week or two. Now it's done, over with."

Cissy eased her foot off the accelerator as they approached the two-lane Chiswick flyover. "There really is a teachers' strike today, you know," she said. "But I gave up teaching five months ago."

"Because of Oliver?"

"I can't bear to lose him, Angie."

"You won't." How could that come out with such assurance? "Is he worried about the business?"

"Very. Not that he tells me a great deal about it. From what I can make out there seem to be hopeless staff and the wrong books."

Angie almost laughed again at Cissy's simplistic judgment. She herself had only the vaguest notion of Jarman's current list of books, and apart from her father's secretary and Deborah Anderson, she couldn't recall the name of a single member of the staff.

"Was last year bad as well?" she prodded gently.

"The last three or four years haven't been good. Last year alone, he said, their pretax profits were down by twenty-six percent. He's blaming himself, of course, although I must say he has some pretty, um, odd people around him."

Angie was surprised. "You know them?"

"Not really, but I've met them on a few occasions, parties and so on. Deborah Anderson is an editor and a sort of editorial manager, a nice, quiet—"

"I've met Deborah. She's been with Oliver for at least twenty years."

"Longer, I suspect. The other two editors are both men, Sidney Niklas and Martin Corbett. Sidney is obnoxious by all accounts and unpopular inside and outside the house. That also seems to go for Martin Corbett. He's the son of Jason Corbett, the printer, who also happens to be a close friend of your father's. A job for the boy, you might say. Editorially that's about it. Cynthia Crew has been selling rights for . . . oh, about three years now. A youngish old maid with airs, if you know what I mean."

"That's what Oliver's been working with?" Angie was aghast. "Why doesn't he get rid of them?"

"This is London, not New York," Cissy said bitterly. "We have industrial tribunals and suchlike. Stupidity and incompetence are no longer adequate reasons to dismiss anyone."

"And my father? How closely is he involved?"

"Enough, from what Oliver tells me. Board meetings, with Sir Richard scowling at the trade figures, aren't much fun, he says. But then neither are all the other meetings. In fact, there's not a damn thing Oliver likes about that place."

Angie realized that she'd closed her eyes and ears to Jarman's so firmly and for so many years that Cissy might as well have been telling her a fairy story. Her own career in publishing had been checkered, stunted by the casual assumption that the wealthy worked for kicks, that paychecks were pin money. Between bouts of enforced idleness, she'd done everything—from selling subsidiary rights to publicity, editorial, and sales. Not even to Lou could she explain why she did not do what everyone expected her to do: start up a company of her own. He, too, had looked askance at the way she squandered her own talents while fostering those of others. She loved publishing but held herself back from its center, not remaining at any job long enough to be absorbed into the system. The system, as she saw it, catered ultimately to the elite, a domain that could have been invented by her father. And she wanted no part of his world.

After many years of careful administration Jarman academic, from which a substantial portion of the family's fortune derived, ran without a hitch. Highly trained staff carried out their research meticulously before commissioning and producing the cost-effective reference books, textbooks for schools, and the wide range of specialist academic books for colleges and universities.

Sir Richard Jarman had set up the trade division in the late 1950's in shrewd anticipation of the escapist trend, particularly toward fiction and popular biographies. He had swiftly established a trade backlist consisting of out-of-copyright classics and books in which the rights had reverted. Before his competitors were aware of it, he had brought Jarman trade into their midst, reaping instant rewards, breaking into markets which did not exist for academic books, using his network of subsidiary companies throughout the English-speaking world to ensure that each title paid its way. The list had reflected his own tastes, and advances always reflected his personal opinion of a book's potential.

It was generally believed that Sir Richard had started the trade list for Oliver. There had certainly never been any question but that Oliver would one day take over its management. He was told that he would read history, as sound a preparation as any for a future publisher. He'd known better than to suggest alternatives. His love of archaeology was put aside for his leisure time. That was somehow an adventurer's profession, a rich man's hobby. Publishing was a gentleman's preserve, and Oliver was to continue that tradition. . . .

Cissy took her eyes off the road again for a moment and glanced at Angie. She recognized the look of battered anger: Jarman's, her parents, Oliver's continuing dilemma. She'd seen that look on Angie's face so many times, and it always scared her. She asked quietly, "What are you going to do?"

"We must help him," Angie said simply, then added, "If we live long enough. Slow down and move over unless you want a punch-up with that Jag behind you."

Cissy turned her attention back to the road and allowed her speed to drop back. "What kind of speed is that?" she demanded as the other car hurtled past them. "At least sixty, my God!" She grumbled about men drivers in general for a few minutes, conveniently forgetting that she had just taken the Citroën well over the speed limit herself. Finally, when she'd run out, she said, "You know what I mean, Angie. What are you going to do?"

Good question, thought Angie. Aloud she said, "I don't know. Ask some questions, nothing to be alarmed about." She knew a fair cross section of London publishing and had a few good friends she could call on for answers.

"Oh, before I forget, your father called last night, and he's asked us all down to the Hall for the weekend. Your mother said you would probably need the rest."

A smile of deprecation pulled Angie's mouth down at the corners. "What Angela needs . . ." Her mother's voice, clipped and precise and wooden. Lady Jarman of Calvert Hall, Belinda Jarman—what did *she* think of the time limit on her son's life? Angie wondered. Belinda. It could have been a soft name, but it wasn't; she never allowed it to be shortened to Belle, to be abused by affection. The handsome Jacobean mansion Belinda Jarman presided over had been in the Calvert family for seven generations, and it was her inherited money that accounted for most of the Jarman wealth. It irked her mother, Angie knew, that Oliver would inherit Calvert Hall and pass it on to his daughter, Pamela, whose name when she married would be neither Calvert nor Jarman.

The mere mention of Calvert Hall, set in the green tranquillity of Sussex, bounded by dense woodland, fields, and orchards, retained the power to wrench Angie painfully back into the past. After all these years, she could still see the sun bouncing off the greenhouse windows, hear the horses clattering over the cobbled yard, feel the finely manicured lawn dewy beneath forbidden bare feet, smell the mustiness of small hidden places, recall the yearning to be forgotten in the endless humming of unseen activity all around. . . .

"You don't mind going down to the Hall?" Cissy was asking.

"I do mind, very much, but it's necessary, especially now." She saw Cissy's instant frown of foreboding. "I'll help Oliver. Believe me, I'll do everything I can."

"Angie . . ."

"I'll help him, Cissy. And this time I'll do it with or without my father's OK."

Cissy had cause to remember Angie's words a few hours later, when Oliver came home. She saw her sister-in-law flinch with surprise at Oliver's appearance, and those words, spoken in defiance a short time ago, echoed hollowly. There was no way Cissy could adequately have prepared Angie, but she wondered if she had deliberately played down the enormous change in Oliver, so that the sight of him would shock Angie into some action. If she had, it had been selfish because she now knew why Angie had returned to England.

The early-afternoon hours before Oliver's return had served an uneasy purpose. In the tranquil comfort of the drawing room in Kensington Square, Angie had been unusually quiet, as if considering something she hadn't yet decided to do or talk about. A combination of rich colors and widely varied textures wrapped her in a quiet warmth. Persian rugs glowed on the polished wooden floor; a chaise longue in dark watered silk harmonized unexpectedly with Queen Anne chairs covered with faded velvet. Fragments of ancient Greek pottery and sculpture—part of Oliver's cherished collection—stood on an eighteenth-century torchère and a delicate drop leaf table.

Angie lay stretched out on the chaise, consciously trying to break down the situation which confronted her into smaller, more manageable proportions. It wasn't working. She was going to need help to find her daughter. And advice. She needed someone she could trust, to whom she could reach out . . . *now*, when self-doubt had already begun to erode her determination. You need a mother, she thought tartly. What Angela needs . . . is a mother. She must have spoken the last words aloud because Cissy asked her to repeat them. Cissy didn't exactly qualify as a mother figure, but who else was there?

Angie said, "I want you to know something."

Cissy was in the process of pouring her fifth cup of tea and had given up asking Angie if she would have one. "Tell me," she said.

"I'll rephrase that. I'd *like* to tell you about a decision I've made. You're not going to approve of it, but I need . . . my hand held."

"Good Lord," Cissy murmured, not knowing what was coming or what tone to take. "You?"

Angie eased herself up into a sitting position. "Why not me?"

"You don't know? How long have we known each other? Practically a lifetime. When have you ever asked me for anything, let alone hand holding? Or anyone, for that matter?"

"I don't understand. You, the two of you, know more about my life than anyone . . . including Lou."

Cissy shook her head adamantly. "I'm not talking about that. You said you needed your hand held, and it surprised me, that's all. Whether you realize it or not, you're like a—a—" Cissy glanced away, images of a fox hunt streaking through her mind. "A small, wild animal, hibernating with its wounds, only venturing out when it has healed itself."

"I've never asked for help, is that what you're saying?"

"Have you?" Cissy wasn't expecting an eruption, but she wasn't prepared for Angie's weary resignation either.

"I guess not. That doesn't mean I didn't need it. Or want it."

Cissy put her cup and saucer down, suddenly afraid of what Angie was building up to. "I realize that," she said gently, "but you do make it difficult for anyone to get really close to you. I can't blame you for a certain amount of skepticism, but that hands off sign you've carried around for years—well, it's a shield that has worked only too well."

Angie was staring at her, wide-eyed, and when she spoke, it was to say, "Ouch" and then: "I'll have that drink now, but make it a whiskey, please."

"On an empty stomach and on top of that analgesic they gave you at the hospital?" When Angie didn't answer, she added crossly, "You're exactly as Oliver describes you—*difficult*. And I would add a 'bloody' to that."

Angie laughed. "You're right."

"Argue with me, for God's sake!"

"Why? You're right."

"That's what makes you even more difficult: You're so *bloody* honest I could strangle you." Cissy jumped to her feet and went over to the drinks cabinet.

What were they talking about? What Cissy said made sense. Angie had sought safety in Lou to the exclusion of everyone else. And before Lou she had peered out from her lair with suspicious eyes. True. She associated Lou with a warm, inviolable safety; their love affair had been deep and consistent, without jealousies and dangers. And without blood-surging excitements. Was that why the glimpse of Paul Angelou's power had turned her on so instantly? She'd been unable to banish Angelou from her mind, even in the midst of so many other preoccupations. Was the small, wild animal to emerge from its hibernation only to invite another attack?

Angie shuddered and took a deep swallow of the drink Cissy handed her. Before she changed her mind, she said,

"I've come back to find my daughter." Crazy not to have anticipated Cissy's look of horror. It would have been nice to leave now, give Cissy time to digest the news and, if she could, come to terms with it.

"Oh, Angie." Cissy slumped back in her chair. "Why now? I'm thinking selfishly, but why now?"

"I'm not sure myself."

"I'm not going to ask you if you've considered all the implications because you must have done. But why now? Has it got anything to do with what happened to Lou?"

"Not directly. It was in any case something we planned to do together."

"When?" Cissy got up again and began striding about the room. "When were you and Lou going to do it?"

"We'd been talking about it on and off for two years. He was waiting for me to decide . . . when I was ready."

Cissy's voice was hushed with shock. "And you're ready now?"

"I told you you wouldn't like it."

"It's got nothing to do with liking it. All I can see is pain . . . for you and Oliver."

"I don't want Oliver to know, not for a while anyway. Will you help me?"

Cissy lifted her shoulders in a gesture of resignation. "Of course, I will. What can I do?"

"I need a lawyer, someone who's quick and discreet."

"Christopher Chetwynd," Cissy said without hesitation. "He's Oliver's lawyer and a family friend. He'll be honest with you; he'll tell you if it's possible for you to find your daughter after all these years."

"Thank you. What are you thinking, Cissy? Am I wrong?"

"Not wrong, my love, but I'm afraid for you . . . and Oliver. You share different parts of the same nightmare, you know. His problems are so deeply embedded in that time. . . . Maybe this way you'll both have a chance, who's to know?"

Angie understood Cissy's sense of helplessness just then. This was going to hurt Oliver, and neither of them wanted that. Later, in the flat, fading light of early evening, Angie realized why Cissy's first concern had been for her husband, that everything else had to take second place. Oliver looked like an old man. The pale, sallow skin bore wrinkles and sagging pouches of flesh which had no place on a man of his age. His gray eyes looked feverishly bright, and from time to time Angie saw him drifting away into a desolate world of his own. Two small table lamps threw soft shadows into the deepening gloom, and Angie felt a guilty relief at not being able to see him very clearly.

"This is a *comfortable* house, Oliver. I hope you never sell it," she said irrelevantly.

"Whiskey?" He took his own glass over to the cabinet for a refill.

"A small one," Angie said. With an effort she tore her gaze away from the tall, shambling figure. He bore no resemblance at all to the boy she'd grown up with, shared tree houses, night feasts, and *Lady Chatterley's Lover* with. As Cissy left the room, murmuring something about dinner, Angie said, "I have to tell you that you look terrible, Oliver." He didn't know that Cissy had told her about the tests he'd undergone.

Oliver leaned over to give her the drink and peered down into her face. "You don't look so good yourself. Cheers."

"I'm serious."

"So am I. Angie, you haven't come back expecting the merry hell of it all to have been a bad dream, have you?"

Angie smiled across at him. "I don't know about that. In my rare moments of lucidity I *can* tell the difference between the grays and the rosy pinks. Not that well, mind you. Just enough to duck clear."

"Lucidity?"

"Clarity of thought and action, as Father would say. The swing and the follow-through. Don't laugh."

"I wasn't going to."

"Time destroys so many illusions," she said wistfully. "Nothing new, but so many grand illusions go. I had them once. I still have a few, I suppose, scrappier but still there. About all this. I'm becoming maudlin . . . stop me."

Cissy came back to tell them that dinner was ready. Oliver said suddenly, "Stay here tonight, Angie. Cissy will drive you over to Chelsea tomorrow. Pointless to traipse all the way over there tonight."

Her flat was not far from Kensington Square, but as they both looked at her expectantly, Cissy with more than a hint of tension, she nodded. "I *am* tired." Too tired to prevent Angelou from invading her thoughts, too tired to rebel against this pitiful charade. With the day nearly gone, so much said and learned, they were all still pretending something else:

Angie that she wasn't hopelessly shocked each time she looked at Oliver, Cissy that the prospect of Angie's search for her child need not affect her husband, and Oliver that the shooting pains in his legs were due to poor circulation and nothing more.

After dinner Cissy left them again to prepare one of the spare bedrooms for the night. After a few minutes they heard her call from upstairs, "Ready when you are."

"Don't go up yet, in case Father calls," Oliver said. "Parental devotion!"

"If he does, tell him I'll talk to him in the morning. And ask him to give my regards to Mother while you're at it." Oliver looked up from massaging his calf muscle and regarded Angie with troubled suspicion. "It's all right," she said with an impatient laugh. "It doesn't matter anymore."

"I knew you'd say that."

"I'm not just saying it. I think I finally really believe it."

From the doorway Cissy watched Oliver draw Angie upright and crush her fiercely in his arms. "Go to bed, Angie. We'll talk tomorrow. God, you're skinnier than ever."

Angie pulled back to study him in turn. "They'd have to hunt to find their pound of flesh on you, too. Apart from this . . ." She patted his stomach where the material of his shirt was gaping slightly.

"Middle-age spread," he said, grinning over her shoulder at Cissy.

"Uh-huh." Light-headed, aware of an overwhelming lassitude, Angie made an effort to shut the door quietly behind her. Upstairs in the large spare bedroom, a nightdress and bathrobe were laid out on the bed. A pitcher of water and two glasses stood on the bedside table. The window was open. Without breaking her stride, she shut the window, drew the curtains, and took off all her clothes. Then she pulled the bedcover back and slid straight between the sheets. The linen smelled evocatively of sunlight and starch. Home.

7

☐   The meeting took place at the Viceroy Security Building in the City of London, where Paul Angelou had his offices. Harry Baird had arrived expecting to see a lavish setup but nothing as studiedly luxurious as this.

On the fourteenth floor a sleek young secretary with the sort of looks and accent he associated with double-barreled surnames ushered him into a small anteroom behind smoked-glass sliding panels.

A dazzling smile was thrown his way. "Is there anything you'd like, Mr. Baird? Tea . . . coffee? It's just gone four-fifteen, and Mr. Angelou will be with you very shortly."

"Coffee, if there's any going," Harry said automatically.

"There's *always* some going, Mr. Baird."

Good Christ, she made him feel fusty and frayed, as though he were twelve years old again and serving behind the counter in his father's tobacconist's shop in Clapham. He ran his finger around the inside of his shirt cuffs, pulling first one and then the other down. It wasn't necessary. The shirt was custom-made from Turnbull and Asser; his suit, from Tommy Nutter. Hell, he thought, amused and annoyed, it was a long time since anyone had made him feel even slightly unsure of himself.

An air conditioner hummed somewhere. The *Times, Financial Times, Wall Street Journal,* and a current edition of *Punch* lay neatly stacked on a low table. Harry sat down and looked around for an ashtray. He finally decided that the glass container the size of a hubcap was indeed an ashtray and not an empty ornament. Too bad if it wasn't.

He lit a Silk Cut just as the coffee arrived: silver pot, bone china cup and saucer, a glass of iced water on the side. And again the smile. No sugar. How did she know he took it black, without sugar?

No sooner had the glass doors hissed shut than they opened

again. "Mr. Angelou will see you now, Mr. Baird. Follow me, please . . . and do bring your coffee."

Angelou's office was the size of a tennis court. It had three distinct areas: a softly lit corner was hemmed in by a large couch and two armchairs; at right angles was a huge television set, faced by more armchairs and sidetables. Most of the space was, however, given over to the office part. A telex machine gurgled efficiently in the background.

As the man behind the desk rose to shake his hand, Harry thought wryly that compared with this office, the plush reception area looked like a parking lot. And that Paul Angelou was nothing like he'd imagined. He saw a tall, slender, yet powerfully built man whose expression he could think of only as austere. In the subdued light he could detect graying at the temples. White shirt, dark suit and tie. Angelou could have been any one of the thousands of moneymen in the City if it hadn't been for the extraordinary sense of power that emanated from him. From the watchful, hooded eyes to the immaculately manicured fingernails Paul Angelou was, even at this first encounter, quite unlike anyone Harry had ever met.

"I trust the urgency of my request didn't put you out too much, Mr. Baird," he said now.

Harry took a mouthful of coffee and placed the cup and saucer on the desk in front of him. "Not at all, Mr. Angelou, although I was naturally surprised to receive your call."

Paul was interested to note that Baird had made no attempt to hide his curiosity. The man had a round, boyishly open face and an aura of inquisitiveness that belied his skill as a negotiator. Paul was also interested to see that the City's newest whiz kid had not seen fit to trim the curly, slightly overlong hair and affect the somber pinstripe City uniform. The hair made him look younger than his thirty-two years, and the light gray suit was more in keeping with advertising than finance.

"I assume you've asked me here because of that last takeover," Baird ventured with a disarming grin, and added, unnecessarily, "The one we were in competition over, that is."

Paul sat back and let his steepled fingers hide a tightening of his lips. "Your *success* with that takeover is *precisely* the reason you're here."

"You surprise me, Mr. Angelou," Harry said lightly.

"Touché, because you surprised *me*. If I didn't know your senior director so well, I'd have suspected some—"

"Dirty dealings? Sorry to disappoint you, but the boss knew about my every move. I'm not saying he would have approached the objective in quite the same way, but there was nothing shady about it."

"I know that," Paul told him, "but without you he would have lost the bid, and my own people *did* lose it. There are cumbersome traditions in City corridors which you seem to be able to sidestep. I would like to know how my adviser was outfoxed, Mr. Baird. I would like to know how one of the best financial brains in the City found himself in second place."

Was that a compliment or a criticism? Certainly it was a question Angelou had no right to ask. Harry was beginning to enjoy himself. Could it be that this man's legendary astuteness was just another City myth? "I'm not at liberty to divulge that sort of information," he replied blandly, "as you well know."

They looked at each other in silence. Paul Angelou's face remained expressionless, and Harry had the disquieting impression that he was being tested.

"What are your ambitions, Mr. Baird?" Angelou spoke suddenly. "I take it you *are* ambitious?"

For a moment Harry thought he'd missed something. To gain time, he pulled out his cigarettes and raised a questioning eyebrow. He might as well have been soliciting a reaction from one of the exquisite prints on the wall. "My ambitions are of the kind that make confidences the absolute and unbreakable rule," he said with care. That was clearly *not* what Angelou wanted to hear. He added, "The game is there to be played, and I happen to play it very well. The stakes are high, and I like to win."

"Does sixty thousand pounds a year, even with considerable additional bonuses, strike you as being adequate recompense for your . . . winning?"

Harry laughed, annoyed once more but now fascinated by the other man's seemingly simple approach. The salary was correct, but then it didn't take much effort to get that sort of information.

"Let's put it this way, Mr. Angelou. I'm thirty-two years old, a junior partner in a reputable firm of merchant bankers. I have a wife and two children and support aging parents. I live in a comfortable house in St. John's Wood, drive a BMW, and holiday twice a year in the Bahamas. Without being fastidious about the word, I would call that adequate.''

"Then I can only assume you enjoy your work," Paul said flatly.

"Totally. In a devious, Machiavellian way, it panders to my every fantasy.''

"Fantasies of power?''

"If you like. Power and danger, the gamble . . . yes.''

"I appreciate your honesty, Mr. Baird.''

Harry shrugged, appearing calmer than he felt. He had, over the years, perfected a mask of good-natured deference for those in whose company he felt ill at ease. The mask was well in place now. "It's a change to meet a man who asks quite such blunt questions, Mr. Angelou.''

Paul stood up, surreptitiously pressing a button on his desk. "I think we understand each other," he said, and then, as his secretary came into the room: "Join me over here, Mr. Baird, it's rather more comfortable.''

When they were seated in the deep luxury of the leather armchairs, each with a glass of gin and tonic, poured with polished deliberation by the secretary, Paul raised his drink. "To more than adequate rewards.''

It occurred to Harry that not once had he seen Angelou smile. Inscrutable was a word he rarely found applicable. It was now. Before he could say anything, Paul went on. "I'm going to put a proposition to you, Mr. Baird, one which I think will interest you. If it does not, I expect it to stop here, in this room, and I will ensure that our paths do not cross again. Ever. Is that understood?''

A small knot of excitement lodged in Harry's throat, and a veneer of unreality descended on the entire proceedings.

"Without going into great detail now, let me tell you a little about my background. I was less than two years old when my family came to England from Greece, and we were penniless. By chance more than design, my father began a small business by collecting and selling paper, magazines, comics that came into this country as ballast on American ships. Being an astute man, he sold some, which would now be labeled soft porn, clandestinely. In the case of comic books he would sell them for, say, fourpence each and, when they'd been read, buy them back for a penny. Sometimes he'd resell them, but again, once he realized that paper was in chronically short supply, he started selling them for pulp and, later, pulping them himself. The comics and periodicals were fine, but it was naturally the men's magazines that brought the most profit. They paid for a house in Soho, a private education for me. My father owns various properties and businesses in Soho, including an office block, restaurant, and nightclub and, although it's not generally known, a video arcade selling pornographic books and videos.''

Paul Angelou spoke as though he were reciting a list of telephone numbers. There was not a shred of emotion in his voice; not once did his gaze wander from Harry's face.

''You don't appear to be surprised, Mr. Baird. Let me add, though, that the Doric Video arcade is legitimate. None of his dealings is, I have ascertained, illegal. What I have decided to do, not without a great deal of thought, is one of two things: if it can be done discreetly, I should like to see the holding company and all its subsidiaries go into liquidation. If that is not possible, a takeover and subsequent dispersal of the assets would be in order.''

Harry realized that his heart was tripping erratically. His lips formed a soft ''phew,'' and the only question he could think of asking was ''Why?''

''There is more than one reason. The only one that need concern you for the moment is the probability that in the near future I shall be adopted as a candidate for a vacant Conservative seat. I hold twenty-six percent of stock in my father's holding company. Suffice it to say that my father's business connections could prove to be embarrassing. He is an old man and doesn't see things too clearly any longer. Times have changed, and the men he once trusted now have sons who wouldn't think twice about selling information. Any information. I intend to put a stop to that in any way I can. And you can help me.''

''Tricky.'' Harry was suddenly chilled by the icy detachment with which Angelou had declared himself. Christ, it was his own father he was talking about!

''I can give you twenty-four hours to think about it, Mr. Baird. No longer. Here''—Paul scribbled on a small gold-edged notepad—''here's my private number. Call me tomorrow afternoon, before five o'clock.''

Harry pocketed the slip of paper, bemused. ''What's the hurry?'' he asked. Already he knew that Angelou was looking for something other than a straightforward solution. If he was after a simple takeover—well, he could do that himself.

Just how far would Angelou go? he wondered. "Twenty-four hours hardly allows time for any . . . serious consideration." He was stalling, he knew; he was also trying to tell Angelou that he, Baird, was not to be taken lightly.

"If you feel pressured by having to decide within twenty-four hours, Mr. Baird, please say so, and this meeting will be at an end. On the other hand, should you decide to accept, I shall expect a detailed proposal from you at our next meeting in a week's time. Nothing in writing, ever."

Harry balked. "I'll need more information—"

"You'll have everything you need before we meet, including details of current loans lodged with the bank as collateral. I want Angel Publications and Doric Video in particular out of business. That should be enough to be going on with. Think about it."

The shutters came down; the meeting was over. Harry remained seated for a moment, trying to gauge his own response to the preposterous proposal. Then he got up and was halfway across the room, heading in the direction of the door, when Angelou stopped him.

"Oh, by the way, the rate for the job is two hundred and fifty thousand pounds. If you accept, you will receive half this amount immediately and the balance on completion. In addition, I will see to it that you receive five percent of any money vested in the name of Arion Angelou."

Harry turned to stare at him uncomprehendingly. For the first time Paul Angelou showed his teeth. "Adequate, Mr. Baird?"

It wasn't what Harry would have called a smile.

When the white telephone on his desk rang at precisely four fifty-five the following day, Paul Angelou knew who it was.

"Good afternoon, Mr. Baird."

A laugh of appreciation greeted this. "I've decided to take you up on your offer, Mr. Angelou."

"Good. Your first briefing will be next Wednesday, at three-fifteen. I'll let you know where."

"I'd prefer it if you didn't call me at my office . . . or at my home. Perhaps I should call you?"

"I will let you know where, Mr. Baird."

The dull monotone took Baird aback. His own cautious deliberations had lulled him into a sense that once he had accepted the proposition, there would be a modicum of ease between them. Angelou used words with the accuracy of a pedant, and Baird wondered how many steps ahead had been planned without his knowledge. The prospect of matching Angelou move for move in the days ahead was as heady as the small fortune that lay at the end of it.

"I'll wait to hear from you then," he said.

"Oh, and Mr. Baird, bring with you the name of your bankers."

"I bank with the company I work for, but they're not my bankers, if you know what I mean."

"I'm not interested in the details, just a name or an account number. If you need an introduction abroad, I will arrange one for you."

Angelou replaced the receiver, and Baird nodded at the humming instrument. He'd been told. Like an office junior, he had wanted to give Angelou a taste of his scheme, both parts of it. The first part was legal and relatively simple and could cost Angelou a great deal of money. The second part was dangerously illegal and could cost both of them their freedom.

8

☐ Soho was Cory's playground. From Argyll Street to the Haymarket, from Beak Street to Cambridge Circus. He knew where the games were being played, which plainclothesmen took money and where the girls were. He knew the clubs, the dens, where to get anything from heroin to hash. His accumulated knowledge gave him a sense of omniscience, a swagger that belied his careful nature. He knew that his foreignness was an asset, that a diffident, boyish grin found him friends and trust. He sought trust, and he respected honor, the kind of honor bestowed on his grandfather, Arion, not really his grandfather, but it pleased them both to say it. Honor came Arion's way in many different guises, from small gifts of fresh fruit to the best table in a restaurant, from whispered confidences to a generosity with time. Corythus Angelou wanted nothing more than to inherit Arion's mantle.

He woke up late that morning, feeling lucky. He needed to; last night had not been so good for him. Win or lose, he'd gotten into the habit of reviewing the run of the cards the morning after, trying to pinpoint what he'd done wrong. Or right. He saw the speed with which he had lost his money last night as just an accident; normally he would have changed tables, sought out a different dealer. But he had walked into the casino with a gut feeling that tonight was his night, and previous experience had taught him that instinct was as important as keeping track of the cards as they came out of the shoe. What had gone wrong?

The dealer hadn't been able to make out whether the young man was trying to impress the girl at his side or whether he simply did not know how to play blackjack. It hadn't been long before the professional players began to leave the table.

"The bank pays nineteen." The dealer took Cory's two ten-pound chips and used them to pay out on two other bets.

Cory ignored the disappointed murmurings of the girl beside him. On a winning streak earlier he'd offered her fifty pounds to play roulette with. She'd giggled her refusal, and he was glad now because he had less than that left himself.

There were two other players at the blackjack table: a pretty, pregnant woman and a man who carried on an endless monologue about his luck and the lack of it. At the moment the dealer was unbeatable. Before drawing the nineteen, he'd pulled two consecutive blackjacks and then twenty-one with five cards.

Cory was blackly determined to sit out the dealer's winning streak. He drew a seven, the woman a king, and the man an ace; the dealer drew a ten. Cory's second card was a four, followed by another four for the woman and a nine for the man. They were using four packs of cards; since a third of each pack consisted of picture cards, the chances that the dealer would draw a jack, queen, or king were good.

Cory took a deep breath and doubled his stake, using his last twenty-five pounds. Double up on eleven, one of the cardinal rules of the game. Law of averages, he told himself. If the dealer could pull a picture, so could he . . . and then he'd have twenty-one. But it was a small card, a two, bringing his total to thirteen. The best he could hope for now was for the dealer to bust. The woman turned up a card on fourteen and got a jack. The man stuck on nineteen.

"I can't believe he'll pull right," Cory said softly, to no one in particular. The dealer drew a nine.

The woman rummaged in her purse for another twenty-pound note, and the man left his two chips in their square. He hadn't won or lost.

Cory turned to the girl. He couldn't remember her name. "Have you got any money? I'll pay you back tomorrow . . . or tonight." He smiled at her, contriving to look slightly abashed.

"Not much, Cory," she said hesitantly, "only five or six pounds, and I have to get home."

What did Leo see in this girl? he wondered. She could not have been more than seventeen, with spiky black hair and eyes red-rimmed from the smoky atmosphere. Why on earth had he agreed to keep an eye on her? Leo was probably out somewhere with what he called the "big boys," cooking up some crooked deal or planning a robbery. Cory couldn't understand Leo's compulsion to supplement his already considerable income by tweaking the nose of the law.

"Kicks," Leo said contemptuously, wondering how the hell Cory had found out. "For you it's gambling. I take a different kind of chance."

Leo Bass's clandestine activities would not have interested Cory particularly had it not been for the six thousand pounds he owed Leo. It was Leo who had introduced him to the managers of all the major London casinos, Leo who had left them all with a warning: "Corythus Angelou. His grandfather is only a millionaire, so be nice to him."

That first time Cory had watched all the gambling with a jaundiced eye. Roulette, he decided, was for the mentally retarded, craps was so complicated he couldn't have cared less, and the fruit machines were simply there to eat your silver.

He'd tried blackjack because it appeared to be an easy game to play, and he'd come away winning eleven pounds. It wasn't the money but the challenge that intrigued him. It was like a familiar storybook being opened on page one each time the dealer spread the cards out; page two began a different story each time.

He had been playing the game now for seven months, winning a little, mostly losing. He was told that the casinos were

forbidden by law to extend credit, but raising money was no
problem. Leo seemed to have an endless supply, and when
Leo cut him off, there was someone else, a man Cory had
never seen, only heard about. This man was also a friend of
Leo's, and the money came to Cory via Leo. It was a good
arrangement and would have gone on indefinitely if the magic
figure of twenty thousand pounds had not been agreed upon
as a limit. At the beginning that sum had seemed outrageous
to Cory. Blackjack was a game in which you did not have to
speculate more than five pounds at a time. To lose twenty
thousand pounds, one would have to work hard . . . or be an
idiot. And he'd done it.

Still . . . one good night, and he could pay it all back,
including Leo's six thousand pounds.

"Six pounds." He counted the notes the girl dropped on
the table and gave one back to her. "One chip, that's enough.
I'll win for sure."

"I have to get home," the girl whined into his ear.

"Do not concern yourself," Cory said loftily, using Arion's
speech rhythms. He centered the chip carefully into the square
before him. "I will arrange everything."

Leo had arrived back in time to take the girl off his hands.
He'd looked pleased with himself. In tuxedo, complete with
frilled shirt and gold cuff links, he'd scarcely listened to
Cory's by now familiar complaints. When the girl went off to
collect her coat, Leo took Cory's arm. "The men want their
money, my old son," he said quietly.

"Men?"

"Him whom you're into for twenty and me whom you're
into for six. The men. All right?"

Cory shrugged now and rolled out of bed, recalling Leo's
light, bantering tone. Today he had things to do, and tonight—well, tonight could be the night he'd come up laughing.

He showered and dressed with care, light slacks, dark shirt,
open collar, soft Italian loafers. He seldom dressed without
the awareness that what he carried on his back was worth
more than most people earned in a year in the village of
Mandraki. The thought brought him not so much pleasure as
the iron determination never to go back.

The first thing he did that morning was check in with Olga,
offering himself for errands, deliveries that would demean
him but that were necessary. She told him that Arion had

visited her earlier. Nothing more. Olga studied him as he
stood before her, assuring her with dignity that his day was
at her disposal. She saw a slim, rather beautiful young man
will full, smiling lips and incredibly lustrous brown eyes. He
charmed her, even though she knew that his docile, winning
manner was assumed especially for her. He had a way of
presenting himself in any role that suited him and could adapt
them too easily, she thought. Today his stance and demeanor
told her that although he had other, more important tasks, he
was ready to do her bidding.

From the look on Olga's face, Cory could see she only half
believed him. She only wanted him to drive the van down to
Hounslow to pick up a consignment of Italian pepper salami.
She always gave him detailed and explicit instructions, as
though she didn't trust him to do it right. He was vaguely
irritated by her open, freckled features. Maybe his irritation
showed because she surveyed him coolly today and did not
laugh at his exaggerated mannerisms. But she had Arion's
ear, and he would have to watch himself.

By the time he delivered the four boxes of salami to the
delicatessen, Olga had gone upstairs to prepare lunch for her
children. Cory left the key of the van on a back room table
and told the girls he'd be back later. The fact that Olga had
mentioned Arion's visit still nagged at him. Had word of his
gambling losses reached the old man? No, it couldn't have.
The amount itself was unreal to Cory; had it been five hundred pounds, it would have caused him more concern.
Twenty-six thousand pounds was Monopoly money, not to be
thought of as real. He also refused to contemplate the possibility of Arion's finding out. He would lose everything: his
position of respect, his freedom, and, most of all, Arion's
protection. And he needed that more than anything.

As he made his way thoughtfully down Dean Street, he
worked out a strategy for soothing Leo's ruffled feathers. The
Englishman was beginning to make unpleasant noises, using
Arion's name in a threatening way. When he said things like
"You're going to have to get the money from him sooner or
later because the interest is piling up," Cory stopped listening. Never.

He paused outside Ani's. If anything were wrong, Scotia
would tell him. The restaurant was crowded, but Scotia nonetheless took his arm and drew him inside. Cory was about to
say that he had not come for lunch when he saw his "grand-

father." Across the room he could see a look of caricatured surprise on the old man's face.

"Eh, Cory, come," Arion beckoned, smiling.

He'd heard nothing. Cory almost froze with the relief of seeing that smile and, even at that distance, the look of love. He went over.

"You have met Frank Sheldon?"

Sheldon, the agent, yes. The two men were inexplicably close; it came to Cory that his grandfather would confide in this man, and he didn't like the idea. He shook Frank's hand and heard Arion say, "Have you eaten? From the sounds you made this morning, I expected not to see you today."

Cory spread his arms out in an enveloping gesture. "But as you see, I am here. And I will eat when I get back to the shop. Olga is waiting for me."

"Before you go, listen. Your uncle Paul and Suzy are with us tonight. You will be home, yes? Ani asks you especially."

Cory touched Arion's arm lightly. "Do not concern yourself," he said, using Arion's phrase impudently. "I will do everything I can to be present."

Arion grunted with delight. "Respect, my boy," he called after Cory as he walked away. "You will show respect for an old man."

"Good-looking boy," Frank commented as the door closed behind Cory.

"Ah, yes, but it troubles me, that way he has."

Frank knew what Arion meant, and he laughed. "You have that way, too, Ari. Where do you think he gets it from?"

Arion appeared not to have heard. He said slowly, "They look like brothers, Cory and Benjamin. But such a difference. Paul's son is—how you say?—steady, like his father. He works hard and does not worry his parents. Twenty now—"

"And reading law at Cambridge." Frank finished his sentence. "Don't say it all seems like yesterday, because it does. It was like yesterday that Cory came over here, and how long ago was that? Four, five years?"

Frank saw a smile at this. It crept over the old man's face and rested briefly in his eyes. "Five, yes. He keeps me young, that boy, like a true grandson. But Ani worries about him. You know he helps out in the two shops? He is good, and everybody loves him, I am told. When he is *there*, everybody loves him, but who knows where else he is?"

"Relax, Ari, he's a good boy. He knows how to look after

himself, and anyway, what could happen to him here in Soho? You have friends everywhere, and they know that the old lion still has teeth and will bite if the cub comes to any harm. Yes?''

"Yes, my friend."

Too quick, too glib for Arion. "You're worried about him, too, aren't you? Is there anything I can do?"

"Thank you, Frank, but no. I will discuss it with him. One day soon . . ."

Frank swirled the last of his brandy around in his glass. Some of the old energy and mischievousness were missing today. Probably because Paul, that pompous son of his, was coming to dinner. Arion was a man who should have been surrounded by family, children, and grandchildren. He loved noise and intrigues, tearful reminiscences and pretended ferocity.

Was he lonely? Frank wondered.

9

☐ The first major decision of Lisa Barrett's life had been her decision not to become a doctor. Or, rather, how to tell her parents that she had decided not to become a doctor. When she was eleven, her mother began to talk about the future. She took to hoarding mysterious items of furniture and stationery that might one day be of use to Lisa. These things, neatly boxed or covered with dust sheets, were stacked in one corner of the attic. Lisa was aware of the growing pile, but lack of interest, combined with a fear of spiders, kept her from inspecting it. Guilt occasionally made her add to the collection herself. Mostly she backed away from the idea that it had anything to do with her.

If George and Irene Barrett didn't exactly plan, they anticipated. This perfect child of theirs had much to give. She was brilliant, loving, and honest; she would have the world at her feet.

When Irene Barrett said, "When Lisa takes over the practice one day . . ." Lisa's stomach would turn over in a languid roll. It took no more than a mention to make her feel queasy. For as long as she could remember, the house and everything in it had smelled of Dettol and a sickly, sweet odor that she always imagined was blood. It wasn't blood, she realized later, but nevertheless worried that she herself was wrapped in the odor when she first began to menstruate. She bathed obsessively and suffered the periodically savage cramps with stoicism.

George Barrett's surgery occupied a small wing of the family house in Worcestershire. Attached and yet completely separate, it enabled her mother to stand on the doorstep each morning and kiss her husband good-bye, even though she generally saw him three or four times during the morning and then for lunch. The routine was so well established that no one, not even the faithful receptionist, considered it ridiculous any longer. When her determination faltered, Lisa would remind herself that she could be walking that same path from front door to surgery door seven days a week if she wasn't careful.

George Barrett was one of two doctors in the village. By common consent rather than prior arrangement, the younger doctor had inherited those patients who lived on the outlying farms and hamlets. Both would occasionally be summoned to oversee the birth of a heifer or listen to the cough of a goat. The receptionist was fond of saying that the young doctor "would do." Secretly she admired the unobtrusive way in which he'd taken the burden of traveling from George Barrett's shoulders.

During the school holidays Lisa helped out with the filing and the repeat prescriptions. Both parents were under the mistaken impression that she enjoyed these duties. Her father's patients brought her chocolates and jigsaw puzzles, cheered by the demure beauty of this blond child.

The child hated every minute of it. The old men who leaned over her smelled of a damp, closed-in sourness; the old women, of perfume and talc. She hated their sneezing over her and coughing until the phlegm gurgled in their throats. And she hated to think of her father having to change bloody bandages and peer down at septic tonsils.

When the time came to choose her A-level subjects, she told her parents quietly that they were to be English and drama. Her father's teeth clamped more firmly around his pipe, and her mother held out a plate of biscuits.

Lisa felt compelled to say, "I'm sorry," but her father waved any explanation aside. He knew that her decision had not been an impulsive one. Not then, or ever, did either of them raise the subject again.

Armed with a B.A. certificate, which her mother promptly appropriated and framed, Lisa was faced with the second major decision of her life. Her degree was just that, a piece of paper that did not qualify her for anything. From a minute rented room in London's Bayswater, she spent two months applying and being interviewed for jobs. Her father sent her a check once a month, and her mother supplemented that with food parcels and every make of disinfectant known to man. The knowledge that her daughter shared a bathroom horrified her. Assault, rape, and being run down by a double-decker bus were secondary considerations in her nightmares.

There were no vacancies for what Lisa wanted to do. She had no experience in newspapers or magazines and baldly refused to contemplate two or three years of secretarial duties as a way in. At the beginning of the third month, depressed by the meagerness and squalor of her surroundings, she bought a copy of the *Writers and Artists Yearbook* and from a public call box in Leicester Square, set about calling publishers and literary agents. In a perverse frame of mind she began with the literary agents. Her approach had so far been methodical. She now chose names at random, names she liked the sound of: Deborah Rogers, Abner Stein, June Hall. Frank Sheldon was the seventh she tried that morning.

Like all the others, Frank Sheldon led a protected life. Her second tenpence piece was running out by the time his secretary gave up and put her through to him. She labeled him immediately as one of those secretive, manipulative people who used silence like a weapon on the telephone. She spoke. He listened—at least she hoped he was listening. She spoke until she felt too pathetic to go on. A separate dialogue was running through her head, furious words directed at the disembodied breathing of Frank Sheldon. The pips went.

Defeated by his silence and her own anger, she said, "I don't suppose there's much point in wasting any more money on you."

There was a halfhearted chuckle at that. "Put another tenpence in. Where are you? And why are you using a call box?"

"Leicester Square, and the rest is a long story."

"Don't you know that this isn't the way to apply for a job
. . . even if there was one going? You should write in, en-
close a CV, it's—"

"I know. Do you know how many letters I've written, how
many hundreds of copies of my CV I've sent off?"

"Hundreds?"

"Well, maybe not hundreds." Lisa moved her head and
stared down at the mouthpiece. Why am I talking to you? she
thought. I don't like you. At least the others were civil enough
not to talk to me at all. "Well?"

"The other thing you should know is that ratty telephone
calls in the middle of the morning aren't a great incentive to
potential employers."

"If I'm ratty, it's because you're all practically invisible. I
think I've gone off the idea of publishing altogether."

"Oh." She could sense, rather than hear, his amusement.
"Well, if you change your mind, you'd better come and see
me."

"What?"

"Are you deaf as well as ratty? If you start walking now,
it shouldn't take you more than fifteen minutes."

Lisa replaced the receiver. Bugger you, she thought, using
the words ornately spelled out in red spray paint in front of
her. A cup of coffee and a taxi were called for. Bugger you,
Frank Sheldon.

She kept her hands jammed in her raincoat pockets as she
was shown into his office. He'd think she was even crazier if
he saw how violently they trembled.

Her first impression of his office was of chaos. Paper, small
mountains of it, was piled on every flat surface. Mounds of
it, bound, loose, boxed, precarious. In total contrast, his large
desk was clear of everything except two telephones, a notepad, an enormous blotter, and mug stuffed with pencils. And
an ashtray. No one had offered to take her coat.

"Sit down. I don't know your name. . . ."

"Barrett, Lisa Barrett."

"Do you smoke, Miss Barrett?"

She shook her head. "My father's a doctor and—" She
stopped. The dialogue began again. My father's a *doctor*?
Why don't you tell him you have a mole under your left breast
and seven pounds sixty-three pence in your purse?

He was looking at her the way she imagined he'd look at

an unruly child, half-irritated, half-amused. He understood quite well that she was nervous and seemed to approve of it. Brown hair, nice, heavily lashed brown eyes in a square, handsome face. Not what she'd imagined. Lips not quite smiling, the width of shoulders and chest blurring the brightness that erupted through the window behind his desk.

"What can you do, Miss Barrett?"

"What?" It wasn't chaos after all. She recognized a personal order quite suddenly in everything.

"You rang me and asked for a job, and I'm asking you, not unreasonably, what it is that you do."

This was it. Her hands came out of her pockets. "Anything—no, not anything. I have a degree in English and drama. I can type, but I don't want to be a secretary. Or a telephonist. Or—"

"Enough of what you don't want to do." His cheek came to rest on the palm of his hand, flattening out the hint of a smile. "What sorts of books do you read? What do you enjoy reading?"

She told him and began to relax as he listened without interrupting her. She had not the faintest idea what sorts of books the agency handled, and when he said, finally, "Those aren't all just titles you've memorized, are they?" she laughed with him.

"I've read them all, I'm afraid."

"Zane Grey?"

"My first love in junior school had plans to become a gaucho. I thought the least I could do was familiarize myself with stirrups, chaps, and lassos."

"And did he?"

"Become a gaucho? Good God, no. He's a computer engineer, and he lives in Purley."

"You keep in touch with him?"

"He writes. Not often. I don't think he ever realized that I was more likely to run off to South America and become a gaucho than he was."

"Good grief, a ratty gaucho. That's quite an image."

"You're laughing at me," she said morosely.

"Not at all. I'm impressed by the range of your tastes. In fact, I'd go so far as to say that anyone who has read and enjoyed Nietzsche and Mario Puzo would have been wasted as a gaucho."

Lisa sighed. She liked him. Her visit hadn't been a total loss. At least she'd seen the inside of a literary agent's office.

"Publishing is not very well paid," he said. "It's hard work, and a lot of it has to be done in your own time, out of the office."

"I don't eat much, and I lead a quiet life."

He was suddenly serious. "Can you be nursemaid, critic, and ego booster at the same time? How much patience do you have, Miss Barrett, not only for getting the book right but for sympathizing about the wife and the bank manager who don't understand, the size of the gas bill, complaints about eccentric editors, bad dust jackets, lack of sales, no publicity, bad reviews, no *love*? The buck starts and stops here. Literary agents are a combination of nanny, Al Capone, and God. And that's only as far as the author is concerned. To the publisher he's a greedy middleman, a regular item on their expense account, but still someone who ought to be gently treated because he doesn't actually know what he's doing. If a book is uniquely brilliant, a publisher will say he can't sell it because uniquely brilliant equals minority appeal. If a book is a unique blockbuster, he'll say he could have sold it better had the *previous* not-quite-so-unique block-buster not spoiled the market. Am I getting through?"

"That you can't win? Why do you do it?"

"Because I love it," he said. "I love every neurotic author and most neurotically ambitious editors. But most of all, I can't wait to hear what new excuse will be invented for late royalty statements. 'The computer's gone home sick' has just about run its course."

Lisa smiled tightly. "It sounds sensationally . . . awful."

"It is."

"Try me."

"You can't know . . ."

"Please try me."

"A month's trial?"

"Two," she said quickly. "And no gaucho jokes."

"You make a lot of demands for someone who doesn't know a rights clause from a hole in the wall."

"I can read! I graduated with honors in English!"

"That simple, is it? Another thing, rattiness is a sole pre-rogative of authors in this game."

"Right," she said pleasantly.

He looked at her suspiciously and shook his head. "I must

be crazy." She didn't contradict him. "Right," he said. "Let's try it."

Lisa's heart quite literally skipped a beat. Her hands went back into her pockets.

"Take this typescript away with you, and read it over the weekend. It's a second novel by an author whose first book has not yet been sold. I want to know if we should go on representing him. No need to do a report, just tell me on Monday. I take it you can start on Monday?"

Lisa read and later sold the novel she read that weekend. She was accepted into the agency with the minimum of fuss. As she suspected, Frank Sheldon left her to find her own way, create her own space. He answered her questions thoroughly, aware that she'd tried various avenues before coming to him. It wasn't touchiness or pride, he understood, just her own way of doing things.

He found out later that she'd taken the contracts files home with her each evening. At the end of three months her research enabled her to negotiate new contracts with ease. She pored over publishers' catalogs, identifying the strengths and weaknesses in their lists and chose editors with extreme care. Frank was impressed by her application and taken aback by her privacy.

A job meant the end of the room in Bayswater and a small, one-bedroom flat in Camden Town. The only item she bought from a store was a king-size bed that dwarfed the tiny bedroom. It encroached on the cramped space, too luxurious among the other wobbly, rough-edged pieces of furniture. Why had she chosen a double bed, she wondered, once it had been delivered? What had she expected? So far there had been three men in her life, actually a boy and two men. The boy, shivering in the cold drafts of her digs, was inept and afraid of what they were doing. She marveled at the clumsy indignity of it, bled a little, and was sore for a few days. Later all she could recall was the little-boy smell of his skin. The first man presupposed that she knew as much as he did and left her lying stiffly confused and guilty. The second man she used, testing her body against his, trying to build on the sensations that tugged at her from nipple to groin. She persevered for so long that he naturally assumed she could not get enough of him. He called her many times after that one night together, perplexed by her excuses. She never saw him again.

"He asked me if you lost your cool in bed." Why had Frank repeated that? she wondered. The idea of Sidney's speculations made her shudder, but she was honest enough to admit that the exasperation she felt was because she could not answer that question.

How could an insensitive oaf like Sidney guess so accurately? And Frank, in his curious repetition of it? Frank's women were self-assured, with a casual sophistication he took for granted. She had met one out of the five or six who regularly called him: Diana Marsh, an interior designer, petite and pretty . . . and sophisticated. Lisa knew about the others because of the flowers he ordered, the tables he booked at nonpublishing restaurants, the professionally wrapped gifts she would sometimes see on his desk. His divorce had been a traumatic, emotionally messy affair, she'd been told. After fifteen years of marriage and two sons, his wife had simply drifted away to Norfolk in the company of a gentle, ineffectual man; after he in turn had drifted away, she continued to grow vegetables and make homemade wine . . . and paint.

Lisa would have to deal with the accusations Frank had thrown her. And at the right time she would find out what had prompted Sidney's question. In the meantime, there was more than enough consolation in the knowledge that she was good at her job. She knew it. And Frank Sheldon would have to live with it.

10

☐   Paul loathed these family meals. Every time one was in the offing, his level of irritability jumped dramatically. Much as she loved Arion and Ani, Suzy had come to dread the meetings, too. The silences between Paul and his father grew longer; their understanding of each other, less and less. She decided, too, that she had not imagined a new source of friction between them: ever since Sir Richard Jarman had suggested putting Paul's name forward for adoption when their local Conservative MP retired in a few months' time, Paul had made excuses to cut down on their already infrequent visits. Tonight would be the first time, and at Suzy's insistence, for some months.

The big blue-gray Mercedes had no more than inches to spare on either side as Paul negotiated the narrow Soho streets. He stared straight ahead, his lips drawn in a tight line of disapproval. There had been a time when Suzy would have leaned over and touched him, brought up some irrelevancy to try to dispel the mood. Now she no longer tried. Perhaps it was the only way he knew how to get through the hours ahead.

Susan Angelou had been in love with her husband for twenty-one years. This fact surprised her no less than it astonished her friends and family. They had all somehow wanted more for her. She never knew precisely what, but she'd always been aware of an expectancy.

Their first meeting still had an immediate, ethereal quality about it, a treasured dream unfolding into reality. A Sunday in July, the lazy warmth of the air trapped beneath a marquee, the childhood sounds of insects, chatter, and everywhere familiar faces.

"Darling, let me introduce you to Paul Angelou, a recent, um, newcomer to the firm." Geoffrey McClure, rotund and pinkly balding, took his daughter's hand and drew her forward with a tenderness at odds with his legendary brusqueness. His pride lay in the knowledge that the tall, exquisitely beautiful girl could more naturally have been sired by any one of half a dozen of the handsome men present, and it amused him to see, as always, the slight shock of surprise register in Paul Angelou's eyes.

Suzy had heard about Paul Angelou. His name had come up many times in recent months. Her father spoke of his "sound exploits," suggesting a combination of gambling and dour decorum. Commodity broking was not a game. When a new arrival made his mark in such staid circumstances, the others spoke of caution and luck and early days.

What she saw on that afternoon was not what she had expected. In retrospect she could never say exactly why, but Paul Angelou took her breath away. His dark hair was neatly parted; his dark eyes were slow to assess and move on. His gaze remained so intent through her father's introductions that she felt her own smile falter. As though detecting something in their silence, Goeffrey McClure's arm tightened possessively around his daughter's waist. Then Paul inclined his head slightly, and Suzy laughed.

"How nice to meet you at last, Mr. Angelou. My father has told me—"

"Nonsense, my dear. You'll give the young man ideas, and next thing I know he'll be demanding an exorbitant amount of money."

"You were annoyed," she told Paul later that afternoon.

"What makes you say that?"

"Your whole body was"—she paused, groping for the right word—"condescending."

They were sitting on a low wall at the bottom of a small terraced rockery. He declined to remove his jacket or loosen his tie. "Condescending." He repeated the word thoughtfully. "I don't think that's quite what I felt at the time."

"Then what?" she prompted. A strong brown hand rested on the gray stone. She wanted that hand to touch her; she wanted to make him smile.

"I was thinking," he began, now turning to look across at the house into which most of the other guests had retired, "that you should not be listening to such a conversation."

It was the last thing she'd expected to hear. "Why on earth not? It's not exactly a secret that my father thinks very highly of you."

"I meant, Susan, that he seemed to be under the impression that I would always be in his . . . employ."

She suddenly lost the desire to entertain him. Her hand went involuntarily to his and came away again abruptly. He sat as still as a lizard in the sun.

"Does that surprise you?"

"A little. Does it have anything to do with me?" Her breath caught in her throat. This time his eyes remained on her face, and his lips relaxed in a suggestion of a grin. It was the most sensuous movement she'd ever seen.

"It *will* have something to do with you. Shall we go inside now?"

She followed him. She was eighteen, and she felt like a dusty schoolgirl. She was conscious that her entire body was damp with perspiration. It was almost fright she felt. Not once did he reach out to help her up the steep incline. Ten minutes later he made his excuses and left.

She existed in a daze of confusion for two months. Hungry

for information about him, she questioned her father at great length. He told her what he knew about Paul and his family, but it wasn't enough. That Paul could be living and breathing and doing other things with other people was intolerable. She called him twice. On both occasions he told her that he would be in touch with her soon. On the third occasion he agreed to dinner.

Suzy spent the afternoon choosing and trying on clothes. Nothing looked right. She was too skinny, her hair too yellow, her eyes neither blue nor gray. Finally she chose a light cream skirt and a flamboyantly red silk blouse, earrings but no necklace. He had booked at L'Étoile and was there when she arrived, looking stern and stiff.

"How often have you done this?" he asked crossly as soon as she was seated.

She looked up. "Done what?"

"Phoned a man who was clearly not yet ready to see you again?"

Suzy gripped the stem of her empty wineglass and felt the blood seep from her face. "Never," she said evenly. "I wanted to . . . see you."

"You're not a child, Susan." His tone was exactly like her father's. "It's unbecoming, and I expect more from you."

Already exhausted by the emotions which were tearing at her, she said, "You expect . . . You don't even know me; how can you expect anything from me?"

He sighed with what sounded like total exasperation. She watched him, ensnared by the disapproving features. Her mind groped blindly for a way to soften them. She wanted to pull his tie loose, open his starched collar. She wanted to disarrange the silky hair and see what his body looked like beneath the immaculate clothing. . . .

She blushed and turned away. "You're right," she whispered. "Perhaps it was . . . unbecoming. If it wouldn't embarrass you too much, I'd like to leave."

"No, stay." It sounded like an order, unforgiving. "We'll have our meal, and I'll explain a few things to you."

"That's not necessary."

"It *is* necessary," he said, contradicting her as he beckoned the waiter over, "since you behave in such an extraordinary fashion. I've decided to ask you to marry me."

Suzy nearly laughed. It was like some monstrous fantasy. It crossed her mind that he could be majestically mad.

"Why?" she asked when he'd ordered for himself and for her, without asking.

"My father is a rich man." He made it clear that he was going to do this in his own time. "Apart from my education and shares in his company, which I have no wish to retain, I've taken nothing from him. He was born in Greece, as I was. He owns a few . . . places in Soho, he's a shrewd man, and he's also a peasant and basically a peddler. I want no part of that. I chose my profession carefully, and I'm good at it. I want sons to inherit my name and my money and everything that goes with it. The position will come later. At the moment I devote my time to money, the accumulation and investment of money—"

Suzy felt something wildly alien stir in her. "Stop it!"

"No, you'll hear me out. I have no time for games, Susan. I don't have what comes naturally to you and your kind. I am the son of an immigrant, and there are doors that remain closed to me. I want them opened, you understand? Even the doors I have no wish to pass through. Do you know what I'm telling you?"

The cold ambition and bloodless words nauseated her. She nodded, speechless. She *did* understand, and she was repelled by her reaction.

"Had you known all this when we first met, would you still have called me?" He relented by running his finger lightly over her whitened knuckles. "You asked, Susan, and you'll soon learn that I always answer questions."

Was he joking? The place was beginning to fill up. Suzy thought she recognized the couple sitting on their left. "What about me? Where do I come in?"

"You want to know how I feel about you? I can tell you because that is the simplest answer of all. I want you. I've wanted you from the moment your father introduced us."

What do you mean, want? Had she spoken those words? What did he mean, want? Want in bed? Want to own?

"I can see through your skin. Look, your hand against mine." He took her hand, forcing her to look down. Her pale fingers nestled halfway across his palm. "I'm almost afraid to touch you in case something breaks off."

"Do you love me?"

His grip tightened in a spontaneous gesture, and she caught a glimmer of the man behind the façade, an instant of recognition. His smile, when it came, was like a benediction, a startling glimpse of the boy, the sensualist inside the zealot. A sweet, heavy warmth spread through her limbs.

She dared another question. "Don't you want to know if I love you?"

He threw his head back and looked down at her through slitted lids. "I know it already. I knew it before you did."

"You arrogant bastard." Her delight took the sting out of her words, but he didn't like it.

"No, never that."

"I believe you. And yes, yes, I will marry you."

"Good," he said matter-of-factly. "Now eat; your food is getting cold."

Later he kissed her good night chastely. She held on to him and offered him her parted lips. He left her with a solemn pat on the shoulder and a promise to call.

Over the following few months she became accustomed to behaving in ways which would please him. He was unlike any man she'd ever known. She remained outspoken but not enough to annoy or embarrass him. She was careful not to display her emotions and found that she could regard the precision of her new curbed life as something temporary. She became almost perfect for him.

He refused to sleep with her before their wedding night. This seeming indifference to the physical side of their relationship went undiscussed. He remained distantly heedful of her reputation and left her with no option but to agree to a certain night, time, and place.

Their wedding night was like nothing she could have imagined. His body was spare and long-muscled, the color of rich oak. His chest was covered with dark, springy tufts of hair; everything was hard and clenched and unfamiliar. She wanted to explore, to touch and bite and nestle. Assuming, without any real knowledge, that there would be time to do all these things later, she was happy enough to accept his gentle caresses. She saw him studying her, turning her, as though inspecting her flesh for blemishes. He stroked her with his fingertips and kissed her deeply. His body brushed hers and, when she moved in invitation, eased away. Her moistness brought his attention back to her breasts, and then she could feel his shoulder muscles like bands of iron beneath her flattened palms as he tried to control his entry. The sensation made her smile and stretch and laugh when he asked, "Does it hurt?"

Her hands went from his shoulders to his hips; she had wanted this for so long that she could almost withdraw from it now, stand aside and isolate each separate sensation, from her heel caressing the back of his calf, to her ear pressed into his palm. It was crazily perfect, complete. Then, without warning, he plunged down, and her breath became a silent gasp of pain, so sharp and deep that it was indistinguishable from the immediate waves of pleasure that spread out from that place of hurt.

He murmured something she couldn't hear, and she moved her hips in a slow circle, wanting with a prickly urgency to go back to the beginning and do it again.

"Lie still," he said as she sought his mouth, the words muffled. She obeyed, confused, as he rearranged her splayed limbs as a prelude to achieving his own climax.

That's the way it was, ordered and controlled. She still expected it to change, that he would come to welcome some initiative on her part, that one day he would allow himself a moment, let himself go, and entrust himself to her. Until then he brought her a wild delight and a peculiar peace, and she loved him.

From the outset she remained unimpressed by his steady accumulation of wealth. Amused by her indifference, he deluged her with useless luxuries, observing her sober acceptance, content with the amiable sweetness of the smile that told him it pleased her only because it pleased him.

"Why do you do this?" she asked once, in the third year of their marriage, gazing at a most graceful filigree bracelet. "When you do this, I feel you've gone away and left . . . this in your place."

"I thought it would please you," he replied gruffly, nettled.

"Darling, it does. It does please me but not in the way you mean it to."

"Are we quarreling?"

"I'm not. Are you?"

He didn't understand what she meant. They shared what he considered a normal married life, dull at intervals, punctuated by misunderstandings, livened by her constant interest in everything he did. She probed into the way he managed his company, drawing from him detailed information about the people who worked for him, their wives and how many children they had. She needed to be involved; he saw it as a desire to meddle.

She put the bracelet down beside the food mixer and went to him. Her body curved against his, and her hip rocked the table as they moved. "Mind the jelly," he warned.

"The jelly, yes, that's important. Are you thinking of Benjamin right now?"

"Why do you ask that?"

"Because . . ." She hesitated, unsure of herself. "Because your thoughts run in such neat channels, darling. Jelly . . . Ben. No jelly, no pudding for Ben. So, is there time to make another bowl?"

"I don't understand you, Susan."

"Try. I want to be close to you. Talk to me. I'm not some statue, I have no idea of how a wife should behave, and I don't want to be just someone you come home to. I love you"—she drew away and licked the corner of his mouth—"all day, when you're in the office, when you're driving, when you're sleeping. You set your love aside . . . now when did you come in? An hour ago? You have washed and shaved and changed your clothes, and now you have the time to love me."

Paul stared at his wife in bewilderment. Her skin was so fair it was almost transparent to him. "Why did you marry me?" he asked stiffly. "I never pretended to be anything I wasn't."

"I married you because I loved you. I still love you, and I want to go to bed with you. Now. Not tonight. Not every Monday and Thursday. You're the only man I'll ever know, Paul. Why shouldn't I know you completely?"

She had tried, even then, to set a pattern for their lives together. But as the years passed, she learned instead to accept the way he loved her. She no longer spoke of her own desires or the way in which she wanted to be loved. If she resented the finality of his authority, she kept it to herself. An exact repetition of days satisfied him. She filled them as best she could. And that was still the way it was.

Ani was waiting on the doorstep. Concealed in the shadows, her strong, hawkish face would be eager, lit with love. Suzy turned to say something to Paul, anything that would jolt him out of his darkness, but he was already frowning into the distance. It would take him a least ten minutes to find a suitably safe parking space, and she had long since learned to live with his displeasure at having to cope with this chore.

Ani kissed her on both cheeks and then on the forehead. "Come in, come in. My son will come later." She could never understand why Paul needed such a large car. When Benjamin was a baby, yes, but not anymore. To her it was more like a ship than a motorcar.

Suzy stood encircled in Arion's arms for a moment. He pressed her face into his shoulder, and she sniffed at the blend of cigars, soap, and aniseed. How could this man be Paul's father? He exuded love like a musk; it was in his eyes and in every gesture he made.

"You look so beautiful," he said, eyeing the elegant white linen suit she wore. The only splash of color came from a string of carved turquoise Victorian beads around her neck. "I am sorry Benjamin could not come with you."

"He is, too, Ari." She held on to him for a moment. "Next time, he promises next time."

"Ah, yes, next time. For the young there is always a next time. Cory says that, too. 'Tomorrow, Grandfather, tomorrow—' "

"Is he here?" Suzy had forgotten about the possibility of Cory's presence this evening. If she'd remembered, her misgivings would have increased tenfold. Paul could barely tolerate being in the same room with the boy, his revulsion almost palpable. Cory was too Greek; there was too much of the peasant in him. . . .

Suzy caught sight of the dinner table through an open door. "Ani, no! So much! So much trouble . . ."

"No trouble, *cara*. Who else do I have to cook for?"

Paul came in and stood at his mother's shoulder. Suzy saw his eyes glaze at the sight of the food: dolmadakia, spanakopetes, kotopita, cucumber with yogurt, shrimp with feta, artichokes and aubergines. . . . He leaned forward to kiss the top of Ani's head. She was having none of that. Her gnarled hands went over both ears, and she pulled his face down to kiss him on the mouth. He straightened, pulling at his tie with embarrassment, and Suzy stood watching them all, away from the group, as Arion came over to shake his son's hand.

In the living room Arion turned to her. "A drink, Suzy. Ouzo?"

"Not ouzo, Father. She—"

"She would love ouzo, Ari. She is old enough to know

what she wants, and tonight it's ouzo.'' Suzy made a grotesque face at Paul.

The clear liquid changed to a milky white as Arion added water. "And you, Paul?"

"Whiskey, if you have it."

"We have it, my son," Arion said dryly. He poured a small ouzo for himself and a glass of sweet red wine for Ani.

Paul had taken one of the armchairs and was sitting stiffly upright. Suzy sat in one corner of the large sofa, with Ani at the other.

Paul looked at his father with a critical eye. The old man was noticeably more stooped, and his clothes had begun to look too large for him. Ani's eyes followed him everywhere. It irritated Paul to see that she had obviously prepared the meal herself. His earliest memory was of his mother standing in front of the decrepit old stove that had long since been replaced with the Aga. She had spent most of the daylight hours baking fresh pita for the café, then working far into the night to prepare the skewered lamb kebabs and salad to go with them. It shamed him that his friends saw her flushed, with bits of dough and splashes of fat dotting her apron. He cringed at the all-pervading smell of garlic and other herbs that were an indelible part of his childhood. Everything smelled of food: his clothes; his books; his hair. On his way to school he discarded the sandwiches she made for him, not sliced bread but pita filled with offensive aromas. He bought tasteless cheese rolls and ate them with pride. When he had no money, he went without.

When she wasn't cooking or cleaning, Ani was crocheting an endless stream of round doilies. They lay dotted around on every conceivable surface in the house. As if the lumbering claw-footed furniture were not bad enough, every ornate gilt frame, every ashtray and ornament stood on a doily; even the silver cups he'd won at school, until he made a foul-smelling bonfire out of every doily he could find. The destruction confused Ani and enraged Arion. He'd experienced a rare moment of fear, standing in front of his father. Never before and never since had he seen that expression on the old man's face. It was more than anger, more than despair. If Ani hadn't jerked him away and taken both Arion's fists to her breasts . . . She, too, had seen the final assault on his spirit.

Eventually he stopped bringing his friends to the house, and once he discovered that his father was a wealthy man, he insisted on going to a boarding school. Ani didn't believe him. He caught her studying him intently. She anticipated his every wish and coaxed Arion into quietness. This was an unheard-of thing. What kind of parents were they that their only son wanted so much to leave their home? Paul countered this by simply withdrawing from them completely, eating and working in silence and alone until the strain began to affect Ani's health.

The old man had never forgiven him. To Paul's way of thinking, Arion didn't have much to congratulate himself over either. He played God by bringing over members of his family from Greece and setting them up in businesses in Soho. They all depended on him, he made them love him, and Paul could not make him realize that they were out for what they could get from him. The nightclub, Prax, two food shops, Ani's, Angel Publications importing some of the magazines he was forced to look at daily. They leaped out at him from every street corner, the mindless rubbish distributed by Angel Publications. There were some of quality, tucked away, slow sellers. He saw only the others. And Doric Video . . . that pornography. Good God, it would serve him right if someone were to tell Ani exactly where the old man's money came from.

And now there was even more to lose. If he ever found out, Sir Richard Jarman would not only opt out of the preliminary discussions about the prospective vacant Tory seat, but he would probably abandon their long-standing business relationship as well.

"Paul." Suzy was getting up. "We're ready to eat if you are."

Arion motioned Paul aside as the two women went ahead into the dining room. "The mantilla I telephoned you about— you have brought it?"

Paul looked askance at his father. "I didn't have time to send anyone out for it, but one of the secretaries said she would look out for the shop when she was next in Little Italy."

"That is good of you," Arion said softly, turning away to hide his disappointment.

The meal was magnificent; the conversation, stilted and halting. At ten-thirty Paul brought the napkin to his lips in a gesture that was by now familiar to them all.

"Are you going to Mandraki again this summer, Ari?" Suzy asked brightly, trying to postpone their departure.

"We have plans, yes. Michaela has not seen her son for many months—"

"Why doesn't Cory go back by himself? Why do you have to travel with him, for God's sake?" Paul asked angrily.

"Because it is something we . . . need to do," Ani answered.

"What do you mean?" Suzy forced a smile into her words. "Isn't the journey becoming too much for both of you?"

"It is far, yes, but it is our home and we long for our people."

Suzy glanced at Paul. Dear God, the combination of Cory *and* Greece was making her feel quite ill with apprehension.

"Ari, tell them, please."

Arion had the look of a naughty schoolboy. "What? What must I tell them?"

"The mountain," his wife said, with rare impatience. "Tell them about the mountain."

"The mountain?" Arion shrugged. "I bought it."

Suzy burst out laughing as her disbelief and delight collided with Paul's look of horror. "You bought a mountain? In Greece?"

"With land around it and a house that they are building, sure. We will, as you English say, go there to retire into our old age."

"But not for a long time yet," Ani added.

"Fantastic." Suzy couldn't resist the idea. "You bought a mountain. I love it. Please ask me to visit you."

"We will depend on your coming, my girl," Ari said. "The house will be big, with many rooms for everybody—"

"Everybody in the village, you mean," Paul interrupted. "My God, you've got it all planned, haven't you? You'll leave the leeches behind here and start all over again there. Can't you see them for what they are? Even Cory's got you fooled, a small-time spiv—"

"Enough!" Arion roared suddenly.

Suzy jumped, and Ani's hand flew up to cover her mouth. "Ari," she said fearfully, "you must not—"

"Sit down, *cara.* Please sit down and do not concern yourself. Cory is of our blood as much as Benjamin is of our blood. I do not understand this word 'spiv,' but I am not so old that I cannot guess what it means. You have a reason for saying this, Paul?'' He now spoke quietly.

''Proof?'' Paul gave a short laugh of derision. ''You want proof?''

''Proof, no. I do not want anybody spying on him. Tell me what it is that you know, and I will decide what to do.''

Silence. Suzy squeezed her eyes shut, willing herself away from this moment. ''Paul, for God's sake!''

Ani's distress and Arion's calm infuriated Paul. His wife's face was ashen. ''Come on,'' he said. ''We're leaving.''

It was always the same. ''Apologize,'' Suzy whispered fiercely as she followed him out into the hall. ''Please, Paul, apologize. Don't leave it like this!''

He whipped around. ''Are you coming or not?''

She stepped back, stunned by the venom in his voice. ''I'm coming. Wait for me in the car.''

She turned and went back into the dining room. Arion was talking to his wife in a low, soothing voice. She was nodding. The movements spilled her tears onto the tablecloth.

Suzy kissed Arion and put her arms around Ani. ''I apologize for him, Ani. Sometimes I don't understand what's going on inside his head. Yesterday he went straight to the office from the airport. . . . He must be tired. He's not like this all the time.''

''I know.'' Ani shook her head in bewilderment. ''Is what he says about Cory true?''

''Of course it's not true,'' Arion said furiously. ''We will not talk about it anymore. Our son is mistaken. Go to him, Suzy.''

''Arion . . .''

''No, no. Go. We understand. Truly.''

''Truly?''

''Truly.'' Arion smiled. ''Do not concern yourself.''

''But I am concerned. I don't understand—'' She broke off as the Mercedes's horn blasted long and loud outside.

''Next time it will be better.'' Arion took her arm and steered her toward the door. ''Next time, as the children say.''

Suzy got into the car and slammed the door. ''That was cruel and uncalled for. You are a bastard at times, Paul. Why did you do it?''

''Tell them the truth, you mean?'' He slid the car into gear and it lurched forward, throwing them both back into their seats. ''You work it out!''

"Do you know something about Cory? Something you haven't told me?"

He didn't answer. Instead, he switched on the car radio. She leaned forward and snapped it off. "I asked you a question."

"Leave it, Susan."

"I'll do anything I can to prevent them from being hurt, Paul. Now is there anything you haven't told me?"

"Nothing," he replied curtly.

His profile was stark against the harsh streetlights. She imagined every muscle in his body drawn taut. He was not a violent man. She had never seen him raise a hand to Benjamin, but at times like this an image of explosive violence always came unbidden to her mind. All it needed was a trigger, some point of pressure. . . .

She turned away, withdrawing herself consciously from him. Tonight he had inflicted bruises that would remain discolored for a long time. She did not understand why he'd done it, nor could she work up any sympathy for him. This time he would have to do without her support.

11

☐ The long, horizontal lines of Calvert Hall wavered in the early summer haze. Steep, ornamental gables stood centered between exotic onion-domed turrets, strange features in the otherwise severe aspect of the house. The domes and the oval niches, once adorned with classical busts, drew wry comments from those who saw the courtyard house as "classically disguised"; they knew full well that generations had added to and modified the H-shaped structure according to the tastes of the day. Constructed of diapered brick, with plain cornerstones, it rose at the end of a great winding driveway which was wide enough for two limousines abreast. The architectural influences of Calvert Hall lay scrupulously detailed in the three-by-four-foot ledger of the Hall, Belinda

Jarman's bible. For future generations she wrote in minute detail of her decision not to replace the transomed windows with sash windows and took the opportunity to describe the lead glazing bars and swinging iron casements just in case, in the unforeseeable future, Oliver or his descendants decided to counteract her decision.

Oliver had no particular feeling for the vast, drafty house with its majestic staircase and unoccupied wings. He and Angie had been subjected to an intimidating sense of isolation as children in the Hall. It was laughable to imagine Pamela growing up there. Pamela, his observant and practical daughter, was the one who had first noticed the way he still skirted any piece of furniture that wasn't a kitchen table or chair. The untouchables of Calvert Hall haunted Angie even more than Oliver because he had found it easier not to slide on the mirrored floors and to knock before entering a room in case Benn might be carrying the English Delft bowls or the nineteenth-century Staffordshire teapot. Sèvres porcelain and Louis XV chairs had taught Oliver not only to walk but to keep two feet of space between himself and anything that didn't move.

Now a soft cushion of larch and yew needles deadened the sound of the tires on the gravel as Oliver's Volvo drew to a halt facing one of the tall leaded windows on the ground floor.

"Drive up to the library," Belinda Jarman would instruct newcomers. It was the best room for visitors to see first, embellished as it was with richly decorated plasterwork panels, an exquisite seventeenth-century japanned cabinet on an ebonized stand, and the Calvert coat of arms emblazoned above the ornate, marbled fireplace.

Cissy, sitting in the back seat, leaned forward to touch Oliver's shoulder. "We're early, darling. We should have stopped for a while somewhere."

The clock on the dashboard read twelve-fifteen. "We could always sit in the car and wait until someone asks us in. What do you think, Angie?"

"I hope you're smiling." Her heart seemed to shift with the sounds and textures of the place. Two rooks and a starling stared at them from the branch of a silver birch. They looked glossy and well fed.

"The last time we were here was in the winter." Cissy was checking her lipstick. "It was lovely even then."

Angie sneezed.

"I hope you're not coming down with anything," Oliver said. "I can't understand how you got the time wrong."

Angie didn't say anything. She'd spent three-quarters of an hour standing coatless on the pavement in the midmorning London chill, waiting to be picked up by Oliver and Cissy. She had not got the time wrong, but in allowing an hour and a half for her meeting with Christopher Chetwynd, she'd overestimated by half. She hadn't known what to expect or how much information he would require. Sitting in his office, listening to the sound of her own voice, she'd had a momentary, suffocating fear. This man was a stranger; he conducted himself more like a doctor than a lawyer. He was polite and guarded, listening, nodding now and then. She began to relax only when her words ran out and the ritual of the law took over.

"It could be a slow process," Christopher Chetwynd said. He was a young man with prematurely graying hair and a cold presence. His office was dark and cramped, an unwelcoming place of business. "The law protects the child in these cases. In fact, I'm not altogether sure what your rights would be . . . if any."

Was he trying to put her off? Angie said, "That doesn't concern me at the moment, Mr. Chetwynd. I'll cope with that when—later. All I want you to do is find her and tell me where she is. And discreetly, please; I don't want anyone barging in."

Chetwynd sniffed and brought out a maroon handkerchief. He touched the tip of his nose delicately. "I appreciate the need for discretion, Mrs. Wyatt, but nineteen years is a long time. We'll have to check local registers, church records, the social services. Are you sure you want to do this?"

Instead of answering, she asked faintly, "How long will it take?"

"That's difficult to say. Two months, maybe considerably longer." He didn't approve, she could see that. She wanted him on her side, not as a confessor but as someone who would recognize her vulnerability and draw from her what she really wanted to say: I just want to know what she looks like, how her voice sounds, and how much she's loved by others. I need you to believe that I'll do nothing to harm her.

She said, "I know I want to find my daughter. Help me. Please."

He filled two lined foolscap pages with closely written notes and put sparsely worded questions, neither helping nor hindering her.

"You were a virgin when this event took place?"

Event? He made it sound like a social gathering. "Yes."

"You had no reason to suspect these two young men of anything other than boisterous friendliness?"

Angie could not understand the reason for his questions and found it impossible to soften her answers. "Suspect them as rapists? It was the last thing on my mind. They were drunk, all three of them."

"What did they look like?"

"Why?"

"If, as you say, either could have been the father of your child, their physical characteristics could be . . . relevant."

"Do you mean as a last resort, if she's not identifiable in any other way?"

"That's precisely what I mean. It's an extremely remote possibility, and I'll understand if you don't feel up to describing them."

Angie gave him the descriptions he wanted and at the end of it said, "Please don't ask me why they weren't prosecuted because I can't answer that." It was so obviously a lie that Christopher Chetwynd actually smiled.

"That was going to be my next question, but from what you've told me, I think I can draw my own conclusions."

She said, "Thank you," and wondered what conclusions he would come to. Nothing approaching the truth, she guessed; but that aspect of it was no longer important, and as she was going to see both her parents in a few hours' time, it was just as well not to think about it.

"Finally, Mrs. Wyatt, I feel obliged to repeat my earlier question: are you quite sure you want to do this?"

"I've had nineteen years to think about it," Angie said. "I'm not asking you to accept any responsibility, moral or otherwise. Just find her."

She left his office with the impression that he'd agreed to set the wheels in motion only because of his loyalty to Oliver. That one brief smile was all she'd got. But it was done. Unless she instructed him to the contrary, the investigation would take its course. . . .

Oliver was patting her knee now, pulling her back. "Cheer up, old girl, it'll soon be over."

Her lips curved in a half smile, mockingly. Old girl . . . He was already beginning to speak the way they did. She looked up at the rooks again. They made her think of chess, and chess made her think of bridge.

"Lou taught me how to play bridge," she said inconsequentially, to delay going into the house.

"Something you swore you'd never do." Oliver got out of the car and opened the door for his wife.

Cissy drew him inside and kissed his cheek. "Courage, old boy. We have to help Angie through this. She needs . . ."

Angie moved away from the car before she could hear the rest. She walked back down the driveway, then crossed a perfect circle of lawn on which a sundial stood. "What Angela needs" had been the words that had preceded her banishment all those years ago from this place. "What Angela needs is discipline; she needs the company of other girls and the sort of authority she'll respect. Do you agree, Richard?" It wasn't an opinion her mother sought.

Her father, impassive, slow to smile, nodded without lifting his eyes from his plate. She and Oliver were seldom addressed directly by either parent, and Angie's glance now went automatically to Oliver for an explanation. The ten-year-old was frowning. The look said that whatever it was, it was settled. Panic engulfed her.

"You're lucky, Angie," he told her later. "When you grow up, you can do anything you want. I can't." How often in the following months had Oliver attempted to instill in her a dream that would make leaving Calvert Hall a wonderful adventure? "I really want to be an archaeologist."

The word was serious to a seven-year-old. "What's that?"

"Digging for things. It's exciting. I'll go to Greece—"

"No!" Her vehemence frightened him.

"You can come, too, if it's really exciting."

Don't leave me here! was what she wanted to scream at him. Don't leave me with them.

Stupefied by the knowledge that she was being sent away, she became a battering ram of questioning protest. Why? It had to be something unspeakable. Donny, the groom, told her that rich people always sent their children away to schools, then shrugged with embarrassment at not being able to explain why Oliver had been spared this ordeal. She asked Mrs. Petters, the cook, who said, mysteriously, "You don't know you're born, girl." She scraped both knees deliberately and went to Benn, bleeding. The iodine the butler swabbed on brought tears to her eyes but no comfort. They both knew what he meant when he said, "Think about the holidays, miss." It was something she would have to endure. If Benn didn't know, no one did.

Years followed in which only holidays, going home, had any real meaning for her, growing up apart from Oliver, then spending the first few days of each reunion easing back into the old world of whispered fantasies and shared landscapes. The hall became smaller; they outgrew their hiding places. The cook's daughter cooed with envy each time she unpacked her small suitcase, admiring an ordinary scarf, two-inch-heeled shoes, the tennis racket they made her bring home. "Take it," she told the girl. "I'll tell them I've lost it." The frame was slightly warped, two strings gone. One girl had left with a crash course in physics; another, with history. Angie Jarman they sent home with a tennis racket, bemused that the daughter of a lithe and athletic sportsman had no desire to compete.

"He was a Blue," they told her: sculling and rugby. Academically an upper second. An achiever. By chance or design, her father had done just about everything right: inherited well, married well, produced an heir on time, before—as Angie saw it—a disastrously errant sperm collided with an equally dozy egg to produce what neither parent wanted, a daughter.

She knew, deep in her heart, that Oliver had been allowed to remain at the Hall because he blended and accepted and conformed. She condemned him for being manageable yet hid behind him when she could; they always found her wanting, spitting defiance while her brother remained silent.

Belinda Jarman invariably summoned and questioned her children separately, in the tone she used when she inquired about kitchen breakages. Richard Jarman had them stand before him, together, the time allocated for such childish aberrations being strictly limited. Angie shocked Oliver by telling him, with a glutton's hunger for honesty, why she hated them. Then, alone, sweated at the lie. For the lie to be true, she would miraculously have to change into someone else, one of those people who assumed they were loved and never questioned their own rightness and reveled in the uncomplicated happiness of not caring.

So she hugged her hurt and watched from a distance; the

changes she saw aroused curiosity rather than envy. The Humphries girls, all three of them, went from jodhpurs to cashmere overnight, it seemed. Angie would anticipate her mother's order to ride over to their closest neighbors at Trenton March to pay her respects to Lady Isobel Humphries by doing just that, unbidden, on her first day at home. Julia Humphries, her former playmate, treated her brief visits and monotonously polite questions with barely concealed impatience. Dressed for comfort in one of Oliver's denim shirts and wearing boots she had twice salvaged from a pile of assorted items waiting to be incinerated, Angie wondered at this softly blond creature who had not so long ago crawled through hedges with her, always amiable enough to take on the feeble roles neither she nor Oliver would tolerate. "Such *nice* girls," Belinda Jarman would murmur, having summoned Angie away from the stables, the barn, the tent in the orchard. "Theresa and Marcia and Julia—such sensible girls. Dear Isobel is indeed fortunate."

Without her being particularly aware of it, Angie's own body rounded; as the seemingly endless school years passed, the planes of her face lost their childish plumpness, although her eyes still expressed a wariness which her contemporaries interpreted as aloofness. In her fifteenth year, on the last day of term, she feel in love with the English master, a man she'd despised with a monstrous passion for six years.

The following day at the Hall, when Oliver found her paler and even more disheveled than usual, he said, "I think you've got a crush on him."

"A crush?" The banality of the description enraged her. "A *crush*?"

He should have known it would hit her hard. Everything did. She had no capacity for self-protection. "It happens. It's normal, and it happens to all of us. It hurts, but at least it doesn't last forever."

Angie had spent the holiday weeks in an orgy of innocent speculation, only to find that Oliver had been right. It lasted for less than three months. There were times when the sound of the man's voice made her knees tremble, when the idea of touching his flesh brought her out in goose bumps.

After that Oliver wrote long, scrawled letters which made so many references to "glands" that she finally looked up the word. "My glands, *all of them*, work just fine," she wrote back, miffed by his assumption that some of them might still be lying dormant. Nonetheless, the word became their euphemism for anything to do with sex.

"Do you suppose she has glands?" They were standing at the library window, watching their mother lecture the tree surgeon, who was too polite to interrupt.

"Shouldn't think so," Oliver said without hesitation.

"He must, though," meaning her father.

"A man always must."

Always? She was still trying to work that out when her father appeared. Once in a while he would descend for a weekend on Calvert Hall and spend an hour or so infuriating the gardener by pruning the roses badly. They watched him rescue the tree surgeon and then take his wife's arm to lead her back to the house. In a high-necked sweater, corduroys, and Wellington boots, he didn't look like her father, just someone who appeared in her life two or three times a year. . . .

Angie shook herself free of the memories and retraced her steps. Oliver was taking their suitcases out of the car, and Cissy was watching her with a look of open concern. No one was looking forward to the next two days.

In response to her knock, Benn opened the door, and his crusty old face appeared where it shouldn't have, on a level with her shoulders. He peered up at her and grinned, taking her hand in both of his. "Miss Angela," he huffed, drawing her inside.

Ah, Benn—shocked again, intolerably pained by what she saw. He was as hunched as a monkey, arms dangling, head askew. She made herself smile but couldn't hide the fact that her hand, still enclosed in his, shook. He would expect her to make light of it. She said, "Either I've grown a foot or you've shrunk. If you'd been this size when I was a child, I wouldn't have been so intimidated by you."

"Then it's just as well I wasn't," he said, dropping her hand. "I had enough trouble with you as it was."

Angie laughed. "So you did. Benn . . ."

"Nothing to worry about; old bones, bad back." Just that.

"Pain?"

"Only when I look up at tall people."

Angie laughed again and went out to help Oliver with the suitcases. They left them standing in the hall and followed

Benn into the drawing room. He retreated, saying, "Her Ladyship will be down shortly."

"Shit," Cissy whispered uncharacteristically, "I always feel like genuflecting when he says that."

"Why didn't you tell me about Benn?" Angie turned to Oliver. "How long has he been so . . . crippled?"

Cissy answered. "It's progressive, I'm afraid. Osteo and rheumatoid arthritis . . . nothing can be done. I'm sorry we didn't warn you."

Oliver was already pouring generous measures of sherry, half listening to the exchange, when Belinda Jarman came in. Perfectly groomed and relaxed, she smiled at each of them in turn and offered her cheek to Angie.

"Mother." Angie leaned over dutifully. Face powder and the whiff of some expensive soap, the rustle of silk on silk and the glacial gray-green eyes . . .

Angie bungled her retreat by colliding with the corner of an armchair. She realized that she had been expecting to find her mother changed, older, plumper, grayer. What she actually saw was a woman of almost willful elegance, slender and upright, an emphatic beauty. Lou's mother had worn designer jeans in defiance of the gray in her hair, running shoes, and a caftan to go to the supermarket. . . .

"Do sit down, my dears. How was the journey, not too tiring, I trust?"

"Better than it would have been tomorrow," Oliver said. "Sherry, Mother?"

"Thank you. Yes, Saturday would not be a terribly good day to drive over. Your father is taking the train this afternoon, I believe."

"Oliver tells me he prefers the train these days because it gives him time to read," Angie said.

"Quite. He works much too hard." Belinda looked across at her daughter as though she were somehow to blame. Her husband's absence in London was something Belinda Jarman had come to accept. She preferred it that way. She saw to it that their house in Cadogan Square remained permanently staffed, but that was as far as she went. London was an abominable place. How anyone could make a life for themselves there was quite beyond her. . . .

Angie shut her eyes. Lethargy was already spreading through her veins. A dinner party this evening, tomorrow a fete, Sunday another lunch . . . God, all those meals and smiles and silences and savageries.

Lunch was a spread of cold meats and salads accompanied by a chilled rosé. Belinda Jarman did not believe in lingering over the midday meal. There was nothing to be gained by wasting the precious early-afternoon hours. Friday meant at least three hours in the library, coping with the worst of the paperwork, then instructing Rosemary, her secretary from the nearby village, on the following week's events.

She looked at her daughter, who had taken no more than three or four mouthfuls of food. The vividly patterned sweater she wore was wrong for the country, and the skirt was of good quality but too long and too big. A wineglass stood empty at her elbow. Belinda noticed, too, that the girl still had the irritating habit of placing her elbows on the table and leaning her chin on interlocked fingers.

Unchanged. Without appearing to be incompetent, her daughter seemed to blunder through life. There was an acute intelligence behind those dark eyes, so unlike her own, but as Isobel Humphries had once remarked, the girl seemed to live through the topmost layer of her skin, instinctively, unable or unwilling to rationalize her actions. How extraordinary it was that both her children resembled their parents so little. Oliver, she supposed, was as good-looking as his father but without a vestige of his strength. Angela had the strength but not the direction. Their closeness was almost unhealthy, Belinda decided, watching Oliver incline his head, listening intently to whatever it was Angela was saying. Well, they had no one but themselves to blame for the chaotic state of their lives. Richard, she knew, planned to take Oliver aside sometime during the weekend. It was all so hideously embarrassing. The boy would simply have to pull himself together. She made a small sound of resentment deep in her throat. Such profound weakness was repellent to her. Still, as with anything unpleasant, it was something they would have to face up to.

They had not done too badly with Angela's problem all those years ago. She and Richard had devoted as much of their time as was possible to deciding just which course of action would be best for their daughter and the child she carried.

Their first decision on their return from London that night was not to report the incident to the authorities. Benn had managed admirably. Their second decision was to take the precaution of summoning the family physician. Normally so discreet, he had nonetheless urged them to take action against the two boys. "It was a particularly brutal rape, Richard. It's simply luck that she wasn't more badly injured or, in fact, that her ribs weren't broken. I'm required by law to report such cases." Thank God Richard had been able to dissuade his friend from doing just that. It would have solved nothing. If there had been any way in which those boys could have been punished without dragging the Jarman name through the mud, there would have been no question about going to the police. Rape was difficult to prove; why put Angela through the torment of endless questions and ultimately a court hearing? Neither Belinda nor Richard voiced their other reservation: no one actually *knew* what had happened that night. Oliver could not enlighten them, and Angela's account of the events was in many ways too simple. She'd been physically abused—of that there'd been no doubt—but how had it all begun: with some teasing kisses, a stirring of passion that had got out of hand?

And then, faced with the fact that their daughter was pregnant, they had once more come up with the most eminently sensible solution. Abortion was out of the question: Belinda's Catholic tenets forbade it utterly. "The boys need not know," Richard said. He had spent valuable time researching their backgrounds. George McFee was the son of a Scottish welder, and he was the brightest law student of his year. Andrew Colquhoun was the youngest son of the Colquhoun whiskey family. Admittedly the Colquhoun ancestry was somewhat dubious, but their current standing and wealth were beyond doubt. They would not take the tarnishing of their son's name lightly. "It would only complicate matters at this late stage, and God knows, we don't want a fuss," Richard said.

Belinda agreed. "Their careers would be ruined and Oliver . . . well, he could well come out of the whole thing with an irredeemably damaged reputation."

It wasn't that they didn't take advice. While Angela spent the months of her pregnancy alone in Cardiff, where one of Richard's oldest and closest friends lived, they made it their business to talk to those they could trust. In the event, it had been relatively simple because the solution lay much closer to home than they would have dreamed. What a terrible time they'd lived through, trying to decide just when Benn would bring Angela home. Ideally, of course, the child should have been born in Cardiff. Belinda had never quite forgiven the brusque Welsh doctor with the lilting accent she swore he used solely to make her ask every question twice. In the end it had been all right. Although Benn had been gray with the fatigue of driving to and back from Cardiff nonstop, he had insisted on taking Angela to the private nursing home himself. The timing could not have been better: no more than three hours had elapsed between their arrival and the first labor pains. . . .

"Does anyone mind if I take a nap?"

Cissy's voice made Belinda realize she'd been frowning. "Of course not, my dear. You'll find your rooms in order. I do hope they've had time to unpack your things."

"Thank you, Belinda. Oliver?"

"I thought we'd go for a walk." Angie pushed her plate back with relief and caught Cissy's nod.

"Good idea." Oliver filled his glass from a fresh bottle of wine. "I'll wait down here while you change."

"You'll need boots, both of you." Belinda, too, was relieved to see the meal over. "Well, I'll see you at tea then. Your father should be here by then."

By the time Angie changed into slacks and sweater, Oliver had finished most of the wine. He slipped his trousers into the top of his boots, took her hand, and led her first to the stables.

"You were always a better rider than I was—how was it you broke your arm twice and I never fell off once?" They were admiring the huge gray hunter being walked around the paddock by a stable lad.

"I broke my arm because I was stupid," Angie replied. "I thought there had to be more to riding a horse than controlling it from the saddle."

"Like what?"

"I never did find out. Let's take the path through the woods."

They walked in silence for half a mile, past slender ash trees trailing long strips of bark. Drifts of bluebells washed around the roots of elm and oak, foxtail and couch grass grew resplendently at intervals, and early dragonflies skittered about at their approach.

"Martin." Oliver pointed to a low branch.

"Not a swallow?"

"Uh-uh, see the the way the tail forks?" They watched the bird disappear. "Definitely a martin. Cissy and I spotted two tawny owls the last time we came out here. They were standing back to back, touching, like bookends. She's amazingly ignorant for a schoolteacher, actually . . . can't tell a magpie from a crow."

"She's not a schoolteacher any longer." Angie stopped and accepted a cigarette.

"She told you? I wasn't sure she would."

"Why shouldn't she? I also know about the tests you had, but I had to drag that out of her."

"I'm sorry about that. We agreed to wait a while—"

"Stop it, Oliver! There's no more time left, and you know it!"

He strode away from her, and she let him go, following slowly. A spiral of anger and frustration had been building up inside her for the past few days. How could she persuade him to live when he clearly had no desire to?

She had set out to learn all she could about Jarman publishing, and what she heard she could scarcely believe. With the help of Fran Forsyth, a literary agent she had known for many years, she managed to lay her hands on a few of the more recent Jarman catalogs as well as the complete stock list. More than five years had passed since she had last seen one, and she could see very little change in the quality and scope of the list. A very obvious attempt had been made to get into the nostalgia market, but from the wrong end, as far as she could judge. The nonfiction in general was worthy but staid, and the fiction, while vaguely promising, had no real style.

Fran Forsyth had answered her questions over lunch. She knew Angie well enough not to inquire too closely into her motives.

"What does the trade think of Jarman's?" Angie asked.

"Solid. No surprises."

"Boring?"

"Boring. They tend to wait for things to come to them; they rely on their reputation."

"Are their advances adequate?"

"For what they get, yes."

"What does that mean?"

"Let me explain something before we get into that. Oliver is well liked, loved even, by a lot of people. He's straight, in a way not many people are in this business, as you know. 'Honorable' is, I suppose, the word I want, and that can be a drawback. He doesn't go after the books he wants, never makes a fuss. If someone like le Carré came his way, well and good; if not, not. He doesn't poach, and says, 'Good luck,' to anyone who nobbles *his* authors. I'm not saying he doesn't care. It's just that . . . oh, I suppose he's not getting the sort of backup he needs. You know this business as well as I do. When people start talking, there's no end to it. Oliver is surrounded by"—Fran hesitated, then added, unsmilingly—"vipers."

It was so melodramatic that Angie spluttered into her coffee. "Vipers?"

"It doesn't take a genius to put two and two together, my dear. Sidney Niklas is a lout. Not a bad publisher if he gets his own way, but a lout nonetheless. I'm told he has the largest collection of pornography in the country. . . ."

It was getting sillier. Cissy had said more or less the same, but Fran was on the inside.

"Oliver apparently refused to publish the porn when Sidney first joined Jarman's, and for all I know, the rot set in then. He laughs at Oliver, publicly and privately, and there's no stopping him."

"Because Oliver drinks?"

"Perhaps, but I think mostly because Oliver doesn't realize what's going on. No one is going to tell him, and Sidney reckons he's safe. He is."

"You're making me feel ill. What about the others?"

"Martin Corbett is hardly worth considering. He does as little as is humanly possible, and everybody knows why he's there. Not only is he idle, but he's actually stupid. Deborah? What can I say? Nice, meek, a worker . . . I don't think she has anything else aside from her job. Dotes on Oliver, well liked but not respected for her taste in books."

"Anyone else?"

"Not really. Cynthia Crew does the best she can, I guess. A bit prissy, uptight, not a natural for selling subsidiary rights, but competent."

"Dunne Morrissey?" Angie asked softly.

Fran sat back and her face lit up with humor. "Dunne? Lovely man, wouldn't know a best-seller if it got up and socked him in the mouth. Reviews, that's what he cares about. Sales are incidental. If a reviewer says a book's good, he'll spend money advertising it. If the Hull *Evening Gazette* prints an unfavorable criticism, that's it, the book's dead. Doesn't have an original thought in his head.''

''And that's Jarman's? Good Lord, Fran, how did all this happen?''

Fran didn't know, and Angie suspected that Oliver didn't know either. . . .

He was waiting for her now, seated cross-legged on a fallen mossy tree trunk. He might have been waiting to show her his latest tree house, daring her to climb a sheer and slippery trunk.

She came to stand in front of him, close but not touching. ''You do know that it will kill Cissy if anything happens to you?''

Oliver shook his head. ''It'll hurt, but nobody dies from heartache. You should know that.''

''Don't be too sure. I still have erotic dreams about Lou.'' She did, and their intensity always surprised her; although sex with Lou had been utterly satisfying, it had been a somewhat companionable activity. . . .

Oliver reached up and yanked her down beside him. ''What made you think of that?''

She shrugged. ''Cissy without you. To wit, don't opt out and leave her to fantasize about you.''

''Redemption or damnation. Which is it to be?''

''Both, probably, in equal measures.''

''I've missed you, Angie, and I'm so sorry about Lou. Have I told you that?'' His words weren't exactly slurred, but the wistfulness made her think he was more than slightly drunk.

''You've told me, and I'm sorry, too. It was supposed to last forever. I miss the . . . delight. And my safety net's got a bloody great hole in it.''

''It won't kill Cissy, you know.''

''Go on, tell me it's the best thing for her, that she'll marry again and live happily ever after, that Pamela won't miss her father, that—''

''I'm not saying any of that. I want you to help me, Angie.''

''Oh, no.''

''You don't know what I'm going to ask you yet.''

''I know, and I won't help you. If you think I'm going to

help you persuade Cissy that everything's all right, sweep it all under the carpet, you're crazy. I've thought about this a lot over the last few days, and as far as I'm concerned, it's a simple either/or situation.''

He didn't believe her. ''An ultimatum? Don't be ridiculous.''

It *was* ridiculous, melodramatic. Only the detachment that came from years of being apart gave her the courage to say it. ''I'm not strong enough to watch you die, Oliver. I can't make you want to live, but I can take some of the weight away, make it easier for you to—''

Oliver put his arm around her shoulders and drew her close. ''Not possible, Angie.''

''The hell it isn't.'' She pushed him away angrily. ''There's no more putting it off, don't you understand? For the first time in our lives, we can't go back!''

''That's not an ultimatum; it's a fact.''

''Here's another. Unless you're in that clinic within two weeks, you'll never set eyes on me again. I swear to God, Oliver, I'll walk away and you'll never see me again.''

He was used to the way she spoke; he thought he could read between her words. He laughed. ''You wouldn't.''

''Watch me!'' she snapped. ''I'll do it even if it means giving up what I came back for. Do you want to die?''

''Leave it out, Angie.''

''Do you?'' she persisted.

''I haven't made up my mind yet.'' The despondency in his voice belied his apparent frivolity.

''Well, take your time,'' she said bitterly. ''Don't let me rush you.''

''What *did* you come back for? Did Cissy write to you?''

''I came back to find my daughter.''

Oliver reared up as though he'd been stung. He slid off the trunk and hugged his knees to his chest. ''You don't want to . . . do that.''

''Don't I? I'm telling you now because it might affect your decision—''

''Why? Why, after all these years?''

Exactly Cissy's question. Angie's tone softened. ''I can't answer that. Lou perhaps. Growing up at last in middle age, coming to terms with what happened, I don't know. It wasn't your fault, just as it wasn't my fault, whatever anyone else says. It happened. We've spent over half our lives trying to forget it. I was raped. Lou made me face that simple fact at least. And it is a simple fact. It's happened before, and it will happen again to thousands of women. I was raped, and I had a child. My daughter is nineteen years old, older than Pamela, and I've never seen her. I intend to find her, Oliver, and I want you around when I do.'' She finished in a rush, before her throat closed entirely.

"That simple, is it? Are you crying?"

"Of course, I'm crying," she groaned. "And of course, it isn't simple. It's whatever you make of it, and you might never meet her. . . ."

"You're fighting dirty, Angie. You can't get to me like that. You're making a mistake, trying to find the child—if that's what you're *really* planning to do."

"You think I'd *lie* about that, *use* her to force you out of your corner? For God's sake . . .''

"I'm sorry."

"You're *not* sorry!" She was livid in the face of his listlessness. "I'll tell you something else—"

"I don't want to hear it."

"Jarman's. I'll run it until you're ready to come back."

Oliver scrambled up awkwardly and backed away from her. She followed him, dragging the sleeve of her sweater across her eyes.

"I'll take over until you're ready to come back," she repeated, blinking to get the stumbling figure into focus. "Do you understand what I'm saying? I'll sit in for you, I'll keep it going—"

"Don't be so fucking heroic, and stop crying. I don't want you to take it over, to sit in for me!"

"*Why not!*" she screamed at him.

"And don't shout. You've been away a long time . . . what makes you think he'd agree?"

"He? Father? He has no choice. It's me or nothing, and believe me, he won't bring anyone else in. I'll make sure he doesn't."

"*How?*" He was incensed now, sober and pale.

Angie hesitated, fearful that she'd pushed him too far. "You won't like this; but I've been asking questions, and I've heard things about Jarman's that bring a black mark the size of bloody Everest right to his doorstep."

"*Our* doorstep. What things?"

"Things like staff, like selecting the people you work with, like Sidney, like Martin Corbett, like discouraging bids in auctions, making you get permission to offer anything over ten thousand pounds.''

Oliver turned away from her, swaying. ''Where did you hear all that?''

''I'm sorry . . .''

''Tell me, Angie.''

''It's common knowledge. Those people you work with have made sure it's very common knowledge.''

''Sidney?'' Oliver looked dazed.

''And Martin Corbett and, for all I know, Cynthia Crew and Dunne Morrissey.''

''I don't believe it.''

''Please believe it. What do you say?''

''He'll never agree.''

''Leave that to me.'' A surge of relief brought a smile to her lips. ''What do *you* say?''

Oliver came and draped his wrists over her shoulders, and she felt his chin come to rest on the top of her head, nodding when she asked once more, ''What do *you* say?''

12

☐ Sir Richard Jarman skipped tea, showered, shaved, and put in two hours of work before going downstairs. He was dreading the evening ahead. The date had been fixed weeks ago; he had had no idea when he'd invited Paul and Susan Angelou and Jason Corbett that Angela would be back or that they would be confronted with Oliver's problems. The other guests, apart from Lady Isobel Humphries, were in fact mere acquaintances. It was a shame that Isobel had insisted on coming to see Angela; her deafness would make the evening even more awkward.

He paused on the landing to inspect the knot in his tie. He would much rather have returned to his study to complete the figures for the next board meeting. Belinda was waiting for him at the foot of the stairs. She looked nervous as he placed his dry lips against her cheek. "I wish you'd been able to put Isobel off," he murmured.

"I tried everything, but Theresa and her family are back at Trenton March for the summer, and for some reason—"

"Theresa Humphries is back from France?"

"Theresa Hillier, Richard. Just for the summer, Isobel says. But don't worry, Isobel is only deaf, not gaga, you know."

"I'm not convinced. Why tonight, when Angela is here?"

"Well, Angela and Julia were quite friendly when they were young." Belinda brushed nonexistent fluff from his jacket. "Not the two older girls, of course, especially not Theresa. It's not that strange that Isobel would want to see Angela after all these years, is it?"

"Perhaps not, but the sooner Theresa and the child cross the Channel again, the better. Well, into the fray, m'dear."

"You go on, Richard. Angela is waiting for you in the library. I'll give you a few minutes alone together."

Angie was thinking that she would have to go on a shopping expedition soon. Apart from the dress she was wearing, the clothes she had left behind in her flat in Chelsea were not only dated but strangely impersonal. Perhaps Cissy would accompany her—

"Angela." She turned to see her father standing in the doorway. He towered over Benn, who was nodding at some unheard request. Angie stood up, glad now that she'd taken the trouble to find the one elegant item in her wardrobe: a Jean Muir that was as much in style now as it had been five or six years ago. It was a long navy silk jersey dress with a slashed neckline and a slightly bloused top. The color enhanced the flush on her cheeks and darkened her eyes.

Watching her father walk toward her, Angie was taken, as always, by the arresting quality of the man. He looked like a powerful patriarch in a soap opera, tall, silver-haired, and unapproachable. Would he kiss her, this sophisticated, remarkably handsome man who was her father? Would he smile?

Richard Jarman did both these things. He did them to cover a sudden confusion because he scarcely recognized his daughter. She looked pale and drawn, despite the spots of color in her cheeks, and her thick hair was unexpectedly lusterless. She was regarding him with a look that was at once quizzical and aloof. As they drew apart, it also struck him that she was a very beautiful woman when she cared to present herself as one.

"How are you, Angela?" he asked. "Have you got something to drink?"

Angie raised her half-empty glass and said, "Thank you, yes."

"I see you're still wearing a bandage. Have you had your arm seen to since you arrived back?"

"The dressing has been changed, and it seems to be healing all right."

"Good." He was about to say something else when Benn appeared with his drink. "What is that you're drinking, whiskey? Would you like another?"

Angie winked at Benn. He nodded and turned away before her father could see the exchange. When he was out of earshot, Angie said, "He must be in a great deal of pain. Should he still be doing this?"

"You of all people should know how . . . pigheaded he is. We haven't been able to persuade him to retire. You can try, if you've a mind to."

"I wasn't thinking about retirement, just . . . easing off. But as you say, he *is* stubborn."

"We were surprised, your mother and I, by your sudden decision to return home. May I ask what prompted it?"

Angie hesitated. "It was time for a . . . change. I must say you've hardly changed at all, you or Mother. I was expecting—"

"Well, five years isn't such a long time, is it?" he interrupted. "I—we were all very sorry to hear about your husband."

"Lou, Father. Louis Wyatt."

"Of course. Tragic business. I take it you managed to tidy things up over there before leaving?"

Angie inclined her head at him before taking a sip of her whiskey. "Do you mean the apartment, belongings . . . *things*?"

"Of course," he said again. "There always seems to be so much more to do when it's so sudden."

"I wouldn't know about that. It *has* been a year. As far as the apartment is concerned, I instructed my lawyers to pay the rent, locked it, and brought the key with me."

"I see." Disapproval etched itself deeply in his face. His body slid all the way back into the armchair, putting more distance between them. It was not going well. There was already a disruptive, impatient air about her, and it annoyed him that she still paid no more than lip service to the niceties.

For her part, Angie recognized the movement for what it was: failure to pass the first test question. It hadn't occurred to her to sublet the apartment or to assess the accumulated objects of her life with Lou. The income from her two trust funds was more than enough to keep them both in perpetual comfort. Lou had been awed by her wealth, at least at the beginning. Later he'd come to take it for granted, much as she did.

"You're rich. I love it." He couldn't stop laughing when she told him. "Why didn't I know this before? I'd have married you sooner."

"I was afraid you wouldn't marry me at all," she confessed.

He planned world trips for them, a house in Mexico, a yacht to take them around the Greek islands, a walking tour around England because it looked so tiny on the map, a year in Ireland. They dreamed of these adventures together in the sure knowledge that their life together was just starting. . . .

"I hear he was a remarkably good editor," her father was saying. "Bennett-Poore, wasn't it?" Angie nodded. She could think of nothing to say. "A fine house, Bennett-Poore. I've known Alec Beane for more than forty years. Fine publisher, developed a backlist second to none. I think you'll find, though, that the current batch of general books leaves something to be desired. But of course, they did make a killing on that awful diet book—"

"Why are we talking about Bennett-Poore?" she broke in pleasantly. "At this precise moment I don't give a damn about Bennett-Poore's general list."

"Angela!" His hand went to smooth down his tie in a gesture so familiar that she shut her eyes against it. He *was* trying, she knew, and she was being unreasonable.

"I'm sorry. I'm *sorry*." What was it Cissy had told her? You make it difficult for anyone to get close to you. What would her father say if she told him about her meeting with Christopher Chetwynd earlier that day? Nothing. Just as he'd said nothing about Oliver. "I'm sorry," she said again. "This is silly . . . we have nothing to say to each other."

"That's not true. Your mother and I have been . . . extremely concerned about you.'' He now glanced in the direction of the doorway as if willing someone to appear there.

"Why?'' she asked dully.

"Why? Well . . . because you were in New York and you married Lou . . . Louis . . .''

"Louis Wyatt. New York is an extremely civilized place, Father. If Lou had not been—if Lou hadn't died, I would never have come back.''

He was embarrassed. "Come now.''

"You don't believe me? In that case, perhaps you'd tell me what there was to come back *to*.''

"We all have to make our own lives, Angela.''

"Yes, of course. The famous Jarman dictum. Go out, my son, and make your own life. Do anything you like as long as it's publishing, as long as you create yourself in my image.''

"That's enough!'' His gray eyes flamed with fury. She baffled him. He had never understood her, what she wanted from him. She was now so close that the air thickened around him. Always braver than Oliver, running ahead. He could see her now, dark hair streaming behind, followed by a skinny, leggy Oliver, shouting caution. It should have been the other way around, something he could never forgive either of them. Girls didn't behave like that. Sweaty with exertion, carrying a frog, a beetle, things that should have made her squeal with fright, bringing them to him as if she expected—what? He never knew. Later she challenged him with her scorn, thinly veiled by obedience. But it was always a measured obedience, lasting only as long as was absolutely necessary. Silence was the only concession she made to maintaining peace. And it was implicitly understood that it was never anything but a concession. Belinda once called it marking time, at a loss, as he was, to understand why she behaved the way she did. There was nothing ladylike about their daughter. She walked too fast, spoke too quickly, and all her energies lay just below the surface, crudely visible. And yet there was some part of her he recognized even now, something of himself that he could scarcely remember any longer. Like a slant of sunlight, it crossed his vision now and then, but he had drawn a shade down on it so long ago that it was no more than that, a faded flicker. . . .

It hurt Angie to see the anger in his eyes, but it was better than nothing at all. She thought they should talk about Oliver, of the inescapable fact that Oliver might die. But he did not want to be reminded, she knew that, any more than he wanted to be reminded of the name of her dead husband. He didn't approve of death; it was a sign of weakness; it threatened him with time-wasting emotions and formalities.

"Richard . . ." Belinda Jarman called huskily from the doorway. "We're all in the drawing room when you're ready."

He got up, relieved. "Angela?"

"I'll join you in a moment. I'm sorry if I upset you. I didn't mean to."

"You've had a lot to contend with."

"Yes. We'll do this another time."

Richard Jarman looked down at his daughter's stricken face with something akin to distaste. She had more of him in her than Oliver did. She was an implacable fighter but one with too many weaknesses. Emotional, vulnerable, yes, but still with a core of granite that would outlast them all. He thought he could see pity in her eyes just then, and a perplexity. . . .

From the depths of her armchair Angie watched her father move away. Fifteen minutes, after five years, were all they had managed. She sat as if turned to stone and for the second time in a week found herself holding back her tears. He had not seen her cry since the day he confronted her with the news that she was pregnant. Her mother had been somewhere else, upstairs, leaving the indignity and shame of the report to her husband. They had not decided what to do, he told her; she would be informed as soon as decisions could be made. He hadn't seen then that all she'd wanted to do was crawl into his arms and be held. He hadn't seen her outrage. He seemed to think that in some way she had precipitated the assault; she'd been there, she was a woman, and she should have known better than to go off with those young men. He hadn't mentioned Oliver, the state Oliver had been in. He hadn't mentioned the blood and bruises and the loathing she felt for this growing thing inside her. None of that, only shame and secrecy and guilt . . .

By the time Benn came looking for her, she had finished her whiskey and was adjusting the high ankle strap on one of her shoes.

"Shall I do that?" he asked.

"It's fine now. But sometime, perhaps tomorrow morning, you could change this bandage for me? You can't have much use for that first-aid kit any longer. Do you still have it?"

"Naturally," he replied, eyeing her keenly. "I knew you'd be back and that I'd need it again." And when Angie giggled, he added, "You sound as mischievous as you did when you were ten years old."

"And you're still as grumpy. Could we spend some time together this weekend, do you think?"

"I'm not going anywhere. Now I suggest you join your family. They're waiting for you." It would not have surprised her if he had taken her hand or reached up to brush the hair from her forehead.

As she entered the drawing room, Richard Jarman turned away from Cissy and addressed his wife. "Does everyone know who's coming tonight, Belinda?"

"I think so. You've all met the Murchisons, haven't you?" She waited for their nods. Like schoolchildren, they stood together in a group. Angie seemed to remember that all the Murchisons ever spoke of were animals in labor. "And Isobel Humphries. Poor dear, she's now deaf as a post, but she particularly wanted to see you, Angela. And—"

Her husband interrupted her. "Lytton Askew is our MP. . . ."

"Quite. The others are friends of your father's."

"Jason Corbett is a friend as well as a business colleague, but I would hardly call Paul Angelou and his wife friends, my dear. I've known Paul for some years, though. He's a broker . . . share a club or two."

Angelou *here*? Angie glanced quickly at Cissy, who shook her head, indicating that she hadn't known. Oliver was blissfully unaware of the tension in the room. Angie stepped away from them both; a surge of adrenaline made her fingertips tingle. Perhaps now was a good time to take a walk with her whiskey, a stroll outside with Benn. . . .

She smiled at her father and heard herself asking, "Does he make a lot of money for you, this Angelou?"

"We've had one or two successes, yes. I'm afraid I don't know his wife at all, but I'm told she's the daughter of old Geoffrey McClure. Sound chap, known Geoffrey for years."

The front doorbell went at that moment. The first guests had arrived. Belinda and Richard Jarman glanced at each other in a wordless communication of some thought. Angie caught the look and wondered about it. They were ill at ease, unsure of themselves. Oliver had seen it, too. He grimaced at Angie just as the Murchisons came bustling in. They were two rawboned individuals who had clearly dressed in haste and driven over in an open car of some kind. Edith Murchison was taller and bigger than her husband. She'd applied a liberal amount of powder to her cheeks, where it now clung with unattractive stubbornness. They looked uncannily like brothers. As they were introduced to her, Angie caught a not unpleasant odor of horses and dried sweat.

Lytton Askew's bulk moved slowly alongside the frail woman he was escorting. The MP's expression was one of oversolicitous concern, his step exaggeratedly slow. Oliver rescued Lady Isobel Humphries and led her to a straight high-backed chair. Askew was immediately confronted by Edith Murchison, who pressed her sherry glass deep into the folds of her bosom and began to describe the difficulties they'd encountered with their last breech-born foal.

Cissy clutched Oliver's arm. "Rescue me if I begin to make a fool of myself."

"If it'll get us out of this, I'll join you. Perhaps they'll send us off to bed without our supper?"

"Some hope." Angie came up behind them, intending to make her way over to Isobel Humphries.

Oliver hooted with laughter, then said, "Stay here, both of you. I'll bring Jason over."

Because her father had described him as a friend, Angie had expected to see an older man, a small, neat, colorless businessman. Jason Corbett was precisely the opposite. She judged him to be in his mid-forties and at least six feet two. He wore a lightweight dinner jacket with the air of a man not completely at ease in formal dress. He was built like a prop forward, deep-chested, with powerful arms and shoulders, and as he came toward her, Angie noticed that he walked with a slight limp, favoring his left leg.

He brushed her hand lightly as Oliver introduced them. Under a thatch of graying fair hair, the imprint of youthful good looks lingered in his face. A conniving charm lurked in the densely blue eyes and in the full contours of his mouth.

Angie watched him kiss Cissy fondly before she and Oliver were accosted by the smaller of the two Murchisons.

"Rugby?" Angie asked, indicating Corbett's right leg.

"Cricket."

"You don't look like a cricketer."

"That's what my ex-wife said when they carried me off the field on a stretcher."

"Oh."

"Yes. She meant—oh, well, never mind . . . you didn't look like a cricketer anyway." He also didn't look like a man who would place his son in a job where he was not wanted. "I seem to surprise you, Mrs. Wyatt," he said as though he'd read her thoughts. "Why is that?"

"I could say it's because you don't appear to be anything like your son, from what I've heard of him. But I think it's probably because we're going to get on rather well."

He wasn't displeased. "How do you make that out?"

There was a barely discernible Yorkshire accent in his voice and, unless she was mistaken, a strangely intimate manner in the way he was using it. "Instinct?" she said, wondering why he hadn't picked up on her reference to his son.

"Perhaps. Do you like the opera?"

"No."

He nodded. "Oliver tells me you're something of an expert on coproduction deals."

"I've set up a few. It's a job that requires patience rather more than skill, as you know."

"But you did it well."

"Yes," she admitted, grinning up at him. "Are you by any chance sounding me out for a job?"

"Do you want one?"

"I don't think so"—Angie paused as she saw her father bearing down on them—"but you never know."

"Jason, I'd like you to meet another two guests who've just arrived. You'll excuse us, won't you, Angela?"

Angelou. She had to shift only fractionally to see him standing just inside the doorway. "Of course."

He *did* look like a gangster, she thought, surprised. Her second impression of him that night was also a leftover from their first meeting: perfection. It surrounded him like a skin and extended from the exquisitely tailored dinner suit he wore to the exquisitely delicate woman at his side. Susan Angelou was quite beautiful; she would not have been out of place on a catwalk, modeling the clothes she wore: a gossamer-light full-length divided skirt with a loose top in a very fine wild silk, the color of buttermilk. Her hair was done up in a chignon; a yellow topaz pin on her shoulder matched the large topaz ring on her finger and the topaz-encrusted rope twisted around her wrist. There was a cared-for, cosseted look about Susan Angelou that did not altogether surprise Angie.

Jason Corbett had made no move to follow her father back to the group which included her mother and the Angelous. He'd been watching her. Angie stepped back, shock registering like a hammerblow at the look of astonished comprehension on his face. She stiffened and spun away from him, moving toward Cissy. Her insides felt chilled, and her face suffused with heat. What had he seen? What chance did she have of coping with Angelou herself if someone she'd spent fewer than ten minutes with could read her reactions with such ease?

Fighting an urge to leave the room altogether, she made her way to where Isobel Humphries sat, erect and alert. The old woman wanted to talk about her granddaughter. Angie pulled up a chair and sat close to her, so that she could speak directly into her ear. In the event, she said hardly anything. Isobel Humphries spoke without looking at her, without taking breath.

"Not yet twenty, you know, such a pretty, lively child. The energy . . . Theresa claims to be exhausted and doesn't emerge from her room until midmorning. Gives me a chance to talk to the girl. They live in France, you see, come over two or three times a year. Christina. Tina, they call her. So different from Julia's two; mind you, one of them is a boy, a man really. Odd creatures, men, never had much to do with them. Three daughters, you see. First time we'll have a doctor in the family. Had clerics, the occasional Cabinet minister, but never a doctor. It's a pity, I think, that Christina will attend the Sorbonne, but there you are, the young tend to make decisions so easily these days. Fearless and quite rightly. Such a pretty, *pretty* child, a light behind the eyes, you might say. Here I am, doddering into my eighties, and I feel at times that I have you all back with me—you and Julia and Theresa. It does make one wonder, my dear girl."

Isobel Humphries's voice trailed off, and Angie felt a hand on her shoulder. "Angie, have you met Mr. Angelou? My sister, Angela Wyatt."

Angie gently disengaged her hand from the old woman's grip and rose. She was momentarily thrown by the undercurrent of poignancy in Isobel Humphries's voice. It was almost as though she had been sharing her joy with a purpose, imparting the sense of a life just beginning in order to offset one recently ended.

"We've met," Angie said to Oliver, and then smiled at his confusion. "On the plane coming over."

"Fine," Oliver said vaguely, and turned to find Cissy.

"Did your arm require more stitches, Mrs. Wyatt?" Paul asked when they were alone.

"You don't miss much, do you? No, there wasn't much damage. As a matter of fact, this"—she held up her arm—"is coming off in two or three days. The bandage, not the arm."

He stood as still as a statue, legs slightly apart, amused. He had expected to see her here tonight, but her presence had jarred him nonetheless, and he was both attracted and displeased by the unwelcome sensations. His recollection of her at the airport was clear and yet blurred, perhaps because he had picked over their conversation so many times since returning to London. Her honest apology at Heathrow had not exactly surprised him, but his reaction to it had. Then, as now, he had the feeling that her spirit had lain unaroused for so long that all it needed was a spark for it to flare into life again. An arrogant assumption on his part? Well, she knew he was arrogant anyway. Not to her or anyone else would he deny it. But he could not understand why she reacted so fiercely to everything he said. How could he be *touching* her without having come anywhere close to her essence?

Angie reached for another drink as Benn moved among them, carrying a small silver tray. Over Lytton Askew's shoulder she caught sight of Jason Corbett; he was deep in conversation with Oliver, but she had the uncomfortable feeling that he'd been studying her again.

She pulled her gaze away and said to the silent Angelou, "Are you always this talkative?" She thought he'd accepted the rebuke gracefully until he said, "I was thinking that you probably should not spend too much time here at Calvert Hall."

"Sharp," she retorted. "Why not?"

"It doesn't suit you."

"I grew up here; it's my home. If I appear to be ill at ease, it's because I haven't been back for a . . . long time."

That wasn't the reason. Paul knew she was lying, but he didn't know why. Beaumont Gracie's first report, which he had since reread, had told him a few things about her, but nothing in depth. He had an appointment to see Gracie on

Tuesday, and he almost regretted having to talk to Angie now; once Gracie had told him what he wanted to know, she wouldn't be able to get away with such a dismissive statement.

"I can see your brother growing up here, but not you. You seem to be . . . camping out."

Angie laughed loudly. "*Very* sharp," she said. "You're not wrong. What about you? Do you feel at ease here, in this room, with these people?"

"Yes."

"I believe you, but then there's something of the chameleon in you. You do blend, beautifully. I'm not sure about your wife, though. I think you should rescue her from our local MP."

Without looking around, Paul shook his head. "Susan cut her teeth on people like that."

"The pompous, boring brigade? Poor girl."

"Not at all. Some things are unavoidable, she understands that."

"She's very beautiful," Angie said honestly. "You're a lucky man—no, I take that back. Luck had nothing to do with it. Am I right?"

"I wouldn't say that, but luck has certainly played a larger part in your life than it has in mine."

She had to admire his technique; it confounded and provoked her. "Do you always do your research so thoroughly?"

"Research?" he repeated. "That sounds like a euphemism for creeping around asking questions."

"Isn't that what you do?" she asked, without heat.

Her question, idle as it was, struck home. "I like to know who I'm—"

"Dealing with?"

"Hardly, Mrs. Wyatt." He came close to smiling, wondering a little at his own frankness. "I've had, uh, dealings, as you put it, with your father for many years now—"

Again she didn't allow him to finish. "Yes, I know that, but whatever information you have about me would scarcely have come from him. I haven't seen my father for more than five years, but I suppose you know that. And he never met my husband. Quite aside from that, he doesn't exactly volunteer personal information. Do you know what I think? I think you prepare yourself, Mr. Angelou. For everything.

Nothing and no one takes you by surprise. Don't you find it boring?''

He was undisturbed. "Do I look bored?"

She accepted the invitation and studied him openly. She could see nothing in his eyes, no humor, no hint that he recognized the absurdity of this conversation. After a moment's hesitation she said, "I think you scare me a little."

"Honesty is not necessarily flattery."

"I didn't mean it as a compliment. That you should take it as one scares me even more."

"Scared? *You?*" Oliver loomed up at her side, drawing Susan Angelou closer. "Angie is not always to be believed, Mr. Angelou."

"You surprise me." There was faint irony in Paul's tone as his eyes left Angie's. "This is my wife, Susan."

"Daughter of Geoffrey McClure," Angie muttered under her breath. She said it to get back at him, and his quick glance told her he'd heard.

Before she could say a word to Susan Angelou, Benn came in to announce dinner. Paul turned on his heel. Oliver took Susan's arm once more, and Angie followed them. Nice, she decided, outwitted once again by Paul's withdrawal. It was sleight of hand, a booby trap, a trip wire. Four whiskeys, and you're amused by the wallpaper. Five, and you'll be stirred by this pantomime of an evening. Confrontational. American word, Lou's word. It had mattered intermittently that he hadn't liked that in her, less as he began to understand her need for it. Paul Angelou had enjoyed the skirmish, at least until the last jab. The gist of her speculations was quite clear to her but she knew she could not afford to accept any challenge . . . except one.

Oliver was enjoying himself. His smile floated across the table at Cissy now and then. Sitting opposite him at the large round table, she responded by moving her lips with words no one else could hear.

After three glasses of claret to take away the slightly gamey taste of the guinea fowl, Angie began to feel light-headed and more energetic as the evening wore on. Heavy Georgian silver, starched damask napkins, candlelight that softened and highlighted, changed and shadowed, Benn ensuring that the level of wine in the fragile crystal glasses remained at precisely the correct level, while keeping an eye on the girl who had served the meal without mishap.

Angie was acutely aware of Isobel Humphries next to her. The old woman touched her arm from time to time, a soft, consoling gesture; she'd given up trying to hear what was being said and now concentrated like an aged bird on the food before her.

Although Angie couldn't see him properly, it was clear from the silence farther down the table that Lytton Askew was no longer responding with polite interest to either of the Murchisons. Seated at the far end of the table, Belinda Jarman made concerted efforts to draw the Murchisons' attention away from Askew. It made no difference: they simply addressed each other and Askew as if she weren't there at all. Richard Jarman was content to converse solely with Paul Angelou, sitting on his left.

Separated from her husband by Cissy and Jason Corbett, Susan Angelou was smiling. Whatever Jason was saying, he was saying it with a straight face, without gestures or emphasis. But he was obviously amusing Susan. Angie watched the woman with unabashed interest. Paul's wife had made occasional forays into the conversation around her, but there was a sense of surfeit to her comments. Angie supposed that she was simply not interested in the company, but her reserve suggested something more than just lack of interest. Once she caught Angie looking at her, and her expression, as she glanced in the direction of her husband, had come close to a mutinous rejection of him. At that point Angie realized that, without giving the slightest hint, Susan was and had been totally aware of everything Paul said and was told. Also, that he took this for granted, turning to his wife for a comment without having drawn her into any conversation. There was also the disquieting impression that Susan Angelou might have been anywhere, in a restaurant, at a charity function, a board meeting. Once or twice she made Oliver laugh and took pains to include Cissy in everything she said. Well mannered certainly. Angie could not relate the cool blond beauty to the dark, distanced man. The woman's attentiveness would have been the same had he been holding her in his arms. He seemed to know it, and it gave him an assurance that was almost obscene.

Angelou had been seated almost opposite her; stimulated, Angie turned half an ear to her father's explanation of writing down warehouse stock. As though sensing her attention, Paul nodded and turned to her for the first time during the meal.

"Is there much difference between British and American publishing, Mrs. Wyatt? Aside from the mechanics of producing the books, that is."

"I think not. Print numbers are much larger, and so are advances; but it's basically the same thing: too few really good writers battling for space amongst the rubbish. Not that I have anything against rubbish; I just wish there were less of it. The trade is being inundated with nonbooks, pop star biographies, television spin-offs, a kind of media publishing."

"You're right," Oliver interjected. "The book has in the last few years become the product, like a record or a box of chocolates. People see, recognize, and buy an image. What they don't recognize and are not willing to pay around ten pounds for is quality, obscurely packaged."

Oliver was exceedingly drunk. Susan marveled at his limitless intake of wine and wondered why it wasn't reflected in his voice. "Why obscurely, Mr. Jarman?" she asked.

"Because there are a limited number of things a publisher can do to ensure that a book is bought not by the bookseller but by the public."

"Such as advertising?" Paul addressed Angie once more. "Isn't advertising much more of a tool of the trade in America than it is here?"

"It is, but only because the print numbers are larger and publishers can afford to advertise. Most books published here sell less than ten thousand copies, and a lot sell a hell of a lot less than that. It's a question of economics."

"Would it be possible to make a best-seller?"

Angie laughed. "There's one thing you can never accuse a publisher of, Mr. Angelou, and that's lack of optimism. Every book published is seen as a potential best-seller."

Paul persisted. "That doesn't answer my question, Mrs. Wyatt."

Suzy was surprised by Paul's demanding tone. Publishing wasn't something he was particularly interested in, but he seemed intent on trying to force Angela Wyatt into a discussion she clearly didn't want to get into.

The table had fallen silent. Angie felt Isobel Humphries's hand come to rest lightly but protectively on her arm, and she sensed, rather than saw, Jason Corbett register the movement. He missed nothing. "Your question is unanswerable, Mr. Angelou," she said slowly. "One book can sell five thousand copies and get onto the best-seller lists; another will have to sell twenty thousand before it does. The permutations on which bestsellerdom are based are endless. It's a relative term anyway."

Richard Jarman looked up from the port he was sampling. "My knowledge of trade publishing is somewhat limited, as you know, Paul, but I suspect one cannot make the public read what it doesn't want to read."

"Well, there's your answer, Mr. Angelou," Angie said flippantly.

"You disagree?"

"Perish the thought," she said sarcastically. "I've never been in a position to find out, one way or the other. I'll let you know when I do." She felt a sharp nudge beneath the table: Oliver, warning her off.

Just then, to her relief, Belinda Jarman rose regally and motioned to Benn, who was hovering, hunched, at the sideboard. "Lady Isobel will be ready to leave shortly. Kindly ask Wills to bring the car around to the front."

As the others crossed the hall into the drawing room, Angie signaled Oliver to remain behind. He was making heavy weather of lighting a cigar, coughing into the cloud of smoke that enveloped his head.

"Well, what do you think of Jason?" he asked.

"I'm not sure. He's very . . . observant."

Oliver waved his hand in front of his face to disperse the smoke. "Not as observant as Angelou. Interesting, aren't they? Susan is stunning."

"What do you know about him?"

"He's rich, that's just about all I know. Greek, father rolling in it, too. I understand our old man is serious about putting his name forward at local constituency level."

Angie whistled softly. "An MP? Anything else?"

"That's all I know. Careful, Angie, he could be a wrong un."

"You're thinking glands?"

"Are you?"

"Don't be ridiculous," she snapped. "I wanted to tell you anyway that I'm leaving first thing in the morning. I can't face another two days of this. I—"

"What are you two whispering about?" Sir Richard Jarman demanded from the doorway.

"Whispering? We're not children, Father. As a matter of fact, I was telling Oliver that I'll be leaving in the morning, going back to London."

"I see," he said mildly. "Your mother will be disappointed."

"Wait." Oliver went after his father as he turned to retrace his steps. "I'd like to discuss something with you. What time will you be in the office on Monday?"

Richard Jarman scowled, annoyed by his son's dull, red-eyed glance. "You know perfectly well I'm leaving for Johannesburg on Sunday night. Perhaps if you did not—"

"I'd forgotten."

"Can't it wait?"

"Not for three weeks."

"Then we'll have to make some time tomorrow. I was going to suggest it myself anyway."

"Oh. If it's about the medical reports, we'll be talking about the same thing." Oliver cast a grim look at Angie, then added quickly, "You see, I've decided to take a . . . sabbatical."

Richard Jarman's entire body froze in a comical attitude of surprise. "Say that again!"

Standing behind Oliver, Angie saw him slide his balled fists into his jacket pockets. "A sabbatical," she heard him say. "A year, maybe more."

"A year—don't you think it would have been civil to discuss this with me before simply deciding?"

"It wasn't a simple decision, and it wasn't a decision I could have put off for much longer."

"And what about Jarman's? You can't just *leave*, you can't just—"

"Angie has offered to sit in for me," Oliver said stolidly.

"Angela? Good God, I might have known."

Oliver stepped back. "My decision has nothing to do with her. Why she would even contemplate taking on the job is beyond me."

"Angela!"

"I'm here." She came forward. For a moment she thought he was going to hit her.

"What's the meaning of this?"

"Can't we discuss it later, when your guests have left?"

"Damn the guests. You'll both join me in the library. Now!"

Oliver took Angie's arm. "I'll talk to him. You go and find out some more about your Mr. Angelou."

"He can wait. Come, let's get it over with."

"Are you sure you want to do this?"

"I'm sure."

"Don't pay too much attention to what he says—"

"I won't."

"Angie . . ."

"Shut up, Oliver."

"Well?" The demand met them as they walked into the room. Oliver shambled back to shut the door, and Angie sat down, facing her father.

"Why don't you sit down?" she asked. He was ready to erupt, arms held tightly across his chest, ready to mete out punishment.

"I prefer to stand. Now tell me what all this is about, Oliver."

Oliver took the chair between them, weary even before the discussion began. Thanks to the claret, though, the old man's stare wasn't as intimidating as usual. "I've decided to check into a clinic, a drying-out clinic in Gloucestershire."

"Without consulting me? I assume that by a drying-out clinic you mean—" He stopped, the words catching in his throat.

"For alcoholics, yes."

Angie saw her father's hand fumble automatically for his tie, then drop to his side. He was baffled. He drew a deep breath. "Now look," he said, the effort thickening his voice, "you drink. We all drink—"

"No, I don't drink like . . . you all drink."

"I can't see that it's as bad as all that. There are other doctors . . ."

"I've been told that alcoholics find it impossible to admit to their addiction. I'm drunk now or at least I think I am. Maybe that's why I can tell you that I'm an alcoholic. I've been an alcoholic for more than twenty years."

"I'll repeat what I've just said: There are other doctors—"

"Stop it, please." Angie spoke for the first time. "Are you suggesting that we ignore the results of those tests?"

"No, I'm not suggesting that. What I'm saying is that there

are better people, people with other ideas. Psychotherapy perhaps.''

Oliver's head went back, and he shut his eyes, trying to remember why all this had come up now, why Cissy wasn't here. . . . ''It's too late for that. There's no time left for experiments.'' Where did those words come from? ''They've given me a few months, until the end of the year, and that's not a great deal of time.'' He wanted another drink. ''Angie, would you please ring for Benn?''

''Pull yourself together, man!''

Oliver's eyes fluttered open. For a moment Angie thought he would faint. To her relief, he expelled a deep, ragged breath and pushed himself to his feet. ''Enough. I've told you what I plan to do, and I'm not prepared to discuss it any longer. You can do as you wish. Angie?''

''Leave us, Oliver.''

''Sit down!'' Richard Jarman ordered. ''I haven't finished.''

Oliver paused, and Angie could see the strain run like a tremor through his body. A direct order; it strung him up pitifully. Go! she prayed, willing him out of the room.

He left. She avoided her father's eyes as the door swung shut behind Oliver and they both listened to his heavy footsteps crossing the hall. Then there was only the sound of the clocks ticking.

''Is it true?'' Her father stood with his back toward her, facing the fireplace, hands linked behind his back.

Angie dropped her cigarettes and fumbled with clumsy fingers to retrieve them. ''I've seen the reports. It's true.''

''I don't understand. Why doesn't he—''

''Pull himself together? It truly isn't that simple, you know. At this stage it's like any other drug, a craving. It hurts; he's in pain.''

''I could bring in Sir Evelyn Wilding. He's the best there is for this sort of thing.''

''It won't do any good. Can't you see what's happening here?''

He turned to stare down at her. ''Evidently I can't.''

''Sit down. Please. I—neither of us wants to hurt you. If you believe that, maybe I can explain a little of what's been going on.''

He sat down reluctantly. ''Carry on.''

''Will it come as a surprise to you if I told you that Oliver hates publishing? That he's always hated it? Surely you know he only went into the business to please you.''

"Are you saying he drinks because he hates publishing?"

"No, but that's a part of it. It started at university, but you were never there to see it. He dreamed of archaeology . . . and I mean dreamed because he knew it was impossible. His idea of heaven was sifting soil, the solitude and suspense. . . . I can't imagine, even now, that there's a major dig going on anywhere in the world that he doesn't know about. Maybe he hated himself for taking the easy way out and becoming a publisher, I don't know. It got worse after his friends—after what happened to me. He never really had a chance.''

"Your mother and I have never pressured him into doing anything he didn't want to do. I won't accept the blame for that.''

"I'm not asking you to. All you have to do now is to let him go.''

Richard Jarman rested his elbow on his knee and pressed thumb and forefinger to the bridge of his nose. "Well, I suppose Sidney and Deborah could manage for a year.''

"I think not, Father. I know quite a lot about Sidney Niklas.''

"You've never even met the man!''

"It wasn't difficult to get the sort of information I was looking for. I know one or two other things about Jarman's as well that you're not going to be pleased to hear.''

Richard Jarman passed his hand tiredly over his eyes. "The trade is going through a bad time just now. Everyone's in the same boat.''

"It's not that. It's the people you've employed to work with Oliver: Sidney, your friend Corbett's son. There's no loyalty to Jarman's, let alone to Oliver. You hold on to the purse strings and reduce your managing director to the status of office boy. The list is dull, it's thin and predictable and boring, and there's not a damn thing Oliver can do about it in the present setup. You said earlier this evening that your knowledge of trade publishing was limited. You were right. Auctions are not conducted by money-crazed zombies; typescripts don't thud down on the mat because you expect them to. Jarman's is in a rut a mile wide and ten deep. It has no life and no style because its managing director is walking around with his hands tied behind his back.''

"That's not true!" There was now more fatigue than anger in his voice.

"Why would I lie to you?"

"Oliver isn't a stupid man. He's done well, he's respected, and if he's unhappy about the staff, why hasn't he done something about it before?"

"I suspect because he knew he wouldn't get anywhere. You've never made it particularly easy for either of us to convince you of anything."

"If that's so, it's because I haven't exactly been sitting idly by all these years. How do you imagine Jarman academic is run? By departmental directors? Do you imagine that all there is to it is market research and commissioning texts? Chairing board meetings?"

Angie shook her head. "We're not discussing the academic side at all. I think I know how hard you work, how many hours you put in. You run Jarman academic on a day-to-day basis; the responsibility and the decisions are yours. It's *your* company, and you manage it successfully by all accounts. You involve yourself by choice in the minutiae, but you haven't given Oliver that freedom."

"Your brother hasn't sought it," he said coldly.

"I would."

"I don't understand."

"Oliver has accepted, for the moment at least, the possibility of opting out for a year or so. He may well change his mind if you pursue the idea of Sidney's taking over."

"And if I decide to bring someone else in?"

"Worse. You see, whether he admits it or not and whether you believe it or not, he feels guilty about letting you down. I would be a caretaker, nothing more. It's me or nothing." She stopped, suddenly talked out.

"That's tantamount to blackmail."

"I suppose you're right. In this context the ransom is Oliver's life."

Richard Jarman eyed his daughter with detachment. Was it true? he wondered. The thought that the publishing trade sniggered behind his back was intolerable. Most of what she had said was intolerable. Not only did she know very little about British publishing, but her personality and brand of decision making would make life decidedly difficult for him. And there was something else, something lying closely guarded and hidden behind that beautiful face. What was it?

"I'll have to think about it," he said suddenly, decisively.

Angie got up, too, stubbing out her cigarette in a minute ashtray she suspected wasn't an ashtray at all. "When will you be back from Africa?"

"In three weeks."

"Then I suggest you consider the options right away, Father. Before I leave in the morning, in fact. Oliver will have a lot to do before he leaves for Gloucestershire. This can't wait."

"I've told you I'll think about it," he repeated. "I'll let you know when I've come to a decision. Now I'm going to rejoin our guests."

Once alone, Angie lit another cigarette and had taken no more than two or three puffs when Benn came to find her. He was carrying a fresh drink.

"Thank you, Benn. How did you know it was what I wanted?"

"Is everything all right?" he asked briskly.

"Not quite." She began to laugh, and Benn thought he detected a hint of hysteria. "Are the guests still here?"

"Only Mr. Corbett and Mr. and Mrs. Angelou."

"Do you think they expect me back in there?"

"Oh . . ." Benn wondered what she was laughing at. He hadn't heard anyone laugh with such complete enjoyment for a long time. "Well, I imagine they are expecting you to go back."

"You're right. Walk with me, will you?" Her arm rested easily across his bent back, but she felt him stiffen at the contact. She had a sudden vision of Benn when he had returned, unbidden, to the small nursing home when she was about to give birth to her daughter. He'd come in with a posy of violets, clutching his waistcoat in alarm at the sight of her.

"I'm s-sorry," he sputtered, "I thought—I thought the baby . . ."

The nurse took the violets from his shaking fist and placed them in a cup of water. "The baby is reluctant, I'm afraid. Please don't stay long."

Astonishingly he had remained at her side, even when she'd jerked her head toward the door, indicating that he should leave. When the nurse returned, she had to disengage Angie's white-knuckled fingers from Benn's. "Go now, Mr. Benn," she said gently. "It'll soon be over."

"Shall I remain, Miss Angela?" he asked doggedly.

Even through her pain she realized that he was on the point of passing out. She shook her head, unable to speak, and raised her hand in a gesture of thanks. He left, and they never spoke of that day again. He knew what had happened to her daughter. And he knew that she would not ask him to betray a lifetime of loyalty to her mother and father. How was it that he had stayed on all these years, knowing what he did about her family?

At the foot of the stairs she stopped, turned to face him, and then kissed him on the forehead. "I've changed my mind. Make my excuses, will you? Anything. I'm going to bed."

She thought she saw the beginnings of a smile before he moved away. But maybe not. She'd wanted to carry on the conversation she'd begun with Jason Corbett, but it would have to wait. Paul Angelou, too. She could hear a soft buzz of noise from the drawing room.

They would all have to wait.

Part Two

13

☐ The sign, in blue, read: THE WIDOW APPLEBAUM and beneath it: DELI AND BAGEL ACADEMY.

In the pedestrian precinct of South Molton Street Angie paused to transfer four bulky shopping bags to her right hand before following Cissy in, past the disorientating chevron mirrors and the signed photographs of actors, down to a booth at the far end of the room.

They had spent the past hour and a half at Browns, a few doors away, choosing the basis of a new wardrobe for Angie. Having suggested Browns in the first place, Cissy was then immediately unnerved, first by the prices and then by Angie's unerring eye. Every color, cut, and fabric she selected seemed to have been specifically designed for her: silky skirts with elegant curved seaming, softly flouncing blouses, crepe de chine tops that swirled (where they were supposed to swirl, Cissy grudgingly admitted, having noted each price before Angie disappeared into the fitting room), dresses that brought a smug look of satisfaction to the face of their laser-eyed assistant.

When Cissy said, "Enough!" Angie knew she'd reached one of Cissy's preconceived spending limits; to go beyond that limit would offend her sister-in-law. And she knew she'd made the right decision to call it a day when Cissy said, pointedly, and for the sole benefit of the assistant, "I'm taking you to Marks and Spencer for knickers!"

"Nice clothes," Angie now murmured placatingly as they sat down.

"Pricey!" Cissy snapped.

"No more so than in New York."

"Mmmm." Unconvinced, Cissy glowered at the menu. "It's nearly lunchtime . . . salt beef on rye?"

The restaurant had a good, bustling feel to it; the comfortable bench seats were upholstered in mock pigskin, framed

American posters hung on the walls, and old-fashioned coolie-hat lampshades dangled over the tables. In the booth to their left a girl was showing calendar artwork to two men sitting opposite her; she looked relaxed and pleased with their reaction as she propped each picture up against the back of the bench seat.

"Angie?" Cissy moved aside the flowers arranged in a Paul Masson carafe and leaned forward. "You're not regretting it, are you? I can still hardly believe what's happened."

"You mean, taking over for Oliver?"

"Not only that, but Oliver—he seems to have accepted it all with so little fuss. As for your father, I'm surprised he didn't cancel his trip to Africa altogether!"

Angie smiled. "I didn't expect him to do that, but I will admit he took it rather better than I thought he would."

She *had* been surprised by her father's almost benign composure when he'd summoned her to his study the morning after the dinner party at Calvert Hall. Five days ago? It seemed to Angie that five years had passed since then. Facing him across the small leather-topped writing desk, even before they'd exchanged a word, she'd been conscious of a fleeting pity. This wasn't the way it should have turned out for him either; by his own rigid perceptions of the rules, someone had unsportingly let fly with a low punch. He did not regard her interim solution as ideal, but if he hadn't actually gone on to articulate the words "closing ranks," they were distinctly understood: better a member of the family than a prying outsider.

It was nine-thirty in the morning, and he was casually dressed in a heavy-knit gray sweater with a soft-collared blue shirt beneath it. Angie made no mention of the stripe of ink on his cheek; this unexpectedly companionable air was too good for her to risk the chance of spoiling it with an implied criticism.

"You'll need to be thoroughly briefed," he said. "I'll prepare a statement for the trade press myself before I leave. Perhaps I should have a word with one or two of the diarists—"

"Newspaper diarists? Surely a move like this wouldn't arouse their interest?"

"The move itself, no, but if they got wind of the reason for Oliver's absence, it could well rate a paragraph or two."

Angie lit a cigarette and chose her words with care. "My

instinct is to play it down. After all, it's not as though Jarman trade were a multimillion-pound organization.''

"I can see you know very little about the press in this country. The size of the company is immaterial; it would be the titillating aspect of your brother's problem that would interest them.''

He would be precipitating just the sort of reaction he feared by trying to forestall it in this way. Her stomach knotting with tension, she said, ''That's even more reason for you not to call them over a weekend. Maybe—maybe your press statement could suggest that this arrangement has been under discussion for some months. It's the overnight decision, as it were, the *suddenness* of it that would make them suspicious, don't you think?''

He thought about that for a moment, then nodded. ''You could be right. That's a good idea. Incidentally, I expect either you or Oliver to inform Jason Corbett, personally, about this change. I'd call him myself, but he was leaving this morning for a few days in Italy. You can rely on his complete discretion.''

Angie got up and wandered over to the window. The day was bright and chilly; the west-facing window gave her an uninterrupted view of the orchard and Benn, making his way carefully down a slight incline. He was carrying a basket. The henhouse? Did he still do that?

"Unless I read it wrong,'' she said, ''Jason was on the verge of offering me a job last night. It's occurred to me since then that you might have suggested it to him.''

"Good Lord, why should I do that?''

She turned to see something that could have passed for a grin flit across his handsome face. And then he laughed outright as she said, ''Well, I'm pleased you didn't. That would truly have been the unacceptable face of nepotism: you've got my son, I'll take on your daughter; that way we'll keep them both out of mischief.''

"I hope you bring some of the vividness of your imagination to bear on selecting the books you'll be buying over the next year,'' he said, not at all sharply. ''Now, if you're still planning to return to London this morning, I suggest you go and find your mother before she leaves for Tonbridge Wells.''

And suddenly she'd wanted to stay on, share a late breakfast with him, help Benn collect the eggs, take the hunter out for a gallop. . . . But she'd left—so quickly that it was almost an escape. They had at least established a basis, however flimsy, for a reconciliation, and that was enough to be going on with. . . .

Cissy was describing the cottage in Gloucestershire which she planned to rent for the following few months. It was no more than five or six miles from the clinic into which Oliver had been booked. Pamela would be staying with friends in London.

"She could stay at the flat with me," Angie said.

"You'll have enough to cope with. How do you feel?"

"A bit scared."

"Ha!"

In their own way they'd all managed to interpret her loose control of the situation as the kind of courage and strength she did not readily associate with herself. In the past year she'd come to consider herself to be just about as flexible as a concrete post, that the supple resilience she had acquired, with Lou at her side, had simply calcified. It had been easier to believe that. Safer. Like observing the world from inside a suit of armor: no soft, vulnerable parts exposed, the view so limited as to be manageable . . .

"You don't like that?" Cissy mistook the self-mocking gleam in Angie's eyes and stabbed at her salt beef sandwich with her knife.

"Delicious," Angie said, with her mouth full. "Did you order gherkins? Is there actually a widow named Applebaum?"

"There is a widow, I'm told, but I'm not sure that her name's really Applebaum. I don't suppose you've heard anything from Christopher Chetwynd yet?"

Angie shook her head. "He told me not to expect to hear from him for at least a month."

"That's a long time; it's just as well you won't be sitting around, waiting, with nothing to do. Are you going to see Jason when he calls?"

"Why shouldn't I? He's very important to Jarman's from what I can make out."

"Are you being deliberately dense? He was, as Oliver kept telling me, very taken with you."

"Gee," Angie said sarcastically. Taken? Of all the things you could have seen, you saw *that*? "Was Paul Angelou taken with me as well? Did you notice whether *I* was taken with either of *them*?''

"I've said the wrong thing, sorry." Cissy looked anything but apologetic. "Were you?"

"Nothing to do with you, my love."

"Tell me!" Cissy demanded, annoyance edging into her voice once more. And then, as Angie calmly went on eating: "Angelou! My God, Angie. Be careful."

Cissy, repeating Oliver's warning. Angie didn't want to discuss Paul Angelou. Or Corbett, for that matter. Like everything else, Cissy's views on love and sex were both practical and unromantic. She was assuming, and, as it happened, correctly, that Angie had not been to bed with anyone since Lou's death. That she would be physically drawn to a man like Angelou was normal. If the discussion had gone any further, her advice would have been for Angie to sleep with him and get it out of her system. Simple. In the face of a loved one's dilemma, Cissy's usually rigid moral code could, and did, quite often take a back seat to expedience.

The devil of it was that Cissy's advice, if she'd asked for it, would probably have been good in this case. *If* Angie could have fooled herself into believing that, that would indeed be the end of it. She couldn't.

As Cissy called for the bill, Angie tried to change the subject. "Marks and Spencer?"

Cissy looked at her blankly for a moment, then laughed, a complex sound, deep in her throat, that held more sorrow than mirth. "Why do I feel so responsible for you? I'm not your mother."

"Then fight it," Angie said, reasonably. "Your priorities are Oliver and Pamela."

"And you'll manage, right? Is that enough for you?"

"Just now, yes."

Cissy sighed. "You are a survivor, I'll give you that. But I do worry about you, Angie."

"Worrying about me is very different from feeling responsible for me. I feel quite comfortable about your . . . worrying."

"You do?"

Angie nodded, truthfully.

Cissy brightened. "Great. Then why don't we have another cup of coffee and you can tell me about Paul Angelou? He's worth a *really* serious worry."

Trying, without success, to conceal her amusement at Cissy's unabashed inquisitiveness, Angie collected her shopping bags and was halfway back to Oxford Street by the time Cissy had paid the bill and caught up with her.

14

☐ It was seven-thirty, and the Dog and Duck was crowded and smoky. Leo Bass stood with his elbows on the bar, staring moodily at his reflection in a patch of mirror. A long, patrician face stared back, light eyes, full lips. His hair needed a trim. . . . Damn Cory, he had a million better things to do than wait for the little wop.

"Here," he shouted over to the bartender. "Make it a gin and tonic this time." Beer and gin were not a good combination. He splashed the fizzy tonic over the ice cubes and decided to give Cory another ten minutes. The younger man's swaggering optimism was beginning to get on his nerves. Twenty-six thousand pounds was a lot of money in anyone's language; what Cory didn't seem to understand was that there was no more where that had come from. For his part, Leo would not have minded waiting a few extra weeks for the money Cory owed him personally. Where else could he invest six thousand pounds at a compound interest rate of thirty-two percent? *And* get a flat five percent introductory fee from his principal, Claude Soames, on the twenty thousand Cory owed him?

Leo and Soames had been working in tandem for four years now. Neither was dependent on the income from their joint venture; Leo was the majority shareholder in a string of shops selling wholesale office equipment, and Soames, grossly overweight and softly spoken, operated from the elegant interior of his art gallery in Brook Street. It was Soames's boast that he had never seen the inside of a casino, and it was Leo's that none of the reputable London casino managers knew about his sideline. Leo never made the mistake of "pulling" a punter at the casino itself. The premises were off-limits. He would watch a player, sometimes for months, noting the man's losses and when he began to reduce his stakes. Leo recognized the desperation at the end of a losing streak, when all the gambler could think about was getting more money to stay in the game. Cory Angelou was perfect. He was naïve and hopeful, and he had access to a great deal of money. They couldn't lose with him.

Leo saw Cory come into the pub and lowered his head, pretending he hadn't.

"Hey, Leo." Cory's arm went over his shoulders.

"You're late." Leo shrugged away. "You're always late, do you know that?"

Cory signaled the barman for a beer; a practiced, ingenuous smile was easy to maintain, but he had to be careful that this Englishman did not read what was in his eyes: contempt and fear.

Leo downed half the contents of his glass. "Well, have you got the money?"

"Drink up and we'll go somewhere else," Cory said softly. "It's noisy in here."

"Did you hear me? Am I talking to myself?"

Cory paid for his beer and motioned Leo to follow him. Outside on the pavement he turned to the older man and said easily, "Now we can talk."

"I'm listening." Leo's expression was sour as he looked across Greek Street to where a plump black girl was leaning seductively against the hood of a parked car.

"I haven't got the money, Leo. I decided not to ask my grandfather."

Leo kept his eyes on the girl. "Just like that, eh? Well, it's not so easy, my old son, because my principal is getting very nervous indeed."

"Leo, listen. I will arrange everything. Do not concern yourself."

This was the most difficult part of the job; persuading punters that their time was up. "You've got to be soft in the head, Angelou. This isn't some Greek backwater; this is an outfit you're into for twenty thousand pounds, money which I, personally, have guaranteed. That is, of course, quite apart from the six thousand you owe me. Do you think I'm going to tell my principal that you have decided not to ask your grandfather for the money? I *could* tell him that, I suppose—if you want one or two of his friends to turn up on your doorstep, I mean. *They'd* have no problem in telling your grandfather, and after they'd told him, they'd be obliged to break your arms in ten places. Nothing personal, a warning to others, you understand. Now tell me again, please, what it is that you intend to do.''

Cory grinned at him, a trusting, angelic parting of the lips. Leo turned away in disgust. He gulped the last of his gin and placed the empty glass on the pavement between his shoes. ''You find that funny?''

''No, no. Come, we will eat, and I will tell you what I'm thinking.''

The prospect of food had a slightly mollifying effect on Leo. He'd had a glass of wine and a slice of cold quiche at a wine bar at noon and nothing since then. ''Where?''

Cory left half his beer on the pavement and strolled off, turning the corner into Bateman Street. Neither spoke until he stopped outside Ani's.

''Here?'' Leo was surprised. ''Have I missed something or did you go back to the casino last night and win a fortune?''

Scotia must have seen them through the smoked glass because he came out onto the pavement and drew Cory inside. Cory introduced him casually to Leo. ''My friend and I would like to eat. We will be quick.''

The restaurant was crowded. Scotia showed them to a table tucked away in a corner and took their order for a selection of meze followed by baked fresh shrimp with feta cheese. He came back a moment later with a large flask of red wine and steaming pita wrapped in white linen.

Leo sat back and looked around surreptitiously. ''So, you're into these people for money, too?''

Cory laughed. ''This is my grandfather's place.''

''I'm glad to hear it . . . and to see so many happy customers. It wouldn't take long to make twenty-six thousand pounds in a place like this.'' He picked up the menu, glanced at the prices, and did a quick mental calculation. ''Average forty pounds for two, about twenty-five tables . . . let's see . . . lunch and dinner, thirteen straight days, and you'd be clear.''

Cory wasn't listening to him. ''Leo, have you got some money for me?''

''I didn't hear that,'' Leo said, thinking that perhaps the young Greek was mentally retarded.

Cory repeated the question. "Two hundred, that's all. I will try again tonight, and if I do not win enough, I will do something else."

"Tell your grandfather?"

"Not that. Something else."

"What!" Leo demanded, lowering his voice as Scotia made his way toward them, carrying four small meze dishes. He watched Cory thank the man profusely and then, as though a switch had been thrown, turn back to the business of the moment.

"We will take the money and the insurance company will return it to my grandfather."

Leo picked up his fork; his head buzzed with confusion and irritation. "What money? Where from? Here?"

"Not here. I will tell you tomorrow—"

"Uh-uh, you'll tell me now. Another two hundred pounds just on your say-so? Forget it."

"Very well. My grandfather's warehouse. It is very big, and there is only one man watching at night. . . ."

Leo stopped eating. His mind raced ahead. He hadn't been out on a job for months, and like a junkie, the prospect of a fix galvanized him. He had begun to suspect that his friends were holding out on him; because they couldn't understand why an obviously successful businessman would want to put everything on the line by breaking and entering, they didn't quite trust him. They were professionals, thieving was their business, and Leo was an amateur. . . .

"What sort of warehouse?" he asked.

"Books."

"Books?"

"Books, but also a safe. A very big safe."

Leo drew a small leather-bound notebook from his inside jacket pocket. More like it, he thought, much more like it . . . but wait, what kind of money were they talking about and why should anyone keep thousands of pounds in cash in a warehouse safe?

"My grandfather is Greek" was the only explanation Cory had to offer.

It was too ridiculous not to be true; the old man either didn't trust banks or was engaged in defrauding the taxman. It would never have occurred to Leo that Arion would set aside a large amount of ready cash in case someone—family or friend—should need it; or that he'd use the warehouse safe simply because it was ancient enough not to have a time lock device, giving him immediate access to the money.

"Sounds good." Leo opened his notebook. "Give me the address of the warehouse."

"Why?"

"Because I might just go and take a look at it, that's why!"

"Leo." Cory placed his knife and fork neatly on either side of his plate and spoke so quietly that the other man had to lean forward to hear. "You will do nothing. You will wait, and you will do nothing."

Cocky little bastard. Leo began to say something but thought better of it. Cory was watching him with a look that almost sent a shiver through his body. The lustrous brown eyes looked quite dead.

Leo nodded. "All right. Just as long as I know it's there, right?"

"Right," Cory said. "Just as long as we *both* know."

15

Arion could not sleep. His head ached with recurring premonitions of disaster. Beside him Ani lay on her side, her breath deep and even. Two o'clock had come and gone, and Cory was not home.

"Ach," Arion grunted as he swung his legs out of bed. "The boy will hear from me."

In the kitchen he cut a large slice of honey cake and made himself a forbidden cup of instant coffee. How was it that a man could not live out his old age in peace and contentment? What had they done wrong, he and Ani? Had they not cared enough?

Arion knew the answer, and it brought him scant consolation. The cave of despondency he found himself in was dark and airless. Ghosts from the past crouched in the corners; past lives vied with each other for identity. Those who stepped out from the crowd, claiming his attention, were from a time

he could recall without effort. He saw the house of his childhood, starkly whitewashed against the umber hills, inhaled
the heat and sweet smells that rose from the earth. The sound
of the sea was inextricably mixed up with the pulsing of Kon-
stantin's generator, the only source of electricity in the village. His uncle delighted the children by giving them cubes
of the ice it so mysteriously produced.

Arion saw the men sitting beneath the ragged tarpaulin of
the *kafenion*, the women outside their own houses, close enough
to talk and share the chores. The women were a constant vision
of his childhood, shelling peas, pistachios, patching, embroi-
dering, and crocheting exquisite shawls for marriages and births.
Their houses faced the sea, the gentle sweep of the bay. With
eyes narrowed against the glare of the sun, they could see the
men on the quayside and identify them by the shape of a hat,
the color of a bandanna.

How close those memories were. These days he did not
even have to reach for them; they were there in his waking
hours and in his dreams. . . .

Mandraki lay cosseted between the swell of two hills. From
the calm waters of the Ionian Sea the village stretched back
into a rising, terraced semicircle and, beyond that, into the
ruggedness of open plains. Because they shared one doctor
and their priest, the villagers saw the outlying districts as part
of their own world, although a shepherd or a farmer did not
find much to say to a fisherman. Spiros Kolliou, the priest,
lived in the largest house in the village. He was a tireless man
of sixty-five, with arthritic hands that caused mothers to tremble with the fear that one day the newly born infant he held
over the font would slip through his fingers onto the flagged
stone floor.

No one could remember a time when the village had not
supported its priest. Arion and his brother, Christos, were
responsible for the collection of fresh fruit and vegetables.
Sometimes the boys were given corn; other times courgettes
and aubergines, a few fresh eggs, a gift of mustard, a bottle
of resinated white wine. Their grandmother tended the flowers in the church; another family made the candles; yet another saw to it that the priest's vestments were starched and
not too threadbare.

Spiros Kolliou gave away most of what they brought him.
Children and animals wandered through his house and church,
always finding a new, cooler place to hide, to sleep. After the

evening service he would share a glass of ouzo with the fishermen and, later, coffee and sweetmeats with the women.

Arion's parents, Rano and Irene Angelou, had both been
born in Mandraki, as had their parents and grandparents.
Irene's sister's husband owned the *kafenion* in the square;
Rano's brother was the schoolmaster. There was a cousin who
traveled and brought back letters, another who worked in
leather and shod the donkeys. Rano instructed the children in
the science of fishing, the treachery of the currents in other
seas, how to distinguish one fish from another, how to open
an oyster and grill *maridhes* over an open fire.

Arion's brother, Christos, married within a year of his sev-
enteenth birthday. He chose Andrea, a quiet, pretty girl whose
father and brother struggled to make a living selling the produce of their orchards. Arion did not envy his brother, in
either his choice of wife or his way of life. Christos was a
placid, equable man who needed nothing more from life than
to exist quietly with his wife and their children. Arion wanted
more, without quite knowing what. He had begun to look
outward with a restlessness that brought knowing nods from
his father and a curious acceptance from his mother.

Across the bay and to the north lay Corfu, an island that
was rich with foreigners and, because of them, glamorous.
He was nineteen when he made his one and only journey to
Igoumenitsa and from there to the island. Away from his
village for the first time, apprehension gnawed at him. In
Igoumenitsa no faces smiled in recognition; on the boat to
Corfu he stood alone, chilled by the unconcerned glances of
so many strangers.

He remained in the harbor town of Corfu for three weeks.
There he found that the people spoke Italian as much as Greek
and seemed to have little time to converse in either language.
In the mornings he earned some drachmas by meeting the
steamers from Piraeus and Brindisi and carrying the passen-
gers' luggage; at night he washed dishes in the waterside
cafés. The afternoons he spent wandering through the narrow
streets of the old town. He gazed in awe at the royal palace
with its giant columns and arches and strolled through the
exotic gardens of the Citadel and lit a candle in the chapel of
Panayia Mandrakina.

Arion met Anya Cavalieri on the steamer going back to
Igoumenitsa. She was thirteen and was being taken by her
parents to visit relatives in a mountain village not sixty kilo-

meters from Mandraki. Anya's Italian father spoke halting Greek. More often than not her mother would laugh and explain more precisely what he meant to say. More out of politeness than any real interest, Arion asked how long they intended to stay in Greece.

Sergio Cavalieri shrugged philosophically. "Who knows? It is an expensive journey from Naples for me, but my wife has not seen her family for many years."

Beatrice clutched her daughter's hand. "It is more than that. There is much to fear in Il Duce's country. The man has ambitions that do not—"

Sergio's stern glance silenced her. The child looked up at Arion and said seriously, "I will stay here with you."

Her parents laughed, and Arion came close to blushing, struck by the girl's calm assurance. She was not a beautiful child, but it occurred to him even then that she would be a beautiful woman.

Anxious now to get home, he accompanied the Cavalieris for part of their journey and promised to visit them when he could. He thought no more about them until news filtered through to Mandraki of Mussolini's attack on Ethiopia the following year, and then Beatrice's words came back to him. He should have sought out the Cavalieri family sooner, he realized, if only to reassure them.

He found them in good health and indeed with no knowledge of what had been happening in the world outside the remote mountain village. Sergio's Greek had improved, and Beatrice had taken to wearing bright, flowery peasant skirts, hiding her thick dark hair beneath a kerchief. Anya was little changed. Slightly taller, more angular, she listened intently when Arion spoke and sat close to him when she could. He stayed with them until guilt forced him to leave. His own father needed him. The Cavalieris were safe with Beatrice's people, and maybe the rumors of conflict were no more than the exaggerated stories of old men.

During the next four years Arion wrote and received two letters from Beatrice. They were uneventful years, a time of waiting for the world to go to war. The villagers began to stockpile what foodstuffs they could; every cellar and cold store was festooned with garlands of dried beans and onions and garlic. Sacks of pistachios, salted for preservation, were tucked into corners, great stone urns of olives in brine stood sentry over strips of fish caked in rock salt. The women preserved fruit in any container they could find; green quinces were piled high; precious coffee beans secreted with the utmost care.

Arion fell in love with Anya that second time he traveled to their village. She was eighteen, a sturdy, beautiful girl who told him with devastating honesty that she had been waiting for him. "I knew you would come," she said shyly. "I told my mother and my father that you would come."

It was too late for the Cavalieris to return to Italy, and there was little talk of any real desire to do so. The village had become their home, and at least there was no fighting with guns here, no fear of questioning officials, no uniforms. They decided that their village would be safer than Mandraki in the event of war. Sergio and the other men discussed such an unthinkable possibility in the manner of children playing a game, moving inanimate objects from one place to another, the only logic being their own.

Arion courted Anya, annihilated by love. That she loved him, too, was something he dreamed about each night but found impossible to comprehend in the daylight. Father Spiros married them in the summer of 1939. Irene Angelou wept until called upon to console Beatrice, who was wailing in a foreign tongue. Arion's father and Sergio became very drunk on the combination of ouzo and eternal friendship between the two families. Arion's sinews ached with fright. Not once during that long, long day did he open his mouth without having to unclench his teeth; not once would his tongue let go of a word.

They spent their first night in a tiny hut on the beach because Anya had missed the sea so much. The small harbor could not have been more different from the Bay of Naples, but she was enchanted by the sounds. They listened to the waves, heard dogs barking in the village, and discovered joy in each other. Her mouth loosened his tongue, and her body lapped against him, soft, quick. She had no angles; everything was downy and giving. She made him cry.

Christos and his friends helped him to finish the small drystone house he had begun building on the outskirts of the village. He and Anya moved in a bare two weeks before their son, Paul, was born.

Three months later Mussolini's armies crossed the Albanian border into Greece, and less than four months after they had been driven from Greek soil, Hitler's war machine rolled in.

The coffee was cold on the table in front of him. The memory of that day in April 1941 still made him sweat.

"Ari." Ani's voice from the doorway was softly scolding. "It is four o'clock in the morning. Are you ill?"

Arion started, his eyes suddenly misting over with tears. "Go to bed, Ani."

"What is it?" She walked across the room with her arms open, the gesture of a mother offering comfort to her child. She wrapped her arms around him, and his head went into the hollow of her shoulder. "What is it, *caro*?"

How could he tell her that the images of those years were as fresh as if it had all happened yesterday? There were things he had shielded her from then and still held back from her now. . . .

Overnight, it seemed, the village swelled with strangers. They slept anywhere they could, in the stables and under the trees in the square. They huddled beneath upturned fishing boats and built shelters with rotting driftwood. These were people who had come down from the mountain villages, starving in that first winter of occupation. The people of Mandraki shared what they could, but they knew their own stores would not last forever. The fishermen distributed their catch each evening. Sometimes there would be a handful of coffee beans in return, an egg or even, on the rare occasion, a chicken.

The Angelou family guarded its two goats fiercely. The animals provided the only milk they could get for Ani's baby when her own milk ran out. The Cavalieris left their village and brought their few belongings to Mandraki. Arion gave them his house and moved his wife and son in with his parents. Irene Angelou displayed an increasing fury at the suffering the as yet unseen Germans were inflicting on her country. She cursed them at length, much to Father Spiros's displeasure.

"They, too, are children of God," he protested.

"Then where is God?" she cried. "Where is He that He does not stop this murder?"

Until the first detachment of German troops walked into Mandraki, the villagers had still believed that somehow the horror of what was happening in the cities and mountains would pass them by. It was not to be. Spiros Kolliou, alerted by a hysterical parishioner, went out to meet the invaders. They brushed him aside and commandeered the schoolhouse and the houses surrounding it. Captain Ernst Krüger refused to exchange one word with the villagers until his men had reconnoitered the area and set up sentry posts.

That night the place was without light or activity. Every door was shut; windows were hung with thick material. The only sounds that could be heard were the tramping of boots, the raucous shouts of foreigners.

The following morning the searches began. Young and old were made to leave their homes and gather together in the square. While their houses were being ransacked, a bored soldier meticulously took the name of every man, woman, and child. Arion stood with his wife and son, his parents close by. Beatrice and Sergio were seated on a low wall, white-faced in the heat.

"You must tell them we are Italian, not Greek," Beatrice insisted. "That way they will not harm our family. That way we will all be safe."

But Sergio had seen these German soldiers, he had heard them talk, and they were not men he would trust with the lives of his family.

The soldiers finished their searches. From each house they took something, some paper, a label, an old newspaper, a book. Captain Krüger, a young man of no more than thirty, summoned Spiros Kolliou to the schoolhouse that evening. Seated behind the desk, he let the priest stand while he shuffled through an untidy mound of paper, smoked a cigarette, and chatted to his men. A half-empty bottle of cognac stood at his elbow, the remains of a meal next to it.

Finally he looked up and said, "You have traitors in this village, Father. I see from the records that you have lived here for many years, and you will therefore know the names of these people. I expect a list on my desk tomorrow morning."

"Traitors?" Spiros Kolliou nearly laughed in the young man's face. "These are simple people, my son. They know nothing of politics and causes. All they want to do is to bring up their children in peace—"

"Peace?" Krüger rapped. "Is that why their cellars contain enough food to feed my men for a year? Is that why I see this—'' He held up a yellowing piece of newsprint. "And this?''

The priest leaned forward in an attempt to see what he was being shown. "What are they?'' he asked.

"Propaganda! Propaganda that makes a mockery of our cause.''

"You are surely mistaken. I can assure you—''

"I have heard enough. Tomorrow morning, Father. *Raus!*''

There was nothing the priest could do. He visited as many of his parishioners as he could that night. They were dazed by his words and looked to him for an answer. He had no answer but to bless them and commend them into God's keeping.

In the morning the soldiers came for him. They escorted him once more to the schoolhouse, where the young captain, freshly shaved and smiling, held out his hand. "The list, Father.''

"I have no list, my son, for I know of no such people. My congregation are God-fearing—''

Krüger made a clucking sound with his tongue. "Bring him," he ordered. "Into the square, everyone!''

An hour later the small fishing boats had been beached, the *kafenion* shut, the children hushed by the activities. The sun beat down on them all, but it was mostly the soldiers who sweated in their heavy uniforms.

"There are traitors in this village," Krüger said. He looked over the faces deadened with fear and felt nothing but anger that he was here, among these illiterates, while the real war was going on in other places. He was here only because he had the misfortune to speak their language. "I have requested the names of these traitors from your priest." He paused, allowing them to draw away from each other, one family away from the contamination of another. "But he says, untruthfully, that he knows of no traitors to the Führer's cause and leaves me to uncover the names of those who support the *andartes.*''

"*Andartes?* The resistance?'' Old Ioannis Spiridon, crouched almost double over his walking stick, shuffled forward. "There is no such thing.''

"Silence! Not forty kilometers from here three of my comrades have been killed, mutilated and killed by these people who do not exist in this place. How, then, is this, old man?''

"Forty kilometers?'' This time it was Raidne Calchas who

protested. She was the same age as Irene Angelou and had two daughters, who now stood in terrified silence on either side of her. "There are many villages in the area. Those you speak of—"

Ernst Krüger raised his hand to silence her. "Quite so," he said with quiet satisfaction. "Many from other villages far away have arrived here in the past few months. Is this not true?"

Spiros Kolliou stepped out from the crowd and spoke for the first time. "That is true, Captain. And we welcomed them. These were not *andartes* but poor people driven from their villages in search of food and shelter—"

"So you say, in the expectation of finding a fool who will listen to you. These people will step forward." Krüger read out five names from a small notebook. With each name the crowd pulled back. Their glance turned down and away. It couldn't be happening. Krüger called out the names of Nestor Telamon, the blacksmith; Georgio and Theo Pelias, fishermen; Elias Leos, the watermelon grower; and Chloris Diodedes, a childless woman whose husband had gone to look for work across the border in Albania. Of the five named, only the woman was a newcomer to the village.

The soldiers surrounded the small group and followed closely behind Captain Krüger as he made his way back to the schoolhouse. The rest of the morning passed in relative silence, but by the time the sun dipped behind the hills, the area around the schoolhouse was deserted. Families left their homes and slept in uncovered carts rather than listen to the screams that went on far into the night.

So it began. Krüger seemed to select his victims at random. Those who insisted on their innocence were brought out into the daylight, already crippled by *falanga*, beaten on the soles of their feet until they could no longer stand. In the square, as an example to the other villagers, they were stripped and beaten more decorously with cornel rods. A few were allowed to see their priest for a final blessing before being led out into the hills. The villagers crossed themselves swiftly and guiltily when they heard the volley of shots. Those who "confessed" under *falanga* also died this way, toppling into shallow graves dug with their bare hands. The people they named under torture were rounded up immediately. It seemed to those who waited and suffered that their God had forsaken Mandraki.

In September of 1941 Arion knew what he had to do. One day soon they would come for him, and Ani would be alone. His son was not one year old, and although the journey would be hazardous, he had no choice. Beatrice and Sergio were stoic in the knowledge that they would probably never see their daughter and grandson again. His own mother wept briefly and began to put by items of food and clothing. His brother, Christos, kissed him many times. It would not be long, he said, before they were all together again.

Arion had one thought in his head; to get Ani and Paul safely to Naples and into the care of Sergio Cavalieri's family. Then he would return to Mandraki and do what had to be done.

They traveled on foot across the border into Albania and from there through Yugoslavia and northern Italy, hoping to reach neutral Switzerland. They walked mostly by night, keeping away from towns and villages yet miraculously finding people who were willing to share with them what little food they had. Few places they passed through had not been touched by the war. Sometimes there was a blessed ride in a donkey cart, a stable to sleep in, even abandoned houses that stood starkly neglected in the chaos of the countryside. Ani always imagined the previous occupants of these houses safe. She convinced Arion that these unknown people had deliberately left behind warm clothes and tinned food for them.

The journey lasted for eight months. Toward the end they walked blindly, carrying a child too weak to cry. Ani rarely spoke, conserving all her energy with a dogged determination to survive. By the time they stumbled into the Red Cross camp for refugees on the Swiss border, Arion was only semiconscious. The man who came forward to greet them was young and clean and healthy. Arion handed over his son and turned with infinite slowness to help Ani. She was too far from him, standing shocked and gaunt, swaying forward as the puddles of water splashed up over him when he fell headlong.

It was two weeks before he was able to tell the authorities his name.

"Just as well you didn't get to Naples," a serious young doctor said. "There's very little of it left."

Arion did not tell Ani this news, nor did he tell her that he was already making plans to travel back to Mandraki. He left the news as long as he could, and when he did tell her, the night before his departure, she said, "Yes. Come back to me, Ari. I will wait here with our son and you will return to us."

Traveling alone was quicker and less hazardous. With a forged Italian passport he was safer but not quick enough. His mother and father were dead, his brother had disappeared, and his wife, Andrea, and their children had gone into hiding in the caves of the mountainous region to the north. Irene and Rano Angelou had been fortunate. Having been "named," Arion was told, his parents were simply taken out into the hills and shot. Spiros Kolliou wept with him, and then, feverishly dry-eyed, Arion heard about the Cavalieris. They had not been so lucky.

"Because of their name, Ari," the priest explained. "The soldiers decided that an Italian family could not live here and be true to Il Duce or to the Third Reich. They took them soon after you left and kept them for weeks. You do not need to know more, except that Sergio was allowed a last blessing here in the church before they took him away. He and Beatrice gave no names."

"And Beatrice?" Arion whispered.

"Beatrice waited outside the church. She could not stand by herself, so the soldiers held her and laughed when she cursed them and the God who was a comfort to her husband in his last hour. She died with hatred in her heart."

Arion learned years later that the priest, too, had died, one evening, surrounded by the solemn children of Mandraki. By then the Germans had gone, and the villagers had burned the old schoolhouse to the ground and built a new one. And still later Arion learned that Christos, his brother, had joined the ELAS resistance movement and had been killed in an ambush.

Andrea, Christos's wife, had moved back to Mandraki with her children and was now a grandmother many times over. Corythus was her youngest grandchild, and she had persuaded her son to give him into Arion's care because the boy had so much of Christos in him.

Arion never told Ani about the manner in which her parents had died. "They were shot, taken out together and shot with others. It was quick."

As with everything else he did and said, Ani accepted this as the truth. After all these years he half believed it was true himself. . . .

*   *   *

Ani was pulling at his arm, urging him back. He wanted to remain there for a while, to mourn the end of it.

"It's Paul who makes you stay awake," she was saying, shaken by the unfocused look she saw. "I will not ask him here again, Ari . . ."

"Paul?" That brought him back to his adopted country, this house, this son who was a stranger to them both. "No, how can it be Paul? He is a fool, a man without God."

Ani found herself smiling at the indulgent tone. "*Your* son is these things?"

"The son I love, yes. You would fight with me at this hour?"

"Come to bed."

"I'm coming."

"Now."

He followed her, stopping to listen at Cory's door just in case the boy had slipped in without him hearing. He hadn't. Arion lay on his back with Ani close beside him. She rubbed his belly and maneuvered his heel cozily into the curve of her instep. He could hear the sea in her voice, the dogs barking. . . .

16

☐ Lisa was right. The novel was good. It was more than just a sensitive look at a small rural community, and Elliot Stone had written it in spare, sinewy prose that left stark images imprinted on the reader's mind. Frank was surprised that the abundance of detail did not hamper the headlong story line, that the novel's pedantic accuracy did not make it indigestible. He was also taken aback by the extraordinarily steamy sensuality Elliot Stone conveyed on the page. Altogether it was an accomplished, at times brilliant piece of work.

Frank had finished reading *Night Work* within two days of Lisa's having left the typescript on his desk. Perversely he kept her waiting for his reaction, and more than a week went by before she came into his office to tell him that Elliot was becoming edgy.

"Why is that? You've told him what you think of it, haven't you?"

"Well, yes, but . . ."

"Tell him you'll call him next Wednesday." He saw her disappointment. "We'll probably have to discuss strategy before you call him with a plan for submitting it. When are you free?"

"Apart from lunch on Tuesday, I'm here."

Frank consulted his diary. "What are you doing on Tuesday evening?"

"Nothing as far as I know."

"Then we'll have dinner and discuss it. I'm meeting Arion for a drink earlier, so let's make it Ani's at eight o'clock."

Lisa nodded, concealing her surprise. These days there was a marked coolness between them, a standoff that intrigued her. She had begun to spend more time in the office, drawn by the prospect of another unpredictable dialogue. She realized, essentially, that she wanted to know what he thought of her and why he was acting so strangely. And she was just beginning to understand why so many in the business found Frank Sheldon a puzzling and unconventional man.

Lisa had already decided to auction *Night Work* to the highest bidder. Frank would not object to that in principle, but he might well question the method she was going to propose. Would he? She had no idea what effect the novel had had on him, but that was another matter altogether. He'd finished reading it, she knew that. He was too professional to leave a typescript of that quality lying around unread in his flat for a whole week. Whatever his reasons for making her wait, he was keeping them to himself. Lisa would have labeled his behavior petulant had it not been for the fact that it had stopped her as effectively as a brick wall. She had no wish to oppose him, to prove him wrong, only to find out what lay behind his curious actions.

Frank spent Monday behind closed doors with the company auditors. Ruby, his Mohican-haired secretary, made a face each time she emerged from his office with a tray of empty coffee cups. She reported, with glee, that one of the two auditors wore sandals with tartan socks and that the other was obsessed with dispersing the smoke from Frank's cigarettes and that the quiet was unnatural. They looked like undertakers inspecting a corpse.

"With your hair and your imagination, you should write a novel," Lilian, Lisa's secretary, commented. A weekend of experimenting with colors had produced strands of bilious green in the central aisle of Ruby's hair.

The two women had worked together for more than a year, and Lilian remained permanently shocked by the other's appearance. She had once confided her misgivings to Lisa. "Ruby's practically a genius; how can she be so stupid?" Lilian knitted her own sweaters and gloves, made her own skirts, wore nothing that did not match perfectly. "What would you say if I came in like that one day?"

"I'm afraid it would cheer me up," Lisa had told her. She noticed the next day that Lilian had changed her regular lipstick color from an unnoticeable red to a deep, noisy pink. The gesture made, she then proceeded to lick her lips clean and remained colorless for the rest of the day.

Thinking about that as she walked through Soho Square the following evening, Lisa fumbled in her handbag for a pocket mirror. She'd come out of Tottenham Court Road underground station windblown and gritty-eyed. Now she stopped to peer self-consciously at her reflection, just satisfied that her eyes weren't watering and that the hint of color on her own lips remained even.

Ani's was new to her. She had never met the celebrated Arion Angelou or had a meal with Frank. She had dressed with more care than usual, choosing a subtly draped dress in a gray and white Liberty's voile. And now she was trying to ignore a sharp sense of anticipation. By the time she reached the restaurant, nerves had taken over. She scolded herself, standing in front of Ani's, but nevertheless paused nervously before pushing the door open.

"Mr. Sheldon's table," she told the smiling man who took her raincoat. As she waited for the tab, she glanced around the room, noting with pleasure that there was no sound of background music.

Frank had taken a chair facing the door. He saw Lisa come in and gestured to Scotia.

"She's here?" Arion turned and started to rise when he felt a hand on his shoulder.

"Don't get up, please," Lisa said. "Hullo, Frank."

"Lisa, this is Arion Angelou. Ari—"

"Yes, I know. Lisa Barrett. Frank has told me much about you."

"Really?" Her lips parted in a wide smile, and Arion decided that she was either an extremely accomplished actress or a woman who had not yet begun to practice guile.

"Would you like a drink?" Frank asked.

"White wine, please."

"Have you been here before, Lisa?"

"Never, but I can see now that I should have persuaded Frank to invite me sooner."

"I tell him that he is not good at sharing, but does he listen to me?"

"I always listen to you, old man."

Arion was not what she had expected. Nor was Frank, in Arion's company. It was more than the way he looked, the lack of edge and irony in his voice. The space between and around the two men seemed nonexistent, and Lisa was disconcerted by what she instantly perceived as their regard for each other. It crossed her mind that her presence could be intrusive, but then, as though sensing her disquiet, Arion took her hand. "This," he said, waving his other hand casually around the room, "was a café when I first met Frank. We had latka and coffee, and we talked about the people who brought me books—"

"You're a publisher?"

"Ari owns Angel Publications, but it's a distribution company, not a publishing house. When he first started up, people used to send him their typescripts, thinking he would publish them. He passed them all on to me, and I sold my first book without an office or a telephone . . . probably from this very spot. I remember the advance—"

"Who could forget that? Seventy-five pounds. It was a fortune."

Lisa thought they were sharing a private joke and looked from one to the other. "You mean seven hundred and fifty, don't you?"

"No, no. No mistake. Seven pounds and ten shillings commission was enough to live on for more than two weeks. We had a celebration, do you remember, Frank? Ani was there, and your girl, Molly."

"And they had to put us to bed." Frank shuddered. "I'd never tasted wine before, let alone retsina, followed—*followed*, mind you, by ouzo. I had a hangover for three days."

"And we still celebrate Frank's books, you see. The next one will be your book, the one Frank is talking about."

"Night Work?"

"Night Work, most assuredly."

He liked it! She turned toward Frank just as someone stepped between them, leaning over the table to take Arion's hand.

"Carlo, you know Frank. This is Frank's Lisa. Carlo Barzini, a good friend."

The angular Italian stood awkwardly between them, reluctant to release Arion's hand. They spoke an unintelligible mixture of English and Italian and Greek. Arion eventually patted the hand which clasped his, and Barzini stood back, still smiling. He exchanged a few words with Frank, bowed formally to Lisa, and raised a hand in salute to Arion once more.

"An old friend," Arion said when he'd left. "He is—how you English say?—eccentric. He does strange things, Carlo."

"He loves you, Ari," Frank said.

"I love him, too, my friend, but if I take everything he offers me, I will be able to open a shop." He glanced down at his watch. "And now I must also leave you. Ani is waiting for me."

Lisa wanted him to stay. "Don't go," she said impulsively.

Arion stood up and leaned over to whisper, "I must, but I will see you again very soon, Lisa. I will telephone you. You will leave this man to work in the office and come and eat with me yourself. We will talk." He made it sound like a delicious conspiracy.

"Get off with you, Ari," Frank snorted. "You're a corrupting influence; he just wants to fatten you up, Lisa."

"And I'll probably just let him," she replied primly.

"He *will* call, you know," Frank said as Arion left.

"I hope he does. Have you really known him for so long?"

"Twenty-three years, long before Molly and I were married. And yes, he really was responsible for starting me off as a literary agent."

"Who was that man, Barzini?"

"It's a long story, but during the war Italians in this country were classified as aliens and many had their property confiscated. Arion bought, very cheaply, a piece of land near Charing Cross Road and found out only years later that it had belonged to the Barzini family. He gave it back, taking exactly what he'd paid for it, even though property prices had gone sky-high. It sounds dramatic, I know, but the Barzinis have never looked back and have never forgotten. You must have noticed that video arcade, Doric—well, that's the property. Ari calls Carlo eccentric because he wants to share what he has; not crazy, he's just grateful.''

"It doesn't surprise me, what Arion did, I mean."

"Don't mention it to him, please. He doesn't like the idea of anyone being beholden to him."

"Of course not," Lisa said absently, trying to recall what there had been about the Greek that had made her feel cocooned and safe.

Scotia suddenly leaned over them with the menu, and Lisa sat back with a jerk. The moment had passed. Frank watched her as Scotia went through the menu, pointing out his particular recommendations. She'd been completely unaware of her surroundings, ambushed by Arion's magic. Frank savored the look of concentration on her face and wondered if she'd even noticed the familiarity with which Arion had spoken her name.

"She's so young." He'd said it to Arion more than once.

"And you are an old man at the age of thirty-eight?"

"Thirty-nine next month."

"Thirty-nine, forgive me. At such an age I am surprised you can still feel love."

Something close to fear had intruded into his thoughts about Lisa. He no longer knew what to say to her. It wasn't a game, not playful sex, not the beginning of something he could explore without risking the penalty of losing her. And no amount of self-ridicule could ease the physical ache that made her presence barely tolerable. It wasn't like that with Diana Marsh, whom he had known for more than three years. He wasn't in love with her, nor she with him; nothing on the surface had changed except that Diana seemed to sense a growing distance between them. And she was right.

Frank sighed. He regretted now that he'd promised to meet Diana at Heathrow at eleven-thirty that night; still, it wasn't something he could easily have refused.

He listened to Lisa order prosciutto and melon, followed by podarakia arniou. "Good choice," he said, and nodded to Scotia, indicating that he would have the same. Then he sat back and lit a cigarette.

"May I have one?"

"You don't smoke."

"I do, now and then."

"Your father's a doctor—"

"You remember that?" She frowned at him. "I could have bitten my tongue."

"I'm glad you didn't. I thought it was very sensible of you."

"Childish . . . I was terrified of you."

It wasn't what he wanted to hear. "Fancy," he said dryly. "Are you still terrified of me?"

"I'll answer that when I've heard what you think of Elliot's novel."

"I think you already know. It's good." He paused to take in the relief on her face.

"Just that? Good?"

"No, you're right. It's very good, sensational in parts. A salable literary novel, something of a rarity, especially in the Sheldon stable, right?"

Lisa flinched. "I'm sorry, that was pompous of me. I apologize."

"Accepted. Now tell me what your thoughts are on submitting the book."

"Auction," she said quickly. "A limited auction to, say, four or five publishers."

"Why not spread it wider? Let more people read it?"

Lisa hesitated. The ease of the discussion unnerved her. He looked as though he were enjoying it. "I've considered that, but with this particular book I think it would be good if we let the other publishers find out about it and come knocking on our door. I don't honestly think there's any way we can limit the auction to four or five publishers, but we *can* play hard to get."

Frank permitted himself a faint smile. "You have learned a lot, haven't you?"

Lisa shrugged. "Psychology. Good psychology, wouldn't you say?"

"Oh, I agree all right. I'm just happy we're on the same side."

It was Lisa's turn to smile, and it was a wicked, triumphant grin. "Just one thing, Frank. Jarman's is on my list, but I don't want to send it to Sidney Niklas."

Frank *was* enjoying himself. She was like a child playing

games in an adult world. "Why not? Because of what I told you?"

"I'd like to tell you that wasn't the reason, but I can't. Let's leave it at that." She searched his face for any sign of having said the wrong thing. She saw nothing but tolerant concentration.

"Fine with me. Who, then, at Jarman's? Not Martin Corbett. Deborah Anderson, maybe . . ."

"Not enough clout. I'd like to send it to Oliver Jarman personally."

"Good idea. How well do you know him?"

"Not very . . . in fact, only to say hullo to."

Somewhere, even after their two brief meetings, was imprinted an image of Oliver Jarman. She remembered him as rangy, with large well-kept hands, blunt fingers, hair graying in a fanlike spread from his temples upward. She had been looking forward, with pleasure and some trepidation, to establishing a professional rapport with him.

Frank felt a tremor of alarm. Had he imagined her sudden shift of interest? Settling a score with Sidney was one thing; having a thing about Oliver Jarman was another.

"I have a lot of time for Oliver," he said softly. "Don't be too hard on him."

"I hear he . . . drinks." She knew next to nothing about Oliver Jarman. She wanted to talk about him.

"Oliver's probably an alcoholic, and he has other problems, too. His sister has just come back from New York, where her husband was killed in a car smash. Sir Richard Jarman is a shit of the first water, and the trade list isn't looking too good. So go easy, all right?"

Lisa sliced off a chunk of melon, folded some ham neatly into a square, and popped both into her mouth. "Do you think I should take him out to lunch, make proper contact?"

"Since when do you consult me about your lunch dates? In any case we've been invited to their launch of that flower book soon."

"Not me," she said cautiously.

"Both of us. One invitation. Lilian has forgotten to put it in your diary. You can give him the typescript then."

"At the party? I don't think that's a very good idea."

"Why not?"

"All right," she said, disappointed. She'd been looking

forward to having an hour or two alone with Oliver over a lunch table.

"Who else is on the submission list? Meredith's?"

"Marvelous melon." Lisa put her elbows on either side of her empty plate and rested her chin on laced fingers. "I've decided against the Meredith's."

"Why? They've just paid thirty-five thousand pounds for the Piedowski novel, haven't they?"

"Exactly. And that doesn't entitle them to see our next big book. I suspect Peter Meredith thinks it does, though."

This time Frank tried hard but unsuccessfully not to laugh at the sheer impudence of her statement.

"Well, at least I know you're not bored," she said stiffly as the sound of his laughter boomed across the room.

"My God," he said finally, "those poor bastards out there, they don't know what's about to hit them."

"You make it sound like a suicide mission."

"I'm not sure it isn't. So, Meredith's is out, Jarman's is in. Who else?" He whistled silently between his teeth as he listened to Lisa's strategy for the auction, and then he raised his glass to her. "Enough. Machiavelli should have taken lessons."

"Oh, just one other point I think we should discuss. I've been considering a trip to New York. I don't want *Night Work* to go through Farley Esterhuys."

"I see. And you'll conduct the American auction whilst you're there?"

"Right. Although I've never been there before, I do know most of the New York publishers."

Frank ate in silence for a few minutes. You asked for it, he told himself, and now you've got it. He knew that Farley would not be good for *Night Work*, but to exclude him on their first big book for months would enrage him.

"Well?" Lisa asked.

"Well, what?"

"Do you agree to the trip?"

"Only if a pro rata share of the expenses for this jaunt comes out of your own commission," he said flatly.

The notion that he would object on that level had obviously never occurred to her. The darkly fringed blue eyes widened in surprise. "I thought you'd balk at disposing of Farley, not bring up my commission again. Two and a half percent is peanuts. Why are you making it so hard on both of us?"

I wish I knew, Frank thought. Scotia's exquisite lamb suddenly had a stringy, tasteless quality to it, and he had trouble swallowing what was in his mouth. He was goading her again, and again he couldn't stop himself. Caution nevertheless tugged at him.

"I take it you think that's unfair?"

"Unfair, no. More as if you're—" she hesitated, trying to find precise words, "trying to push me off into a corner, to punish me for—"

"Success?" he interrupted sharply. "Assuming, just *assuming* this novel does well, you cream off your two and a half percent of the income regardless and I fork out two thousand pounds of the agency's take to subsidize your trip. That's a good slice of the agency's return, wouldn't you say?"

"No, it's not that. We're not talking about money; at least I'm not. The trip can come out of my share, but the fact is we're moving in opposite directions. Maybe we're incompatible." The word shocked her into a moment's silence.

"Maybe we should call it quits?" He smiled wolfishly across the table, no less astonished than she was by the turn in the conversation.

She drew back defensively. "No!"

"Why not? I didn't ask you to sign a piece of paper; you came in as a free agent, and you're still that. You're on a high at the moment, and I'm just wondering whether you've been pushing for a break."

"No!" she said again. "That's not what I want."

"The trouble is, I don't really know what you *do* want. A partnership, is that it?"

"What?"

"A partnership, Lisa. Is a partnership what you're after?"

Her fork clattered onto the plate. He wasn't joking. Her self-confidence drained into a trickle of consternation. "No, at least not this way. I enjoy working at the agency; I enjoy working with you. Why are you being so *bloody*?"

She meant it. He knew her well enough to see that the confusion and hurt were real. She never backed away, and he had never in his life wanted to touch anyone as much as he did just then. "Lisa . . ."

"No, Frank. I'm going to have to think about this. It's time we—"

"I'm offering you a partnership." She shook her head. "You don't want it?"

"No!" How many times had she said no in the past few minutes?

"Why not?"

"Because . . . well, because it wouldn't work. It's not that I'm ungrateful, but I don't want to tie myself down in a relationship that's so . . . scratchy. I'm sure you don't want that either, and in any case I don't understand why you're offering it now, when all you seem to be able to talk about is *my* commission. There has to be a very good reason for this sudden desire to share *yours* with me. I can't help feeling you're not being honest with me."

I'm in love with you. Is that honest enough? "If I told you that you were well on the way to becoming one of the best literary agents in London, you'd understand, wouldn't you? You wouldn't ask for an explanation and demand honesty. Is persuasion by flattery all you will accept?"

He lifted his shoulder as if her reply would be of no interest to him. Inwardly he directed a curse at himself for having underestimated the perverse side of the female nature, particularly this female. She wanted everything, he understood, but strictly on her own terms.

"Are you leaving all that?" She glanced at his plate with unblinking solemnity, as though the question were somehow relevant.

He nodded. "Do you mind if I smoke?"

"We never finish our conversations. I'm enjoying this, so why don't you talk and let me finish eating?"

She ate with relish, and he wondered vaguely how she kept her weight down.

"Why are you smiling?" she asked suspiciously.

"Just thinking . . . My ex-wife spent most of her time thinking about food and how to avoid eating it."

"She wouldn't have been able to resist this," she said matter-of-factly, nudging her empty plate toward the center of the table.

"Oh, I think she would have enjoyed resisting it. You clearly have no great interest in food and therefore enjoy it when it's good. She was obsessed with it and enjoyed nothing."

"Masochism?" Lisa asked with a sober smile. "It takes us all in different ways."

"What's your way?"

She dropped her eyelids, and Frank was aware that he was

holding his breath. "Getting to where I'm going in my own way, I suppose."

"What the hell does that mean?"

"If it's too easy, it doesn't count. What you said just now about a partnership, you were right. I want more, much more."

His eyes widened in mock astonishment. "Does that mean that you want to take the agency over?"

Lisa laughed. "Not that. I want to *share* it with you." He was looking at her with a relaxed, attentive expression, but his question had not been as idle as it had appeared. She was still far from discovering what lay behind his curt accusations. Despite that, it occurred to her that not once during the evening had she wanted to be anywhere else, except here.

"Maybe I'll go to New York with you," he said.

It was so unexpected that Lisa's "Yes" came out in a sibilant splutter.

"What's the matter?"

"Nothing. You surprised me." Stunned was more accurate. Immediately she thought of seven uninterrupted hours with him on the plane, booking into the same hotel, more evenings like this.

"Not a good idea?" It wasn't a good idea at all and he knew it. For both of them to be away from the agency at the same time was absurdly impractical.

"It's a wonderful idea, Frank. Does that mean I'll have to pay a pro rata share of *your* expenses, too?"

Frank covered his mouth with his napkin, thinking she must have seen through his pathetic maneuverings. "Touché. But there's always the chance people will think I've come along to hold your hand during the auction."

"That occurred to me too but I don't mind if you don't mind." She *should* have minded, she knew, but for some reason the risk of losing some of her independence seemed eminently worth taking just then.

"OK, I'll think about it," Frank said and then, as Scotia began to wend his way through the tables toward them: "Sweet trolley?"

"Just coffee, please."

"Two brandies and coffees," he told Scotia.

"It's been a long time since somebody tried to get me drunk," she said with alert pleasure.

"Good God, is that what I'm doing?"

He had an uncanny way of making her feel childish, but Lisa wished quite suddenly that there had been a motive behind the two bottles of wine and the brandies. *And* the mention of accompanying her to New York. Unless Sidney Niklas was alone, people on the outside seemed to assume they slept together anyway. The notion of Frank as a lover made a weird kind of sense. Although she had never thought of him in that way before, she decided that she would like his compact body, enjoy the feel and weight of him. Then she forced her mind away from the thought. He'd probably pat her bum, place warm milk on the bedside table, and sleep on the couch. . . .

Frank noticed the color in her cheeks deepen and wondered if she had indeed had too much to drink. They finished the brandy in a companionable silence. He glanced at his watch. Ten-thirty. He beckoned Scotia, who came over with the bill. Frank scrawled his signature at the bottom left-hand corner and handed it back. "A taxi for Miss Barrett, my friend."

"There's no need—" A dull disappointment hit her. He had a car outside, and she had naturally assumed he would drive her home.

As if reading her thoughts, he said, "I would have driven you home except I have to collect someone at the airport at eleven-thirty."

"Of course."

"It's true, odd as it sounds." He helped her on with her coat, shook Scotia's hand, and led her outside. It had been raining, and the night was cool and fresh. Frank took a deep breath and let it out slowly.

"Thank you for the meal," Lisa said formally as she moved toward the waiting taxi.

Frank observed her suspiciously as he held the door open. "Are you all right?"

Lisa did not reply. Nor did she look back as the taxi sped away.

17

☐ Angie had expected Paul Angelou to call sooner, but at the same time she was amazed that he had waited no more than ten days. When the telephone rang at seven-thirty, pulling her out of a dream-distorted sleep, she cursed him and the swelling silence that greeted her.

"It's Paul Angelou," he said finally.

She had to stop herself from replying, "I know," and gave a noncommittal "Yes" instead. It was as if he'd known that she had spent a haunted night trying to escape from him. In her dreams he spoke intermittently with Lou's voice, arousing her unforgivably, until she recognized his dark face above her, eyes lit, narrowing smile. He had invited all the ghosts back. . . .

"I hear you're working in London and you're going to be here for the next year."

"Your information is, as ever, immaculate." Angie eased herself into a sitting position on the bed, pushing the pillows behind her back, active because the sound of his voice, everything about him created chaos inside her. Everything.

"You know why I'm calling."

"Where are you?" she asked. He had a wife; where was she at this hour of the morning?

"I'm at my office. I want you to have lunch with me today." The words were emphatically impatient, demanding.

"I want"—not "Would you like to?" His arrogance weakened her resolve and infuriated her. More than a little of the contempt that came out in her next words was directed at herself. "I don't think I like you very much, Mr. Angelou."

"It's not compulsory. And the name is Paul. Say yes, because you will, sooner or later." He thought he heard a laugh, but it could have been something else. "Please," he added, ungraciously.

"Later then."

"I want to see you." Stern, as though she were there only to carry out his wishes. "Why not today? I have a free lunch."

"How inconvenient for you. What makes you think *I'm* free?"

"I know you are."

"Not today," she gasped, terrorized by her own reaction. It would happen. That had been a tacit understanding from the start. If not today, then next week or the week after that.

He went on as if she hadn't spoken at all. The Brasserie St. Quentin, twelve-thirty . . . Brompton Road. "Are you making a note of this?"

Angie crashed the receiver down, her palm slippery with sweat.

She didn't want him in her bed, she told herself, or anywhere near her. No, that was so obviously untrue that she actually laughed. She slid down under the duvet, tossing one of the pillows aside, lying flat on her back, thoughts jumbling. He was a married man, she scarcely knew him, and she *did* want him in her bed. Her resentment had nothing to do with morality, rather the realization that he had reached her at all—and now, when her mere presence in London had quadrupled the complications in her life.

She had been spending each day in the office with Oliver. The only point of contention between them so far was her adamant refusal to tell the staff just yet that their managing director was opting out for a year or more. She couldn't tell Oliver, but she knew instinctively that two people in particular—Sidney Niklas and Martin Corbett—should be given as little time as possible to undermine his decision to leave.

"I don't understand," Oliver said in exasperation. "What are you supposed to be doing in the office every day? Making the tea?"

"Tell them I'm writing a report on British publishing or that I'm briefing you about American publishing. Anything. It doesn't matter. I'll sort it out later."

Although Oliver was an efficient administrator, Angie could see that there were whole areas on the lower levels of publishing that he had no tolerance for. The production department seemed to work in a vacuum; typescripts filtered down to them from the editorial department and reemerged as bound and jacketed books. And apart from a once-a-week meeting, the editorial staff, too, seemed to pursue separate lives, quite independently of other key departments. Three things struck her immediately: the first was the high cost of setting and printing. So much for her father's old friend Jason Corbett; he was certainly one of the first problems she would have to tackle. The second was just how few books there were in the pipeline. Unless she did something about that, and quickly, the turnover for the year ahead would be catastrophic. The third was the negligible sum spent on advertising and promotion.

She said nothing to Oliver and declined his suggestion that she get to know the staff by lunching them individually. She would get around to that in her own time and with a selected number of people. Not even for Oliver would she contemplate spending an hour and a half listening to the gibes of Sidney Niklas or the bored complaints of Martin Corbett.

Angie grunted her annoyance in the brightening light of the morning. And how had Paul Angelou found out about her taking over? Was there *anything* he didn't know? She'd overheard his wife telling Oliver that they had a son, grown-up but not much older than her own daughter. Angie found that she could quite easily visualize what the boy looked like: a cross between Paul and Susan, dark-skinned and blue-eyed. She could see him more clearly in her mind's eye than she could the child she'd borne herself. She remembered Christopher Chetwynd's questions and the revulsion she'd experienced having to describe George McFee and Andrew Colquhoun. Which one had implanted the seed? An aid to identity . . . as if she'd need it. There had always existed an illogical certainty that she would know her daughter, in spite of the countless, shifting images she'd failed to breathe life into all these years. She could picture Paul's son, whom she'd never seen, but like an Identikit with endless overlapping transparencies, her daughter's features eluded her. . . .

She swung out of bed and stood for a moment in the doorway of her bedroom, surveying the flat. She'd bought it as a pied-à-terre. Set high above a neat square of Chelsea green, it had begun to take on a temporary air. It was a place to sleep in, to work in but not to come home to. It had been furnished by a friend whose tastes had run to angular furniture and the juxtaposition of clearly contrasting colors. He had underlined the contrast by choosing fabrics of such different designs and weaves that nothing felt comfortable to her. It was a designer's flat, and Angie didn't like anything about it. Another, albeit slight complication, she thought.

The telephone rang again just as she stepped into the shower. Probably Cissy calling to confirm another shopping date the next day. Angie let it ring, blowing water out of her mouth, sightless in the steam. She remained there until her shoulders stung and the water began to run cold. Everything that was happening around her, whether she liked it or not, was happening to some extent because of her: Oliver's decision to leave Jarman's; her father's not to stand in his way; Paul Angelou. Unwelcome as these involvements now were, they were manageable in a way they would not have been a few months earlier. The difference had to do with her own determination to allow herself, if necessary, to be defeated. That, in itself, would be some kind of victory.

Fewer than four hours later she was trying to reclaim that calm, watching Paul Angelou. Neither hurrying nor dawdling, he made his way across the restaurant toward her. He wore a plain dark blue suit and a subtly striped shirt that gave out a hint of pink. She smiled up at him, thinking that Lou had always looked as if he'd just stepped out of a tumble dryer.

"You're smiling," Paul said, sitting down.

"Isn't that what one normally does on such a friendly occasion?"

He leaned toward her. "You were looking at me and thinking about something else. What was it?"

"My husband," she replied, surprised. "I was thinking that he deliberately bought clothes that didn't fit him."

"Why?"

"I've no idea. Maybe it pleased him, just as your . . . perfection pleases you."

Anyone else would have laughed at that. Paul merely turned toward the waiter and said, "Two whiskeys, with water, no ice."

Angie balked. "I might have preferred vodka."

"Do you?" In short snatches his glance dropped on those sitting closest to them. He seemed to categorize, assess, and dismiss them as safe in an instant. When he turned back to her, she was lighting a cigarette. She aligned the lighter neatly in the center of the white and purple packet and decided that he had probably worked out the reason for that one, too: she was having trouble keeping her hands occupied.

"How's your arm?" She was wearing a silky, long-sleeved shift that obscured her body from neck to knee. He was once again aware of the extraordinary mixture of colors she wore; this oriental pattern was, if anything, more striking than the outfit she'd worn at Kennedy Airport. "Is there a scar?"

"Slight, but I'm told it will fade with time."

He would have asked to see it had the sleeve of her dress not fitted snugly around her lower forearm. "I suppose you'll soon have lunch appointments every day of the week. I understand that publishing is a very sociable business."

"We do talk and eat a lot, yes."

"And you enjoy that?"

"It depends on the conversation and the food," she said lightly. "I thought you might suggest Ani's today. I hear it's very good."

"Who told you that?"

"Does it matter?"

"My father's restaurant was not . . . appropriate."

Angie drank some of her whiskey, outwardly composed but inwardly disoriented by his total concentration on her every word. "You make this sound like a clandestine meeting."

"You're being facetious."

Good God, he didn't like it, and it showed. "To be frank, I don't quite know what to say to you."

"Why is that? Do you find me intimidating?" There, at least there was a touch of humor behind those words.

Angie shook her head. "It's probably because almost everything you say is a question, a demand. You . . . unsettle me."

He remained smoothly unperturbed. Some people played the honesty game with devastating purpose. Was she doing it, trying to disarm him? No, there was nothing remotely indifferent in her glance. Instead, he detected an underlying weariness about her that made him think she had neither the imagination nor the energy for games.

"I admire your honesty, Angela."

"Do you? Shall we look at the menu, or do you know what I like?"

He shrugged. "You're a meat eater, anything but game. You like salads and fruit, not cheese so much. And you prefer red wine to white."

"Bloody hell," Angie whispered, making sure he heard. "I'm no longer awed by your intimate knowledge of my habits, so you can just cut that out."

"I'd recommend the rack of lamb."

"Fine."

"No arguments?"

"None."

He leaned toward her again and asked, conspiratorially, "Is that good?"

"Oh, yes." She laughed with him, joy coming from nowhere. Oliver's brief warning flashed through her mind. Glands, yes, but more than that. Angie thought she recognized fear—his as much as hers. For those few moments she was bewitched by it, taken over by their mutual elation.

He ordered their meal with a slight smile on his lips, rejecting the petit pois in favor of the haricots verts, the spinach in favor of leeks simmered with wild mint. Then, as though peace had not intruded into their conversation, he said, "You were angry when I called you. You were expecting me to call, and yet you were angry. Why?"

"I can't explain it. You . . . touch me, Paul, and I can't afford to get involved. Maybe that's too simple . . ."

"Afford?" He picked up the word coldly. "What do you think I'm going to ask you for?"

Angie winced. "I didn't mean it like that." She wanted to add, Don't spoil it, but the temporary ease was already over. "They tell me you're thinking about standing for Parliament—"

"Why are you changing the subject? I asked you a question."

"Then stop asking me questions!" she bristled. "I have no intention of letting you badger me, Paul." He drew back. Was he afraid she would raise her voice and embarrass him? She tried something else. "Have you known my father long?"

"Six or seven years. That was the first time I—we'd been invited to Calvert Hall."

On safer ground Angie relaxed and reached for another cigarette. She understood him to mean that the prospect of becoming an MP had been the spur for the invitation. He was probably right. "My father doesn't encourage close friendships. Business relationships, yes—" she stopped, distracted by the sight of him flicking her lighter on and off. "You're using up all the gas. Am I boring you?"

"By talking about your father? I don't think so, but you're

wasting your time. I suspect I know Sir Richard Jarman rather better than you do.''

"That I can believe," she said sarcastically.

"And I certainly get on with him better than you do."

"Almost everyone does. Is it that obvious?"

"It was to me, that night. But only because I was seated next to him and couldn't take my eyes off you."

Angie laughed. "If I'd realized, I'd have behaved better."

"I thought that was why you didn't come back, you and your brother. He had had too much to drink, but you—did you have another date?"

"Date—that reminds me of school dances, posies. No, no date."

Then it would have to have had something to do with Oliver's leaving Jarman's and Angela's taking over. Only that would have accounted for Sir Richard's white-faced anger when he had returned to the drawing room. The information about Oliver's "sabbatical" had come to Paul via Beaumont Gracie's very swiftly completed update on his earlier report on Richard Jarman. Although Gracie had not had much time in which to cover the ground thoroughly, the update had contained at least one bombshell.

Gracie had evidently considered the job done. He'd been surprised and alarmed to receive a summons from Paul so soon after submitting the updated report. Apart from the additional—and specifically requested—information about the son and daughter, the document was substantially unchanged.

He had been further surprised by the compliment with which Paul had greeted him. "A thorough investigation, as usual, Gracie. An interesting family, wouldn't you agree?"

Gracie had given him a confused, hesitant look, as though there were a specific penalty for agreeing; he had long since been dissuaded from volunteering an opinion or asking a question.

"I'm curious about Mrs. Wyatt's child," Paul told him, squaring off two notepads on the desk in front of him. "Where did that information come from and how reliable is it?"

"Totally reliable, Mr. Angelou. It was a bonus, you might say, coming as it did from a friend in the force, long retired, memory intact."

"Your friend, he was in the area of Calvert Hall at the time?" Paul glanced down at the open folder. "Forcible rape, not reported. How did a policeman find out?"

"Oddly enough, from a barmaid who was friendly with the cook's daughter."

"Too clichéd not to be true, I suppose. Did he say why the rape was not reported?"

"He assumed it was simply to avoid a scandal, especially as rumor had it that Oliver Jarman was lying drunk in the back seat of the car not two hundred yards away."

"I see." Paul experienced a fleeting sympathy for Oliver but no surprise at Richard Jarman's handling of the situation. He didn't know what he felt about the rape, except no pity for Angela; she would not have thanked him for that. "Does your friend happen to know where the child is now? Who the adoptive parents are?"

"No one does," Gracie said earnestly. "Since it wasn't part of my brief, I haven't pursued it. In any case, there wasn't enough time. What I can tell you is that a lot of trouble was taken to keep the identity of the adoptive parents a secret."

Paul folded his arms and contemplated the pained expression on Gracie's face; he looked like a perpetually disoriented grandfather. "Can you find her?" It was less than three weeks since Paul had met Angela Wyatt, and already the tranquil assurances of his previous life were being undermined. What he planned to do was instinctive.

"Sir?" Gracie's heavy eyebrows lifted.

"You say that no one, not even her mother, knows where the child is. I'm asking you to find her. And before you ask why, I have my reasons."

What was the old man thinking? Paul wondered. Would he object or demand to know exactly why Paul wanted him to find the girl? If he had, it would have been totally out of character, but Paul was nonetheless relieved when Gracie rose from his chair. "I can find her."

"Sit down, Gracie. That's only half of it. After you've found her, as you go along, in fact, I want you to ensure that Angela Wyatt's daughter is thereafter untraceable through the regular channels."

"I am to obscure evidence?" Gracie made the question sound as unpalatable as possible.

"Scorched earth policy, Gracie. Not obscure. Get rid of."

Gracie knew better than to object outright. "Destruction of public records—I would suggest that a reasonable alternative would be a form of . . . falsification."

"Whatever. But do it quietly and quickly. Very quickly."
Paul silently applauded Gracie's self-control; the only gesture
of disapproval came in his pause at the door, although they
both knew there was nothing more to be said.

Alone, Paul had locked the Jarman file in his desk and
pocketed the key. By instructing Beaumont Gracie, he was
drawing Angela Wyatt to himself in some indefinable way. It
was more than a compulsion to know everything there was to
know about her. He'd gone beyond the point of trying to
diagnose or rationalize his feelings; all he did know was that
he wanted to *absorb* her in order to deflect the undoubted
power she had over him. By taking her over he could perhaps
control her and, therefore, himself. The child was a part of
her other existence, unimportant as yet. Circumstances would
indicate just when and how he would use her.

"He's waiting for you to taste the wine," Angie said now,
nodding toward the waiter, who had just cleared his throat
for the third time.

"Leave it," Paul told him. "If it's no good, I'll let you
know."

"And thank you," Angie added, making the point that it
was quite unnecessary to be so brusque.

"Is it mere coincidence that Oliver's sabbatical comes just
as you return from New York? Aren't you taking a lot on
yourself?"

Angie swallowed a sharp retort just as their food arrived at
the table. Glad of the breathing space, she heard Paul assure
the waiter that they had indeed decided to skip the hors
d'oeuvre and that medium rare was the way he'd ordered the
lamb.

When they had been served, Paul looked at her over the
rim of his glass and said, "Well?"

"It's none of your business, Paul." Angie lifted her own
glass. "This wine is very good, don't you think?"

"It's common knowledge that Oliver is an alcoholic. I have
certainly known it for many years now."

"Please understand, I'm not discussing Oliver with you or
anyone else."

Paul sliced into his lamb, separated the meat, and inspected it closely. Satisfied, he raised his head to give her a
look of glancing arrogance. "I think you came back to London for a reason. A specific reason."

Angie picked up her own knife and fork. The two of them seemed to be in some remotely inaccessible place, somewhere it would be impossible to escape from, walk out, and see humdrum daytime faces, dogs and cars and children. He had reduced her to a woman completely on her own. She ate in silence, conscious of his brooding expectancy.

"You're not making it easy, Angela."

The soft accusation came close to unnerving her finally. She felt small and mad just listening to him. *Am* I doing it? Am I making this happen? "Please listen to me, Paul. For reasons of your own, you've gone out of your way to find out quite a lot about my life. That doesn't mean you know anything about me. And it doesn't give you any rights. Do you understand? I don't like what you're doing. You're casting me in a role . . ." She faltered, lowering her voice. "For God's sake, you're putting me on the defensive for no good reason! I'm here, and the reason for my being in London has nothing whatsoever to do with you. If I wanted to tell you, I'd have volunteered the information. So stop, please. Be nice."

Nice was an odd choice of word, almost exotic in its unsuitability. Over Angie's shoulder, Paul watched a large woman in a paisley-patterned dress coming toward them; he would know soon enough why Angela had come back to London.

"Angie." The big woman's voice took a moment to intrude on Angie. "Surprise. How lovely to see you again so soon."

Jolted by the familiar voice, totally out of place, Angie rose to her feet and turned to face Fran Forsyth. Before she could gather her wits, Fran said, "You're looking good, so much better than when I saw you last."

"I . . . thank you. Fran, this is Paul Angelou. Fran Forsyth."

Angie caught the look of chilling disdain on Paul's face as Fran held out her hand with a friendly "Hi."

"Why don't you sit down and have a glass of wine?" Angie asked.

Fran glanced over her shoulder. "Well, thank you, I will, if you're sure it's all right. I'm waiting for Michael Goodwin. He's always late."

Paul looked up, held Angie's glance for a moment, then signaled the waiter for another glass. Other than that he gave no indication that they weren't alone.

"Michael Goodwin." Angie turned back to Fran, who raised her eyebrows in a soft, questioning look. "Isn't he the moneyman, the sort of English Paul Erdman?"

"I never thought of him like that, but you're right. Maybe I should use that comparison when I submit the proposal for his next book."

"Paul is a commodity broker," Angie said as the waiter arrived with Fran's glass and filled it.

"*Are* you?" Fran asked with exaggerated interest, now distinctly aware of the frost. Angie was almost relieved when Paul merely nodded his answer. It would have been all right had Fran, in the ensuing silence, not pursued it. "Then you must have heard of Michael Goodwin."

"Why?"

"Well . . . same business, I suppose. Money—"

"I don't read fiction," Paul interrupted flatly.

"He doesn't write fiction," Angie said.

"I've still never heard of Michael Goodwin."

Fran drained her glass quickly. Before she could protest, Angie filled it again. "I haven't thanked you properly for all the information you gave me, Fran. It was extremely useful. Perhaps we could do this alone, another time?"

"Of course." Fran glanced desperately over her shoulder again. When she saw the man who had just come through the door, she jumped to her feet. "There he is. I'll call you, Angie. Thanks for the wine."

Angie watched her hurry away, big, amiable Fran Forsyth. She watched her position Michael Goodwin at the table, so that she, Fran, would sit with her back toward them. Angie then pushed her own plate away and lit a cigarette, knowing it would offend Paul.

"Did you know she was going to be here?" he asked.

The lamb in front of her was by this time no more than lukewarm. Small spots of fat had whitened around the haricots verts. "Knightsbridge isn't exactly publishing territory," she said.

"That's what I was thinking. An unlikely coincidence."

"You're suggesting I planned an . . . interruption?"

"Did you?"

"Not only is that an absurd notion, but I can see no reason for it. All I have to do is get up and leave."

"Then why don't you?"

Angie recoiled at the ferocity in his voice. Even so, his

fury suffused her with caution. Its irrationality brought a leaping desire to feel him, gentled, in her arms. "I wouldn't like to leave it like this."

"That woman . . ."

"She's a friend, Paul. A warm, decent person. Doesn't that mean anything? She's harmless."

"Not so harmless, intruding on my time—"

"*Your* time? I invited her to join us."

"You invited her here today."

Angie's patience ran out quite suddenly. *"What for!"*

"Keep your voice down. I'll pay the bill, and we'll go somewhere else."

"What do you mean?"

"We'll go somewhere else. Or don't you want to leave your warm, decent friend?"

Angie looked around the restaurant, noting the calm faces of the other customers. At the far end of the room, in the corner, Fran's shoulders were peculiarly hunched. "No."

"I want to see you alone."

"We are alone."

"We *were* alone until that woman showed up."

Part of her wanted to see this out. "What would happen if I told you I *had* arranged for Fran Forsyth to be here today?"

"I would forgive you."

Angie laughed at the unpredictability of that statement. "Then maybe I should confess."

"Why are you laughing?"

"Not because I'm amused, let me assure you." She bent over to pick up her handbag. "I'm leaving now."

"Why?"

"There's nothing left to say. There's nothing to talk about. Stay, please. Finish your meal."

"Are you going to talk to that woman?"

"Apologize for your behavior? I think not."

Paul nodded. "If you're going back to the office, I'll give you a lift."

"Thank you, no."

He got up anyway as she turned to leave and followed her halfway across the restaurant before veering off to the right. As she closed the door behind her, Angie saw him at Fran's table, leaning over, smiling, animated. She knew he wasn't apologizing. He was buying Fran with that smile. He had decided that she would serve his purpose better as an ally.

Against whom? Confused, Angie turned away and began to scan the slow-moving traffic for a taxi. She felt a masochistic envy of Fran, still there, beleaguered by his charm, having no reason to suspect his motives.

Later that afternoon, sitting in the office with Oliver, she wondered what she would have done had a taxi not appeared just then. Started walking in the direction of the underground? Or gone back into the restaurant?

18

☐ It was more than three months since Arion had set foot in Prax and more than seven years since he had possessed a key to either the front or back doors of the nightclub. James Bonnier had, from time to time, attempted to explain the intricacies of the electronic security system. Arion pretended not to understand the workings of the system because he had no desire to carry around with him any key but the key to his own house.

Prax was situated near the apex formed by Shaftesbury Avenue and St. Giles. Like Ani's, it was a mixture of the opulent and the intimate. It had been a derelict warehouse housing the overflow of books and magazines destined for the pulping machines, and only Gallic flair and optimism could have seen the ramshackle building as anything other than a potential heap of rubble. James Bonnier had approached Arion about the site on behalf of a consortium of businessmen who had envisaged an arcade of boutiques, a wine bar, and a coffee shop. Bonnier spoke of the project with such listlessness that Arion felt compelled to ask him why.

"Who wants another batch of expensive boutiques selling tat?"

"Tat?" Arion had never heard the word before.

"Cheaply made, overpriced rubbish."

Arion liked the aura of grave honesty about Bonnier. He was a short, burly man with barely a trace of accent in his voice. Under a helmet of dark, curly hair, his face was unmistakably French to Arion: full, sensually shaped lips, a hawkish nose, and eyes that could not conceal a quick, hot temper.

Building a nightclub on the site and using the existing dimensions of the warehouse had been James's idea, one with which Arion had readily concurred. James had used the vast floor space with cunning. A large wedge-shaped stage occupied the northeast corner of the room; tables separated the stage from the area of the spotlighted dance circle. A twelve-foot bar stretched along the west wall, and another, smaller bar lay tucked away in a softly lit corner. James's objective had been to make the stage visible from any part of the room but also to give those who had not come for the show enough space and silence in which to converse.

Arion had been horrified by the price of membership to Prax. James, in his typically sardonic manner, said, "You're right, of course. The membership fee *should* be increased, but you know how it is these days."

Arion had nothing to complain about. James and his wife, Gina, managed Prax as carefully and with as much imagination and energy as if it had been their own. Unlike Scotia, however, they had accepted Arion's offer of seventeen percent of the shares in the enterprise.

A small group of musicians were rehearsing on the stage when Arion walked in. An exaggerated riff on one of the electric guitars alerted James Bonnier to his presence.

"Was that a signal?" Arion grinned at James as he hurried over.

"Why didn't you tell me you were coming? Gina is out—"

"I am here to say hullo only."

"Then please sit down. How is Ani?"

"She's well, and she gives you both her love."

"Gina will be sorry she missed you. Is anything wrong?" James was a shrewd and intuitive man. This was not one of those times Arion dropped in for a chat and a glass of wine. He could tell from the dullness of the old man's glance, by the lethargic movements.

"Wrong? No, I think nothing is wrong, but I would ask you about some things, *mon ami.*"

"Come into the office . . ."

"No, no. Here is good. The musicians are good."

James glanced over his shoulder and got a long trilling note from the piano for his efforts. "Good, yes. Jokers, too. What sort of things, Ari? You know all you have to do is ask."

"Cory." Arion looked at James closely as he spoke, watching the man's reaction carefully. "Does Cory come here often?"

James lit a cigarette. He didn't like the seriousness with which the question had been asked. "Not often, Ari. Once or twice a month maybe."

"What does he do when he is here? Is he with friends? Does he bring girls with him?"

Was that it? Had Cory got some girl into trouble? "Friends, boys and girls. More boys, though. They drink a little, dance a little, and then they go. No trouble."

Arion hesitated. "These friends—you know who they are?"

"I'm afraid not. Is it important? I can find out. What's Cory been up to?"

Arion sighed and pushed himself slowly to his feet. He shook his head. "I do not know. Maybe nothing, my friend, but I wish I knew who—who these friends are."

"I'll ask around. Leave it with me." James saw apprehension cloud Arion's eyes. "Don't worry, no private detectives or anything like that. I know a lot of people in this city."

"I know. That is why I have come to you. Please telephone me, James."

"Won't you stay for a glass of wine at least?"

"Another time. Now I must leave." He paused, then said harshly, *"You will tell me."*

"Of course." James held his alarm in check. He squeezed Arion's arm gently. "Why shouldn't I tell you?"

"I have a feeling that my age prevents the truth from being told."

"You would doubt a Frenchman's word of honor?"

"Never. Thank you, James." At the door Arion turned to give him a reassuring smile. "I will hear from you," he said.

19

☐ Deborah Anderson was drinking her afternoon tea in Cynthia Crew's office when Sidney Niklas shouldered his way through the door. His fleshy face was contorted and pale as he turned to kick the door shut behind him.

Cynthia raised her eyebrows, and her hand went up to pat her perfectly rigid hairdo. Nothing pleased her more than to see Sidney in a rage.

He towered over Deborah. "Guess fucking what, girls?"

"Sidney, please . . ." Deborah began.

"Do you want to hear the news, or do you want to take your sensitive and virginal ears out of here, Deborah?"

Deborah flinched and bit down on her lip. He really was the limit, but she had no intention of leaving before she heard what he had to say.

"I need a drink." Sidney began pacing up and down between Cynthia's desk and the filing cabinets.

"Well, you won't get one here," Cynthia said waspishly. "What is this news you're so steamed up about? Another girl stand you up?"

"What would you know about it, either of you?" He scowled down at Deborah. "And you—you can say good-bye to your pathetic lustings. He's leaving—sabbatical, he's calling it."

"He? Who do you mean? What are you talking about, Sidney?"

"Oliver bloody Jarman, Cynthia, that's who I'm talking about. Our alcoholic, mind-bendingly boring managing director."

Deborah felt a sickening jolt and closed her eyes. Sidney was lying. This was another of his obscene jokes. "Sidney, please . . ."

"Don't puke, Deborah, for Christ's sake. Go to my office

and bring the bourbon in the cupboard. And glasses . . .
you're going to need a drink as much as I do.''

"I don't believe what you're saying.''

"Don't worry.'' He sat down in her chair. "I'll wait until
you come back before I tell you the *really* good news.''

She was gone for less than a minute. Sidney waited until
she had poured out three measures of bourbon before he
raised his glass to Cynthia. "The king is dead, long live the
queen.''

"Dead?'' Deborah's face turned gray.

"Not dead in that sense, idiot! He's going away to dry out,
somewhere in Gloucestershire. They say if he doesn't go,
daddy will no longer have a son and heir. Some heir!''

"Cheers, Sidney.'' In the midst of Sidney's fury and Deborah's panic, Cynthia saw herself as omnipotently objective.
"So, what happens here? Who'll take over? I suppose it isn't
you or you wouldn't be so—''

"You guess right, and you may live to regret that. You've
met Angela Wyatt, girls? Sister, widowed, childless . . . want
me to draw you a picture?''

"Good Lord, *that's* why she's been coming into the office.
They might have told us the truth, don't you think?'' How
would this affect her? Cynthia wondered. She got on well
with Oliver, well enough, but another woman? Feeling less
sure of herself, she asked, "Who told you all this, Sidney?''

"Never mind who told me. OJ is going to announce it all
this evening at the party.''

"Oh. Oh, that's why we've all been invited,'' Deborah
whispered. "I thought it was odd . . . when is he leaving,
Sidney? When is it going to happen?''

"It's *happened*, for Christ's sake!''

Deborah's hand went over her mouth to cover an involuntary cry as she got up and stumbled from the room.

"Do you have to be so bloody obnoxious?'' Cynthia demanded.

Sidney poured himself another drink. "I wonder if Martin
knows.''

"I doubt it, unless he's heard it from his father. What do
you know about Mrs. Wyatt?''

"Nothing except that she's been living in New York for
years, married an American who worked for Bennett-Poore.
Knows fuck-all about British publishing—not that Oliver
knows a lot. Christ, I'm leaving . . .''

"Don't be a fool, Sidney. Your kind of job doesn't grow on trees out there. Why don't you wait and see what she's like to work with?"

"I don't mean leave Jarman's. I meant I'm leaving now, and I'm going to get drunk. I may or may not turn up tonight. Don't hold your breath."

"Oh, I shan't," Cynthia said sweetly. Like hell he wouldn't turn up for the fun. And he'd turn up halfway sober, too. Not even Sidney would take on an unknown member of the Jarman family without at least some of his wits about him.

20

☐ Harry Baird said, "If you want it done, once and for all, Mr. Angelou, no comebacks, this is what I suggest. Two things."

They were sitting in Paul's Mercedes in Cleveland Square, parked between a GPO van and a rust-ridden Volkswagen. Locked in the safe behind Harry's desk at the office was a strongbox containing all the information he would need about Angelou's father's holdings. The chronological and heavily detailed notes gave him names, addresses, ages, balance sheets, and investment portfolios. How the hell Paul Angelou had managed to lay his hands on all this was a mystery. Harry even knew what the old man's house was worth and what it cost him to run. If he had had any misgivings about Paul Angelou's determination, they'd been dispelled when he handed the documents over.

"The equity in the Angel holding company is seven point two million pounds. Your father owns thirty-five percent of the shares, you hold twenty-six and the balance of thirty-nine percent is held by other shareholders. I propose that you instruct us through Marcus Clifford to sell fifty thousand shares at whatever price. At the moment the shares are seventy-eight eighty pence in two and a half thousand shares. On this basis,

Marcus could sell your block at, say, seventy pence." Harry paused to light a cigarette and open the window.

Paul Angelou stared straight ahead. When he spoke, it was more of a remark than a comment. "And Marcus will go on selling blocks of between twenty and fifty thousand shares at intervals; this will lead to a bear raid. The jobbers will take defensive measures, and within two weeks the shares will be worth no more than fifty pence."

"With a little help from the odd rumor at the right time; nothing serious, just a word in the ear of other shareholders that this might be a good time to sell. Angel Publications is a public company, so your father is not protected by a pre-emption clause, which means, of course, that he can't buy time to forestall a panic by buying up the shares others will want to offload. In any case, he won't have the money to do it because his shares stand as collateral for various loans. By the time the banks call in his loans, they should be down to around fifty pence. It shouldn't be necessary to sell more than a hundred and fifty thousand of your own shares; such a relatively small number wouldn't make it obvious at all to your father that you had in fact started the run on the shares."

"You said 'once and for all.' It seems to me that quite a lot could go wrong. Angel Publications isn't exactly unprofitable. A clever speculator could do his homework and see a bargain."

"Naturally, but that includes you, Mr. Angelou. If I didn't know better, I'd suspect you of doing just that. You said you wanted to instigate a takeover; a raid on the shares will ensure that. Who will eventually own the majority of the shares in the holding company is not my problem. Nor, as I understood it, yours. I don't have to remind you, either, that you could be down some three hundred thousand pounds if Marcus doesn't read the market well whilst he's negotiating for the sale of your shares."

"Leave that to me. What's the second part?"

"Arson," Harry said, flicking his cigarette out of the window, noting with satisfaction Angelou's sharp movement of surprise. "Specifically, your father's high reputation versus the possibility of his being investigated for arson. Shall I go on?" He put the question deliberately, needing just then to elicit some sort of response from the taciturn Angelou.

"Kindly continue."

"At any given time your father's warehouse contains between five and six hundred thousand pounds worth of stock. Turnover of stock is rapid, but to judge from the records you've given me, half a million pounds is a good guess. The warehouse must be destroyed.''

"Let me—''

"I haven't finished yet, Mr. Angelou. Arson it will be, and arson it must be seen to be. Do you understand? That is your 'once and for all.' The evidence of arson will be *your* insurance that the phoenix doesn't rise from the ashes, to put it crudely. Just one small indication that it wasn't an accident, a chance clue, nothing obvious. No insurance company will pay out a cent if arson is even suspected, let alone proved. And as the shares begin to plummet, the fire will provide the finishing touch, because suspicion will naturally fall on your father. The timing of the sale of the first block of shares will be crucial. It should come no more than a week before the fire.''

Harry hesitated, waiting now for Angelou to say something. When he didn't, he went on. "I'm not putting this forward lightly, believe me. It's a gamble, and it's dangerous. And the decision rests with you. I would emphasize, though, that this way you not only get rid of the old man's company, you put a stop to his even *trying* to salvage it. His reputation will preclude a serious police involvement. It could be uncomfortable for a while, the hint of criminal activity, but I would bank on that being the worst of it.'' Again Harry paused, trying to read Angelou's silence. "In view of your political . . . ambitions, I imagine you will want to consider the problem of adverse publicity. All I can say on that score is that if you have access to any strings in Fleet Street, now is the time to pull them. Well, there it is. Depends on what it's worth to you.''

"And to you, Mr. Baird.'' Paul turned toward him, hiding a slight smile. Apart from the warehouse, nothing Baird had said had come as any surprise to him. "The media need not concern you,'' he said. "Go ahead.''

Harry was shocked, despite himself, at the instant decision. "I suggest you take some time to consider the implications.''

"The implications are perfectly clear to me. I will be in touch with Marcus Clifford in the morning. The rest is up to you.''

Harry shook his head. "The rest? The second part, the warehouse?"

Paul leaned forward and turned the ignition key before glancing into the rearview mirror. He was looking at himself when he said, "Burn it."

21

☐ The taxi sped along the Carriage Drive, on the southern perimeter of Hyde Park, and found a bunched-up line of cars as it drew abreast of the Achilles statue. The driver turned around and said, "I hope you're not in a hurry, luv," and, having mistaken her for a tourist, added, "at least you've got something pretty to look at." Hyde Park. It *was* pretty in its lush midsummer greens, which ranged from lime to emerald green and olive.

Angie smiled and nodded at the driver. She had wanted a word with Oliver before the guests arrived, but it would keep. He wasn't leaving for Gloucestershire for another two days yet, and since he'd vetoed her suggestion that she accompany him and Cissy down, she'd have to find some other time.

To her surprise, Angie felt a mild flutter of nervousness and quietly upbraided herself for reacting to a situation over which she had no control. It was done. Tonight's gathering had originally been planned to promote a strikingly illustrated book on Britain's rare plants and flowers. Oliver had bought in copies from a well-known packager, and Angie thought privately that he had agreed to buy too many copies at too high a unit price. Jarman's would need all the review space and praise it could get. To that end the guest list included not only reviewers but booksellers, literary agents, and a smattering of other publishers.

Cissy, too, would be there this evening. It had been her idea to announce Oliver's impending departure at the party. "I'm not coming to hold your hand," she'd reassured him. "I'm coming to make sure that you tell them. Leaving Jar-

man's, even for a year, is so long overdue that I won't believe
it until I hear you tell everyone."

Angie could scarcely believe it either. He already looked
better. During their intensive briefing sessions she had had
the feeling that he was shedding layers of care. Once or twice
it had seemed as though he would change his mind. "These
aren't just pieces you're going to be picking up, Angie.
They're bloody great boulders."

"That's right, scare me."

Would London publishing accept or even tolerate a virtual
outsider as head of Jarman trade? Did it matter? Angie had
recognized the source of her tension and could only admit to
herself that it did matter, at least for the moment. If it had
not been too late, she would have suggested moving tonight's
publicity-oriented party from the boardroom to a club or a
restaurant. Until the last two weeks it had been years since
she had set foot in the Jarman building. She now found it
unexpectedly nerve-racking to anticipate walking in not as a
visitor to be announced but as someone with an office, a
secretary, and a nameplate on the door.

The traffic ahead thinned out, and they were moving again,
edging into the right-hand lane in order to cross Park Lane
into Mayfair. The space and openness of London directed
her thoughts abruptly away to the simple grid structure of the
streets of New York. Angie loved that city for its generosity
and vibrant anachronisms, for its squalid violences and bad
humor. London caught her differently. It was not a place she
loved, and it would demand of her a responsibility she had
been happily free of in New York. Matronly, inhabited by
those of her own kind, its core eluded her. The very Englishness of its multiracial population mystified her. It evoked none
of the New Yorkers' vocal pride in their city; its heart
thrummed equably, it tolerated the clogging of its veins each
day without rancor, and it accepted all those who wished to
make any part of it their home. And yet, she knew, it would
spew out what it found ultimately indigestible; it could poison
and kill by its silence.

Silence . . . London without Oliver and Cissy, especially
while she was waiting to hear about her daughter from Christopher Chetwynd, would be a lonely place. The thought was
a disturbing one because she knew how easily she could withdraw, how deeply solitude attracted her, and the reckless
means she could use to dispel that attraction. Her atavistic

fear of Paul Angelou had something to do with this. She could see herself letting go, being embroiled by his persistence and arrogance, his goading. Already he was edging her toward a reckoning she wasn't ready for. . . .

The taxi pulled up with a jerk. "There you go, miss, number thirty-two. Sorry about all that."

Angie got out of the car and handed the driver two five-pound notes. He went on apologizing, as if the traffic congestion were somehow his fault. As she took her change and handed back a tip, she said, "Why are you apologizing?"

"Traffic's so bad sometimes that the punters go paranoid on me. Reflex, I suppose. Sorry." He grinned at her and moved away. He'd apologized for apologizing.

Angie stood back and looked up at the huge stark white building in front of her. RICHARD JARMAN & SON, PUBLISHERS, she read, advancing toward the double glass doors. That was all, a brass nameplate, one foot square, on the left. She stopped in front of the sign, her reflection showing up healthily ruddy on its glossy surface. What was that expression—fright? Yes. She laughed, getting a wide, if confused, smile from the doorman as he greeted her.

"Has my brother arrived, Dennis?"

"A few minutes ago, Mrs. Wyatt. Not many others, but they'll be trickling in soon enough. Will Sir Richard be coming?"

Please God, no. She said, "He's still in Africa. We're expecting him back next weekend, I think."

"He isn't much one for these kinds of dos." Dennis pressed the lift button.

Angie agreed. "You're right."

As the lift doors sighed shut, she sighed, too. I'm not much one for this kind of do either, she thought, wishing that the next few hours were over and that the lift were going down instead of up.

A quick glance around the room told Frank that Lisa had not yet arrived. He collected a scotch and water from a white-jacketed waiter and turned to find Oliver Jarman at his elbow.

"Good of you to come, Frank. Have you met my wife, Clarissa?"

"Clarissa?" Cissy raised her chin in protest. "I haven't been called Clarissa since—since infant school. Cissy, Mr. Sheldon."

She stood very close to Oliver. Her grip was warm and soft, her expression open and guileless. "Hullo, Cissy. I'm afraid I respond only to Frank. That's it, no second name either."

"That's good, uncomplicated. I was named after an aunt whose heart stopped after she'd smoked two pipefuls of opium in a nursing home in Cheshire."

She said it so matter-of-factly that Frank burst out laughing. "I'd like to drink to that lady. Was she called Cissy, too?"

"Oh, no, no one dared. Formidable woman, pulverized everyone she met, except Toby. Toby was her husband, a brigadier, I think. He saw to it that her pipe was buried with her. Then he sold everything he had and died in Turkey from an infected finger two months later."

Oliver put his arm around his wife's waist. "Do you believe that story, Frank?"

"Certainly. No one could invent anything so bizarre."

"In that case, let's just say that Cissy could have been one of the most imaginative novelists of the century."

Cissy made a gesture of resignation. "Oliver has no sense of the dramatic truth. If Clarissa had choked to death on a boiled potato and Toby had wilted away from a broken heart, he'd have no trouble accepting it. Skepticism . . . a condition of the male publisher."

The room was beginning to fill up as they spoke, the level of noise rising perceptibly. Frank recognized and knew most of the people present. It was a tribute to Oliver that the specialist reviewers had turned out in force; also, an impressive number of literary editors—such was the demand for their time that while they normally accepted all invitations, they chose which functions to attend only at the last moment. Most of the established literary agencies were represented, together with a few editors from other publishing houses. That struck him as odd, but before he could begin to think about it, he saw Lisa come into the room. She hesitated, confronted by groups of people and strings of sound. Then she saw Frank's raised hand, and a smile of relief touched her lips.

"You're looking . . . very nice," he said as she came within earshot.

"What?" She leaned in close to him, and he could smell the clean fragrance of her hair.

"I said you're looking very nice."

"Oh." The compliment caught her unaware, and she searched his face for some sign of mockery. She hadn't quite forgiven him for the other night, but it was good to know he actually noticed what she wore. She had considered going into an overdraft for a Katharine Hamnett dress but had finally chosen separates for their practicality: a pair of beautifully cut Cacherel trousers with a matching cotton-knit sweater.

"Is that *Night Work*?" Frank indicated the bulky parcel she held.

"For Oliver, yes."

"He's over there with Dunne Morrissey. Why don't you give it to him now? Too heavy to carry around all evening."

Lisa knew precisely where Oliver Jarman was, and she wasn't ready to approach him yet. She wasn't sure he'd even remember her name.

"Well?"

"I'd like a drink, Frank. Is that whiskey? I'll have the same."

"Wait here and I'll see what I can do." He resisted the urge to add something sarcastic.

"Well, well, if it isn't the lady Lisa," Sidney breathed into her ear. He cupped her elbow and forced her to turn around. His large bearded face was a few inches from her own. Whiskey, garlic, and cigars on his breath . . . Lisa stepped back automatically and collided with someone behind her.

"I'm so sorry." She spun around, trying to keep the fury out of her voice.

"No damage," the other woman said, brushing at her skirt. "You're Lisa Barrett, aren't you?"

"Uh-uh," Sidney interjected. "*The* lady Lisa Barrett."

The woman ignored him. "I'm Angela Wyatt. I've been hearing a lot about you."

Lisa's mind galloped into a dead end. Angela Wyatt? Familiar but only vaguely. A reviewer, someone from the magazines?

As if she could see the frantic searching, Angie said, "I'm Oliver's sister. Don't be embarrassed. There's no reason on earth why you should know who I am. I know how disconcerting it can be, believe me."

Lisa nodded wordlessly. Dumb! She damned Sidney Niklas to hell and could have hugged Frank as he edged between her and the editor.

"Your drink." He held out a glass of whiskey, and she snatched at it gratefully.

"Thank you. Frank, this is Angela Wyatt—"

"Oliver's sister. I've looked forward to meeting you for a long time, Mrs. Wyatt. It's strange, don't you think, that after all these years in the business we've never met before?"

Her frown clashed with a half smile. "Nothing in this business surprises me any longer." When she lifted her glass, he saw that her hand and lower arm were wet. Without a word he brought out a handkerchief and dabbed at the moisture.

"My fault," Lisa said, wishing she could go out and come in and start all over again.

"I'll vouch that she's normally the least clumsy person I know," Frank said.

Angie moved forward and spoke into his ear. "Coming face-to-face with Sidney Niklas will do it every time, Mr. Sheldon."

Frank let out a whoop of appreciation and pocketed his handkerchief. The reserved, haughty look was gone, and in its place was one he would have described as collusive. A beautiful woman, he decided, taken aback that he should even notice such a thing with Lisa standing beside him. She wore a loose saffron patterned dress, caught at the hips with a broad terra-cotta scarf. The light cotton material skimmed her body rather than just hanging from her shoulders. It was the second time in the space of minutes that he'd noticed a woman's clothes. He further surprised himself by saying, "On the strength of that, I'd like to buy you dinner, Mrs. Wyatt. Are you going on anywhere after this?"

The unexpectedness of the invitation caused not a split second of hesitation. "Unless Oliver has arranged something else, I'd be delighted to join you."

"Lisa?" But she'd gone. A few feet away she stood facing two young men who fidgeted and nodded intently at her. She was still clutching the typescript.

Frank's disappointment was so obvious that it startled Angie. He wanted Lisa Barrett, and the girl had no idea. The message was so clear to Angie that she wondered at the girl's insensitivity. There had been no lack of intelligence behind those cool blue eyes, but there was a certain innocence. . . .

Frank turned back to her. "I can't seem to get Lisa to hand that typescript over to Oliver."

"I'll take it, if you like."

''I'm afraid it has to be Oliver. Lisa doesn't want Sidney to get his hands on it.''

''Trust me,'' Angie said with a small laugh. She half suspected that Oliver would have told his close friends in publishing, people like Frank Sheldon, that he would be handing over to her. She knew that he had broken the news to Jason Corbett that morning, but she had not had the opportunity to learn of Jason's reaction. How would Frank react? she wondered. He would approve. She was so sure he would approve that she told him, quickly and quietly, what he would have heard in a few minutes when Oliver made his announcement.

When she'd finished, he said, ''Yes. It can't have been an easy decision . . . for either you or Oliver.'' He remembered Oliver telling him about the death of her husband, and he'd imagined a woman's shock and grief . . . but a contained, aristocratic woman—someone, in fact, like Oliver's wife, not the person who had just passed on such a painful confidence.

''It was necessary . . . and urgent,'' Angie said. And to herself: Why am I telling you all this? And why aren't you surprised to be hearing it? But already an unambiguous trust of Frank Sheldon was beginning to build up in her head. She wanted to go on talking to him, but people pressed in closer, making it impossible for anything they said not to be overheard.

''Later,'' Frank said as someone tugged at his sleeve for the third time.

Angie nodded and out of the corner of her eye saw Jason Corbett zigzagging his way toward her through the crowd. He didn't look particularly happy, she thought, and felt a pleasurable anticipation for the first time that evening.

He took her hand and, holding on to it, said, ''Should I be offended that you made no mention of this that night at Calvert Hall?''

''I didn't know,'' Angie said. ''Not for sure.''

He looked as though he'd just arrived home after a day at Lord's. He wore gray flannels, a dark blue blazer, and an open-necked white shirt. ''Would you like me to put on a tie?'' he asked, having noticed her glancing appraisal. ''I have one in my pocket.''

''Of course not.''

''For what it's worth, I think Oliver has made the right decision.''

''Yes.'' Was it her imagination, or did he look slightly

flustered? They were being forced to stand so close together that unless she tipped her head well back, she couldn't see his face properly. When she did, curious about the hint of aggression in his voice, she saw nothing approaching ill temper in those light, shocking blue eyes. Which was just as well. She needed time to work out precisely what was happening on the Jarman/Corbett production front. Something was very wrong, but until Oliver was out of the office, there was no way in which she could gauge the size of the problem. She needed comparative estimates, a thorough breakdown of setting and binding costs. . . .

"I've been trying to work out why you thought fit not to let your staff into the secret before today," Jason said. "It's unlike Oliver to be so . . . secretive."

Secretive. The word was ugly, and to Angie so were its connotations. She bridled. "Let me assure you that there were very good reasons for not announcing it officially until today. Your son—"

"Did I mention my son?"

"Perhaps you should have done! What other possible interest could you have in Jarman's staff?"

"I've worked with them . . . *all* . . . for years," he said coldly.

"In that case, I'm surprised you can't work it out for yourself. I—we all want Oliver in that clinic by Saturday. By *not* telling the staff, I've ensured just that."

"Commendable, Mrs. Wyatt . . . if I knew what you were talking about." He was genuinely mystified, and Angie was appalled by her own behavior. She *liked* him; she'd been looking forward to seeing him again. How could she be so nonsensically touchy?

She saw Oliver at the other end of the room. He was raising his arm, calling for silence. Jason turned and saw it, too.

"You already know what he's going to say," she said, and that, too, came out almost as an accusation.

"Let me get you another drink before he starts." He took her empty glass before she could protest and moved away, edging sideways through the crowd. A head taller than anyone else, he scanned the room for sight of Martin but couldn't see his son anywhere. The boy wasn't happy about Angela Wyatt's appointment; neither, it seemed, was Sidney. She didn't seem to be all that delighted herself. Nerves? No, unless she was a better actress than he gave her credit for. Then

what? Fear for Oliver's well-being, no more, no less. He could
see her being trapped into this situation but at the same time
not resenting it entirely; she was neither victim nor martyr.
Her reaction to his criticism about not informing the staff had
lain somewhere between the two. And she'd been on the point
of apologizing. He hadn't waited for that. A degree of defensiveness was understandable, but what continued to intrigue
him, as Oliver began to speak, was just how keenly and decisively she'd responded to Paul Angelou that first night. The
air had been electric. Her fingers, caressing the smooth, intricate grooves in her wineglass, had been somewhere else,
on some*one* else: Angelou. And she knew he'd seen it and
understood it. That was possibly, in part, what she now resented. But even as the thought crossed his mind, he knew it
wasn't so. She would, if anything, have been amused by his
observance of the byplay. She might even have been aroused
by it.

Cut off from her now, Oliver's voice quite loud in the stillness, Jason replaced the two glasses of whiskey on the table
beside him. This was not the time. Too much was happening
around her; in a very real sense she wasn't in control. His
decision to cut out after Oliver's speech was partly due to a
reluctance to complicate this evening for her further and partly
because he could, with equal reluctance, envisage himself
being fitted into some temporary gap in her life. And just
now he found neither option tolerable.

There was a stunned silence when Oliver announced his departure from Jarman's. Angie kept her gaze focused on him
as heads turned in her direction. She squared her shoulders
under Sidney's venomous glare and the speculative glances of
others she had not yet met. It amused her to see that Lisa
Barrett was still holding on to the typescript. Martin Corbett
stood in sullen contemplation of Oliver, Cynthia Crew was
smiling tightly, and Dunne Morrissey wore his habitually bemused expression.

"Christ, I'm glad that's over," Oliver said as whispered
conversation started up again. "How do you feel, Angie?"

"Like a bug under a microscope. Cissy?"

"I normally hate parties like this, but I'm quite enjoying
myself."

"That's because you know it'll be the last one for a very
long time," Oliver said.

"Where's Deborah?" Angie asked. "I've seen everyone else."

"In the loo, crying her eyes out," Cissy said.

Oliver was amazed. "You're not serious!"

"Don't tell me you didn't know!" Cissy tugged at his tie accusingly. "She dotes on you, and you've broken her heart!"

"How did I do that? Should I talk to her?"

"Tomorrow perhaps. In any case, she won't come out of the loo. I've tried."

"That's a relief. Have you seen Sidney, Angie?"

"Have I! *And* young Corbett."

Oliver gave a halfhearted laugh at the touch of iron in her voice. "They're not so bad, Sis. You'll find—"

"I think I know what I'll find. But don't worry, the length of rope you've allowed them is not about to be cut in half overnight. This is a caretaking operation, not a takeover, remember? I'm sorry Jason couldn't stay, though. . . ."

"Oh, he asked me to tell you that he'd be in touch—ah, here's Lisa. Have you two met?"

Oliver had been surrounded by people all evening. The party would be drawing to a close soon, and Lisa had still not had the opportunity to talk to him alone. His wife was a permanent fixture at his side. She said, "Unless someone else has stepped on her toe and spilled whiskey all over her, yes, we've met. I feel doubly foolish after what I've heard because I've brought you a typescript."

"You weren't to know," Oliver said kindly. "Perhaps Sidney could—"

"Not Sidney," Angie interrupted. "Why don't you leave it with me, Miss Barrett, and I'll try to read it over the weekend?"

"Lisa, please. It's not really that urgent, but thank you."

"Is it on auction?" Oliver asked.

"I'm afraid so. The others won't be getting their copies for another few days—"

"I'm sorry we didn't get the last novel you offered."

"So am I, but Meredith's would have paid whatever it took. This is something else, though. It's a first novel, and I think it's uncannily good."

Angie watched this exchange with interest. Oliver was asking questions without any real interest in the answers, and Lisa was intent to the point of trembling.

"Can you tell us anything about the author?" Oliver asked.

"Elliot?" Lisa seemed taken aback by the question. "He's a teacher."

"Old? Young?" Oliver prompted.

"About thirty-five, I guess."

"Lucky man."

"Why?"

"Well, to have written a marvelous first novel and to have you as his agent."

She said honestly, "I haven't done anything yet."

"How many publishers are seeing the book?"

"You're one of four," Lisa replied shortly, avoiding his eyes. Where was Frank? He was never there when she needed him. She could feel sweat break out on her upper lip, the air close around her. The sweater had been a mistake. . . .

Angie spoke. "I'm curious to know why you included Jarman's in the auction, Lisa, since I understand they've hardly ever come in with an offer."

"I knew Oliver would like this book."

Cissy laughed uneasily. "How on earth did you know that?"

Lisa resisted the temptation to touch her wet forehead and swallowed a knot of nausea. "I suppose I should have said I hoped he would like it. Would you—" She turned to him, unable to stop herself. "I can get an extra copy of the typescript if you'd like to take it away with you."

The slight to Angie was not intentional, but it provoked a moment of uncomfortable silence. Angie rescued her again. "Good idea, Oliver. Why don't you take this copy with you and Lisa can let me have another in a day or so?"

Oliver nodded, less surprised by Angie's gesture than the persistence with which Lisa seemed to be addressing him. "Well, that's settled then," he said gruffly, touched by her youthful gravity. He felt Cissy close up against him and pulled her arm up under his.

The automatic reaction was not lost on Lisa. She'd really wanted to impress this man. She'd anticipated this meeting with him for a long time, given herself some witty and succinctly telling lines of dialogue . . . and then fallen flat on her face. She summoned her will and turned to look for Frank. With any luck he'd say or do something that would annoy and thus divert her. She found him. He was standing with his back toward her, talking to Cynthia Crew. She willed him to turn around, then abruptly changed her mind, excused herself from the small group and left the room, following the taped signs to the cloakroom.

There the fluorescent lights were cruelly revealing. She took one look at herself and groaned. Was there anyone in the room who hadn't seen what a fool she'd made of herself?

She leaned over the washbasin and washed her face with soap. Then she turned off the hot tap and splashed icy water over her face and let the water run for a few minutes over her wrists. Bodies should not let one down in such a treacherous way, she thought, feeling slightly better. She took a small compact of Clarins makeup from her handbag and spread the light foundation sparingly over her cheeks. It wasn't as though she'd even fantasized about Oliver Jarman.

She washed her hands again and then slid them up beneath her sweater, pulling it away from her damp skin. She left the cloakroom confused and cold despite the heat that radiated from her skin. She was going back into the Jarman boardroom, and she was going to talk to Oliver again.

By nine o'clock there were no more than nine or ten people left in the room. From his vantage point over the shoulder of a diminutive drunken features editor, Frank could observe those remaining.

The evening had proved more instructive than enjoyable. In retrospect, it wasn't surprising that Oliver had decided to opt out for a time. There hadn't been many people in the room who believed that he was truly leaving on a sabbatical, although no one but Sidney voiced an opinion. Sidney had complained to anyone who would listen.

Frank saw Angie listening to Leonard Gascoigne, a bookseller. She stood perfectly still and straight-backed, an empty glass in her hand. Now and then a twist of the lips would pass for a smile, but beyond that she gave no indication that she was involved in the conversation at all. Watching her, Frank revised his earlier estimate of her; she was quite stunningly beautiful but with something very fragile lurking beneath the calm exterior. How the hell had she come to play the thankless role of catalyst?

Oliver and Cissy were laughing loudly at some remark made by Bob Stuart, a young paperback editor. They were still laughing as he shook hands and turned to leave. In the far corner of the room Sidney was belaboring Fran Forsyth about the stupidity and greed of literary agents who were sending hardback publishers to the wall. She was trying to edge her way out of the corner, and Frank considered rescuing her; but he had no wish to switch Sidney's attention to himself.

The only other person left was Lisa. Will Benson, doyen of literary editors, was patting her on the shoulder with one hand and reaching for his walking stick with the other. She walked to the door with the old man, and as she came closer, Frank saw that she was flushed and obviously in some distress. He drew her aside.

"What's the matter?" he asked. "You look feverish."

Her eyes went up to his face, the way they always did, even when he was with someone else and not even looking at her. There was a forceful quality about Frank Sheldon's face, she thought distractedly. The face was smiling. The smile was wide and warm and threw his skin into a million tiny wrinkles. She felt safe under his gaze, free to be as she felt, jumpy. Because of the way she was looking at him, he struck an affected pose. "Do I pass?"

"Silly . . . it's hot in here."

Frank placed the backs of his fingers against her forehead before she could object. Her skin felt clammy. "I think you're coming down with something."

A severe case of terminal idiocy, she thought, wishing he'd leave his fingers where they were so that she could lean into him. . . .

"Why don't I get a taxi to take you home?"

Lisa pulled away from him. "You're always getting taxis to take me home," she said thickly. "Don't fuss, Frank."

"If you say so. I'm taking Angela Wyatt to dinner when this is over. Would you like to join us?"

Lisa scowled and confused herself further by demanding, "Are you taking her to Ani's?" There was more than a suggestion of betrayal in her voice.

Had she had too much to drink? "I haven't decided yet. Why do you ask?"

"Will your friend be there?"

"Arion? I doubt it. Has he called you yet?"

Lisa shook her head.

"I'll remind him—"

She choked back a desire to hit him. "Don't you dare!"

"That's better. I haven't had a rise out of you all evening."

With that her shoulders went down, and her smile caught

him like a fist. "Why do you watch out for me so? I'm not a child, Frank."

"And don't I know it," he murmured.

She appeared not to have heard him. "This has been an odd evening, not what I expected at all. Is it true what Sidney says, that Oliver's going into a clinic to dry out?"

"It's true. And I'm afraid he's in for a very hard time. I think it's time we left. Are you joining us?"

Lisa's eyes darted to Oliver. He looked tired. She hadn't had a chance to talk to him again. She wanted to walk over and say good-bye but she knew no words would pass through her lips, which felt dry and swollen.

"Lisa?"

"No. Thank you, no, Frank."

"Are you going home?"

She didn't answer. She turned on her heel and strode quickly from the room. Out in the street she walked in the direction of Berkeley Square and kept on walking until the chill of the night air seeped through her clothing. It felt good. She drew in a deep, uneven breath. She didn't understand what had happened back there; it was as though she'd magicked herself into a stranger's body—a disageeable stranger's body. She'd managed to present herself to Oliver Jarman as an empty-headed adolescent; she'd confused his wife and, albeit unintentionally, insulted his sister. What do you do for an encore? Short of stepping in front of a double-decker bus, she could think of nothing.

22

☐ Harry Baird was contemplating another pint when the young man who had been reading the *Times* in the corner came over with a pint of Directors for Harry and a gin and tonic for himself. He pushed aside the gloves that lay next to Baird's cigarettes and placed the beer in front of him.

"You've been nursing that one long enough, Mr. Baird," he said.

Simon Riggs could not have been more than twenty-three or twenty-four. This fact alone was enough to put Harry on his guard. Riggs wore a dark gray tweed jacket over a stone-colored shirt; his tie was held in place by a broad gold clip. Harry registered the chunky body, the soft brown eyes, and the delicately tapered fingers. He found himself drawing back instinctively.

"*Salute*," Riggs said. "Bit off your beaten track, aren't you?" Which meant he knew that Baird lived in St. John's Wood and worked in the City. . . .

It had taken Harry a surprisingly short time to locate Riggs; it didn't mean that Riggs was "visible," just that Harry's contacts were more reliable than most. He'd been nonplussed by the ease of the operation, so much so that he hadn't been sure what to say, how much to let himself in for when he'd dialed Riggs's number.

"Baird, you say?" The voice on the telephone was smooth and unhurried, the accent county.

"Harold Baird, Mr. Riggs. You have been recommended to me, very highly recommended."

"By whom, Mr. Baird?"

"I'm afraid I'm not at liberty to disclose the name."

There was a long silence. Harry waited, weighing the risk he took that the man would hang up.

"Where are you?" Riggs asked finally.

"A pub, the Lancaster in Queen's Gate."

"Be there on Tuesday at seven o'clock. Take gloves with you."

"Gloves?" The phone went dead in his ear.

Harry had been tempted to start out under a false name, but he'd known intuitively that Riggs would simply not have turned up. Riggs had given himself time to do some checking, and although there was nothing to hide yet, Harry had the fleeting desire to get up and leave. Now. As with Paul Angelou, he was sure Riggs knew everything there was to know about him.

"Let's get on with it, shall we?" he said briskly. "I take it you're interested?"

"I'm here, and I'll listen to what you have to say. Then I'll tell you whether or not I'm interested."

Harry told himself he couldn't afford to antagonize this

arrogant young bastard. He needed him. Riggs was by all accounts clever and discreet, a man who gambled his freedom on calculating the odds correctly. His name did not appear on any of his clients' files, and he'd never been caught or even suspected of a crime. . . .

"It's a warehouse," Harry said softly. "I want a warehouse destroyed."

"Destroyed?" One slender finger came to rest squarely in the middle of Riggs's lips.

"Destroyed. Fire . . . isn't that how it's usually done?"

"I wouldn't know, Mr. Baird. How big is this warehouse, and what does it contain?"

"It's big, about twenty thousand square feet, brick and timber, the usual thing. It holds paper, mostly magazines and some books. I have the floor plans."

"Excellent. Where is it, and is there anyone there all the time? A caretaker, a watchman?"

"A night watchman. Middle-aged, lives close by, I understand."

"A good night watchman? Or one who sits in his hole with coffee and cigarettes?"

"That's what I'm paying you to find out," Baird said testily.

Riggs brought out a silver cigarette case and lit an unfiltered cigarette without offering Baird one. He replaced the case in his inside jacket pocket and said, conversationally, "You're not paying me, Mr. Baird. Not yet. When I ask a question, I expect an answer. If you don't know the answer, you'll find out. I will then check your answer against my own investigations, and we will proceed from there. Do I make myself clear?"

"Perfectly." Harry swallowed his chagrin. "I know nothing about the watchman's habits."

"Very well. You used the word 'destroy.' I take it you want the building razed?"

"Totally."

"Insurance?"

"Something like that. I also want some evidence of arson left behind."

For the first time Baird saw a spark of interest. "Let me understand you correctly. This is not just a fire; it's a deliberate fire, right?"

"Right. Don't make it too easy, though. I don't want a can of paraffin left lying around."

"Paraffin? You jest, Mr. Baird. Where is this warehouse?"

"That comes with the floor plans and other details. Let's talk about your . . . fee."

"Fifteen thousand pounds. In cash, half up front, as they say, the rest after the event."

"That's a lot of money."

"That's a lot of warehouse."

Harry watched the effeminate fingers slide up and down the stem of the glass. If he had been asked to identify Riggs out of all the men in the crowded pub, this young man with this soft, pale skin and languorous movements would, without any doubt, have been the last.

"Agreed." Harry reached for his briefcase under the table, but once again he hesitated before handing over the large buff envelope. Once Riggs had that, he, Baird, was an accessory. "The night watchman—he's not to be hurt."

"Violence is no part of my business, Mr. Baird. Do you have a private number where you can be contacted?"

Baird gestured toward the envelope. "It's all in there. I'll arrange for the money to be paid over once I hear from you."

Riggs slipped the envelope between the folds of his newspaper. "Excellent," he said again. "Well, stay put, Mr. Baird, enjoy your drink. You'll be hearing from me."

As he turned and walked out of the pub, Harry noted the perfect cut of his jacket. Not a crease, not a spare millimeter of material was evident across the shoulders. He took a long pull at his beer. His mouth felt dry, and the beginnings of a headache tightened the muscles of his neck. Fear, like a circling vulture, threw a shadow over the bright lights and muffled the sounds around him.

If anything went wrong, he was a dead man. Between Paul Angelou and Simon Riggs, he didn't stand a chance.

23

☐ The rhythm of their lives had changed perceptibly. Susan Angelou could not put her finger on it, but the axis had somehow tilted. Paul had begun to come home earlier; he'd taken to phoning her in the middle of the day. Once he even asked her to join him for lunch in the City. There was a faintly expectant air about him. It was as though he were clutching her to himself while looking over her shoulder at something else.

Suzy conceded that she liked this shift, although she had no idea what had brought it on. She thought at first that it had been a killing on the market. She almost persuaded herself that this was the reason. But deep down she knew it wasn't. If it had been, their weekends would not have been spent without the intrusion of frantic telephone calls. Her father, always the first to congratulate his son-in-law, had not been in touch for a month or more.

What then? She studied the shadowed contours of Paul's profile silhouetted against the light from a small table lamp. In the shifting shadows shed by the television screen, the sternness had softened into an expression of boyish concentration. He gave himself so totally to everything he did.

"Paul?"

"Mmmm?" He wasn't listening.

"I saw Ani today. I went to visit her."

"How is she?"

"Worried. They're both worried about Cory."

"There's nothing I can do about that," he said flatly.

Suzy watched him for a moment, then sighed and went upstairs. In the bedroom she began to pin up her hair. Then she turned on the shower and came back to the dressing table. She paused to stare at herself in the mirror before spreading cleansing cream over her cheeks and forehead. She often wondered what her life would have been like if she had not been born blond and blue-eyed. Paul would not have fallen in love with her, she knew that, and at times it rankled. He had subdued so much in her, even something as relatively unimportant as her dress sense. He preferred her in light colors, creams and pastels, which not only accentuated the whiteness of her skin but added to her virginal looks. It was just as well that her own tastes in clothes did not run to frills and plunging necklines; he didn't approve of frivolous designs, colors, and textures. She sometimes yearned for the colors she'd worn as a teenager, crimsons and fluorescent blues, pinks and yellows. Her wardrobe now contained not a single item that could possibly displease him. The more austere the covering, the more pleasure it gave him to strip it away, layer by layer, until he found her bare skin. She had also become accustomed to concealing the instant desire he provoked when the ritual began. She had even begun to take an arbitrary pleasure in trying to anticipate his advances, thereby giving herself time to prepare her mind and body for restraint.

She wiped the cold cream from her face and turned her thoughts to Ani. Paul's mother had looked old and weary today, and Suzy was reminded again that she and Ari would not be around forever. She often thought with dread of her own parents' dying, not being there, but much as the very idea of it pained her, it was inevitable. That Arion and Ani should die was not inevitable. Their life-force was somehow different, more enduring. It was nonsense, she knew, but the prospect of their deaths was nonetheless unthinkable. There were times when she would tell herself that she loved them more simply because they were Paul's parents. But that was a fallacy, an explanation she'd invented for herself. She would have felt the same way, had them lodged in her heart, had they been unrelated, total strangers.

Paul was sitting on the bed, fully dressed, when she returned from the shower. He watched her draw the pins out of her hair.

"Has the program finished?" She still found something disturbing about his quietness after all these years.

"What's on your mind, Susan?"

She lied. "I was thinking that you and I might go away somewhere this year. Benjamin is spending two weeks in Venice with the Stevensons, and God knows it wouldn't hurt you to get away from London for a while."

"A holiday? Is that it?"

She pushed damp tendrils of hair from her forehead and tightened the sash on her dressing gown. "That's it."

"Come here." He patted the bed beside him. "Do you have any place in mind?"

She knew he wouldn't like it, but she tried. "Greece."

"Why?" he challenged, leaning back on one elbow. He drew the robe gently down from her shoulders and let his fingers trickle down her bare spine.

She felt foolish, facing away from him. "Because . . . oh, Paul, because you were born there, and they say it's so beautiful. . . ."

"Who says that? My mother?"

"Of course, but not only Ani." She twisted around, amazed to see him relaxed and smiling up at her. "I would like to see it for myself. Will you come, too?"

Without answering, he urged her down and carefully kissed her lips.

"Paul?" He went on kissing her. The material of his jacket was uncomfortable against her bare breasts. She eased away. "What are you doing?"

"I'm making love to my wife," he replied reasonably.

"Now?"

"Why not?"

"In case you've forgotten, we're due at dinner in less than an hour."

His response was to cover her mouth again, and this time Suzy's arms went around his shoulders, pulling him closer. He was acting as if she'd always denied him her body. After years of making love at least twice a week, he couldn't now seem to get enough of her. Heat gathered in the small of her back. Why now, she wanted to ask him, why now, after so many years? Nothing had actually changed. They were still the same people, doing the same things, but in *this*, the rhythm of their lives had changed the most. It was almost as though he had discovered someone else in her. Suzy's eyes flew open as her mind recoiled from the thought.

Paul felt her involuntary movement and drew back. "No?"

He was so close to her that she had trouble focusing. "What?"

"Do you want me to stop?"

"No, I—what's happening?"

"I'm making love to my wife."

She shuddered, clenching her teeth against his lips. She wanted to demand an explanation, reassurance. She wanted to know why he was making love to her now, fully dressed.

Later that evening, sitting opposite him in the crowded restaurant, she decided that she really knew nothing about this man. Lily and Thomas Ardrey, their oldest friends, were delighted by his good humor, his carefully chosen confidences, the *control* he asserted over them all. He orchestrated the evening with finesse, held them and wooed them with his charm. What would happen when this mutual lust came to an end? The word surprised her and sent a flash of alarm through her veins. Less than an hour ago, in that same suit, shirt, and tie, he had been thrusting into her. His breath had mingled with hers in small explosions of exertion. Afterward he had straightened his clothes and gone downstairs to wait for her. The entire episode was at odds with everything she knew about him.

He caught her looking at him now. What did those dark eyes see, she wondered, as he moved solicitously to fill her glass and touch the back of her hand with his fingertips? Whom did they see?

Paul was conscious of his wife's troubled stare and felt himself stir once more as she lowered her eyelids almost shyly. He wanted her again; she must have seen it. Not even in the first years of their marriage had he been so preoccupied with her physical presence. He didn't understand it any more than she did. At first he had the idea that he was testing himself, challenging his imagination to substitute Angela Wyatt for Susan. But that wasn't so. He saw only Susan beneath him, felt only her familiar movements. The more his obsession with Angela Wyatt increased, the closer it drove him to Susan. Fear? He didn't discount the irrationality of his desires. The compulsive need to make love to his wife was to disclaim awareness of that other hunger. It wouldn't work indefinitely; already there were moments of truancy, when it needed effort to pull himself back. He could no more deny the clamorous ache he felt for Angela Wyatt than he could the revitalized love he felt for Susan.

24

☐ A yolk-yellow sky, hanging like a painted backdrop; a landscape which seemed to be inhabited by other, unseen creatures no less fantastical than the one that peered out of the picture: the Ken Kiff painting suggested an orderly wilderness, frightening, yet as satisfying as a childhood fairy tale.

From where she sat, behind Oliver's desk, the broad strokes of color attracted Angie's eye; an office wall wasn't the ideal location for the small painting, and she wondered now if the fact that she couldn't clearly define the mythical creature's outlines at this distance accounted for the tingle of disquiet she felt each time she glanced at it. She took a moment to think about that, not wanting to hear Christopher Chetwynd's voice in her ear.

". . . and so I'm afraid it's going to take rather longer than I anticipated."

"What sort of problem?" she asked, turning away from the picture. She hadn't planned to call Chetwynd this morning and now regretted that she had. His responses to her questions, delivered in smooth, dry tones, were neither obstructive nor helpful. He had no intention of detailing the setbacks.

"I am assured that the delay is temporary, Mrs. Wyatt. As soon as I have anything concrete to report, I shall do so."

Angie nodded and heard herself thanking him, politely, for his efforts. "I'll wait," she said, as though there were a choice.

She replaced the receiver, surprised that the lawyer's charmless reticence had done no more than dent her sense of well-being. She *could* wait if she had to, and she would endure the waiting without impatience unfurling into anger. The calm optimism, she knew, had to do with being here, in Oliver's office, doing his job, unraveling a situation that was at once formidably complicated yet simple. She saw quite clearly where the solutions lay; the challenge was now to find ways of implementing them.

Angie had spent the first two weeks after Oliver's departure in the office with the door shut. She canceled the editorial, production, and sales meetings and gave herself over to reading through the past year's minutes of those meetings. She familiarized herself with the current list and made a careful note of which books were serviced by which editor.

From the editorial minutes she was also able to glean which books had been sold to paperback and book club. It came as no surprise to find that most remained unsold, their advances heavily in the red. Dunne Morrissey's publicity budget seemed to bear no relation to the salability or otherwise of the individual book. In confidential memos to Oliver the eleven-strong sales force placed the blame for low unit sales on dull dust jackets, lack of promotion material, the general sameness of each season's books.

The evidence of Oliver's patience stunned her. The minutes reflected so many conflicting opinions that she marveled at the fact that Jarman's had a list at all. To satisfy her own curiosity, she tried to follow the progress of one particular novel, from its first airing at the editorial meeting to its publication more than a year later. It was a first novel about Robert the Bruce, submitted to Deborah, who'd read it and assessed it as "good, for a first novel, promising writer."

By the second editorial meeting Sidney had read it. His opinion was that the young female novelist had not come close to inhabiting the lusty world of the Bruce. A week later Martin had added his reservations to Sidney's.

At that point Angie called Deborah in and explained to her what she was trying to do. Deborah immediately took the explanation as a criticism, and Angie had to spend the next twenty minutes reassuring her. Finally she got what she wanted.

"I'm curious," she said gently. "Three people read that book—you, Sidney, and Martin. Why was it then passed on to Cynthia for yet another reading?"

"We thought she would be able to tell us what—what the paperback and book club chances were."

"And?"

Deborah frowned, scoring the soft wood of a pencil with her thumbnail. "Cynthia said she might be able to sell it to a paperback house that had a costume drama series or maybe a specific interest in Scottish fiction."

"I see. What happened then?"

"Well, I brought it up at the sales meeting—"

Angie laughed incredulously. "You consult the salesmen before you buy a *novel*?"

Deborah flushed. "Most of the time," she said.

There was no point in upsetting Deborah any further, so Angie let that go. She said, "I know you eventually bought the book, but do you know what happened to it afterward?"

"I'm sorry, I don't know what you mean. I remember having a lot of problems with the jacket design. . . ."

Clearly Deborah had no idea that the novel had been a disaster in terms of sales. Or maybe she simply had no access to the computer printouts. Once the overheads had been built in, the book showed a loss of close to two thousand pounds. The saga made Angie's head ache. The book had been talked out, tired, dead before the ink on the contract had dried.

Night Work lay at her elbow. Jarman's needed it even more than she had originally thought. The system creaked. If her plan to put in a preemptive bid for the novel was successful, there was at least a chance of working some of those rusty bolts loose.

Toward the end of the second week Jane Bullivant, her father's secretary, asked to see her. She came in looking flustered and nervous. There was no mistaking her surprise at the transformation of Oliver's orderly office into something resembling a paper-strewn obstacle course. There were typescripts balancing precariously on the leather sofa and perhaps a dozen box files spread in three piles on the floor; in addition, some bulky orange authors' files lay fanned out on the carpet, a dull patch of color against the fawn. Jane's glance went to the desk. There was no sign of the telephone.

"Sit down, Jane. And don't worry, I know where everything is."

"Just as well. Mrs. Wyatt—"

"Since when have I been anything but Angie to you? Have you forgotten how long we've known each other?"

"Eighteen years, to be precise."

"That long?" Angie had a good idea why Jane was looking so uncomfortable, and since none of it had anything to do with Jane personally, she felt quite sorry for her. "I know we haven't had much time to talk, but as you can see, I've had a lot to catch up on. How are you?''

"Embarrassed, if you must know. This isn't something I'd choose to do, but I've been asked to . . . convey to you the very real level of unhappiness outside this office.''

Angie made a show of drawing her brows together. "What do you mean?''

"The staff wants to know what you're doing, what your plans are. I think it's fair to say they're apprehensive. Oliver ran a pretty democratic outfit, and there are naturally fears that any newcomer will feel obliged to clear out the old hands and start afresh.''

"Is that what you think, too?''

"I'm here to save my sanity. If another person walks through my door to ask what you and Sir Richard are planning to do, I swear I'll scream.''

The telephone rang somewhere at Angie's feet. She leaned over and switched the call back to her own secretary. "If you must say something, I suggest you tell them it's business as usual. My job here is precisely as outlined on the notice boards. I'm standing in for Oliver. I'll change what I think needs to be changed, but I have no intention of polarizing Jarman's. The meetings will begin again next week, and we'll go on from there. All right?''

"May I pass that on?''

"Of course. But tell Midge first on your way out. I imagine she's been on the receiving end as well, although she hasn't said anything to me. By the way, how long has she been with Oliver?''

"About three years. Any problems?''

"On the contrary, she's very efficient. A bit dour perhaps but then one can't have everything.''

Jane Bullivant smiled for the first time. "You know you can call on me at any time if you get stuck.'' She glanced around the office again. "Just as well we're not unionized. This could be fairly described as an industrial hazard.''

"It's more hazardous than you'll ever know, Jane, but thanks for the offer.''

Angie got up and stretched with satisfaction as the door shut behind Jane. Although she had not meant to make the staff quite so nervous, it had been her intention to create a certain amount of wariness. Oliver had been badly served; she didn't intend to make the same mistakes. . . .

Now Angie glanced at her watch; she had ten minutes before she was due in her father's office. She was not looking forward to it. Not only was he going to balk at her intention of going after *Night Work*, but he was going to take what she had to say about Jason Corbett and his printing prices as a personal attack on his integrity.

Angie stubbed out her cigarette and gathered up two slender folders. Walking along the corridor, she thought longingly of a few quiet hours with Frank Sheldon. During these last weeks he had helped her to a knowledge of the London publishing scene, its intricate politics and delicately balanced power structures. With quiet generosity and patience, he made himself available whenever she needed him. His company pleased her enormously, and she sought him out as easily as she would have a close girlfriend. His humor and frantic honesty about Lisa Barrett delighted her. He played it as a comedy, ridiculing himself for his mismanaged lust. Angie found herself confiding in him without having to weigh her words or fear a scornful reaction. In so short a time he probably knew more about her than either Oliver or Cissy—except for the rape, and when the opportunity arose, she'd tell him about that, too. He was also, albeit unwittingly, helping her get through the time waiting to hear from Christopher Chetwynd. She loved his unobtrusive masculinity and the fact that he had, so obviously, nothing to prove.

What on earth would he make of the dark corner inhabited by Paul Angelou? Of her sustained shock at not being able to rid herself of it? He spoke in all innocence, and without any prompting from her, about Arion Angelou. The closeness of his relationship with the old man didn't strike Angie as strange, but the obvious dislike with which he spoke of Paul did. She never asked him why, and apart from mentioning that she'd met him, she never introduced Paul's name into their conversations. It troubled her, not the deliberate omission but the feeling she had of hoarding and protecting a sinister secret. She didn't bring up Paul's name because she wasn't ready to admit the depth of her desire to be taken over by him, to allow herself to become completely absorbed. There was no part of her consciousness that accepted as anything more than a temporary aberration the fact that Paul Angelou made her feel more alive, more vital than Lou ever had. . . .

Jane Bullivant gave her a bright smile and said, "Hullo, lovely day, isn't it?"

Did Jane have sinister secrets? Angie couldn't imagine it. She was married to a British Rail executive, had been for nearly thirty years. Angie said, "If you hear a scream, it'll be me."

"I wouldn't be too sure about that"—Jane laughed—"but I'll listen out anyway."

Angie walked into her father's office, smiling. Maybe the sounds *everyone* made were shot through with the same deceptions.

Sir Richard Jarman was less than pleased to find himself confronted by his daughter so soon after she'd moved into Oliver's office. To give her her due, though, she had done her research meticulously, and the facts she presented to him were more than borne out by the abysmal trade figures.

Then she was asking, no, asking was not quite right, she was informing him of her intention to make a preemptive bid on a novel that was being auctioned.

"By that I take it you intend to ask the agent to withdraw the book from the auction?"

"If she accepts my offer, yes."

"Why do you think that's necessary? Why not simply bid in the auction like everyone else?"

Angie couldn't make out if he was just curious or actually disapproved of the ploy. "There are two reasons for doing it this way. If the offer is tempting enough, the agent will accept it; there's always the chance that if the auction runs its normal course, she won't get nearly as much. There's also the chance that we ourselves will be outbid if the auction continues. The other reason is, I suppose, publishing politics; preemptive bids aren't that common. It will be good PR for Jarman's and will encourage other agents to consider us in much more commercial terms."

As she spoke, he had the impression of reined-in enthusiasm; she wasn't allowing herself to let go, but what she said made sense. He didn't appreciate the marketplace aspect of trade publishing. If she enjoyed it, as she clearly did, let her get on with it.

"Thank you," she said dryly when he told her just that. "That's only part of it, and ten thousand pounds isn't nearly enough to acquire the rights to *Night Work*."

"Ten thousand pounds?"

"Oliver was obliged to consult you on any offers he made over ten thousand pounds. It happened so seldom, though, I'm not surprised you don't remember the . . . ruling."

She was wrong. He *did* remember it, and as far as he was concerned, the arrangement had worked perfectly well. "What are you driving at?"

Angie took a deep breath. "I would like to offer the agent a two-book contract for a hundred and thirty thousand pounds: sixty-five thousand for *Night Work* and sixty-five thousand for the author's second novel." She saw immediate astonishment on his face and went on quickly. "It's a unique novel, literary enough to ensure blanket reviews and commercial enough to top the best-seller lists for months."

The figure was outrageous. How could she be so sure of the novel's potential? "I can only assume that you have an excellent supporting offer from a paperback house," he said.

"I'm afraid not, but only because I haven't approached a paperback house. I want to acquire the rights for Jarman's and *then* auction the paperback rights."

The size of the gamble began to take on proportions he would normally have found unacceptable. He was almost inclined to say, "Go ahead," and then watch it all come apart in her hands, crumbling like a house of cards. In many ways she was courting just that danger. "I don't understand why you don't tie up paperback support now, before you make the offer."

He was taking it rather too calmly, Angie thought, almost as though he weren't considering it seriously. She said, "Visibility again. A successful paperback auction would attract more attention to Jarman's. It isn't only the literary agents we have to convince but also the paperbackers and the book clubs—"

"I don't approve of personality cults," he interrupted.

"I hope that doesn't mean what I think it means," she said quietly. "I'm not here to show Oliver up, to prove that I can run the company any better than he could; if you believe that, we have a very difficult year ahead of us. My first priority is to buy books; at the moment we don't have any sort of publishing program. And if you're concerned about agents' expecting to get large advances for every book they submit, well, all I can say is, don't be."

"Nonetheless, what you're suggesting . . . a hundred and

thirty thousand pounds is a lot of money to invest in one
author. This isn't New York.''

"It's a lot of money for New York, too." Angie smiled at
him.

He looked down again at the tabulated figures before him,
devastating evidence that she was right. Not only were there
too few books, but the realistically projected earnings set
against each title were pathetically inadequate. In spite of
himself, he found a nub of admiration for her thoroughness
in compiling the document.

"Very well," he said at length. "But before you indulge
in your buying spree, I want to see a budget, a full forecast
of—''

"You'll have one. Thank you.''

She wasn't through yet. As she riffled through the papers
in one of the files on her lap, he noticed the thin red scar on
the inside of her wrist. Unsightly on such a beautiful woman.
Would she have something done about it? Surprised that the
thought had even crossed his mind, he continued to study her
in the silence. Maybe it was the soft crimson blouse she was
wearing, but there seemed to be a glow about her, a visible
renewal. Her thick dark hair had regained its luster; there
was a hint of physical pliancy in the way she sat.

What she was looking for was the provisional estimate for
the production costs of *Night Work*. He took a copy from her
and spent a moment skimming down the line of figures. It
should have looked good, considering the print run of fifty
thousand copies, but it didn't. Once she had his agreement
on that, she told him quite simply why.

The setting, printing, and binding costs had been taken
from a standing tabulation of prices supplied by Jason Corbett. It hadn't taken her long to find out that Corbett quoted
the same price per page for setting fiction as he did for setting
everything else, from designed and illustrated nonfiction to
original trade paperbacks.

"Are you suggesting that Jason Corbett has been pulling
the wool over my eyes all these years?''

"Not at all. The only estimates *you* see from him are those
for academic books. And they're competitive, I won't deny
that. What the trade department has been accepting for years
is not only uncompetitive but downright greedy. If your friend
has sacrificed anything on the academic side, he's more than
made up for it on the trade side.''

Angie vetoed her father's suggestion that he take the matter up with Corbett. It wasn't his problem, and she made it clear that she expected the questions to come from Corbett himself when he began to realize that Jarman trade was looking elsewhere.

Richard Jarman knew he had no option but to agree. No matter what he thought of her and her methods, Jarman academic could not disassociate itself from the trade side altogether. In a curious way he could even admire his wily old friend for having got away with it for so many years.

Why had there been no liaison between the two production departments? How could anything as blatantly obvious as this not have come to light earlier? The answer was chillingly simple: the instruction to use Corbett's had come from him personally. He had expected his wishes to be carried out to the letter. They had been.

When she left, he looked again at Corbett's figures in relation to the other two outside estimates she'd obtained. He did not like the implication that he'd been hoodwinked. Left to himself, though, he would even now accept the disparity between the two sets of figures. He would not consider jeopardizing the excellence of the academic figures to bail out the ailing trade side.

He put the estimates aside and stabbed the button on his desk, once, sharply. When Jane Bullivant came in, carrying pad and pencil, he was facing the window, his back toward the vast expanse of his desk. He must have heard her because he swung around immediately. His handsome features were set in a stony expression.

What the hell happened here? Jane wondered as she took a seat. The engraved silver cigarette box on his desk was open, and he held a freshly lit filter-tip between fore and middle finger, close to the knuckles. She hadn't seen him smoke for more than fifteen years.

Back in her office Angie eyed the clutter on her desk, for the first time slightly demoralized by the sheer volume. How had Oliver managed without more working surfaces? She did not particularly want to reorganize his office by ordering more tables and shelves; on the other hand, it wasn't exactly the done thing for a managing director, even a stand-in one, to be seen sitting on the floor leafing through a three-inch-thick computer printout file. Appearances . . . the hell with it.

She sat down and on impulse tipped Oliver's pending tray out and found the scrap of paper on which she'd scribbled Paul Angelou's telephone number. "Viceroy Securities." Very regal. She was still looking at it, cheek resting on the heel of her hand, when Midge walked in.

"Fran Forsyth called," Midge said. "And you asked me to remind you to call Lisa Barrett about the auction."

A note, written in Midge's neat handwriting, lay under Angie's hand. It read: "Fran Forsyth called. Call L Barrett re auction." The double reminder—as though Midge related the chaos in the office to the state of her mind—served to lift Angie's mood, and she smiled up at Midge's serious face. "Thank you."

"Shall I get them for you?"

"Not just yet. I'd like to make a start on this morning's mail. Do sit down." She balled up the piece of paper with Paul's telephone number on it and opened her fist in her skirt pocket, nudging the fragment down with her knuckles.

Midge looked at her expectantly.

"Right," Angie murmured.

The number was still there, unused, when she got home that evening. And Paul Angelou was waiting for her.

He was sitting in his car, his wrists angled over the lower curve of the steering wheel. Angie saw him as she leaned into the taxi to pay her fare. By the time she collected her change, he'd locked his car and was waiting for her at the lobby door. He followed her in.

"I want to talk to you."

Every normal avenue of conversation was closed to her. You should have let me know you were coming. Have you been waiting long? How did you know where I lived, that I would come home tonight?

He wore a plain light gray roll-neck sweater under a navy jacket. He had made an effort to appear less formal, and Angie wondered what lay behind it. In the lift he concentrated on the floor numbers as they flicked on and off, his hands linked in front of him. Angie stared at him woodenly, not at all surprised by the forcible hammering of her heart. She wasn't prepared for him, but he wasn't a man who would take that into account.

The lift doors opened on the seventh floor. She hadn't pressed the button. Distracted, she fumbled for her key. "Give it to me," he said. It wasn't a particularly small landing. Out of the five doors, he went without hesitation to the right one.

Once inside, she turned the light on unnecessarily. "Take your jacket off. Would you like a drink?"

"No. Yes, whiskey."

"Help yourself, over there. Same for me, I won't be a moment."

She went into her bedroom, pushed the door halfway closed, and stood with her back to it, groping for the shape and texture of that hour they had spent over an uneaten lunch. Her most immediate recollection was of standing on the pavement, regret battling with reason. She tried to recall his intransigence and her restive refusal, in spite of her desire to the contrary, to yield to it. Every meeting with him so far had ended on a warring note. Why should tonight be any different?

Paul nudged the door with his foot, holding two glasses. "Come out," he said just as the telephone rang, startling them both. "Are you going to answer that?"

"Of course." Angie took the glass from him, sat on the edge of the bed, and picked up the extension.

"Angie?" She glanced quickly at Paul. He stood in the doorway, still with his jacket on, watching her. "Angie, it's Cissy."

"Cissy." She nodded, bringing the glass to her lips. Paul turned on his heel and went back into the other room. "This is an odd time for you to call."

"I just rang quickly to tell you that everything is . . . all right. It's not wonderful, but it's more or less as expected, they say. I don't know what that actually means . . . oh, there go the pips. I'm sorry I haven't got any more money on me . . . I'll call tomorrow."

The phone went dead. Angie couldn't imagine what Oliver and Cissy were going through, and she tried not to think what the agony of withdrawal could do to Oliver's already weakened heart.

She could hear whispering movements in the next room. Paul was moving about, but there was nothing to see, no photographs, mementos. She'd expected him to reappear the moment she put the receiver down, but when he didn't, she went out to find him, shrinking a little when she saw that he'd turned off the overhead light and switched on a table lamp.

"Do you mind?" At least he was sitting down. "Cissy is Oliver's wife, isn't she?"

"You know she is. They're going through a bad time—"

"You seemed very surprised to hear from her. Were you expecting someone else?" In front of him, on the coffee table, lay a copy of *Night Work*. His eyes remained unwavering on the blue and white Sheldon Agency label as he spoke.

"I was only surprised because she usually calls later from the cottage."

He'd hoped she'd gone into the bedroom to change her clothes. She wore a blazing crimson silk blouse and a swirling amber gold skirt with huge pockets; for some reason the outfit made her look formidably businesslike. "Who else calls you here? Frank Sheldon?"

Angie took the ball of paper from her skirt pocket and gave it to him. He stared at the telephone number for a few seconds, then shook his head, without looking up. "All this means is that you changed your mind about calling me."

They observed each other in silence for a moment. She was stopped by the way he looked, overtaken by the reality of his presence. She tried smiling at him. "We can't say two words to each other without leaving a mark. Why have you come?"

"Because I don't like it being like that. I'm not in love with you, you know."

"No." Her smile broadened, briefly. "You could have told me that on the telephone. But don't worry, I believe you. You'll be relieved to know that what I feel for you isn't exactly love either."

"Sex. But then you can get that anywhere, can't you, Angela?"

"Are you asking me or telling me? Incidentally, do you speak to your wife this way? Does she allow you to?"

"My wife doesn't do the things you do."

The dialogue was becoming crazy again. Disbelief threatened to engulf her. She said, "You only think you know what I do. Why on earth don't you ask me instead of building up this obscene fantasy? There's nothing remotely mysterious about me. Why won't you believe that?"

Paul shrugged. It had little to do with knowing what she actually did with her time. He almost smiled himself then, trying to make sense of his incessant goading. She'd laugh if he told her what he really felt: that her very existence was a challenge, the focus of his personal conflict. From his initial indifference on learning about her rape, he was now unable to put it from his mind. He had begun to dream almost nightly of her ordeal; he dreamed of identifying and executing the rapists, although this wasn't what he actually wanted to do. And then he dreamed of taking their place, fathering her child. The fantasy was repugnant in the daylight, as was the knowledge that he had never wanted a woman as much as he wanted Angela Wyatt. He knew he wouldn't force her, but if she came to him, he also knew that he might not be able to control himself.

Angie sat down and took a cigarette from an open packet lying alongside the typescript.

"Where's your drink?" he asked, suddenly shrugging out of his jacket. Without waiting for her answer, he fetched her glass from the bedroom and without asking, topped up both their drinks.

"I don't like this flat very much," he commented, sitting down again.

"Neither do I. I never intended to live here for any length of time."

"Has Frank Sheldon been here?"

"Jesus!" she gasped, stunned again by his insistence.

"Has he?"

"That's got nothing to do with you!"

"You told me to ask you," he said mildly.

"I didn't mean about that. Is that all you're—yes, he's been here, and if your next question is, Have we slept together, the answer is no."

"He doesn't like women?"

"Don't be ridiculous," she snapped.

"Why not then?"

"If we had, it wouldn't have meant anything."

He didn't believe her. "You have no respect for yourself, Angela."

"You know that, do you? I know about Frank's relationship with your father. He's a good man, a good friend and I owe him a lot. We seem to have had this conversation before. . . ."

"And you let him make love to you by way of thanks?" Paul interrupted.

"That makes me feel shabby. No. For the last time, no." Angie told herself that behind that unblinkingly stern expression lay an ambush. Thinking about it, she could almost anticipate the icy shock of fear when the mask of control fell away. "I skipped lunch today," she said, in an attempt to bring some normality into the conversation. "Would you like something to eat?"

"Come with me now. Tomorrow we can—"

"Where's your wife?"

"Susan's away, visiting her son."

Her son? "No."

"What do you do if you don't sleep with him?"

"If?" She raised an eyebrow wearily. It was almost as if he wanted it to be true. "Leave it, Paul."

"Tell me. Do you prefer to—"

"Why do you ask?"

"Because I've done it with Susan, thinking about you."

Angie shut her eyes, but not before she saw the flare of hostility that shook him at this admission. And still, he wouldn't let it go. "What do you think about? Do you think about me?"

"I think about you all the time."

"And?"

"*What!* What do you want me to say?" She was on her feet, furious. Before she could move, trying instinctively to put distance between them, he was there. She sighed as his arms went around her, expecting an onslaught, but found herself loosely held, able to draw back.

He spoke in a torn whisper. "Give me something!"

"I've thought about you, you must know that. I've phoned you a hundred times and imagined you making love to me. You've become an obsessive . . . intrusion into my life, Paul. I know you're married, that you have a son, and that you're a wealthy man. I've met your wife. You've told me, not in so many words, that you're in love with your wife. What can I give you? I'm not—" She stopped.

He found her lips taut and closed and without breath. She forgot everything she was going to say, everything except the sensation of his touch. She drew back to kiss one corner of his mouth and felt his hands pressing down over her back, to her waist and then up again; she curved her body backward, giving him space to find her breasts. He seemed unaware of the movement and used his hands to cradle her face, hold her head still as he urged her lips open. He didn't have to. She could not have moved if she'd wanted to. His tongue probed the inside of her mouth with a kind of slow insolence, and she heard a sound of astonished pleasure strangle at the back of her throat. She strained her hips forward, wanting him hard up against her. He seemed unaware of this, too, intent only on her mouth. He kissed her until she leaned into him, shaking. When he finally stopped, his own breath came in ruptured little spurts.

If he was surprised by her response, he gave no indication of it as he left her and turned to retrieve his whiskey glass. Then, with almost absent-minded affection, he said, "I will enjoy kissing you."

"Will?" She backed into the sofa. "What was that, a dry run?" She sat down and made an effort to stop herself from wrapping her arms around her body, excited and afraid by the speed with which his mood seemed to have changed again.

"It's important to me that you're not sleeping with Frank Sheldon."

Angie slid off the sofa onto her knees. She didn't trust herself to get up and reach for her cigarettes. "Isn't what you just saw proof enough that I'm not sleeping with anybody? Is that why you did it, because you don't believe me?"

He looked relaxed and satisfied, as if he had indeed proved something to himself. And to her. He could do whatever he wanted with her. For now that seemed to be enough.

"If you're going to stay, I'd like to talk about something else. You have a son . . . tell me about him, please."

Again she failed to surprise him. "He's twenty-one, reading law at Cambridge."

"What is he like? Does he look like you?"

"People say he does." He didn't want to talk about Benjamin. "Do you have any children?"

"That's a strange question coming from you. Don't you know?"

"I wouldn't ask if I did." The lie came easily. She had yet to tell him anything about herself that he didn't already know. As far as her daughter was concerned, he knew more than she did now. The latest information Beaumont Gracie had come up with had not unduly surprised him. Someone else was looking for the child, and it could only be Angela. Gracie had expected him to call a halt or at least to leave the rest of the original documents intact.

"Stay ahead of the search," Paul had told him. "Nothing

has changed." Here was one part of Angela Wyatt's life that lay within his control.

"All right," she said, "children are not a good topic of conversation. Why don't we talk about politics. . . ."

"Politics don't interest me."

Angie laughed with disbelief. "Is that why you're standing as an MP? Surely you'd have a responsibility to your constituents? Since my father is a rabid Tory, I can only assume you'll be—"

"Does that mean you're a socialist? In your position?"

"Which position is that: that I have money? Or that my father has a title?"

"Both."

"Let's not argue about it. Why are you standing if you're not interested in politics, though?"

"I've done everything else. If I'm going to be invited to join the most prestigious boards in Britain, I might as well begin from a position of . . . strength."

Angie realized she'd been looking for some redeeming feature in Paul's makeup. This wasn't it. "A stepping-stone. Power for the sake of advancement? Isn't that a bit cold-blooded?"

"You asked me, I'm telling you. Do you imagine your father's reasons for putting my name forward are altruistic? Or for that matter that his own involvement on the sidelines of politics is out of a sense of deep commitment?"

"Commitment, no, but he certainly believes he's contributing to the welfare of the party and, I suppose, of the country. I don't think he'd do it otherwise."

"Then you're extremely naïve. Politics is a peer group club and has the same advantages as any other exclusive club. For someone with my background, it's the next best thing to being invited to play polo with Prince Charles."

Angie didn't smile at the scorn those words conveyed. "Don't you care about *anything*?"

Paul laughed at her emphasis. "You've been away too long, or maybe you actually believe that the class structure no longer exists? Morality? We could discuss that. I've never been unfaithful to my wife. I love my son, and I've never been convicted of a crime. Why are you so surprised that I'd take what I can get from politics? The only difference between me and your father is that it would never occur to him that he *was* taking anything . . . and do you know why? Because he considers it his rightful due *anyway*."

Angie was astounded, by his honesty or his cynicism, she wasn't sure which. "You hate him."

"No. He's important to me. I can't afford to hate him."

"Aren't you afraid I'll tell him?"

"I might be cold-blooded, as you say, but I'm not stupid. You wouldn't do anything to . . . harm me."

"How can you be so sure?" she asked in a small voice. Her hands were trembling again. He didn't answer, just looked at her with wide-eyed complacency. My God, is there anything about me he doesn't know? He was demonstrating his power; now that he was assured of her vulnerability, he felt free to press home his advantage.

As Angie began to rise, he got up, too, reaching for his jacket. "Are you leaving?" she asked, looking up at him.

"When will I see you again?"

"Please call . . . don't just turn up."

"What are you afraid of, that I'll interrupt something?"

She had to smile; he made it impossible for her to say yes or no.

The front door closed behind him. Not once had they parted with any semblance of civility. She was relieved by his sudden exit, emptied as the room was. Yet as she stood there, poised in the silence, she realized that she was listening for the sound of his returning footsteps.

25

☐ There was an innate godlessness abroad, Arion decided, and he had done nothing to bring about any change in what he saw. In ways he could not begin to define, he had somehow contributed to it. It seemed to him, waiting for word from James Bonnier, that it was too late for him and Ani. Their time had passed. There was too much he did not know and things he would never be able to learn. How, then, could he protect his own?

"We will go back." Ani soothed him, kissing his eyelids. "We will go home, Ari, and those who love us will come there."

She was right. A lifetime away would mean little to the people of Mandraki. It would be the same. Nothing changed: the olives were still plucked; the corn was reaped and stored for feeding the animals; the melons were left ripening in the sun; water was drawn from the communal well; the *kafenion*, for all its plastic coating, was as it had been in his childhood. He awoke, shivering in the night, despair and longing bringing agony to his bones. This was not the way, he wanted to shout at his God, this was not the way it had been promised. So much care gone to waste, so many questions he had childishly expected answers to.

Arion sat in his office, a glass of chilled guava juice in front of him, a green salad, now wilting, beside the telephone. What he wanted was the rasp of ouzo hitting the back of his throat, the sound of voices and the sun. Old bones. He mocked himself. Old bones needed the warmth of the sun.

"Ach," he grunted, pushing the salad farther away, ignoring the juice. He patted all his pockets until he found his bifocals on the newspaper in front of him. He placed them on the end of his nose and peered down. He had not been mistaken. Angel Holding's shares stood at sixty-five pence, a drop of thirteen pence in a matter of days.

Why had he not heard from his financial adviser? he wondered. The man whose company could have existed on the fees earned from Angel Holding's alone had not advised him of this mysterious fluctuation.

As he always did, Arion went into the next-door office rather than press the buzzer on his desk and asked his secretary to get his adviser on the telephone.

"He's likely to be at lunch," she demurred.

"Please try." He went back into his own office to wait. The lunchtime sounds of Soho seeped through to him. On such a bright day there was less scurrying, fewer cars blasting out their impatience in the narrow streets.

The three-story house in Greek Street which he had acquired floor by floor over the years was as dear and familiar to him as his family home. Paul had loathed it from the outset. It bore none of the glossy trappings his father could easily have afforded. Two steep flights of stairs left visitors gasping, and although the rooms were light and airy, they were small.

It did the old man's standing no good, it breathed meanness to Paul, a lack of insight, and it shamed him whenever he had to go there.

Perhaps his City friends, after all these years, shared Paul's misgivings? Would his financial adviser also have preferred Arion to take a suite in the glass and chrome perfection of Angel House?

The phone rang, and the other's voice came through the wire hesitantly. "Ari, I've been meaning to call you. How are you, old boy?"

"I am well, and Ani is well. I have been expecting to hear from you."

"Ha-ha, well better late than never, eh? I take it you're referring to the share price quoted this morning? A seasonal fluctuation, so don't worry about it."

"I am worried. Tell me what you know, please." In his mind's eye Arion could see the man, pinched and birdlike, fidgeting.

"Well, hardly anything at all, old boy. Shares have changed hands."

"That I know," Arion sighed. "How many and at what price?"

"I can't be sure about the number."

"Who is selling?"

"There's no way I can find that out yet. Two or three brokers have sold stock, and no one is buying."

"Try to find out, my friend. I want to know who is selling and why they are selling."

"I'm sure it's nothing we should be unduly concerned about, but I'll see what I can do. I'll get back to you soonest."

"I am here for one more hour. I will hear from you before I leave." For the first time in his life Arion felt *used*, out of control. He replaced the receiver and reached automatically into his inside pocket for a cigar. What was it Frank had said about the old lion still having teeth?

Early October, he decided, pushing everything else from his mind. It would be cooler in Mandraki, and maybe they would spend Christmas there. Why not? If he could persuade Scotia, perhaps Olga and her boys would come, too; it was part of their heritage as well. . . .

The urgency wouldn't leave him. It lapped at his vitality and made his heart thud like a hammer in his chest. He got

up and went into the outer office again. "I will be at Ani's,"
he told his secretary. "Please put telephone calls through to
me there."

Arion walked with care down the stairs and out into the
sunlight, the unlit cigar still clutched between his fingers.
Scotia would listen to him, and perplexity would wrap itself
into the folds of his face. He knew only the restaurant business, nothing else. Of City dealings he knew nothing. Of
English gentlemen who controlled small empires like Angelou's he *wanted* to know nothing. Of what lay in Arion's heart
he knew everything. In this, especially, was it not the way it
had been promised, for that knowledge should have belonged
to one man only: his son.

And Arion knew he could no more communicate that to
Paul than he could snatch back the years of his youth.

26

☐ Leo Bass circled the block twice in the borrowed blue
Fiesta. Then he parked in one of the side streets leading off
from the back of the warehouse and strolled casually around
the block. There were not too many people around on a Saturday afternoon in this industrial section of Eltham. To avoid
drawing attention to himself, he walked purposefully, darting
eyes hidden behind dark glasses.

The warehouse was surrounded by a six-foot-high chain-
link fence. Well kept, but without the usual barbed-wire top-
ping. The enormous one-story building stood about twenty
feet from the fence. There were loading bays on each side of
the double concertina metal doors and a small access door
for the staff. Built as an extension in one corner was a dwarfed
brick room, boasting one window. The sign on the door read
PRIVATE, and an ancient rusting bicycle stood propped up
against the elevation of one of the loading bays.

Leo bent over to untie and retie the lace on one of his
shoes. The front gate was secured with a chain and padlock.

Whistling, he continued around the block, crossing to the other side of the street before he reached the small back entrance again. A metal door. It didn't look like much, not thick or too heavy.

Back in the car, he adjusted the rearview mirror and winked at his reflection. It was on.

27

☐ Frank arrived late at the office. It was close to three o'clock before he began leafing through the accumulated correspondence: four royalty statements; two rejection letters, one with a postscripted invitation to lunch. There was also a short letter from Farley Esterhuys which ended on an angry note. He had received Lisa's letter telling him she was going to auction *Night Work* herself in New York. Frank consigned the letter to his file tray. Too bad. That was the arrangement they'd made, open-ended. Nothing, he decided, was going to dispel the mood of quiet pleasure with which he had returned from visiting his wife and the boys in Norfolk.

The weekend had been good, despite thirteen-year-old Mark's reticence, for all the younger Sandy's rebellious demands. Molly, too, had appeared happier, somehow more rounded. She still observed her two sons as though they were strange, rampant intruders who had been left behind by mistake. In less than a year, Frank guessed, Mark would be taller than his mother. In a bemused way she had already begun to treat him as an adult.

He had delayed his departure until Monday morning, breakfasting with the boys, later having to go in search of his wife to say good-bye. She was in the chicken run, hair afloat with feathers. As he approached, he decided the eggs would be healthily brown. They were. His laugh startled her into returning his affectionate kiss.

The sun was shining when he got back to London. A glimpse of the trees fringing Epping Forest reminded him that he was meeting Angie that evening. It had been her suggestion that they meet at the Serpentine in Hyde Park. Next time the zoo, he'd said, not altogether surprised to hear her name a date. . . .

The sound of Lisa's voice just before she walked into his office coincided with the telephone's ringing. She paced around with nervous energy until he'd finished and then said, unnecessarily, "You're back. Have you heard the news?" She had tied her hair back with a red and white polka-dot ribbon that had come partly undone and now hung down across her shoulder. "It happened just after you left on Friday afternoon. I tried to call you over the weekend."

"I was in Norfolk."

"Oh. Well, it's *Night Work*. I've had a preemptive offer, and guess who from?"

"From whom." She was itching to tell him. "Tell me."

"Angela Wyatt. She loves it! But listen to this: a two-book contract, sixty-five thousand pounds for *Night Work* and sixty-five thousand pounds for the next one."

Good God, Frank thought. He said, "Well, well."

He was impressed. Lisa could see it. As well he should be. "And I've accepted her offer. I've spent this morning phoning all the other publishers and withdrawing the book from the auction. What do you think?"

I think I'd like to kiss you, right now. . . . "Congratulations, you made the right decision. It's a marvelous offer. It couldn't have been easy for you. What did Elliot have to say?"

Still standing, Lisa giggled. "Not much. I think he probably fainted for a while. Are you sure I did the right thing?"

"Positive. I must remember to congratulate Angie, too. I'm seeing her tonight."

"Again?" The word escaped involuntarily, and Lisa braced herself for his corrosive snort. For once he let it pass.

"Have you got everything fixed up for your trip next week? I've decided to give New York a miss, by the way. It's all yours. I should warn you, though, that Farley isn't too happy to be missing out on *Night Work*."

Perplexed by this sudden change of plan, Lisa nodded curtly. Did it have anything to do with Angela Wyatt? There was a twinge of something that felt suspiciously like jealousy but which she put down to disdain for Frank's unpredictable behavior.

"You're not disappointed, are you?" Was that sarcasm?

"Not at all," she said stiffly. "What made you change your mind?"

"No one thing particularly. Besides, you're a big girl now; you'll manage." The look of childish bewilderment on her face so surprised him that he added, "It's better this way. You don't really want me to be seen to be holding your hand, do you?"

"Well, if you're not coming, I'd like not to have to see Farley in New York."

"Out of the question," he snapped. "You'll leave your personal feelings aside and take lunch or dinner with him, whatever he suggests."

"He makes my skin crawl!" She turned her back on him and began pacing around again.

"Too bad. You can't pick and choose. This is real life, remember?"

Her immediate reaction was incredulous anger, and her face paled with it. "Real life? *Explain that!*"

"Stop hovering like a demented dragonfly, and I'll try. I thought we'd been through this before." She sat down, and he marveled at his instant annoyance, the increasing facility for communicating it to her. "Without Farley's list we're not exactly dead, but we're gasping. Do you understand that? We *need* him. Maybe we won't need him forever, but at the moment we do. The fact that you disapprove of him and his list is neither here nor there. That he makes your skin crawl is even less relevant. If I could change it, I'd give him the list of Farrar, Straus and the looks of Paul Newman. But I can't, and you're stuck with it. Do you imagine I—" He stopped, hearing his own voice hectoring in his head.

"What were you going to say?"

"Never mind."

She insisted. "I want to know."

He sat back in his chair. Why not? It was time she knew anyway. "Have you ever wondered what we do night after night when he's here? No? Well, I'll tell you. Farley is into girls—the pun is intentional. I take him, because he insists on being escorted, to strip clubs and porn shows. He needs to talk about it, what they look like and what he's going to do to them. Surprised? He likes blondes, small blondes, very young, fresh-faced blondes. Do you know how many brothels there are in Soho?"

"I don't believe you!"

"No?" There was no humor in the sound. "All *you* have to do is have a meal with him. All right?" For a moment he thought she was going to fight him. Maybe she should have, it occurred to him later, driving across town to meet Angie. But she had nodded, the pallor still in her cheeks.

"All right," he said. "Pax. Now, what do you say we have a cup of tea to wash away the taste of Mr. Esterhuys?"

"I think I need something stronger to take it away."

"At four o'clock in the afternoon?" he chided her gently.

"Why not? Isn't that what big girls do?"

He almost believed he hadn't heard her correctly. He chuckled, and the sound exploded into laughter. Christ, she was nothing if not honest, registering delight at his reaction, coming forward to take the glass from his hand.

Safely behind his desk, he saw her down the three fingers of scotch without a word and without so much as a grimace. She actually licked her lips. Then she walked out of the office and slammed the door so hard that the whiskey cup skittered off his desk.

While Frank went into the kitchen to open a fresh bottle of burgundy, Angie stepped out onto the tiny balcony of her flat. Chelsea had become a place for the very young and the very old, she thought, those who dressed to look older and those who dressed to look younger. The style, she observed, seemed unique to Chelsea. The extremes were soft cashmere sweaters and low-heeled court shoes for those who trekked in from Knightsbridge; multicolored drapes like the scarves from a magician's sleeve for others.

Two hours earlier, waiting for Frank at the Serpentine, she had decided to sell the flat and move to North London, buy something bigger, more like a home. She felt like a tenant in the flat, a squatter waiting to be evicted. Standing at the edge of the Serpentine, shivering as an early-evening breeze whipped across her ankles, she realized that the flat itself was one of the reasons why she still felt like a visitor in London.

There were few people about in Hyde Park at that hour. Londoners did not use their parks the way New Yorkers did. In New York she and Lou had joined the evening and weekend strollers, Saturday afternoon shopping, Sunday morning brunch, then winding their way through the tiny boutiques, collector's shops, and galleries, more often than not ending up in Central Park. Moth-eaten Central Park; it had nothing of the lush perfection of Hyde Park, but it was used. New Yorkers jogged and played and roller-skated to music. Londoners lolled and fondled and brought out cold white wine. . . .

Angie went back into the living room and shut the balcony door. Frank lay sprawled on the couch, an ashtray with a small heap of white stubs beside him on the floor.

Frank watched her as she drew the curtains and turned to face him. She looked strangely exotic and remote in the caftan with its front panels of velvet and brocade; the robe was made up of a patchwork of oriental silks with gold binding and reembroidered with gold sequins; when she moved, the back swirled out and gave the impression that she was gliding along on skates.

"I like that very much," he said.

"The caftan? Thea Porter, one of the two things I didn't sling out after Cissy and I spent those three days shopping."

She was wandering restlessly around the room, running her fingers over the shelves and the spines of books. She paused to pick up a small paperweight. "I swear I've never seen this before," she said, putting it down again.

Frank waited for her to rejoin him. He didn't know what to make of her present mood, but she wasn't to be rushed. The revelation that she had a nineteen-year-old daughter had floored him. She had told him about the rape, the child, and her discussion with Christopher Chetwynd all in the space of ten minutes, using short, flatly factual sentences, stumbling now and then over certain words. He allowed her to talk without interruption. Sympathy was not what she was looking for; she was using him, in a way, to broaden her own perspective and to reinforce her belief that she had made the right decision. He wanted to help her, involve himself immediately by telling her about his own children, but before he could begin, she'd switched off, cut short the monologue by leaving the room. She'd spent half an hour in the kitchen, and when she finally emerged, she was carrying a plate of sandwiches which neither had so far touched.

Frank found a clean spot in the ashtray and ground out his cigarette. Out of the corner of his eye he saw her retrace her steps and pick up the paperweight once more. She balanced it thoughtfully in the palm of her hand and then went into the kitchen, where he heard it thud into the dustbin. When she came back, there was a look of satisfaction on her face.

"You remembered who gave it to you," Frank said.

"No, but what the hell, it was ugly."

She'd made up her mind about something. She collected her wineglass, placed it carefully beside his ashtray, and settled down on the floor with her back against the couch. "Talk to me, Frank." When she said that, it usually meant talk about something else, I need to be reminded of other things.

"You have three enviable assets," he said slowly, refusing to be drawn. "Money, beauty, and the ability to rope yourself off."

Angie picked up her glass and began tapping her fingernail against the rim. "Cissy said more or less the same thing not so long ago."

His hand came down and rested on her shoulder. "Do you want to find your daughter because of what happened to Lou? Do you want to move away from here because she might want to come and live with you?"

"I wish I knew. I suppose the answer to both those questions is yes. But it's more than that; I *have* to find her."

"Then why don't you accept that, stop punishing yourself this way?"

"Because the one reason for finding her that I can identify, very clearly, has to do with *me*, and it's a selfish reason, whichever way I look at it. *I* have to know that she's alive and happy. *I* need that . . . consolation if I'm ever to get on with my own life again."

"Why is that selfish? She *is* your daughter, and it's not as though you had any choices at the time."

"I wish that helped, but it doesn't. Sometimes I have this insane idea that if I analyze my own motives too closely, I won't be able to go through with it."

He couldn't be sure that she wasn't backing away from him again. No one deserved to go through such a time alone. From what she'd left unsaid, he could just about imagine her isolation in the years before she'd met Lou and in the months following his death. And what she must be feeling now, racked by so much doubt and urgency that it left her almost breathless. "Do they know about the child?"

"The boys who raped me? I'm not sure, but I guess not. Do you think they have a right to know?"

"I don't think it's a question of right," he said carefully.

He understood why she was asking: had they, too, been cheated in this drama? He wanted desperately to give her the answer she was looking for. "Such . . . peculiar decisions were taken at the time."

"Peculiar?" She twisted around to look up at him, breathing rapidly again, as though she could not draw enough air into her lungs. "That's not what you're thinking. You're thinking about your own children, aren't you?"

She was right. If he and Molly had broken off their affair instead of getting married, she could easily have left with the embryo of his child inside her. He would never have known.

"It's not the same, Frank. This fathering had nothing to do with them . . . those boys. I realize what that sounds like, but rape obliterates everything I would consider normal. I was forced then, and I'm still living without having made any decisions: to name them as rapists; to have the child; to keep the child; to be hidden away without knowing what happened to the child. None of these decisions was mine. Is there something in the male psyche that prevents them from understanding what it's like to be physically violated? Have you ever been threatened? Has anyone ever forced you to do anything, to—have you ever been *helpless*?" She ended the sentence quickly, drawing away from him a little, moving with an inner torment so apparent that his hand tightened to keep her.

"I've been afraid once or twice, but never—or at least I've never considered the possibility of being helpless, which is almost the same thing."

He felt her shiver under his hand. "Think about it, Frank."

"I can't. Not in your terms. I think that kind of helplessness would shame rather than frighten me."

Angie sighed. She got up and retreated to an armchair close by. "Shame is the one thing we can't articulate. Even at the time, if it hadn't been so brutal and even if the decision hadn't been taken away from me, I would have considered saying nothing. I was ashamed. Through no fault of my own, I'd been shamed. I've heard people, friends, say of rape victims, 'At least she wasn't harmed,' the assumption being that one man more or less doesn't make much difference. She'd be better off forgetting about it; it's worse but not much worse than someone pressing up against you on a train."

"That's nonsense," Frank said roughly.

"Is it? Lou understood a little, I think, because he was

affronted by the idea of anyone else, by force or not, being inside me. And he did help me to rationalize it, to accept what happened as fact and go on from there. The trouble now is, Where to?''

"Christ, Angie, why are you being so hard on yourself? Who wouldn't be scared? The implications are . . . formidable. You've considered the possibility that your daughter might not know she's adopted, but what if she *does* know, without knowing the circumstances?''

''And what will happen if she wants to know who her father is? I think what scares me the most isn't any of that at all. It's the sort of person I've become, whether I'll be able to cope with her problems as well as my own. Cissy says I walk around with a hands-off sign around my neck. You say I have—what was it?—an ability to rope myself off. You're both right. It's too late to play the role of mother, but if it ever did come to that, what would this child of mine find?''

Frank hauled himself upright and refilled both their glasses before going back to the couch. "Mine wasn't a particularly astute observation. I was only trying to get you to talk.''

"Apparently I don't do that often enough either. Good God, that sounds pathetic. I'm feeling extremely sorry for myself, you understand.''

"I'm not going to say you're entitled to, but for what it's worth, I can't see how your decision can be wrong. *Your* rights have been abused all down the line, and for all I know, so have your daughter's. You'll have to decide for both of you when the time comes—''

"Whether to tell her if she doesn't already know? I can't think about that.''

"You don't have to, Angie. There'll be time enough later.''

She would have to have enough strength to walk away, that was what she was thinking; that was the blackest part of her nightmare, the one prospect she couldn't yet begin to contemplate. "Lou said it would be like digging into one's family history and taking the chance of finding out that your grandmother was Lizzie Borden. Do you have fantasies, Frank?''

"About Lizzie Borden?''

Angie laughed. "You wouldn't be the first. My own fantasies are so simple they can hardly be called that.'' And they were in black and white, like an old home movie, the subject always too far away, barely in focus. Sometimes she conjured up a six-year-old with red hair and freckles, sometimes a solemn, pale fourteen-year-old with dark hair and questioning eyes. "This wine is going to my head. Are you ready for a sandwich? Smoked salmon, no cucumber."

Frank was hungry quite suddenly, remembering that he hadn't eaten anything since breakfast with his sons. "What are the chances of finding your daughter?" he asked between mouthfuls.

"Oliver's lawyer said good at first, but I understand he's now encountering some problems. He wasn't too keen to discuss them. I'm glad you're going to be here, Frank; I mean, that you've decided not to go to New York with Lisa. That's selfish, but with Oliver and Cissy gone—"

"How is Oliver?"

"Rough, Cissy says. It was never going to be easy, but she says it's worse than anything she could have anticipated. She's taken a cottage in a village near the clinic."

"Have you been down?"

"She won't let me, not yet. Soon, though."

"I'll drive you down."

"Why?"

"Because you don't have a car, that's why."

Angie pushed her tongue against the inside of her cheek to hold back a smile at the gruffness in his voice. If she had any sense at all, she'd fall in love with Frank Sheldon and the hell with Lisa Barrett and Paul Angelou. Paul had sat where Frank was now, demanding and unsatisfied. Like a teenager, Angie felt her cheeks and neck redden at the memory of his pressuring mouth, a miserly gift even if he hadn't meant it to be, a test she had no way of knowing whether she'd passed or failed. She would have opened herself to him then, except that that had no longer seemed to be the objective. She had rejected him on earlier occasions, and she had begun to realize that if he couldn't have everything, he would ask for nothing. . . .

"When is Lisa leaving?" she asked, coming back to Frank.

"Thursday. I think she's beginning to regret her decision to auction *Night Work* on the spot, though. Not an easy thing to do on your first trip. She was flabbergasted by your offer. I don't mind telling you that I was, too."

"It's a wonderful novel, and Jarman's needs it. I can't say my father was delighted when I told him."

"But he agreed, that's the main thing. You're enjoying it, aren't you?"

"Being at Jarman's? Oddly, yes. There's so much to be done, I don't have much time to think about anything else. I'm excited by the possibility of making it *work*, pulling it all together. But I do dread . . ." She hesitated, and Frank saw tension thread its way through her once more.

"Oliver," he said. "How your success in the job will reflect on Oliver's reputation? Let me spare you some heartache on that score. Anyone who's been in the business for more than ten minutes knows that Oliver isn't a book man. I'm sorry if that sounds too simple; but it's true, and it matters. Publishing isn't a profession; it's a way of life."

"And it was never Oliver's way of life. Still, he's spent practically half his life doing it."

"And hating it. We both know that. If printer's ink runs in any Jarman's veins, it runs in yours. It's instinct, nothing you can learn. Do it, Angie, you're *good* at it."

"We'll see. . . . I've got a year to play around with. Incidentally, would you like me to call some people in New York, arrange a few things discreetly for Lisa?"

"Good God, no. She'd have my guts for garters if I interfered. In any case, a few knocks wouldn't do her any harm."

"I envy you," Angie said wistfully, thinking of her own compromised and complicated world.

"It's driving me crazy."

"I can tell. Why don't you say something to her?"

Frank picked up another sandwich and squinted at her. "Because she'd probably run a mile, leave. . . . She can't know what she wants herself."

"She's not a child, Frank," Angie said gently.

"That's what she keeps telling me. Where are you going?"

"To make some coffee. Want some?"

He followed her into the kitchen, grinning behind her back. "Are you sure I'm not allowed to fall in love with you instead?"

Angie switched on the electric kettle and placed two cups and saucers on a small tray. When she turned, her eyes were alight with amusement. "I'm as sure as you are. In any case, the person you're looking at isn't the person you think you're looking at."

"I thought as much," he said, feeling slightly drunk and wanting Lisa. He patted Angie in a brotherly fashion and went back to the couch.

Alone in the kitchen, Angie laughed at herself. They comforted each other like children, innocently, with a lifetime of friendship ahead. He would have his Lisa; unless the girl was blind and stupid, it was just a question of time. And *still*, she thought, and *still*, she hadn't mentioned the other fantasy in her life, the recent Technicolor daydream: Paul Angelou.

28

☐ Cory was still convinced that one night of luck would change everything. There were laws of logic that persuaded him to keep trying, and the harder he tried, the more wrong decisions he made.

Tonight, in desperation, he decided to make the dealer play against him. For an hour or so it worked. To the annoyance of the other players at the table, he stuck each time on two cards totaling anything over twelve.

Cory looked around for Leo as the chips began to pile up at his elbow. Leo was standing with his back to him, playing roulette. It was still early evening, and the club had not yet begun to fill up. Cory felt good. Tonight was the night the tables would work for him. They had to, because it was his last chance to get out of doing what Leo had planned for them. The idea frightened him not because of the danger he would be involved in but because of the possibility of Arion finding out.

Two hours later, when Leo had eventually worked his way around the room and come to stand behind his chair, Cory was down to seventy-five pounds. He began to limit his stake once more to five pounds, waiting for a new dealer to take over and change his luck again.

"I'm going to get a drink. Are you coming?"

"Later, Leo. I was going good for a time; you should have seen me."

Leo lingered, watching the game with a tight grin of contempt. Cory pulled a queen and an eight, the dealer turned up an ace and an eight; on the next hand Cory pulled a ten, a three and hesitated over a third card. Stupid, Leo thought, since the dealer had drawn a six . . . even if the dealer had pulled a picture as a second card, he would still have to draw again. Cory decided on a third card, and Leo walked away when he saw what it was: a jack.

By eleven o'clock it was all over. Cory wanted a drink, but the last hand had taken all his silver and left only a few coppers, which now lay heavily against his thigh. He went to the bar, head swiveling in search of a familiar face. Leo was there, drinking alone. "*Now* I get to buy you a drink, right?" Leo said as Cory joined him.

"Sure. I was just going to get myself one. Tequila Sunrise."

Leo watched the barman mix the multicolored drink and took a sip of his own brandy. He didn't relish what he had to do, but tonight was Soames's deadline, and Cory was still behaving as though the money he owed were two hundred and sixty pounds, not twenty-six thousand. He and Soames didn't want to scare the young Greek off, and they didn't want to take on the law by bruising him a little.

"Cheers," Leo said, raising his glass. Cory grimaced. "Not good, eh?"

"A temporary setback." Cory donned his mask of bravado. He didn't want to chat. What he wanted was a fast two hundred to start again.

Leo saw the heavy-lidded brown eyes rest contemplatively on him. "Don't ask," he said. "Don't even think it. You're in deep enough as it is."

Cory shrugged, but the words sent a shiver of panic down his spine. What the hell was he going to do?

"My principal wants to see you when you leave here. Now don't do anything silly, like trying to sneak off, OK?"

Principal. Leo spoke as though this moneylender were some sort of anonymous god. "Why should I? If you think I'm afraid of your principal, you're crazy. He wants to see me? Well, let's go see him now, OK?" There was too much forced nonchalance in his voice. "Where is he, waiting outside? You want to walk me out in case I get myself lost?" Cory shoved his chair back.

"Relax, sit down. I don't think you realize how much trouble you're in. Twenty-six thousand pounds, that's not pocket money."

"What do you want me to do, cry?"

"For a start you can cut out the cheap answers and listen very carefully to me. Now isn't the time to feel sorry for yourself. Nobody forced you into anything, remember that. You did it yourself and even now, even *now* you would give your eyeteeth for a fiver. But I'll do you a favor and tell you what you're going to hear from my prin—the boss. Today is Monday. You've got until eleven o'clock on Wednesday morning before we walk into your grandfather's office and present him with the bill. All of it, chapter and verse."

Bastards! Leo had tentatively planned the warehouse break-in for Tuesday night. Now they were giving him until Wednesday morning.

"Let me get you another drink"—Leo leaned forward—"because it gets even worse than that. Someone, somewhere might have told you that gambling debts are not covered by any law. Just in case you believe that, I'm here to tell you that it's not true, at least not in your case. What you've signed is not an IOU on an empty cigarette packet, understand? If your grandfather refuses to bail you out, other means will be found to recover the money, and don't ask me if that's a threat, because it is. Please make no mistake about it. . . . I wouldn't like to see anything happen to you or your family."

Bastard! Cory's fists clenched. Bastard. They were all in this together. He made a show of downing the last inch of the drink lying at the bottom of the glass. "I'm leaving now," he said haughtily. "You will please tell your *boss* that I will see him at eleven o'clock on Wednesday morning. Not now."

"Don't be stupid."

"Tell him, Leo! That is my final word."

Leo followed him out of the casino, and Cory's resolve faltered with each step. "You betrayed me," he said softly when they reached his Alfa.

"What the hell do you mean, betrayed?" Leo laughed. "What kind of a word is that?"

"You told him—your principal—about the warehouse, about the safe, didn't you?"

Leo put both his elbows on the roof of the car. Betrayed? It sounded like Greta Garbo dialogue. The excitement Leo felt at the prospect of the break-in had little to do with recovering his and Soames's money. He had had to use all his powers of persuasion to get Soames's agreement. "Going to Arion Angelou would be the simplest and safest solution, right enough," Soames had said. "Why risk a run-in with the police?'' Leo didn't say: Because it's like a fix, better than sniffing cocaine. He said: ''Because we, you and I, get to share whatever money is left over after the basic has been paid off. Who knows, maybe there's a hundred thousand or more in the safe?''

''Well?'' Cory was demanding. ''Did you tell him about the warehouse?''

A grin of pure malice stretched Leo's lips back from his teeth. ''What do you think?''

Cory understood. He could have killed Leo then. He could have battered him into a pulp that bled all over the tarmac. It was what he wanted to do more than anything, yet a cold grip of caution held him back.

Leo recognized the fury, saw it flare and abate. ''My place, now,'' he said. He strolled to the passenger side of the car and waited for Cory to unlock the door.

They drove in silence. When they arrived at Leo's expensively furnished second-floor flat near Marble Arch, Leo drew a folded page of lined paper from his pocket. On it he'd drawn a sketch of the warehouse and its perimeter fence. ''Sit down and look at this,'' he said. ''Tell me where the safe is and what's going on around it. I want to know everything, the forklift trucks, the clocks, the lights. Everything.''

29

☐ At first Oliver knew for certain that he was going to die. He also knew that dying would be easy, much easier than this, a welcome, blessed relief. He stopped hating himself and turned his curses on those who kept him here, confined, drugged, every second an eternity of pain. His eyes watered, his nose ran, and his body convulsed, spewing out what they gave him to eat and drink, denying their insistence that he was here to live, not to die.

From screaming nightmares he woke to find reality harsher; he no longer bit back his cries and his pleas because nothing mattered, not the strangers around him, not Cissy, whose face floated before him. They gloved his hands to stop him from injuring himself. In his mind's eye it was Cissy who was inflicting the agony; everyone who touched him was Cissy, and he reached for her, even when she wasn't there, fingers curling for her throat. He held on, squeezing until his hands stopped shaking. But she wouldn't die; she was always there, pulling his eyelids back, pressing a needle into his arm, wiping his face, holding him as he shook and shook and wept because it was so very cold.

Then he began to dream that it was over; he dreamed that he fell asleep and woke up to light, a soft light unbroken by warped flashes of color. Just light and quiet. Cissy came again. She worked the glove away from his fingers and held them. He wanted to tell her that she was dead, but sleep snatched him away forcibly. And he dreamed of sleep, weightless, sightless, floating safely. . . .

Cissy was telling him a story, a fairy tale about giants, a mountainous island and shipwrecked sailors trapped in a castle, jackknives, shellfish, and gnawing rats, a beautiful princess with long dark hair, epic journeys, and a golden hero with an Arabic name. The plot was Kafkaesque, but she made no concessions for him, continually dredging up characters long since fallen by the way, weaving a monstrous entanglement for him. Drifting in and out of the story, much the same way as the characters, he waited for a happy ending. When it didn't come, he thought she'd plotted herself into a corner, dimly aware of disappointment, of Cissy sitting silently beside him.

For the first time she said, "Are you awake?"

The light was blinding; his jaw felt slack. If the story had been a dream, he could retell it to Cissy. He saw her through slitted eyes. "What happened?"

She thought he meant, What happened to me, where have I been? She said, "You had a run-in with a juggernaut, but you're going to live." The metaphor was no exaggeration as she saw it.

"Cissy?" Was she smiling? "What happened to him, Rashid?"

"You heard all that?" She laughed with delight, and he reached reflexively for her hand. "Well, the sea subsided, he got ashore, rescued the princess, and they lived happily ever after."

"No." He groaned, and his eyelids drooped once more. "He hadn't been adopted or sold into slavery? What's the real ending, Cissy? Tell me the *real* ending."

She told him the real ending a week later. They sat facing each other in the pleasant warmth of a sunroom, a plate of biscuits between them. She wanted to cry, but there was too much light in the room. Even his voice was weightless. Her hands trembled more than his, rattling the teacup against the saucer.

The worst was not over, but he had come through the beginning, the part he'd had to do alone. What faced them both now was not something either wanted to anticipate. "One day at a time," the doctors and therapists repeated; it was up to Oliver, and they knew that nothing would ever be the same for him again, that he would live the rest of his life wanting to lift a glass to his lips. Just once. And once was enough.

Depression clouded his vision without warning. Cissy had come to recognize the look that said: Enough, enough about Pamela's studies, Angie's acquisitions at Jarman's, the outside world that bore no relevance to this place. There was something frightening about the despair, bringing, as it did, a lethargy so deep it left him almost comatose. Her instincts were to chatter, to joke and drag him out of it, but his glance, so bleak, stopped her.

Angie was becoming impatient. Cissy spoke to her sister-in-law almost daily from the small cottage; when they weren't talking about Oliver, Angie sounded happy, at least contented. She still refused to discuss Paul Angelou, but Frank Sheldon's name came up more than anyone else's. He was, in some capacity, involved in her life. The notion of the two of them surprised and pleased Oliver. Maybe it would weaken her determination to find her daughter and reopen all the old wounds; there's been too much bloodletting already. . . .

He said to Cissy, "Would you take the chance, after all these years?"

"Yes." She couldn't imagine any other answer.

"Even if it hurts the child?"

"It's very unlikely she doesn't know she's adopted. There's bound to be some bitterness, but think, darling, *think* what it must be like to have a child and not know her. For all Angie knows, they might have met each other at some time."

"Come now, that sounds like one of Deborah's romantic melodramas."

"Do you honestly think it's a mistake?"

Reluctantly he nodded. "But I wouldn't try to stop its happening."

"Would you help?"

There was a short silence. She was giving him a chance to say no. Finally she said, "I have an idea your parents know much much more about it than they admit. And they admit to nothing, you've told me."

Listening to the words articulated had a jolting effect. That's because I've never asked them. Neither has Angie. *We've never talked about it.* Oliver shifted uneasily in his chair and jerked up the rug covering his legs and thighs. The lingering memories of those days could still drive him into a dark corner. Crouching there was not a new experience. A few drinks would have let in some light.

"What time will Angie be here tomorrow?" He wasn't sure he was ready to face his sister.

"Frank is driving her down; they'll be here sometime before lunch."

A sickening wave of nausea flared out from his chest and surged up into his throat. With it came a trembling that shook his limbs and clamped his teeth together. The spasm left him weak and wet with perspiration. "Can't you put her off?"

"Of course," Cissy said. "If that's really what you want."

It wasn't what he wanted. He shook his head, turning away from the anguish he saw in Cissy's eyes. It was time for her to leave. Tomorrow Angie would be here. Tomorrow would be better.

30

☐ The percentages were against him, and Sidney knew he would have to watch his step. There was menace in the woman's silence, a dispassionate objectivity in her glance. He couldn't help noticing that Martin had begun to spend the odd lunch hour in his office with the door shut, ostensibly reading through piles of typescripts. That he was actually supping from a bottle secreted in the large lower drawer of his desk Sidney had no doubt. That the *Times* crossword lay folded between the typescript pages he had no doubt either.

They'd all been in and had their little chat with Angela Wyatt. Everyone except him. And not one of them was laying it on the line for *him*; not one of them was prepared to disclose whatever it was that she had discussed with them. The longer it went on, the more viciously it twisted at his gut. Bloody, *bloody* woman. Who was she that she thought he could not make her squirm? As the days went by, he nonetheless found himself putting off appointment after appointment in anticipation of her summons. It didn't come. She was interviewing the production people now . . . and still no call.

It was a game, a war of nerves. He knew it, and he knew that she realized he knew it. The knowledge brought him no satisfaction. She had collided with his world inside Jarman's without acknowledging the slightest bump. Women—what they all needed was a good screw. Old adage, good advice. She was no different. The only problem was that he could not imagine Angela Wyatt unclothed and submissive. However hard he tried to superimpose her face and body on other women, the imaginative feat escaped him. If he lost his confrontation with her, there was a dead end ahead, a black spot that blocked out his particular sun.

That morning, despite the hot July weather, he'd donned a tie and jacket. Until a few weeks ago editorial meetings had been just another pain-in-the-ass two hours on a Tuesday morning. Now it was different. Today was to be her first meeting, and he wanted to impress her, to take control and stun her into silence. This would be the meeting that would define their roles. Already he was infuriated that none of the others had dared add any comments on the reports circulated before the meeting. They seemed to have interpreted her bland tick against her initials as one of disapproval. Not one of them had had the balls to take a chance on her reaction.

The secretary Deborah shared with Martin dropped an agenda on his desk half an hour before the meeting. Apart from one American thriller which he had read and circulated a report on, it looked like being a dull meeting, until recently hardly worth turning up for. If it hadn't been for *Night Work* and the ridiculous rumors flying around, he might have considered absenting himself altogether on some pretext.

The others were all there, sitting around the elongated boardroom table when he arrived shortly before ten o'clock. Dunne Morrissey picked nervously at his fraying cuticles. Martin was doodling down the margin of the agenda in front of him. As Sidney turned to stop the hinged door from slamming shut behind him, he almost crashed into Angie, who had followed him in.

She wore a loose, sleeveless shirtdress in brilliant peacock blue and carried nothing apart from cigarettes and book matches. Not even a pencil.

"Good morning, Mrs. Wyatt," Deborah said from her usual place at the farthest end of the table.

Feeling like a schoolteacher on the first day of term, Angie smiled at each of them in turn and waited for Sidney to settle down on her left. In front of her Deborah had placed the circulated reports and the material that was listed on the agenda.

"I'm sorry I haven't been able to reinstate these meetings before now," she said, "but I'm sure you'll understand that I've had quite a lot to, uh, catch up on." There was a faint American inflection in her voice. She spoke so quietly that Deborah had to lean forward to hear. "Right. Does anyone have a spare copy of the agenda for me?"

Deborah got up. "Here's mine. I'll share with Cynthia. You'll also need a copy of the last minutes."

"Thank you. I have had a look at the minutes, and there didn't seem to be anything on them worth pursuing. Any objections if we skip them?"

Silence greeted this until, again, Deborah spoke. "We don't mind."

"Good. Now forgive me if I'm wrong, but it appears to me that there's not much worth pursuing on the agenda either."

"What the fuck," Sidney muttered audibly, pushing back from the table.

Angie turned to glance at him as she lit a cigarette. The bullying features behind the heavy beard made her toes itch. Silence gathered around them until he finally turned a malevolent look in her direction.

"*I* heard what you said, Sidney, but I'm sure those at the far end of the table didn't. Would you care to enlighten them?

No? The response to my comment that there didn't appear to be anything worth pursuing on the agenda has so far been 'What the fuck.' Would anyone like to add to that?''

For the third time in ten minutes Deborah tried to break through the tension. ''I'm sure Sidney means that he doesn't understand, that's all.''

Angie felt her thigh muscles beginning to cramp. She slid forward in her chair and concentrated for a moment on loosening the stiffness, relaxing. It didn't help much. She knew what she had to do; the hostility in the room could only increase.

''Thank you, Deborah. In that case I'll explain. It's not difficult. Item one: a two-page proposal for a new biography of Lindbergh. Who is the author, is this his first book, and if not, what has he written before and who published it? Why has he left his previous publisher? If he's written before, has anyone checked the quality of his work? Has there been a biography of Lindbergh since the Mosley one; does anyone know when that was published? I happen to know it was just about ten years ago, also that it was well received and pretty comprehensive. Is there room for another? In view of the subject matter, a two-page synopsis seems to me to be woefully inadequate anyway. Is there anything at all here that should be taking up our time at this stage? The submission letter is addressed to you, Martin. If I were you, I'd have a word with the agent about the facts of life.'' Angie paused for a moment, waiting for Martin's surly nod.

She scanned the next item quickly. ''Lucinda Eastman, twenty-three novels to her credit, wants to break out of the purely romantic fiction she's been writing. Here we have the first sixty or seventy pages of a historical novel that goes by the title of *The Blessings of Mildred Munro*. I take it you've read what's here, Deborah?''

Deborah nodded, blushing to the roots of her hair.

''Yes?'' Angie prompted. ''Well, what do you think of it? Do you want to publish it? I don't see a report—''

''No . . . I—I thought we could discuss it. It's not bad, and she does want to change her image. The agent says she would consider writing it under a pseudonym.''

''Beside the point surely. Is it any good? Do we want to publish it?''

Deborah cringed. ''No, I suppose not.''

''I'm sure you suppose right. Item three: American thriller, set in the swamps of Louisiana. That's just about all you've told us in your ten-line report, Sidney. Another reading recommended. Why have you wasted a week circulating the material instead of simply getting the book read again?''

''Because that's the way we do it here,'' Sidney replied curtly.

Angie ignored him and went on to shred the remaining items on the agenda. By the time she had finished, Martin had doodled enough projectiles to start a world war, Sidney was breathing through his mouth, and Deborah was on the verge of tears. The only person smiling around the table was Cynthia Crew, concentrating on the enameled perfection of her fingernails.

''This meeting is for discussing serious projects, factually presented. Let's not waste each other's time, please. Now, before we adjourn, there is one thing I'd like to report. As some of you may have heard, I've bought a first novel called *Night Work* from Lisa Barrett at the Sheldon Agency. Midge is having photocopies made; if anyone would like to read it, please ask her for one.''

''Fantastic.'' Cynthia brought her hands together in a soundless clap, like an overgrown schoolgirl. ''I'll get it over to the book club immediately.''

''No. Read it first, and then we'll discuss it. And don't show it to any of the paperbackers yet either.''

''Why don't you tell us what you paid for this little gem?'' Sidney laced his fingers together at the back of his neck and stretched, looking up at the ceiling. ''The rumors are becoming embarrassing.''

''Why embarrassing?'' Angie asked.

Sidney pursed his lips thoughtfully. ''Because,'' he said, aware that he had everyone's attention, ''because they make us look like prize fucking idiots.''

Angie laughed suddenly. Cynthia's mouth curved in a soft ''Oh,'' and Dunne Morrissey's sharp intake of breath left a smile on Angie's face. They were clearly used to Sidney's antics; the only question in their minds was how she would react. She said, ''I haven't heard any rumors. Would you like to share with us what *you've* heard?''

Sidney focused on Deborah, deliberately, coolly; she was the one who was guaranteed to fall apart. ''I heard a two-book contract for one hundred thousand pounds.''

"Without a paperback?" Deborah's voice had dropped by two octaves. "We always—"

Sidney didn't let her finish. "That's the rumor. Perhaps, since we all have a vague interest in what's going on in this company, we could now hear the truth?"

There was still a slight smile on Angie's face. Sidney brought his hands down, and Angie saw him wink at Martin. "You're almost right," she said, "on both counts. I have negotiated a two-book contract, but the total advance comes to one hundred and thirty thousand pounds: sixty-five thousand for *Night Work* and sixty-five for the next book."

"Fuck!" Sidney exploded. "Is that embarrassing or is that embarrassing?"

Angie stubbed out her cigarette. He was suggesting not only that she had paid well over the odds, but that she had done so, selfishly, in order to make her mark. She resisted an impulse to light another cigarette. "Is it the *size* of the advance you find embarrassing or the fact that it's a two-book contract, or both? Or, perhaps, the fact that it's a first novel? Or even that it's Jarman's first successful preemptive bid? Give me a clue, please."

Sidney, finally and reluctantly, turned to face her. "It's pathetic, that's what it is. Makes us look fucking desperate!"

"We need books," Angie said, reasonably.

"Not at those prices, we don't."

"No? Has it occurred to you, since you haven't read the novel, that it actually might be *worth* sixty-five thousand pounds?"

"You buy the first auction book that comes your way and it just happens to be worth sixty-five thousand pounds? Oh, sure. In any case, it's customary for more than one person to read a book before making an offer. Especially when we're thinking of buying without paperback support, *especially* when the advance is so fucking high! As the senior fiction editor—"

Angie interrupted. "Do you mean senior by dint of length of service or status?"

"What?"

"You heard me. Your particular job description is editor, not senior, not fiction or nonfiction."

Martin sniggered and nudged Cynthia. "I like it. Christ, I love it."

"Shut up, Martin." Cynthia spoke out of the corner of her

mouth. To be honest, she was enjoying the spectacle more and more. It was high time someone put that foulmouth in his place.

"It's always been understood that I—that all the fiction comes to me for approval. Apart from Deborah's historicals—"

"Why?" Angie asked pleasantly.

"Why what!"

"Why does all the fiction come to you for approval? Is it some arrangement Oliver agreed to?"

"Oliver?" Sidney's incredulous bark of laughter was enough to bring Deborah to her feet. She left the room in a crouched run. "Oliver wouldn't know—"

"Be careful, Sidney." Against her will Angie felt herself sliding into a black, black fury. "Be very careful."

Damned if he'd back away from her. What she was trying to do was so obvious it sickened him. His next words were, however, more cautiously phrased. "It was an understanding rather than an arrangement. Up till now it's worked perfectly well."

"Would you call the autumn list, the fiction in particular, good?"

"Some of it's OK."

"Some of it? Dunne"—the pencil Dunne was holding clattered away across the table—"if you were given, say, twenty-five thousand pounds to spend on promoting and advertising two books on the autumn list, which would they be?"

Dunne Morrissey shook his head miserably. "I don't think anything warrants that kind of money, Mrs. Wyatt. In any case, my budget—"

"We'll discuss your budget some other time, Dunne. In the meantime, I think we can agree that the list is less than . . . adequate. I want to publish *Night Work* in January, and I want finished copies for export by the end of September. And I want Farnsworth's to do the printing and the binding. I've already spoken to them; it's a tight schedule, but it can be done. I'm also allocating that twenty-five thousand pounds to *Night Work* alone, Dunne, and I'd like to see a detailed outline of how you propose to spend it. All right, Sidney?" She turned a mocking glance at him, aware that Martin had stopped doodling. How long before he told his father that *Night Work* was not going to be printed by Corbett's?

"I'll reserve my judgment until I've read the fucking

book.'' Sidney glared back at her. ''Wouldn't it be nice if we could *all* spend that kind of money promoting our own books?''

''Wouldn't it?'' Angie beamed at him. ''Unfortunately that's not possible. But I do, believe me, look forward to hearing what you think of *Night Work.*''

''I'll just bet you do,'' he muttered, getting to his feet.

''Are you leaving?''

Sidney sat down again, eyebrows raised. ''There's more?''

''This doesn't affect Deborah since she hardly spends anything at all, but I would like you all to look at your expenses more closely. At the moment they're running to about twenty-seven thousand pounds a year among you. That in itself doesn't concern me. What does is the repetition. You're all seeing and lunching the same people. Personal friendships are fine, but I can't imagine that a regular get-together over a three-hour lunch produces anything but a large bill and a wasted afternoon. Also, the time and money bear no relation at all to the number of books being brought in, and that *does* concern me. I'm asking you all to spread your nets wider and more selectively. Please don't force me to impose a limit on you. And incidentally, I don't think that evenings spent drinking in wine bars in the hope of meeting the odd journalist qualifies as a legitimate expense. Those of you who don't have company cars have allowances for petrol, et cetera. . . . Martin, a bill for a hundred forty-nine pounds for taxi fares is hardly reasonable, wouldn't you say? Any comments, anyone?''

No one answered. No one looked at her. ''Very well, that's all for the moment, I think.'' As the others began to leave the room, Angie called Sidney back. ''Stay a moment, would you?''

He came back to the table and leaned over, palms flat, fingers splayed. ''Well?''

''That was unpleasant, Sidney. And it's not going to happen again. You don't like me very much, do you? Why is that?''

''Because you're a fucking amateur, Mrs. Wyatt, and you're throwing your weight around.''

''You have a foul mouth and a nasty habit of patronizing people, Sidney. I don't like bullies. In fact, I think I dislike you even more than you dislike me. The only difference between us is that I have no fear of you.''

"You think I'm scared of you? Is that what you think?"

"It's what I hope, because you should be."

"I don't believe this." He began straightening up, a great intake of breath swelling his chest.

"Believe it, please. And don't take me on. You can't win."

He whirled and headed for the door. "We'll fucking well see about that!"

"Oh, one more thing before you go. I don't much care what you do or say privately, but if I ever hear the word 'fuck' from your mouth again, I'll ban you from every meeting and every sales conference at Jarman's. Don't think for a moment that your abusive language shocks me. It doesn't. It's the sheer, unimaginative, monotonous regularity of it I object to. That's all."

He stood framed in the doorway until she'd finished. She waited until the sound of his footsteps disappeared, then sagged forward and lit a cigarette with shaking fingers. She hadn't meant it to go so far, but at least it was done.

And now she would have to watch her back.

It didn't take long, less than two hours.

Midge announced Sir Richard Jarman a split second before he walked into Angie's office. Angie wasn't at all surprised by the frown or the purposeful stride. Jason Corbett had heard about *Night Work*. For once Martin had acted quickly and decisively.

"Good afternoon, Angela," her father said formally. There were not many things that would have lured Sir Richard into the trade department area.

"Hullo, Father. Won't you sit down? I was just about to have tea—"

"Not for me," he interrupted. "I'm not staying long."

"Well, at least sit down." With a certain degree of wistfulness she thought how good it would be to please him—just once. He was smooth, intent, scrupulous with his own and others' time; for some reason it crossed her mind that he had probably never had to ask anyone for anything in his life. "I suppose this is about Jason Corbett?"

"How do you know? Has he been in touch with you?"

"Uh-uh, but his son attends my meetings, remember?"

Clearly he hadn't bothered to put the two together. "I've just had a call, and Jason is, needless to say, quite furious.

Has this thing been settled? Have you signed the print order for *Night Work*?''

Angie came back quickly. ''It's settled. Why, are you willing to throw another two or three thousand pounds into the pot for Jason Corbett?''

''Everything is black and white to you, isn't it? Always has been. I've told you before, but let me spell it out for you again. Jarman trade is no more than an encumbrance at the moment. It's not earning its keep, and it's soaking up funds I could put to use elsewhere. Even if it were earning its keep, it would contribute no more than a quarter, probably a fifth, to the academic income. That's where the money is, to put it crudely. And profitability depends on printing and binding costs. You know that, and yet you selfishly go ahead and—''

''Wait. Before you go on, I did tell you what I intended to do with *Night Work*. I didn't exactly go behind your back.''

''*After* I had told you how . . . extremely competitive Jason's prices were on the academic side!''

''That's surely your problem. I really can't see why both prices shouldn't be competitive. After all, it works both ways. Jason Corbett needs Jarman academic as much as it needs him.''

''That, Angela,'' he said deliberately, ''doesn't appear to be the case.''

Just then Midge came in with a cup of tea. Angie waited until she'd left before asking, ''He's threatening a price war on the academic books?''

''Jason isn't one to lay his cards on the table, but I'll find out later this afternoon. He's coming in, and he insists on seeing you, too.''

''Obviously a man used to giving orders,'' she said.

''You'll see him, and that *is* an order. From me.''

Angie sat back in the chair and eyed her father speculatively. Bluff? He tugged at his tie, impatience in every movement. ''Very well, but I'll see him alone.''

''Angela . . .''

''Alone, Father. And before you get yourself into a state, I'd like you to consider the probability of the trade side reaching beyond the halfway turnover point of the academic list. Two years, no more . . .''

''Oliver will decide that.''

Angie laughed with honest bewilderment at the look of dismay on his face. ''Of course, he will, but I can't see that he'll have much choice since he's laid the foundations. Why do you hate the idea so much? Competition with academic? Or is it me?'' If it had been anyone else, she would have added, I can make this work. I know I can.

Sir Richard stood up with an abrupt movement, expressionless. "Jason is coming in at three-thirty. He should be with you by four o'clock."

"I'll be here. Incidentally, how is Mother?"

"She's well. You'll report to me the minute Jason leaves this afternoon. Is that understood?"

"Yessir." No concessions asked for or given. It wasn't often that Sir Richard Jarman was confronted by a will as unyielding as his own. There could have been enjoyment in that, a tenderness at least. If there had been a chink, she could have pried at it. How to convince him that she wasn't in competition, never had been?

Angie thumbed through a batch of estimates in front of her. From what she knew of him, she guessed that nothing less than a confrontation based on facts would satisfy Jason Corbett. On top of the pile were two copies of the print order she'd signed for *Night Work*.

A cloying lethargy made her snatch up the estimates and walk through into Midge's office. She told her secretary to expect Jason Corbett later that afternoon and asked her to tabulate the essential figures on the estimates before he arrived.

What else could happen today? Sidney, her father, now Jason Corbett. And tomorrow Frank was driving her to Gloucestershire to see Oliver. Jarman's might take twelve hours of her day, but they were not stultifying hours. Finding the time to read the growing piles of transcripts was becoming a problem, a losing battle. Free-lance readers were the short-term answer, but not yet. She was too new, to the literary agents too much of an unknown quantity. It was as though they were testing her with the quality and range of their submissions, demanding in their own way the admission fee to the club.

She made a mental note to reread *Night Work* in proof to see how much Deborah's editing had improved it. Deborah was, by all accounts, a good editor, orderly but, Angie suspected, not an instinctive one, the way Lou had been. Nor was she. While he had so lovingly labored over the words on a page, their rhythm and associative connections, the blithe and beautiful prose, she felt no compulsion to treat them as

her own. It was enough that they were there, *almost* perfect.
Perfection as an objective held no fascination for her. A tragedy, Lou had informed her sadly, because she recognized and
was able to live with imperfections. But then he'd loved her
because everything she was and did was slightly off-key. . . .

Behind a desk on the fifth floor of the Jarman building, a
stack of dictation at her elbow, the prospect of Jason Corbett,
seventeen typescripts to be read . . . Lou she yearned for.

It was after five o'clock when Jason Corbett was finally announced. Midge opened the door for him and stood aside
with a disapproving look. It might have been because he was
late or the fact that his expression was studiedly grim. He
certainly hadn't arrived determined to flatter Angie out of her
decision. Angie's glance went quickly to the chair in front of
her desk and then to the leather couch, layered with transcripts.

"Mr. Corbett." She met him halfway across the room. He
touched her hand cursorily and waited until she'd moved the
typescripts. He then lowered himself onto the couch with
infinite slowness. "Would you like something to drink? Tea,
coffee?"

"A very dry sherry."

Yes, like her father, a man used to issuing orders. Angie
felt his eyes on her as she poured the sherry and, when she
turned, saw him studying the room in great detail. He took
the glass from her with a nod, nothing more. Rather than sit
beside him at an awkward angle, she chose the chair in front
of her desk and waited for him to speak.

"The first time we met you told me you thought we were
going to get on rather well," he said conversationally.

"I remember that."

"Well, you were wrong. If you wanted an easy relationship, you wouldn't have done what you have."

"I didn't say I wanted an easy relationship. I'll settle for
a working knowledge."

"You've brought some peculiar ideas back with you from
the States, I understand. We do things differently over here—
you're smiling."

"Excuse me, I'm going to join you in a drink." Angie
turned her back on his frown and poured a small quantity of
whiskey into a glass and filled it with water. She placed the

sherry bottle on the table in front of him before sitting down again. "Help yourself," she said.

He did. "Well, what do you have to say to me?"

"I suppose you're entitled to an explanation, Mr. Corbett, so let's start at the beginning. There is and has been for many years an arrangement between Jarman's and yourself. Apart from your friendship with my father, this has been a strictly business arrangement. In exchange for a monopoly on all the books on the Jarman list, you provide the most competitive setting, printing, and binding prices. I have some figures for you." She handed him a stapled sheaf of papers, which he did not glance at. "Look at them when you have time. I'm calling a halt to the arrangement, on the trade side, that is."

"I wouldn't call that an explanation."

"Then look at those figures. *You* wouldn't put up with such discrepancies. I have no intention of doing so either."

His eyes lit up at the prospect of a fight. Angie almost grinned as he leaned toward her, his fist dwarfing the sherry glass, leaving only a portion of the stem visible. "Discrepancies. You're suggesting something . . . dishonest?"

"Not at all. Incompetence on the part of Jarman's more than anything else."

"Meaning your father and Oliver, yes?"

"Don't put words into my mouth, please. You know perfectly well what I mean."

"Your opinion of your brother isn't exactly flattering, Mrs. Wyatt."

"You're trying to needle me, and it won't work. I'll not apologize or explain on that score. I've stated a fact. Kindly accept it as just that."

"Very well. I take it you've made a comparative study of the academic figures, too?"

Angie shook her head.

"Why not?"

"A waste of time," she said shortly. "They're good."

"*Very* good?"

"Very good. Why do you think that entitles you to a back-hander on every trade book, though?"

"*Backhander?*" He said the word to himself, as though he'd never heard it before. "Is that what you think?"

"It may not be a personal backhander, but it goes into the Corbett kitty nonetheless. I simply don't understand why. Reciprocal arrangement, swings and roundabouts?"

"Precisely," he grunted.

"No more. I'm putting a stop to it. From now on Corbett's will be asked to provide individual estimates on the trade side, the same as everyone else."

"I see." He glanced at her with a tiny downward movement of the lips. "You relish the idea of competition. Unseemly in the circumstances. Would you want to win at any cost?"

"Meaning trade over academic? You're not nearly as naïve as you're making out, Mr. Corbett. The academic figures will remain as they are. We both know that. It's a question of mutual interest. We're discussing only the trade figures."

"It's not that simple."

"I'm afraid it is to me. Until Oliver is back and in this office, Corbett's does not have a lien on setting and printing for Jarman trade. I can't put it any plainer than that. While I'm here, I'm going to make this *work*, and I can't do it on the margins you quote. You leave me no choice."

He appeared to consider this seriously, as though she'd introduced a totally new concept into the discussion.

"You would like me to say I appreciate your honesty, Mrs. Wyatt, but if I did, I'd be lying. You're upsetting more than one applecart here." He paused, decided to change his tack. "If I were to withdraw the standard setting cost for Jarman academic and force Sir Richard, as you put it, to ask for separate estimates on each title, he would have to increase his production staff by at least five people. Expensive."

Angie walked around behind her desk for a cigarette. Her earlier inertia was gone, and in its place was a heady awareness of the moment. Impossible, but she was enjoying herself. Jason waved the cigarettes aside impatiently as she offered them. She was undisturbed by the vague threat of her father's displeasure. He was right, of course, but in order to deal with individual estimates, *he* would also have to take on the same number of additional staff. "Expensive," she agreed and paused before adding, "For both of you."

An exquisitely delicate shrug lifted his shoulders. "You're not what I expected either, Mrs. Wyatt. Why are all beautiful women such bitches?"

"As opposed to handsome men wielding big sticks?"

She was rewarded by an uninhibited explosion of laughter. He snatched up the sherry bottle by its neck and held it out to her. "I deserve a strong one of what you're drinking, neat, and then I'll leave."

"No hurry, Mr. Corbett. There was something else I thought we could discuss. Since you're here, I mean."

He waited until he'd taken a mouthful of the whiskey and swirled it about in his mouth. "My son," he said, and the Yorkshire accent was there again, she noticed. "What's he done?"

Careful, Angie told herself. She put a dash more whiskey into her own glass. "Not a lot, Mr. Corbett. May I speak frankly?"

He inclined his head. "He *is* my son." This was by way of a warning.

"That's why I'm asking."

"Is he unhappy here?"

"You don't know? How did he sound when he called to tell you about *Night Work*?"

Jason Corbett hesitated. He must have decided that the two of them had gone too far because he said, "Slightly drunk, if you must know. But it *was* lunchtime."

"That's something else. The very nature of this job is detrimental to Martin. He's not a bad editor, but neither is he a good one. I'm also sorry to tell you that he seems to do very little work. Corridor politics appear to hold his interest more than anything else. He's simply not pulling his weight at Jarman's." She caught a spark of anger in his eyes, also something else that made her regret the harshness of her last words.

"You're gathering a few enemies around yourself, Mrs. Wyatt. Is that sensible?" The voice had gone flat.

"Perhaps not. I take it you include amongst my enemies your son's friend, Sidney? That's something else he must have told you about."

"Sidney's been at Jarman's for a long time; he makes a bad enemy."

Was he advising caution? Angie said, with more decisiveness than she felt, "That's no reason not to take him on, is it?"

Again the shrug, the lowering of the eyelids to reveal slits of pale blue. "Why are you asking me when you've obviously already made the decision?"

"This isn't what I intended, whether you believe it or not. Your son needs help."

He was on his feet in one lithe movement that made her

blink. "Thank you for telling me," he said. "You look as if you're about to say you're sorry. Don't. You'll be hearing from me."

Angie remained where she was long after he'd left. He moved like an athlete when he wanted to. A pulse throbbed in her temple, and she gulped down the rest of her whiskey. She'd hurt him. In her headlong rush to get it all said, to beat him at his own game, she'd vulgarized the exhilaration they'd both felt. She had him down as a street fighter, and she had assumed, stupidly, that he would protect himself. He hadn't, not when it had come to his son.

"Nicely done," she murmured, biting down hard on her lower lip, sick with the feeling that she'd gone in like a charging bull. "Nicely done, Mrs. Wyatt."

31

☐ By the time James Bonnier phoned, Cory had left the house. Arion took the call in the kitchen, reacting softly to James's voice because Ani was pottering about on the back porch, just out of earshot.

"Gambling? I do not understand, James. What gambling?"

"Let me come over, Ari. Let's talk about this, eh?"

"Talk? Yes, I—" His voice broke in confusion. "He puts money on horses?" That didn't sound too bad.

"Not horses, Ari. He plays cards, blackjack at the casinos."

"All the time? Every night? Is this why he does not come home?"

James Bonnier held the phone away from his ear. He would have given anything not to be having this conversation. It was a mistake to have telephoned, he realized now. What he should have done was go over, see the old man, break it all to him more gently.

"James?"

"I'm here, Ari."

"Tell me, my friend. Tell me everything you have found out. I must know."

"Very well. He's a member of most of the big casinos in London. Someone has been giving him credit because—because of who you are. He has been encouraged to play, and mostly he loses. He owes a lot of money, Ari, and this man, I don't know who he is yet, has no patience, I'm told."

Listening, Arion cursed himself for being a fool. How could he not have seen what was going on? How could he have allowed it to go on for such a long time? How could the boy have been living this sort of life under their roof?

"The money, how much does he owe these—this man, James?"

"That I couldn't find out, not exactly, but it runs into thousands of pounds. Give me another day or two—"

"No, no, it is enough. Ask no more questions. I will talk to Cory, and I will . . . do whatever I have to. Thank you." How much did Paul know of all this? he wondered. Could it be that he had known and kept that knowledge from Arion in the hope that it would eventually turn him away from Cory?

Arion thanked James again and hung up. Outside, Ani was humming to herself. The morning was bright and fresh and held the promise of a warm day.

"Ari, look," she said, pointing to perfect miniature peppers growing in a box on the side wall. He put his arms around her waist and pulled her toward him.

"Are they for eating?"

"For prettiness only. Are you leaving now?"

"Soon. *Cara*, if Cory comes home during the time I am away, tell him I want to talk to him."

"He's done something wrong?"

"Nothing, Ani. Please do not concern yourself. Can a man not see his own grandson?"

He left her on the porch, collected his jacket, and began to make a mental note of his route through Soho. He'd make his way down Poland Street toward Bridle Lane and Golden Square. If he had no luck there, he'd head along in the direction of Charing Cross Road. Someone must have seen the boy. . . .

First he made a detour to his office and asked his secretary to cancel his appointment later that morning at his bank. Angel shares had dropped by another ninepence. The shares

were being sold in what seemed to him to be a panic. His
financial advisers were at a loss to explain it, and Arion knew
why the clearing bank had requested a meeting. Its directors
were going to call in his loans.

Perhaps, when he got home again, he would call Paul.
There was more than a silence now between him and his son.
Apart from Paul's feelings about Cory, quite apart from that.
There was no possibility that Paul did not know about the
drop in the price of Angel shares. Why had he not called?
Arion wondered. What was there to gain?

32

☐ The weekend before leaving for New York Lisa drove
her dilapidated Mini to Worcestershire to visit her parents. It
was a long, unbroken drive, yet at the end of it a radiant
energy still enveloped her. Not even the odors of disinfectant,
so familiar from her childhood, could blur the tangible feeling of well-being that swept her into her mother's arms.

Irene Barrett, delighted at the display of affection, put it
down to her daughter's success in London. The girl was losing that reticent, demure look which had made them fear for
her ability to cope. There was still something gangling about
her, a long-legged awkwardness that remained from her teens.
But there was also a new assurance that came from self-confidence, and it showed in her dress, the way she moved and
spoke.

"She's a woman, darling," George Barrett said, as if that
explained everything. "And she's probably in love with some
long-haired writer living in a commune."

The idea horrified his wife. "Do you really think so?"

"No, not really." He laughed. "She'll tell us soon enough,
though."

Upstairs in her bedroom Lisa unpacked the few things she'd
brought along. The small room was aired and fresh, but nothing had been moved. Dog-eared copies of *Jane Eyre, Wuth-*

ering Heights, and *Moby Dick* were dust-free and carefully positioned alongside *Kinflicks* and *Catcher in the Rye*. A tiny pale onyx jar, a present from an aunt, stood alongside a silver cup inscribed "Lisa Joan Barrett. 200 yards freestyle. 1972."

The angle-poise lamp she'd used for studying now stood on the bedside table. The bed itself looked impossibly narrow and virginal. Impulsively she sat down on it, skimming her fingertips over the crisp light covering. In the humming stillness of the afternoon there was a limpid heaviness to everything but the cool material. . . .

Lisa had become aware of her body as never before, and she wasn't altogether sure it didn't have something to do with the hot summer weather. Her skin tautened with a vague anticipation each morning when she woke up to the promise of another sunny day. Since that night at the party in the Jarman boardroom, she had had to face the embarrassing fact that almost everything conspired to turn her on. She was becoming accustomed to that phrase and used it against herself as a form of sarcastic penitence. "Aroused" would have been more precise, but she didn't like the clinical sex-manual connotation of that word. To be turned on suggested frivolity, other more cuddly aspects of sex, simple enjoyment. She suspected that this had to do with her ambivalent feelings about Frank. She hated him. He'd complicated their working relationship for no good reason and seemed to spend all his time trying to enrage her. On the other hand, she was dazzled by his ill humor, by the ease with which he manipulated her responses. She lived in a fantasy of confrontation and anticipation, indignant as an adolescent when his praise wasn't forthcoming, feeling a cold finger bumping down her spine each time she inadvertently caught him looking at her. But while she scorned her sexual delinquency, the very uncertainty of her desires gave her sleepless nights. At times she existed in a welter of longing, waiting for something to happen; at other times she was electrified by random sensations.

Frank's stern-faced recital of Farley's vulgarity had sent her initial fury into reverse. It had taken scarcely any imagination and certainly no conscious effort to become the girl on the stage, *a stripper*, and from beyond the single spotlight to see Frank's expression change from boredom to—she wasn't sure what. She'd felt her loins constrict in a now familiar spasm; if Frank had come anywhere near her at that moment, she would have run from the room. It was almost pain, and it left her jumpy and disconcerted. . . .

Driving back to London on Sunday night, Lisa grappled with the sense that an unknown woman had inhabited her skin for the last few weeks. She decided that there were some positive advantages. One was her newfound patience and capacity to take in the details of her parents' lives. She'd come away knowing the price of bulbs at the local nursery, the breakup of their bridge evenings since old Mr. Harrington had been placed in a home by his son, what a youth officer had told Margery Ackerley's boy when he'd been found grilling their canary over a fire in the back garden. The story about the canary made her laugh for some reason. Her father put his hand over his mouth to hide a smile, and her mother left them alone with a look of grave suspicion.

It had been good. She told herself that she would visit them more often—if her rusty red Mini held out. When she finally got back, her flat seemed vibrantly enclosed, welcoming her into dark, empty places where she wasn't alone. She found her pocket diary and wrote ''Worcs'' at right angles across the entire weekend just gone, then paged two weeks ahead and did the same with that weekend. Then, as if she needed reminding, she saw ''Elliot/celebration dinner'' penciled in for Wednesday evening and ''New York,'' in red, covering Thursday. Her heart still did a sideways lurch each time she thought about the hundred-and-thirty-thousand-pound deal she'd negotiated with Angela Wyatt. She tried not to think about it . . . or the fact that she was going to have to go through the whole nerve-racking procedure again in New York. Without Frank.

Last-minute preparations for her trip took up most of Monday, and drawing up a draft contract for *Night Work* most of Tuesday. By the time she met Elliot Stone for dinner on Wednesday night, her elation at the successful auction of his novel was dampened by tiredness. She had initially toyed with the idea of booking at Ani's, but since it was more than likely that Frank would be there with Angela Wyatt, she decided not to. Instead, they ate at Langan's Bistro, within walking distance from Durrant's Hotel, into which she'd booked Elliot for the night.

Perhaps she should have invited Angela Wyatt along tonight. No, that would have been awkward. The truth was that

Lisa didn't know what to make of the other woman. Unless it had been a deliberate ploy to set herself apart from the others, Angela Wyatt had lavishly praised the quality of Elliot's writing *before* making her preemptive bid. Lisa was accustomed to publishers' holding back on their enthusiasm in the interests of securing the book for the lowest possible advance. Angela Wyatt had then further surprised her by asking how she would react to the novel being handed over to Deborah Anderson for editing.

"Martin Corbett's not experienced enough, and I know how you feel about Sidney," Angie had said honestly. "Deborah is good. I know she's quiet and a bit fussy; but she's a worker, and she gets on well with authors. I'm also told that she's a good editor."

"I don't see how I can object," Lisa said, flattered. If this was the way Angela Wyatt intended to run Jarman's, then Lisa's decision to place Elliot there was even better than she had originally thought. It was still difficult to think about Jarman's as an exciting publishing house, but whatever Angela Wyatt was doing there, the vibes she was sending out already had other agents looking closely at their client lists; if the company was going to be revived, they wanted to be among the first to negotiate contracts there.

Elliot Stone was, understandably, less interested in the reputation of the publishing house than in the advance it was going to pay him. At eleven forty-five he was suggesting another bottle of wine. They sat at a table against a wall covered with a patchwork of prints, drawings, and photographs. The bistro was cheerfully noisy, and the middle-aged couple sitting alongside were now leaning noticeably toward them in an effort to overhear their conversation. They had begun to listen when Elliot had raised his glass and said loudly, "A hundred and thirty thousand pounds. God save America if they match Jarman's."

Now he was more than a little drunk, and if anything, his voice was even louder. Unaccountably Lisa was annoyed at herself for being bored. Elliot was the sort of man her mother would have called "nice." He was of medium height, medium build, dark-haired. Quite good-looking in an undramatic way. It was the monotony of his voice that finally sent a danger signal into her head, that and the fact that he pouted from time to time, reacting coyly to each hint of praise.

"What's she like, this Deborah Anderson?" he asked eventually. "Is she pretty? I work better with pretty girls."

Lisa smiled noncommittally. "Better than that, she's a good editor."

"I hope she's not going to ask me to do a lot of work. I hope you told her that."

Lisa caught the waiter's eye and gestured for another bottle of the house red. "Why don't you wait and hear what she has to say tomorrow, before assuming what it is she'd like you to do?"

There was the pout again. "They wouldn't have paid so much money for a book that had to be rewritten—"

"Who said anything about rewriting?"

"Isn't that what editors do?"

"We seem to be talking at cross-purposes. Let me explain something to you. The editor, in this case, Deborah Anderson, is your contact within the publishing house, someone pretty crucial. Not only does she edit the book, but she sees it through its various production stages. She'll present the book to the sales force and generally be behind it every step of the way. I'm not defending editors, and I don't know where your information comes from; but there are very *very* few books that don't need editing. I'm not talking about a rewrite, just editing."

"But you said they thought *Night Work* was brilliant."

Lisa tried to control her impatience. "It is, but if you recall, I did tell you that there were certain changes that I would have recommended myself. I'm sure that whatever Deborah tells you tomorrow, it won't be anything to be alarmed about."

"I'm not so sure," he countered moodily. "She'll take me to lunch, won't she?"

"What time is your appointment, eleven-thirty? Probably."

"You're not sure?"

"I didn't make the appointment; you did." She saw him flush at her sharp tone. "Look, I'm sure she will. If she doesn't, come by the office and we'll go to a wine bar close by."

"Will you cancel your own lunch?"

She lied, knowing it would please him. "Of course. There'll be plenty of time before my flight. I wouldn't dream of allowing a talent like yours to roam the streets of London.''

''You really think it's good, don't you?'' He made the statement with satisfaction.

''I really do.''

''I suppose they'll want me to do a lot of publicity. It's not something I care about personally. Privacy, Ellen's and my privacy, is very precious. My wife is a fantastic woman. Have I told you she locked me in a room, actually locked me in—''

Three times. Lisa swallowed a yawn. Fantastic Ellen, who vacuumed the cupboard under the stairs three times a week because she so wanted to make the house somewhere Elliot would want to come back to. Now that they were united in celebration, Elliot had brought out a walletful of snapshots. Ellen was plump, pretty, and undistinguished; their two children, a boy and a girl, were neat and toothy.

''We work at our marriage, you know; it's not all easy. I've been tempted many times, let me tell you, and once or twice . . . well, I'm sure you understand, a pretty girl like you.''

Dear God, if he wrote the way he spoke. All women were girls to him. She didn't want to hear about his marriage or his extramarital conquests, still less what he thought he saw in her. She refilled his glass, dismayed that the level of wine remaining didn't seem to go down at all.

He took the bottle from her and filled her glass in turn, spilling the liquid over her fingers without noticing. ''I suppose you have lots of temptations, doing what you do.''

Lisa was conscious that the couple next to them had moved a fraction closer again. ''Temptations?''

''Oh, you know . . . parties and things. People.''

''I meet a lot of people, certainly, but there are fewer parties than you'd think.''

''And I suppose all your authors fall in love with you.''

''Oh, no. Most of them are happily married, like you.''

He didn't take the hint. His next question prompted a swift withdrawal by the couple, a snapped intake of breath. ''Do you think my sex scenes worked?''

''They worked very well in their context.'' And to herself: I don't want to be here. Please, God, make him shut up.

''Why?'' He pouted.

''Why did they work well? I don't really know. I suppose because they read real.''

He persisted. "Erotic?"

Lisa glanced at her watch, wondering what on earth he wanted from her, apart from an invitation to bed. "Erotic, yes."

"Did they turn you on?"

Hah, she almost laughed. They were just about the only thing that didn't turn her on. She said, "They did exactly what you intended them to do, Elliot. They explained and deepened a relationship in a way that put the whole village into perspective."

"Have another glass of wine. You haven't answered my question, but girls get embarrassed, I know."

"I'm hardly a girl, and I'm certainly not embarrassed. I think I should get the bill. You've got a long day ahead of you, and so have I. I'll be halfway to New York by this time tomorrow night."

"You *are* embarrassed!" he retorted smugly.

Lisa signaled the waiter, then allowed her glance to drop. This was going nowhere; another few minutes would see her patience run out. "Maybe you're right."

His shoulders went back, his chin up. Victory? But why? He couldn't be stupid enough to think she was going to bed with him. The waiter came over with the bill, and while Lisa was checking it, Elliot asked him for a cork and proceeded to cap the half-empty bottle of wine. "For later," he said, and winked.

Once outside, he took her arm. "Which way back?"

She led him down Marylebone High Street, with its brightly lit and expensive boutiques, and then turned right, into the dignified calm of George Street. Elliot was humming to himself. Lisa stopped in front of St. James's Church and disengaged her arm. "If you have time while you're in London, you should see the Wallace Collection. It's over there"—she pointed across the road—"just behind Spanish Place."

He stopped humming. Lisa thought she heard him say, "Maybe," before he reclaimed her elbow and began to steer her once more toward the hotel.

"Well," she said, pulling up again as they came to the door. She focused on a pretty hanging basket of flowers and tried once more to ease out of his grip. "I'll hear from you tomorrow—"

"You're coming up for a drink."

"No, it's late, and I'm tired. We'll talk tomorrow."

"Just one. Promise. Come on"—he tugged—"or I'll think you don't like me."

The last resort of the totally insensitive. Could he really be that drunk? As he pulled her through the door, her composure began to desert her. You don't own me! He had already hinted at the inevitable: be nice or I'll go away and find somebody who appreciates me. Unless she put him straight now, it would go on, and there would always be this between them.

She did nothing. They stood silently apart in the small lobby. He swung the half bottle of wine like a trophy. Facing a central, flaring staircase, Lisa decided that if God were truly on her side, Elliot would pass out here and now.

"A drink . . . before a drink," he muttered, propelling her past the reception on the left and down a corridor. "The George Bar . . . it's nice, cozy."

"Elliot . . ."

He stopped in front of the telephone kiosks, suddenly, barring her escape by leaning into her. "You'll phone me—won't you?—when you know what—what's happening in New York."

"Of course, but as I've said, it won't be for another ten days or so."

"Maybe I should come with you."

"No!" She pressed herself against the glass panels of the phone booth. There weren't many people around; the corridor itself was deserted.

"Why not?" His hand went down and cupped one of her breasts.

Lisa stiffened and tried to push him away. "Don't . . ."

"Could be fun . . . don't say you don't like the idea." He moved back slightly to get better leverage, and she tried to edge away. He took this as an invitation and dragged his hand up over her shoulder, then down to her waist and finally to her thigh. She stood perfectly still, surprised that she could control a shudder at his touch.

It seemed to dawn on him quite suddenly that this was not the way it should be, and he raised his eyes to her face. What he saw made him pull away so quickly that he stumbled against the opposite wall.

"Finished?" she asked quietly. "If you want this as part of an agent's service, get somebody else. Do you understand? It's your decision. I'll be in my office tomorrow. *Call me!*"

She left him standing where he was, flushed and open-

mouthed. As she made for the door, she was angrily aware
of an elderly man who had obviously been watching them
from the lobby. Her furious look made him turn away in
confusion.

She found a cruising taxi and got in. Her own ineptitude
stunned her. It wasn't the first time a writer had assumed
ownership; it was a hazard of the game, recognizable in its
early stages. Never before had it gone as far as this. How had
she managed to jeopardize what should have been a simple,
working relationship?

By the time she reached her flat, her anger had abated into
a dull flare of frustration. It would have happened sooner or
later with this particular man. Better to have it out and in the
open. If she'd recognized it as more than a drunken pass, it
would have helped. But she hadn't, and that was that.

She undressed and stood under a hot shower, thankful for
the wall of sound, for the heat that drained some of the tension from her limbs. Despite the fact that she was sexually
immune to Elliot, her body, as so often recently, was reacting. Grumpily she dried her hair to the sound of an LBC
early-morning program and then decided that she must be
ready for sleep.

She wasn't. Irritably she turned on the bedside lamp and
began to read *The Name of the Rose* from the beginning again,
trying for the third time to get into the novel. But the words
blurred, and the light did nothing to dispel the splayed images
that seized her senses. She wanted someone, here beside her,
in bed. God, to go from fear of being frigid to *this*.

She threw the book across the room and rolled over onto
her stomach. She knew she wouldn't be able to sleep; musky
scents of soap and shampoo filled her nostrils, and she
groaned, thrusting her face deep into the pillow as her hips
burrowed down, reaching instinctively for some pressure.

She finally slept as she lay, spiraling down into a dream
about Sidney Niklas. Her purse was open, and money lay
scattered on the floor between them. He wanted her to give
it all to Farley Esterhuys, and he wouldn't say why. He left
her on her knees, gathering up the notes, and when she looked
up again, Frank was there. . . .

33

☐ The warehouse would burn tonight. Paul Angelou shifted his body into a more comfortable position on the couch. He was tired. His eyes ached, and all he wanted to do was escape his own thoughts. It was an unpleasant sensation and oddly disquieting.

It was ten-thirty. The house was quiet and dimly lit. At first the silence had evoked a chafing sense of isolation, and he found himself listening for a sound, some break in the rhythm: the soft thud of a door closing; the sudden hum from the refrigerator; Susan moving about in another room. . . .

He wanted to take Susan and leave, remove her from the possibilities of the next few hours, days. But as he contemplated his inactivity, he knew that was impossible. Tonight had been a long while coming, and it arrived at a time when his life had become a curious circle, without purpose or any real definition. He was floundering. The fire would solve one problem; if everything went according to plan, it should ensure that his parents returned to Greece, leaving him free to pursue his political ambitions unhampered. But that was no longer enough, and he didn't know why.

Paul stirred restlessly, wanting to leave the questions, wondering what the hell Susan was doing so silently in the kitchen. It surprised him to find that he could accept the blunt tautness about her these days. He had never loved or wanted her more, even when she wore a distant, unapproachable face. Their time together had become unaccountably fragile to him because he knew how easily he could lose her.

There was more than an uneasy quiet between them; it was as if she knew something she couldn't possibly know. He would have been hard pressed to decide which he feared more: not seeing Angela Wyatt again or Susan finding out about his involvement, except it wasn't an involvement. Not yet. Nothing had happened. . . .

There, the sound of a cupboard door closing. Satisfied, he let himself drift into other thoughts, not peaceful, but jagged and red, like a spent fury. His contemplation of Angela Wyatt was something apart, a self-contained and enclosed space filled with exotic imagery. Even absent, she reached him with menacing exactness. He couldn't now recall feeling her softness against him, the taste of her mouth or the pitch of her voice. Yet they shared an awesome intimacy. He didn't know her and had no desire to, not in the same way he knew Susan, *safely*. Each time they met it was as though he came away with some part of her—but never enough. It wasn't simply the fact of her, body, breasts, eyes; it was what was going on inside her head, the aching honesty she sometimes allowed him a glimpse of; shutters that in anyone else would have come down were flung open when she was shaken or hurt; she fought him not for coming too close but for seeing her as someone mysterious and remote. There'd been nothing mysterious about the woman who'd slumped against him that last evening; nothing more than desire had set her trembling like a leaf. He told himself that it had been just that, that he could have taken her then without resistance. He had at once been elated by her striking physical response and repelled by her utter lack of shame, thinking that if he could have had her so easily, so could—*easily?* It wasn't fair, or the truth, and he knew it. . . .

Paul felt the beginnings of an erection, a blind stirring that made him shift again as Susan walked into the room. The discomfort did not annoy him, as it would once have done. That, too, lay within his control.

At three o'clock in the morning the sky was black and starless, the air biting. In the aftermath of a light drizzle the tires hissed softly as the car drew to a stop as far away from the streetlight as possible. Leo had switched off the headlights moments before.

From where they'd parked, they could just see one corner of the front of the warehouse. It was situated well away from the street; deep shadows obscured its lower outlines and made the fence all but invisible.

"The watchman will be sleeping by now," Leo commented with assurance. He needed a cigarette but dared not to take a chance on the flare being seen and remembered.

Cory, huddled deep into the upturned collar of his jacket,

thought it was not too late, even now. All he had to do was lean over, switch on the engine, and tell Leo to drive him home. By the time he got there it would almost be time for Arion to get up. They would sit at the kitchen table while Ani made coffee, and they would talk. Arion would care nothing about the money, but his grandson's weakness would bewilder him. Cory could see the look, an old man's confusion and disappointment. Ani would stand behind him as she always did, her hands on his shoulders; they both would look at him and know he wasn't the man they thought he was.

No! His fist came up and slammed against the dashboard. "Come," he grunted. "Let's get it over with."

They were a day late. The rusty Ford Cortina Leo had stolen for the job had needed a new exhaust at the last moment. His own large Peugeot or Cory's Alfa would have stood out like a sore thumb in the area of the warehouse, even at this time of the morning. Leo had told Cory he'd had trouble convincing Claude Soames to wait for another twenty-four hours. In fact, it had been just the opposite; the possibility of a jackpot had made Soames cautious. He urged Leo to take more time, get to know the night watchman's habits, when the police Rovers were likely to patrol the area. Leo had rejected the advice on the pretext that Cory might change his mind, given enough time. What he didn't tell Soames was that as far as he was concerned, no job was worth getting out of bed for unless it carried an element of risk.

He pulled on a pair of soft leather gloves. Cory did the same. They were ready.

In the pitch-darkness of the warehouse, Simon Riggs crouched over the small alarm clock, its face illuminated by the light from his pencil torch. Whistling under his breath, he turned the minute hand forward by thirty minutes. That would give him enough time to check the procedure through one final time and to leave and resecure the metal door at the rear of the warehouse.

It was so quiet that he could hear his clothes rustle as he moved around the outer walls, ducking between the massive shelves that reached up to a height of thirty feet. Paper everywhere. The place was an arsonist's dream. They didn't come much easier than this. Even the safe was not too difficult. He had been tempted to help himself to its contents, then decided against it. Fifteen thousand pounds for a few hours of watching and reconnoitering was enough. It had taken him no more than twenty minutes to do the rest once he'd slipped in through the back. He was proud of his own calm professionalism. He took pleasure in his stealthy movements, continually conscious of himself, as though he were watching himself on a screen.

Satisfied finally that the remaining four devices were perfectly located, Riggs turned to inspect his route back to the gray steel door. He was almost reluctant to leave and for a moment considered waiting for the first flare. He grinned in the darkness. It was a long time since he'd been tempted to behave like an amateur. He wasn't in this for the thrill any longer. It was a business—and a lucrative one.

"Burn, baby, burn." He moved soundlessly on sock-covered sneakers and eased the heavy back door open an inch at a time. Before slipping through, he pulled a black balaclava type of mask over his head and set about relocking the door. When it was done, he crouched in the shadows, waiting. The sound of a car in the distance came to him in muted waves, then silence again.

He ran across the concrete space and pulled himself up and over the fence with the agility of a cat. Then he paused to remove the socks covering his shoes and the mask over his face and walked away.

The chain-link fence rattled, bowed, and sagged as Leo tried to get a toe grip. He spit out a string of expletives. When he was over, he lay flat against the damp grass and went on cursing Cory's equally clumsy efforts. There was a sharp cry of pain and the sound of tearing material as the younger man dropped down beside him.

"It's nothing, tore my shirt, that's all." Cory panted, feeling a warm trickle of blood slip down his midriff.

The light in the night watchman's room was on. From behind ill-fitting blinds, it seeped out, etching shadows that could have been mistaken for boulders. On their hands and knees, the two men crept forward, their stocking masks stretched and ready across their foreheads.

The radio was on; they could hear a mournful sound of violins. It gave Leo the jitters. "The door won't be locked," he told Cory for the second time in ten minutes, "but if it is, I'll say we're the police and he'll open up, all right?"

Cory pulled the stocking down over his face. The instant

claustrophobia made him gag. He reached up and pulled the nylon away from his mouth.

Leo got to his feet and gestured for Cory to stand behind him. He grasped the door handle and slowly pushed it down. They both held their breath as the door moved inward. Suddenly the music was louder, and now they could hear the watchman snoring in concert. The man had cleared his desk and lay stretched out on it like a corpse, hands clasped over his stomach, head resting on a rolled-up sweater.

Cory shut the door behind him, and Leo nudged the sleeping man. "Wake up, Dad," he whispered.

For the first time Cory saw the knife he held. "Hey, I told you—"

"Shut up, for Christ's sake! All we need is for him to hear your lovely accent. How many times do I have to tell you?"

Cory gestured wordlessly toward the knife. Leo grinned behind his mask and made a stabbing movement. Then he punched the watchman on the arm and leaned over so that the first thing he would see would be the knife.

The man woke up from one nightmare into another. He lurched up onto his elbows. "What the hell . . ." he began, blinking, fear running through him.

"Shut your mouth, Dad." Leo pressed the point of the knife against his chest. "You speak when I tell you, and then you keep your voice down, understand?"

The watchman nodded, his fear subsiding somewhat. They both were young, he could tell, scavengers, kids. He was fifty-three years old, and his instincts were to clobber them and send them home.

"The key." The knife prodded him. "Where's the key?"

"Let me sit up." The man swung his legs over the edge of the desk, his eyes level with Leo's. "What did you say?"

"Are you deaf or something? The key, now!"

"All right, keep your shirt on. Over there, hanging on that nail."

Cory lifted the large key ring and handed it to Leo. "Which one for the small door?" Leo held them out. "Come *on*. I'm not playing games with you, old man. Which one?" The watchman pointed to a Banham mortice key. "That's all? Just the one?"

"Just the one. Look . . ."

"Shut it. Come on, get up . . . you're going to invite us in, aren't you?"

"Listen, lads, there's nothing in there—"

"Who asked you?" Leo shoved, sending him stumbling against Cory. "Open the door and get out of here. *Quietly.* Close it behind you." He nodded to Cory.

As they filed into the warehouse, Leo slapped at the watchman's hand as it went automatically to the light switch. "Do something like that again, and you're in trouble, right? Now lock the door again. You"—he turned to Cory—"find something to tie him up with."

Cory almost grinned at the peculiar accent Leo had adopted, the tough guy language meant to intimidate the old man. He found some white nylon twine on the packers' shelf and held the knife while Leo bound the older man tightly, hands behind his back, knees drawn up. The nylon was looped around the watchman's neck and then taken down to his ankles. Cory felt some pity for the trussed-up figure, but it would be for only three or four hours, he knew.

Grunting with satisfaction as he knotted a gag in place, Leo stood up and drew Cory aside. "Where is it?" He picked the knife delicately from Cory's fingers. "Where's the safe?"

Cory nodded toward the small office sectioned off in the right-hand corner of the warehouse. He followed Leo, stepping gingerly in the darkness.

"Some place," Leo murmured. "Spooky."

The safe looked much bigger than Cory remembered. It was an old gray Chubb, its tumbler dial scratched and worn. It stood, cemented into the floor, against the back wall of the office. The only furniture in the room was a scarred desk, two plastic chairs, and a filing cabinet.

"Can you open it?" Cory whispered.

"He's got a voice, hallelujah. Here, hold the torch, and let's have a look."

Leo crouched down in front of the safe and pulled on a pair of surgical gloves. "Not bad," he murmured. "Haven't seen one of these dodos for years, but it can be done, boyo, it can sure as hell be done. Hold that light steady."

The watchman heard a muffled thump behind him and tried to draw his knees up closer to his chest. A rat? His flesh tingled with distaste, and he prayed for this night to be over. He attempted to shift, to move, in case the thing came closer. His shoulder and hipbone scraped painfully against the concrete as he pushed himself around, straining his neck to see.

There was another sound, farther away, but the same sort of sound, a spark of light. A few minutes later the smell of smoke came faintly to his nostrils. For Christ's sake, a fire! He froze, trying to shout through the gag, but it only made him retch. Had one of those boys lit a cigarette and thrown a match down carelessly? He couldn't think. What had started as a soft crackling had become a steady roar, and flickers of red light grew fiercer by the second. The fire was flaring and spreading, inching toward him, and already the heat had brought a film of sweat to his forehead.

His mind leaped in panic. They were after the money in the safe but the office had no windows, so they couldn't see what was happening; by the time they did, he would be dead! The way he was tied prevented him from rolling over. He tried, grazing his forehead, his exertions dragging great drafts of smoke into his lungs.

When he saw the flames creeping up on him from two other directions, he realized that this was no chance happening. His scalp tightened, and he could smell his hair beginning to singe. He cursed his luck and screamed silently into the material covering his mouth. If he could just turn and hold his hands out, the flames would melt the nylon cord. But he couldn't; those bastards had done for him.

You killed me. He shocked himself with the words as the unbelievable agony spread. His hair flamed like a fizzing firework. You killed me. It was his last thought.

"I thought you said it would be easy." Cory felt they'd been in the office for hours.

"Just hold that damned light steady." Leo was on his knees, ear pressed against the safe. He was enjoying himself.

Cory was considering what to say to Arion and Ani when he got home in a few hours' time. He had not slept in his bed for two nights, and he knew that his grandfather had been asking around for him. Earlier that afternoon he'd got two messages, one filtered through Leo, to say that he was wanted at home. What could he tell the old man? He could say there'd been a girl. . . . Arion always understood that, even showed pleasure at the admission. But he'd used that excuse too often, and he'd never stayed away for so long. No, it would have to be something else. . . .

"What's that?" Cory's head swiveled in alarm.

"For God's sake, hold that light—"

"No. No, listen! What's that noise?"

Leo jerked his head away from the safe. "I was nearly there, you bloody idiot. I was—" He stopped abruptly because he could hear it, too, a faint crackling, like a crowd of people walking over dry twigs.

"I can smell smoke. Leo, can you smell smoke?"

Leo scrambled up. "Switch on the light!" he screamed. The air was suddenly hot around them, suddenly blistering in through the cracks, crunching like a huge animal moving forward. "The lights," he screamed again, groping in the dark.

Cory swung the thin beam of light around frantically. The panic in Leo's voice jarred him. He flicked the light switch. "It doesn't work," he said, sounding more calm than he felt. "There is no light."

Leo crashed past him, doubled up, toward the doorway. Cory knew what was happening. In a distant part of his mind he knew that it was all over, that by some fluke he was going to die here, and that it wasn't all that inappropriate. He heard himself say, "Don't open the door," a fraction of a second before Leo did, shrinking back as a wall of white flame barreled into the room, taking Leo where he stood, killing his momentum, shriveling him into a blackened statue.

Cory held his hands up to his face, feeling them blister and shred like paper. The pain he felt was because Arion would find him here, he would know what he'd been doing, and he, Cory, would not be there to explain—finally to explain.

His clothes ignited, and he could no longer see through his swollen lids. He sighed as he toppled, lungs and heart seared. He died wanting Arion's smile on him one last time.

Part Three

34

☐ They arrived back from the clinic in Gloucestershire at ten-thirty. Angie had never been to Frank's flat in Bloomsbury before. She made no comment as she followed him up two flights of stairs and then, as she walked into the large white flat, just "Oh." Everything was white: the walls; the ceiling; even the bookcases and rugs.

"No, you're not dreaming," Frank said. "I've been here just over a year, and I haven't got around to redecorating. The previous owner left the bookshelves and the rugs. Actually I'm beginning to like it."

Angie thought it was like being in the middle of a warm snowdrift. She said, "Mind if I put my feet up? You've done all the driving, and I feel exhausted."

Frank brought her a rug and went into the kitchen, where he set about checking the ingredients for an omelet. Neither he nor Angie had eaten anything since the cold meat and salad lunch they'd had with Oliver and Cissy. He removed a bottle of white wine from the fridge, then changed his mind and sat down with a cup of instant coffee, hoping to give Angie enough time to doze off if she wanted to. In the event, she made him jump by padding in after him, barefoot. The day had taken a lot out of her, but unless he was seeing what he wanted to see, she was beginning to recover.

She seemed to be able to call on hidden reserves of strength when she needed it—like now. The drive to and from Gloucestershire had been the easiest hours of their day.

"What on earth are you doing?" she asked. "Hiding?"

"You looked ready to drop a few minutes ago; I thought you might like to sleep for a bit."

"I'm wide-awake. No, not strictly true, I'm awake, and I'm starving."

He gave up the idea of an omelet and grilled some lamb chops while she made a salad. It was an odd sort of meal, finished off with some fine Brie. They both drank whiskey throughout. When Angie sat back with a sigh of contentment, Frank ventured that it didn't take all that much to please her.

"You're wrong," she said, remembering her run-in with Sidney the previous day, then her father, and finally Jason Corbett. "My tolerance level is"—she glanced down at her bare feet—"somewhere around my ankles. I've been told—"

"Why do you listen?"

"Not everyone is wrong. Don't *you* ever listen?"

He shrugged. "All the time, but I suspect I'm more selective about what I take on board."

"Semantics, Frank. I want to . . . thank you for being with me today. It couldn't have been very pleasant for you, and I'm grateful."

"I'm very fond of Oliver," he said quietly. "And Cissy, now that I'm getting to know her. She's an extraordinary woman."

Angie smiled. Cissy. "She's the one piece of good luck Oliver's had in his life. He couldn't have got through this without her."

Angie had been dreading this day. Cissy was not given to exaggeration, but over the past weeks her tears of rage and impotence had had an oddly comforting effect on Angie. She interpreted Cissy's outbursts as signs of hope and always kept her talking long enough to reassure herself—and Cissy—that Oliver would survive this.

"You'll be shocked," she kept telling Angie. "But please don't let him see it. Pamela insisted on coming over for the first time a few days ago, and she reacted badly. He wants to see you, Angie, but he's not looking forward to it."

In spite of Cissy's warnings, she wasn't prepared. Frank had been courteously silent during the drive to the Cotswolds, allowing her time to think . . . or not. It was barely two months since she'd last seen Oliver but what she feared that what he had been through in that time would have put a distance between them. It could be like talking to a stranger.

They had arranged for a table to be set up for lunch on the lawn, well away from the immense Victorian mansion and other gowned figures trailing listlessly in and out of its French windows. As Cissy hurried across the graveled driveway to greet them, Angie looked past her shoulder for sight of Oliver. He was too far away for her to see him clearly, but she registered the fact that a gaudy blanket covered him from the waist down and was tucked in around his ankles. His hands were hidden. So intense was her concentration that she collided with Cissy and felt Frank's hand close on her upper arm.

"I can't do this," she whispered as Frank guided her across the lawn. She dug one heel deep into the turf so that she could kneel and postpone the moment.

"Yes, you can." Frank urged her up and, without appearing to, propelled her forward.

Oliver wasn't fooled. As she reached him, he said, "You always were an abominable liar, Angie. So don't say it, whatever it is."

His hair was thin, lank, and lusterless. Apart from the gaunt pallor of his face, the first thing she noticed was that the color had seeped out of his eyes. What had once been a brilliant blue-gray was now a chalky imitation that made her think of sightless, shriveled old age.

"Oliver?" She drew his hand out from beneath the blanket, circling the wasted wrist with her fingers, feeling the tendons and bones. It was lifeless. She lifted it in both of hers, and it was weightless and dry, like an autumn leaf. A tired old man, needing visibly nothing, an old, old man on the run-in . . .

"Sit down," he told her, pulling away with surprising strength. "You're blocking my sun. Frank, it was good of you to drive Angie over. It's a long way."

"I like to get away from London occasionally. In any case, your sister is an excellent conversationalist." He winked at Angie and then patted his pockets. "I've run out of cigarettes."

"Come, I'll show you where you can buy some," Cissy said.

Oliver nodded at their retreating figures. "Nice man."

"They're leaving us alone," Angie murmured.

"I realize that. I'm just sober, not mentally retarded, you know." He accepted a cigarette from her. "And stop looking at me like that. The worst is over. From here on in it's a doddle, so they tell me."

"I'd probably ask them to define doddle," Angie said thickly, fumbling for her handbag.

"What are you looking for, sunglasses? Don't bother. It is *allowed*."

"I'm not crying, damn it!" she snarled at him. Oliver nodded. She was flushed and slightly rumpled, great dark eyes awash with tears. "Was it bad?"

"Worse than anything." His gaze fastened on a stand of oaks in the distance. Angie watched him retreat to the edges of that nightmare and then haul himself back. This wasn't the time to cry. The worst *was* over; if he needed anything now, it was for her to share his hope.

"I hear fantastic things about you, Angie. Are they true? I heard about *Night Work*. Christ, that party seems like a hundred years ago. The book is good. . . . I got around to reading it last week. I can't vouch absolutely for my concentration, but I think there's an exceptional talent there."

"The two-book contract doesn't worry you? If the second book isn't any good, *you're* the one who's going to be lumbered with it."

He gave her an odd, sideways glance. "You did the right thing. What about the paperback rights?"

"I'm going to auction them. The only question is, When? Now, or after publication, when the reviews are in?"

"Now," Oliver said emphatically. "Capitalize on what the trade already believes: that staid old Jarman's, under new and dynamic direction, is back in business."

"Cut that out," Angie said sharply. "The glamour bit, buying and wheeling and dealing, that's the easy part of it, and you know it."

Oliver laughed wheezily, dragging a smile out of her. "Of course, I'd forgotten just how easy it was. Listen, I wasn't being sarcastic—well, maybe just a little, because . . . I wish you could see yourself. I wasn't going to tell you for a while yet, but you might as well know now: I'm not coming back."

She was still too shocked by his appearance to feel any surprise at his statement. She wondered if she'd been expecting it. "It's the way you're feeling now . . ."

"No, it isn't. I knew you'd say that, and that was why I wasn't going to tell you. Cissy is just beginning to believe me. And now that I've seen you, there's no question about it."

"What do you mean?"

"Just this . . . and remember, I've gone beyond the hallucinating stage: I don't know what else is going on in your life, but I can't remember ever seeing you more . . . alive."

"Rubbish," Angie said quickly, reaching for the ashtray. "You've decided that in ten minutes?"

"Since you arrived. Body language . . . and more. I saw it when you were walking toward me. It sounds callous, but you're looking better than you did even when you were with Lou. Do you remember telling me once that, with Lou gone, your safety net had a great big hole in it? Well, it's time you realized that you function better without any net at all."

"Oh, very clever," Angie muttered.

"And it's not what you want to hear. But I can't help that. Does Frank have anything to do with it?"

Relieved to be talking about someone other than herself, she told him about Frank and Lisa, amused by his clear disappointment. "Incompatible glands," she finished, and before he could go on to ask her about Paul Angelou, she told him about her confrontation with Jason Corbett the previous day. That made him laugh again as he pictured their father's restraint. Angie said, "He would have liked to sack me on the spot, but how do you sack someone you're not even paying?"

"Are the other production quotes you got really that much lower than Jason's?"

"I'm afraid so."

"The old man must have been fit to be tied. What about Sidney? How are you getting on with him?"

"If you really want to know, I'll tell you. Badly. I'm sorry, but not even for you can I tolerate his presence. And it *is* a presence. One way or another I intend to get rid of him."

"Martin, too?" She hadn't mentioned Martin's name, and when she nodded, he said, "Don't look so guilty. I was too lax. You're the one on the spot; it's your decision."

"I find Jason intriguing, though. I like him, and I don't want to alienate him. He . . . surprises me."

"And not many people do that, right?"

Angie accepted the gently chiding note in his voice. "Is this facility for instant analysis part of the service here, or did you have to pay extra? What are you going to do if you don't come back?"

If. She didn't quite believe him yet. "I'm going to live, Angie. Don't laugh, but we're considering a world cruise. Can you see it? I can't, but if it isn't that, it'll be something else. I'm thinking of applying to Swan Hellenic—"

"Lecturing on archaeology on their cruises? That's a wonderful idea.'' The color in his eyes had deepened. Angie saw it, wanting to applaud and caution him at the same time.

''And you?'' he asked. ''What will you do, stay and take over?''

''I'll do it for as long as I said I would. After that . . . when will you tell Father? Could you leave it for a while?''

''You think I'll change my mind?''

''It isn't that.'' She was thinking of her daughter and a new life, too, of Paul Angelou and Jason Corbett, of herself. ''I need a bit more time, that's all. Christopher Chetwynd should be in touch any day now.''

''I was hoping you would be able to tell me something . . . I mean, some news.''

''Chetwynd keeps telling me to be patient, that these things take time. He's an extremely unforthcoming man, your friend, and I'm not, as you know, very patient.''

''Sit tight, leave it to Christopher. He's a *good* friend. And let me know the minute you hear from him, will you?''

That, too—the rape and her child—had brought Oliver to this place. ''I'm scared,'' she said.

''So am I, but listen, concentrate on one fear at a time. The old man is going to hit the roof when I tell him I'm not coming back. I'm not looking forward to telling him, but at least I won't be within . . . range.''

Close enough to be peppered with shrapnel, though, Angie thought. But safe, safely out of it, leaving her unintentionally, as a sitting duck . . .

''You don't have to make the decision right away,'' Frank was saying now. More than at any time in her life, he realized, she was living and working blind. On the way back from Gloucestershire she'd told him about Oliver's decision and been totally unsurprised by his reaction: ''It's what you want to do, isn't it? What's more, you're damned good at it.''

''Publishing, yes. Jarman's, I'm not so sure.''

If London publishing had satisfied its curiosity about her, she had no idea. Not that the curiosity had manifested itself in any way other than polite invitations to lunch. People in the industry saw her successful bid for *Night Work* as a statement of intent, Frank told her, more than a suggestion that there was an open checkbook on her desk. When she'd laughed in amazement, he'd added, ''At least we've paid you the ultimate compliment of not submitting books we've been trying unsuccessfully to place for years. Don't look so surprised. It's been known to happen."

But he was right. At least she didn't have to make up her mind immediately. She helped herself to another sliver of Brie and nodded her thanks as Frank placed a cup of coffee in front of her. Her silence prompted him to say, flatly, "You're not thinking of going back to New York."

"It's crossed my mind, but that also depends on what Christopher Chetwynd has to tell me. I *could* take up my life there again."

"You belong *here*, Angie. This is where you live."

Did she? Consciously or not, she had been postponing her life, getting through the days, waiting. The child first; everything else would follow from there: the houses Frank had agreed to look at with her over the next few weeks; the growing estrangement from her parents; Jarman's; her risible need of Paul Angelou. All that . . .

"Would you like to come into the other room and listen to some music?"

"Another time, please, Frank. It's late, and I'm tired."

"Stay."

"Here?"

"With me, yes. I don't want you to go home alone tonight. You'll find everything you need in the bathroom, toothbrush, cream, wrap. Go now, before you fall asleep out here."

"Frank . . ."

He wasn't listening. She surprised herself by obeying him. By the time she emerged from the bathroom, wrapped in a heavy white robe, he'd washed and stacked the dishes and was listening to a sonata she couldn't identify.

"The only thing missing in the bathroom is a nightgown," she said.

"Tired?"

"Dead."

He led her into the bedroom and pulled the duvet down. He gave her two of the three pillows and said, "Nice. Very nice," as she slipped off the robe. Scrubbed and damp-haired, she looked like a child, played out. He planted a kiss on one of her eyelids before turning out the light.

She slept deeply and dreamlessly for the first time since Lou had died. She drifted into consciousness once or twice, aware that Frank was in the next room. She could hear him breathing. Once she thought that she might wake him up and talk about Lisa, and it didn't seem a silly idea, and when the telephone rang, she pulled the duvet over her head, having decided, happily, that it was Lisa, calling Frank.

Frank came awake instantly, grazing his elbow on the wooden strut of the couch as he tried to reach the receiver before the second ring woke Angie. He looked at his watch. It was five o'clock in the morning. Unless some American had miscalculated the time difference badly, it had to be bad news. . . .

"Hullo? *Scotia?* . . . What's wrong?"

Scotia was weeping. Frank dropped the receiver and got up to turn on a table lamp. Arion, something had happened to the old man.

"Scotia, it's Frank. What's wrong? *Tell me!*"

The sound of scuffling came down the line, a hurried few words. Then a woman's voice. "Frank? It's Olga. Something has happened . . ." The words would not come out of her mouth either.

"For God's sake," he shouted. "Is it Arion?"

"No, it is Cory. You know Cory. He is—he has been . . . dead, and Arion is asking for you."

"Dead?" Frank looked up to see Angie standing in the doorway. "Where is Ari, at home? Tell him I'll be there. . . . No, no, right now. Ten minutes."

"What is it?" Angie came forward, her fist bunching the robe up around her neck.

Frank looked at her without recognition, the receiver in both hands, like a weapon. "It's Arion. I must go."

Arion Angelou—Paul's father. "Where? What happened?"

"His grandson has died. I don't know how." He still made no move to get up.

"I'll come with you."

"No."

"Yes! I know his son, remember? Maybe I can help. Get up, Frank, get dressed."

She found her dress hanging outside one of the cupboards in the bedroom and hesitated for a moment. The russet garment, sleeveless, with a scooped-out neckline and delicate shoulder straps, looked distinctly frivolous in the circumstances. Then she heard Frank open the front door and quickly slipped the dress on without pausing for any underwear. The silky material felt cool against her bare skin. She couldn't find a comb and settled for pushing the hair out of her eyes as they ran out to the car. Frank said nothing as he drove, nothing as they drew up outside the house that was flooded with light. Two policemen stood on the pavement, the front door was open, and people were beginning to gather in curious groups nearby.

A tall, menacing-looking man with red-rimmed eyes was waiting for them. "Scotia." Frank grabbed his arm. "Where's Ari?"

"In the kitchen, Frank. It's not good, you understand."

"What happened? What happened to Cory?"

"He was burned."

Frank caught his breath and turned to Angie, as though she could provide an explanation. "Burned? What do you mean?"

"In the warehouse. He and . . . others."

Frank exploded. "What the bloody hell was he doing in the warehouse!"

"Nobody knows that, but the police, they think . . . they have told Ari that Cory was stealing."

"Christ! What was there to steal?"

"Money in a big safe, Frank. Money."

Frank looked around in bewilderment. There was so much pain in this house that Angie's instincts were to turn and run. Then Frank took her hand, and she had no option but to follow him down a short flight of steps into the large kitchen.

There were perhaps a dozen people in the room, and the only person she saw as she walked in was Paul Angelou.

They had obviously just got out of bed. Paul held the woman's glance for an endless moment, long enough to register fully the shock of her surprise. Then Frank Sheldon propelled her toward the table where his father sat.

Murder. The word hit Paul. It would be classified as murder. No, accidental death, except that the arson had not been accidental. More than just bad luck, there was almost a sense of divine vengeance about it. What in God's name had happened? How could Harry Baird have been so stupid? Murder. He repeated the word to himself and let it lie exposed in his head. Susan stood behind him, talking quietly to Olga, each asking questions the other couldn't answer. Paul slid away from them, trying to isolate himself from the hubbub, to consider the implications. . . .

Scotia was handing out mugs of black coffee. Angie took

one and moved back until she was standing in front of the
Aga. Heat spilled out, and she shivered. Deep, uncontrollable sobs were coming from the old man, muffled now as
Frank held him. The old woman watched her husband, a
cold, dead look on her face. And Paul Angelou watched them
all.

For some reason it hadn't occurred to Angie that he would
be there. A total image of what she and Frank had looked
like when they'd walked in had been encompassed in the look
she and Paul had exchanged. The collar of Frank's shirt was
turned inside out, he wore slip-ons with no socks, and the
hair on the crown of his head stood up in spiky waves. Her
own hair was a tangled mess. Standing there, Angie felt naked, aware of her flimsy dress, inhaling the musky dampness
of her own body.

"Angie." Frank beckoned her over, and she could see
wetness on his eyelashes. "I think Ani's going to need a
sedative. Try to get their doctor over, would you? And see if
you can find out exactly what happened?"

Angie nodded and turned to find Paul, but he was no longer
in the room. She went to Susan, who was shaking her head
sadly at the diminutive woman at her side; both women had
obviously dressed in a hurry. Susan wore a belted honey-
colored raincoat over a polo-neck sweater and light cotton
trousers, her hair tucked behind her ears.

"Mrs. Angelou." Angie spoke tentatively. "Do you know
the name of the family doctor? Frank thinks that maybe a
sedative . . ."

"Yes." Susan brushed her hand over her forehead and then,
as though she'd just recognized her, said, "Mrs. Wyatt. I
didn't realize you knew my husband's parents."

"I don't." Angie glanced toward Frank, who now stood
behind Ani, speaking earnestly into her ear. There was no
sign that she heard anything he said.

"I'll call Dr. Bergen immediately," Susan said.

Angie took a cigarette from an open packet on the table,
lit it, and followed Susan Angelou out of the room. Paul's
wife disappeared into the front room, and Angie sat on the
bottom step in the hallway, trying to blot out the scene in
the kitchen. She now understood why Frank spoke of Paul
the way he did. Frank was the one who'd held Arion Angelou
and cried with him, Frank who'd registered the boy's death
with confused anger. He wasn't deliberately usurping the son's

place; it was just that Paul seemed to be present for another reason altogether. An accident of birth . . . Angie lowered her head, fighting a real fear in this unreal morning. How far, she wondered, divorcing herself from her surroundings, could the apple fall from the tree? Could her daughter, the beautiful and serious child she dreamed about, be as different from her as Paul was from his father?

Paul came through the front door and was halfway across the hall before he saw her. He stopped. She noted the dark stubble on his cheeks and chin and thought how he must hate being seen like this. She said, "Your wife is phoning for a doctor."

"Good." He sounded angry. "Maybe *he* can get rid of all these policemen. It's a wonder some newspaper reporter hasn't turned up yet."

"Do you know what happened to the boy?"

"Apart from the fact that he appeared to be in the middle of a robbery, no."

He was standing over her, so Angie got up, alienated by his stance and the freezing neutrality in his tone. "That's hard, considering the boy is dead."

"My father is a stubborn old man. Everybody could see it coming except him."

"What do you mean?"

"I mean Cory was a tearaway, out for what he could get from the old man."

"But why should he set the place alight?"

"To cover his traces, I suppose. Bloody fool . . . it's unforgivable."

Angie inched backward until her heels came up against the bottom step. She fumbled for words under his critical eyes. "Unforgivable. That he was . . . careless or that he was killed?"

"Both. Why are you moving away from me?" He bared his teeth derisively at her. "Do I still *scare* you, Angela?"

"I think I want to ask you why your heart doesn't break, even a little . . . for those two people in there." She jerked her head in the direction of the kitchen.

His glance swept over her, at once appraising and insolent. "I hope you're not going to cry. Well, at least there's no mascara left to run."

Angie's hand went involuntarily to her cheek, as if she'd been slapped. His meaning was clear enough: that she was

smudged and moist in the aftermath of lovemaking. Instead
of anger, she felt herself flush with embarrassment. He continued to observe her, humorlessly.

"Get out of my way." She tried to brush past him.

He said conversationally, "You lied to me. Tell me, is he
good? Did you enjoy it?" He didn't move.

"Paul, please . . ."

"Did you enjoy it?" He could have killed her. She had
betrayed him. This had been his inescapable fear, and he
knew that he could not control himself at that moment any
more than he could control her mind or what she did with
her body. He ignored the outrage on her face, blocking her
escape. "Did you enjoy being screwed, Angela? I hope you
weren't interrupted by all this . . ."

"Don't speak to me like that!" she gasped. Murder was
up there in his eyes. Her anger overrode every splinter of
logic. She didn't know how to counter his accusations; she
couldn't begin to explain that she was torn, even now, between a wild desire to touch him and some internal mecha-
nism that stopped her from telling him that she hadn't given
herself to Frank Sheldon.

"You look worn-out," he said. She did. She stood whip-
tired, shoulders forward, tense and quite still. I could tell you
about your daughter now, he thought dispassionately. You'll
never find her; you're wasting your time. Then pity caught at
his throat and stabbed deep into his bowels. She's *paid*. In
the soft focus of his vision she moved, and he stopped her
with words he'd never used before. "How many times did
Frank Sheldon fuck you? Three? Four?"

Angie's throat constricted. "Please!"

He looked at her with contempt for a moment, then stood
aside and said decisively, "We'll discuss this later. I'll call
you."

"What are you talking about? *Call me?*"

"Yes."

"Don't."

"I'll call you," he repeated.

"Don't!"

"Why not? We can talk about my heart, and"—he glanced
down at her bare legs—"I might even buy you some stockings."

The considered insult was somehow even more appalling
than the words he'd used earlier. Angie strained forward and

slapped him across the mouth with all her strength. Then she was stumbling toward the kitchen, rubbing her stinging palm against her hip. She felt like a stray cat that had worn its claws down trying to get out of a box.

Frank pulled out a chair and made her sit down. "Are you cold?" She was shaking. "What happened?"

"I—nothing, Frank. Susan is calling a doctor."

"Thank you." He turned back to Arion; he didn't know who looked worse, Angie or Arion. "This is Angie," he said.

"Angie." Arion tried out the name. "You knew my grandson?"

"No, I—" Her own voice broke as his eyes filled with tears again.

"Forgive me," he whispered, moving into her arms.

"It gets better," she heard herself say, rocked by the nakedness of this grief. "It will never be the same, but it does get better." She felt him nod, and her arms tightened around him as her own trembling subsided. Over his shoulder she saw Ani nodding, too, although she could not have heard.

Ani believed that Cory would walk through the door at any moment and make fun of them all. That she would never see him again was not true. What the policeman had said was not true. That the pain of it might kill Ari was more unreal than anything else. She held herself in for his sake and nodded at the woman who held him. That was good. She knew she would die if she held Ari and felt his tears.

When Arion finally pulled away, Angie's arms were aching. She moved aside for Scotia and whispered to Frank, "Can't you get all these people out of here?"

"Apart from the police, these are his friends. Family. Where the hell is Paul?"

"The son?" she asked bitterly as Angelou's face cut across her consciousness.

"You've met him. I keep forgetting."

"Will they be all right?"

"Arion and Ani? Christ, I hope so. Did you find out anything?"

"Nothing, except that Paul considered the boy something of a crook. He said he'd taken Arion for a ride—"

"Paul never liked Cory. It seems certain, though, that he and one or two others were in the middle of breaking into the safe when the fire started. What's killing Ari is that he found out only yesterday that Cory had lost a lot of money gambling and hadn't told him. Presumably he was hoping to pay off the debts by raiding the safe. Ari can't understand why the boy didn't tell him.''

Before Angie could say anything, Paul came back into the room and strode over to his parents. He leaned over Arion's shoulder and said something softly. They didn't touch.

"The doctor's probably arrived," Angie said, watching Paul straighten up and walk toward them.

"Thank you for coming," he said easily, taking Frank's hand. "I'm grateful for your support. And you, Angela."

She thought for a moment that he was going to reach for her hand, too, and a shapeless longing nearly brought her down at his feet. Her knees actually buckled. She jerked back and felt Frank's arm go around her waist. He pulled her close against his hip and took her efforts to separate herself from him as movements to regain her balance. He simply held her against himself in a casually proprietorial way. What did they look like? Like lovers.

Those seconds seemed to last forever. Her brain felt like a plowed-up field. There was no hiding away from this one. Any halfway intelligent human being would have come to the conclusion that she and Frank Sheldon had spent at least part of the previous night making love. She could so easily have denied it to Paul, offered an explanation, whether he believed it or not. Yet she hadn't. In some corner of her mind lay the distasteful truth: she had enjoyed his intensity, the ruthless clarity of his attack; even in her inarticulate fury, she'd felt herself rammed into a higher gear, invigorated by his perception of her, what he thought he'd seen. . . .

Frank was talking about the police officer who was waiting to interview Arion. Paul was nodding. His eyes dropped to her breasts but appeared to be unfocused, as though he were really concentrating on Frank's words. Then a tiny muscle snagged at the corner of his mouth, and Angie looked down to see that Frank's arm about her waist had twisted her dress around, pulling it tightly across her breasts. Her nipples, blatantly erect, were clearly outlined by the material. For the second time that morning she felt blood flush up into her cheeks. She saw herself as Paul saw her and almost laughed up into his face. None of this is real, she thought; not even *you* have choreographed such a black comedy.

She gently prized Frank's arm away and straightened her

dress. She put a few inches of space between them. It seemed incredible that Frank could not see what was going on.

"The police definitely suspect arson?" Paul was asking.

"That's what the inspector told me, but there's also the chance that Cory or one of the others dropped a lighted cigarette. It could have been an accident."

"I'm sure it was. Not even Cory would have been stupid enough to start something like that deliberately. What do you think, Angela?"

"I never met him—"

"That doesn't mean you can't have an opinion."

"It seems to me that you'll find out soon enough what actually happened."

"Angie's right," Frank said. "At the moment I'm more concerned about your mother and father—"

"That's good of you," Paul interrupted. "I'm sure they appreciate your concern."

Frank made an impatient sound at the gibe, and Angie said, "I'm leaving." She had to get away from both of them, right now. "Frank, please call me if there's anything you need."

Standing in the doorway, Susan saw Angie move away from the two men. She walked jerkily, as though her limbs were being controlled by an inept puppeteer. Susan had become accustomed to people reacting strangely to the handsome, somber man who was her husband, but Angela Wyatt was showing signs of extreme stress, more than could be accounted for by the death of a total stranger.

Susan watched her press Ani's hand and place her cheek for a long moment against Arion's. Then she came toward her, eyes downcast, avoiding—what? Paul? He was still talking to Frank Sheldon, but his eyes followed Angela Wyatt with a look of frightening assurance. Susan sighed and felt the breath leave her body.

It had to happen sooner or later; she'd always known that. He hadn't expected to see Angela Wyatt here; he hadn't had time to prepare himself. She was the woman he saw; Susan knew that now as surely as if he'd formulated the words himself. She was the woman who brought him to her bed almost every night. Susan wanted to say something as she passed her, but Angie didn't look up. Then she was gone.

35

☐ Sidney conceived a plan of action that would bring him immense satisfaction, even if it did not work out perfectly. The idea came to him while he was reading *Night Work*. Sabotage. Ideal in the circumstances, effective and yet relatively safe. He told none of the others except Martin, who could be of some use to him. And because Martin had not yet realized that Angela Wyatt could and would harm him. He was under the mistaken illusion that he could shelter behind his father, that Jason Corbett's clout with Sir Richard Jarman was sufficient to protect him.

Sidney knew better. Sir Richard had stormed in and out of her office; Jason Corbett had come and gone. This morning he, Sidney, had phoned the new printers, ostensibly with a setting query. They had treated him like a benefactor, eager to please. He'd hung up impressed despite himself. She had not canceled the print order; she'd done not a damn thing to extricate herself. Such arrogant self-confidence in a woman irked him. In this particular woman it almost crippled him with fury.

He had spent most of Wednesday afternoon and much of the early evening reading *Night Work*. He did not take kindly to its quality and ended up with two pages of closely written notes. *Night Work* was eccentric, not only in its language but in its languid pace and lack of decisive denouement.

He guessed that the book would appeal to a few of the more snobby reviewers. They would no doubt praise the author for his bravery, for not being diverted or influenced by the prospect of bestsellerdom. Enough of those, and it could become a cult book, one of the great unread, bought for its spine and after-dinner value.

And Lisa Barrett was going to auction it in New York. That meant that Farley Esterhuys was out in the cold. He was a greedy old bastard, Sidney knew, but he would have wanted

Night Work for the prestige even more than the money. And Lisa had done him out of both. It was almost funny, a complicated situation just waiting to be made worse.

On Thursday morning he phoned Elliot Stone and introduced himself. "Kept me reading into the small hours," he lied. "It's the first book to have done that since *The White Hotel*."

"Really?" The man was easily flattered, Sidney thought contemptuously. There was a pause. He wanted more.

Sidney gave him fifteen minutes of undiluted admiration before Elliot swallowed the hook. They agreed to meet for a meal after Elliot's next meeting with Deborah in about ten days' time. He would be in London overnight to clear up any copy editing problems. Perfect. Sidney kept the smile out of his voice. He confirmed the time and left Stone with a final puff for good measure. He was ripe, the narcissistic little shit, there for the taking.

36

☐   Harry Baird was expecting the news of the warehouse fire to be mentioned at the end of a local radio broadcast. He was shaved and showered and not really listening to the first item on the news: bodies, two identified, one burned beyond recognition, the tragedy of a robbery gone wrong, police inquiries, forensic experts on the scene. . . .

"Jesus God!" He sat down on the bed, sock in hand. There was a roaring in his ears as he grappled to make sense of what he'd just heard. It had to be a mistake. Three bodies? Who the hell were they?

He finished dressing and stopped himself from running down the stairs and out of the house. In the kitchen his wife was buttering toast, at the same time looking at the small television set on the counter. "Terrible, isn't it?" she murmured, nodding at the picture of the still-smoldering ruin.

Harry made himself chew through two slices of toast and

drink two cups of coffee. Everything as usual. He nearly choked, grateful now that she accepted as normal his silence in the mornings. He could lose everything they had built up together. All of it.

He stopped at the first phone box he saw and broke a cardinal rule by dialing Paul Angelou's office. He hadn't arrived yet. The operator was quietly insistent that he leave his name. She was unconvinced by the excuse that he himself was unreachable and would try again later in the day. Without much hope Harry tried again, this time Paul Angelou's home number. He was shocked when Angelou answered.

"I'll pick you up at the north entrance of the British Library in an hour," Angelou said. "Wait for me."

Harry stared at the buzzing receiver for a moment, then replaced it. He inserted another tenpence coin into the slot and dialed another number. There was no answer. He tried again. His stomach churned with nausea. If Simon Riggs was one of those found dead in the warehouse, it could be over . . . for all of them.

"Are you telling me it was a coincidence?" Harry raised his voice as an articulated lorry thundered past. *"Coincidence?"*

"I'm not telling you anything except what I have been told. The boys were breaking into the safe; they were trapped. The third person is probably the night watchman."

"How do you know that?"

"I don't *know* anything. The police interviewed the watchman's wife at eight o'clock this morning. He was an hour overdue then. I'd say that was fairly ominous, wouldn't you?"

"Christ," Harry whispered. "What happens now?"

"Nothing." Paul's hands lay loosely in his lap. To Harry he appeared angry rather than nervous, as though this were just another unforeseen hiccup in his plan. "You do nothing and you say nothing and you do not call me again, under any circumstances."

"What about Riggs?"

"Riggs?"

"The man who—" Harry could hardly bear to speak.

"The arsonist? You chose him. If you chose well, he'll know enough to take care of himself. Quite frankly that's your problem, and I expect you to take care of it."

He made it sound easy, not voicing the most concrete of all the dangerous possibilities: that Arion Angelou could be charged, not with arson but with causing the deaths of three people.

"Incidentally, Mr. Baird, you haven't mentioned the current price of the shares. You'll be pleased to know that I checked this morning, in the wake of . . . everything that has happened, and they stand at fifty-one pence."

"I'm not surprised. It's only your father's reputation that has prevented them from falling away to tenpence."

"Don't sell any more. If my father were able to retain control of Ani's and Prax, which are not part of Angel Holding's anyway, he could be sure of a comfortable retirement. But not Doric Video. If the arcade is included in a salvageable package . . ."

"The video arcade? I'm surprised you didn't bother to check. Your father doesn't own that."

"Of course he does."

"You're mistaken. He did own the property but very many years ago. It now belongs to the Barzini family and has for more than fifteen years."

"Are you sure?"

The bland murmured inquiry took Harry out of the car without another word. He crossed the road, dodging the traffic, to get away from Angelou. Even with *that* news, Angelou showed no sign of being touched, either by guilt or by regret. Harry sucked moisture into his mouth. He knew then that he was out of his depth with Angelou. And that there was nothing he could do about it.

37

☐ Ani had fallen into a drugged sleep upstairs, and the house was silent once more. Frank had persuaded Inspector Vincent to leave his questions until the following day. Lee Vincent wasn't too happy about it but went along with the request. The old couple were undeniably shocked and overwrought, and in any case, he had more than enough to occupy himself with for the next twenty-four hours.

"Please take my word for it, Inspector. Mr. Angelou will tell you everything you want to know. As it happens, I don't think he knows much."

"The question of the arson alone is a very serious one, Mr. Sheldon."

"I realize that. Would you have any objection if I drove out to see the warehouse for myself this afternoon? If I go, maybe Mr. Angelou won't feel it necessary to go himself."

"I've seen it. What's in it isn't for the squeamish."

Frank showed the policeman out and returned to the kitchen, where Arion now sat, alone. Olga had washed the dishes and emptied the ashtrays. Two damp dishcloths hung drying on the Aga rail. Someone, not Ani, had placed a vase of early yellow dahlias on top of the fridge. Frank noticed them for the first time and almost recoiled at their lush perfection.

"You surround yourself with beautiful women, Frank."

"Angie? She's very special."

"And your other girl? Lisa?" The question was light, but Frank detected a hint of reproach.

"Lisa is special also, but in a different way. Nothing has changed."

"That is very good. You will wait, and she will come to you." He said it so emphatically that Frank found himself nodding in agreement. Arion was gathering up the remnants of his strength, shifting the weight of his pain. He wanted to talk about love, the humor and chaos of it, not deeply, just enough to get him through the morning. Earlier, fighting against the narcotic Dr. Bergen made her take, Ani had said dreamily, "We must tell them we are coming, Ari. All of us."

He knew what she was saying, that her thoughts were on their planned trip to Greece, with Cory—and he knew what he had to do. Sitting in the kitchen with Frank only postponed the inevitable. "What am I to tell his mother and father? They gave their son to me. How can I tell them, Frank?"

"Let me, Ari. They'll understand."

"No, no, it is something I must do. Only it is . . . hard." It was one of the hardest things he would ever have to do. And only he could do it. He wanted to lift his head and howl out his grief like an animal, and like an animal, he wanted to run and hide from the days to come. "You must go to your office, Frank."

"Lisa's there. Don't worry about me."

"Is she not leaving today? Then you must say good-bye to her. There is much for you to do," Arion said sternly.

"Tomorrow won't be easy, Ari. The police want to talk to you about the fire."

"I know. There are many who want to talk to me."

"If you mean your bank manager, I told him what had happened when he phoned earlier. Don't worry about him. He can wait."

"Ah, you think so."

"What does that mean?"

"I am not worried, and it is not important now. Angel shares are . . . tumbling."

It was such an unusual word for Arion to use that Frank could not help smiling. "Seriously falling?"

Arion nodded pensively. "For some weeks now."

The phone rang, and Frank snatched it up. It was Angie, sounding hesitant until he identified himself. Arion got up and wandered out onto the porch. Frank could see him turn to pick dead leaves out of the flower pots.

"I'm going out to the warehouse this afternoon. Do you mind calling Lisa and telling her what's happened? I'll try to get in before she leaves for New York."

"Would you like me to come with you to the warehouse?"

"Thank you, no. I'll call you when I get back. There's more trouble here than just what happened to Cory, as if that weren't enough. Did Paul mention anything to you about his father's company?"

"No, why?"

"I'm not sure . . . all this happening together, Cory, the fire, Arion's shares."

"Can I help?"

"I'd say yes if I knew how."

"Well, I'm here if you need me. Please use me."

Frank joined Arion on the porch. The old man was holding a fistful of dead leaves. "Ani has so much concern. She always worries too much," he said. "I said to her the other day, 'You must not, it is not good for you, you will drop dead,' and she tells me, 'It is *you* who worries; for me, my days of dropping dead are over.' " He laughed softly, opened his palm, and let the crushed leaves blow away. "Now I must telephone."

He would not let Frank stay with him, not because his tears would shame him but because he had to tell a mother that her son was dead and he could not imagine anything other than the act of conception itself that was more intimate.

38

□ Lisa would always remember setting out on her first trip to New York on the day Arion Angelou's grandson died. She had been glad to leave London, not because of that but to get away and give herself time to think. She spent the tedious hours on the plane doggedly avoiding any thoughts at all. Rather than contemplate the previous few hours in London, she had two gins and a small bottle of wine with her meal, slept, and woke up in time for the in-flight film. A loose connection in her earphones made concentration imperative. She succumbed to a deadened eardrum halfway through, drank another gin, and fell asleep again, only to find herself outwitted by her subconscious. In two loosely connected but blindingly detailed sequences, she dreamed of Frank Sheldon and Angela Wyatt.

First there had been Angela Wyatt's call. Lisa had arrived at the office still smarting from the ugly end of her evening with Elliot Stone; she had taken the call grudgingly, annoyed with Frank for being late, today of all days.

When Angela Wyatt broke the news about the boy's death, Lisa could only think of Arion as she spoke, of his face as they told him, the way he would be feeling now. "When— when did this happen?"

"They're not sure yet, but we heard about it at five o'clock this morning."

We? Lisa's mind spun. Five o'clock in the morning? "We?"

"Frank and I . . ." Lisa heard the other woman's shallow

intake of breath as she realized what she'd said. "I . . . happened to be there at the time. We went to the house immediately, and Frank is still there. He asked me to tell you that he would try to get into the office later."

"Thank you," Lisa said numbly.

"Lisa . . ."

"Thank you, Mrs. Wyatt." Lisa hung up. She placed her palm flat against the receiver, holding it down. It was a gray morning, and her office had suddenly become a place of shadows and corners. She listened to the dull, uneven breaths coming from her own body; it was already a day she wanted to forget.

That was the first thing.

Frank had appeared at six o'clock, tired and unshaven. They met on the landing just as she was about to take her suitcases downstairs. He was surprised to see her still there.

"When I knew you wouldn't be coming in today, I asked Lilian to collect my suitcases so that I could go to the airport straight from here."

He looked exhausted, a little confused by her icy tone. "I'll drive you to the airport."

"A taxi's on the way."

"Well . . ." He hesitated. "Look after yourself."

She relented. "Frank, I'm sorry about Arion's grandson. How is he taking it?"

"I don't think either of them will ever get over it. Today . . . it's killing Ari."

"It's a bad time for me to be going off." Her mood was shifting now that he was here, furring at its hard edges. "If you need me here, I'll stay."

"No. Listen, your taxi is probably waiting downstairs. If *you* need anything while you're in New York, call me."

"I will. Frank . . ." He stood awkwardly, preoccupied, his hands deep in his pockets, peering at her in the gloom. "If you don't want me to stay, would you kiss me good-bye? I feel as though I'm catching a train to Brighton. If you kiss me, I'll know I'm going on a real journey."

He laughed directly at her. "Anything to get rid of you, baby Barrett."

Flabbergasted, Lisa walked into his arms. He held her shoulders, and his lips brushed her forehead. "Thank you," she said morosely. "That's the way my father kisses me."

Frank said no to himself and kissed her lips. He felt them

part under the light pressure, soften, the touch of her tongue.
"That's definitely not the way my father kisses me."

"I should hope not." He wondered what the hell she was
doing.

Lisa hadn't known then, even less now. She'd behaved like
a child, a winsome brat, taking from him when he had nothing left to give, certainly no pleasure after his day with Arion.
And she'd obviously embarrassed him because he'd disappeared into his own office without another word.

Every time she thought about it Lisa groaned, sometimes
quite loudly. She couldn't believe she'd done that, especially
after he'd apparently spent the night with Angela Wyatt. The
recurring memory had wrecked her journey and eclipsed the
excitement she experienced on landing at Kennedy Airport.
Once she was on the ground, however, Frank and Angela and
the whole of London dissolved into unimportance.

Her first thought when she stepped out of the airport terminal was: How can any one place outside of hell be so hot?
The humidity was a living, vibrant force that collided with
her and left her feeling stunned and limp. After forty-eight
hours her skin was dry, and a heat rash seared her arms and
shoulders. She had begun to dread leaving the large air-con-
ditioned room in the Tuscany Hotel. The humidity settled
over her like a bear rug, taking away her appetite and accentuating her Englishness. By the fourth day she had decided
not to be persecuted by her body temperature; she wore fewer
clothes, no stockings, used more moisturizer, no makeup.
She gave up on her hair the day she bruised her nose walking
into a glass door while she tried to pluck lank strands of it
out of her eyes.

New York publishers, on their own territory, charmed her
and laughed at her discomfort. The city was everything she
had imagined: gritty, glossy, and bad-tempered. A cab ride
down Fifth Avenue, from Fifty-third Street to the Flatiron
Building left her carsick; synchronized traffic lights allowed
the huge yellow cabs to blast down the uneven streets like
flying sailboats heaving into a storm. A cabdriver yelled at
her for getting out of the car before paying the fare. When he
heard her accent and saw her nose wrinkle as perspiration
slid down either side of it, he apologized, picked her up again
an hour later, and gave her a free ride back uptown.

Twice in one morning she was stopped by strangers and
advised to fasten the zipper on her briefcase. She saw three

elderly men skateboarding down Park Avenue; a man in a dark suit and homburg sat in the back of a limousine parked outside the Waldorf-Astoria eating a hamburger and watching a small television screen. She was introduced to the exquisite delicacy of Japanese food and the luxury of iced water on every table.

On the day she was due to have lunch with Farley Esterhuys, Lisa considered calling Frank. Ten days weren't enough. She was beginning to enjoy New York, to get some sense of the city's layout. She complained confidently about the crosstown traffic and learned to save cab fare by not flagging down a cab on Madison Avenue in order to go to Greenwich Village. In Greenwich Village she made herself homesick by getting lost around Abingdon Square. An immense black woman directed her back to Bleecker Street and issued a stiff lecture about staying away from Washington Square Park. "Junkies and hoods with knives," she said firmly, wagging her finger. She sounded like Lisa's mother, except that to Irene Barrett a hood was something that went over the head.

Lisa went back to the Tuscany to freshen up after her two morning appointments. Farley had booked a table at the King Cole Room at the St. Regis Hotel on Fifty-fifth, sixteen streets north of the Tuscany. A cab was quite definitely called for, she decided, loitering in front of the air conditioner. It was too early to call Frank. She felt vaguely dissatisfied that he hadn't bothered to call her, at least to find out how the auction of *Night Work* was progressing. "Reasonably well," she would have told him had he asked. Actually she was a bit disappointed at the American reaction to the novel; there was much praise for its literary qualities but scarcely any enthusiasm for its commercial prospects.

She deposited her key at the reception desk, changed a traveler's check for two hundred dollars, and walked across to Third Avenue in search of a cab. As she walked, she wondered if the staff at the Tuscany were being so nice to her because of Frank, who had stayed there over a period of years. Compared with the Waldorf, which someone had told her boasted two thousand rooms, the Tuscany was a relatively small hotel, baroque and elegantly comfortable, with spacious rooms and orgy-sized beds. She was impressed by her one visit to the Da Vinci restaurant on the ground floor and more than impressed by what she had come to think of as their "hey presto" room service.

She declined to check in her briefcase when she arrived at the St. Regis Hotel. She was early, but she could make use of the time to run through her notebook. The King Cole restaurant was opulent. By the time she was shown to her table, the fine film of perspiration on her forehead had dried and she felt less like a sweaty tourist. The central area of the restaurant resembled a sunken dance floor with tables, surrounded by a gallery with more tables. The linen was dazzlingly white and crisp, and the quiet absurdly wonderful.

Before she could open her notebook, Farley Esterhuys walked into the restaurant. He saw her immediately, and the expression on his face was not welcoming. Lisa straightened her back as he came toward her. She caught a whiff of sweetish after-shave as he put his lips against her cheek.

"So, how's it going then?" He sat down, conspicuously overweight but well dressed. "Ordered a drink?"

"Not yet. Just Perrier, please."

"Perrier? Don't worry, I won't tell Frank you drink at lunchtime."

"Just Perrier, Farley." He was wearing a pearl-gray lightweight suit and a silver tiepin. She wondered if the cloakroom ticket lying beside his plate meant that he wore a hat. "It's so wonderfully cool in here."

"Christ, you Brits are so pathetic. This is the greatest city in the world, and you tell me hot. This is nothing. Wait a week or two, and you'll see hot. At least it doesn't piss down with rain like London all the goddamn time."

"You're right." Lisa, benign in the cool, smiled at him and listened as he told her how much he hated leaving New York. He spoke as though the city were his personal property, somehow indebted to him for his presence. He tore open a small roll and popped half of it into his mouth. Was he really as bored as he looked?

"I hear your book's not doing too well," he said, eyeing her slyly.

"Where did you hear that?"

"This is my town, remember? Think you're going to get a taker by Friday? The closing date is Friday, isn't it?"

"I hope so," she replied equably to both questions.

"What have you got so far?"

Lisa wrapped her fingers around the tall frosted glass in front of her, tempted to roll it across her forehead. She was determined not to be discomfited by his snide assumption that she'd fall flat on her face in his town. "So far I've got two nos, one maybe, and three offers."

Farley sat back and flicked a crumb from the lapel of his jacket. "That's not what I heard, and I've got a lot of friends in this town."

"I'm sure you have. Why don't I call you before I leave and tell you how it went?"

"Whatever." He feigned indifference, wanting to dislodge the haughty composure, the dislike she was so unsuccessful at covering up. "You made a mistake, you and Frank. You know that?"

Lisa decided on the turbot. The sooner they ordered and ate, the sooner she could get away.

"I know what you think, that I can't handle lit-er-a-ture." He drawled out the broken word. "Well, I've read your sexy little piece, and it ain't so terrific, let me tell you. It's not our scene, and you need somebody who *knows* how to sell it for you, to explain how to make it travel to the Midwest, that it's a roman à clef about a *real* village, that all the fucking that goes on—"

"I don't have to lie about it, Farley. It *is* very English; the author is—if you'll pardon the expression—an Englishman. What do you want, a north country village with three McDonald's and two Robert Redfords? Shall we order?"

"So, don't believe me; it's OK. Let's wait for Sidney."

Lisa looked up sharply. "Who?"

"Sidney Niklas. He's joining us."

"That's not funny."

Farley laughed with genuine enjoyment. "He said you'd be surprised."

Why hadn't anyone told her? Both of them, Farley and Sidney—she wouldn't be able to cope. She knew it. "I will have that drink now, Farley. A very large gin—I'll add the tonic myself."

Farley motioned to the waiter, still grinning. Every table in the sunken dining area was occupied. Lisa scanned the relaxed faces. They were fortunate, whoever they were, not to be sharing a table with Farley Esterhuys.

"Sidney's on holiday, so he says. He just took off, made me promise not to tell you."

"Thanks."

"Don't thank me until you hear what he has to say about your book. He thinks—"

"Don't spoil his fun," Lisa said sharply. She added an equal measure of tonic to her gin and downed half of it, slowly, the ice numbing her upper lip. Then she plucked the perfect quarter of lime from the rim of the glass and bit into it. "I'm sure Sidney would want to pass on his criticisms himself. As it happens, though, I couldn't be less interested in his reaction."

"Jarman's came up with a big deal, didn't they?"

"Jarman's, yes. Not Sidney."

"I didn't know Frank liked playing those sorts of games."

The gin had found its way into her empty stomach with bustling efficiency. "Damn it, Farley, you know this has nothing to do with Frank. Now cut it out. You don't like *Night Work*. Sidney doesn't like *Night Work*. Ninety percent of the American population may not like *Night Work*. I just don't want to hear about it right now, all right?"

"Getting cold feet?"

"In this weather?" Lisa swallowed hard, repressing an urge to get up and leave. "What time was he supposed to get here? I've got another appointment at two forty-five."

"Really?" He didn't believe her.

"Really. *And* it's down in the Village, so two-thirty will see me—"

"Hullo, pretty!" Sidney's hot breath whooshed down into her ear. He hugged her from behind, and Farley chuckled with delight as she cringed, clapping her palm over her ear. "Surprised?"

"Very," she almost snarled.

Sidney sat down and removed his jacket, winking at Farley. His face was streaked with perspiration, his shirt crisply dry. She wondered if he'd changed in the hotel cloakroom.

"I owe you one, Farl. Our Lisa would never have found the time for me on her first trip to New York."

"What are you doing here, Sidney?"

"I told her you were on holiday—"

"Holiday and . . . other things. Had to get out of that bloody office for a few days."

"Jarman's? Lisa doesn't think it's so bloody. Sixty thousand pounds for *Night Work*—"

He had it wrong. Lisa poured another two inches of tonic over the remaining ice cubes. "Sixty-five thousand," she said. "And the same again for the second book. What's wrong with Jarman's?"

''Where have you been, my lovely? You've met the boss's daughter, the sister, the widow, haven't you? The one who's an item with Mr. Sheldon? I've heard about soliciting for books, but that's ridiculous.''

Farley guffawed, and Lisa directed silent obscenities at both of them. ''I'd like to order, Farley.'' *And then I'd like to knock your heads together. . . .*

Angela Wyatt and Frank Sheldon? Farley tapped his finger against his temple. He didn't like not knowing facts like that. He had met the woman once or twice here in New York and had received no impression of her apart from one of cool distance.

Sidney made an unnecessarily detailed inspection of the menu and then decided on very rare steak. Farley ordered another round of drinks, and Lisa could see Sidney studying her speculatively.

''So, tell me, Lisa,'' Farley persisted, ''Frank and Angela, huh?''

Those two names linked together so casually were beginning to make her head ache. ''Ask Sidney,'' she said. ''I know nothing about it, and even if I did, I wouldn't discuss it here.''

''See? Scruples. I told you, Farley. This one is something else.'' They were talking about her as if she weren't there. ''Where are you staying, Lisa?''

''You don't know?''

''Yeah, I do. Tuscany, Thirty-ninth and Park. Nice, is it?''

''It's fine.''

''I'm at the Algonquin.''

''Of course,'' she said sarcastically.

Farley was bored by the exchange. This was his third meeting with Sidney in the five days since he had arrived in New York. He wondered if he could trust this unclassy Brit. What reason did he have, apart from wanting to embarrass Lisa, for saving that bit about Frank and Angela Wyatt until now? Farley didn't appreciate that at all. Especially as he'd played his part in Sidney's little plot to discredit *Night Work* in particular and Jarman's in general. He had not allied himself with Sidney too closely just yet in case it all blew up in his face. The theory was fine, but the reality risky. More than one editor had called him after Sidney had been to see them. Was it true that Angela Wyatt had been conned into overpaying for *Night Work*? That she was so desperate to make her mark that she'd ended up paying an advance she couldn't hope to recoup? Jarman's never spent that kind of money without paperback support, and there was none for *Night Work*; was it true she couldn't *give* the paperback rights away?

Farley knew the answers to all these questions, and he told each of the editors something slightly different, allowing the poison to spread spontaneously. He faked concern for the venerable house of Jarman under Oliver's sister and left them with the impression that he himself had refused to handle the American auction because the Sheldon Agency was expecting big bucks and he knew no American publisher would be foolish enough to be taken in.

Farley tried again. "I never figured Frank, though. What's with him and this Wyatt woman, Sidney?"

"Apart from encouraging the odd one hundred and thirty thousand pounds into the agency?"

"Action?"

"On a regular basis—that is, if she doesn't abscond with his accoutrements."

They were doing all this for her benefit. Lisa broke into their laughter, addressing Farley. "Angela Wyatt aside, why do you hate Frank so much?"

"Am I drunk, Sidney? No? Good, I thought not, because I'm going to answer that question. For your information, Frank Sheldon is a condescending son of a bitch who patronizes the likes of Farley Esterhuys. Does it surprise you that I know that? It shouldn't. Because I've known it for years, and that's one of the reasons why I turn up on your doorstep twice a year . . . to make Frank Sheldon squirm. And he takes it because he needs my books. *You* need my books, but that sort of money doesn't come for free. You pay for what you get, understand?"

"You both make me feel sick."

"Hey, that fish is twenty-eight dollars a plate—"

"What's Frank done to *you*, Sidney?"

"He allowed you to go over my head with *Night Work*. That's one thing at least."

"I'm tired of saying this. It was my decision. Nothing to do with Frank."

"OK then, I just don't like him, good enough? You going to tell him or what?"

Lisa was shocked at her own composure. They were like

two evil schoolboys, hissing over a live dissection. "I can see you would *like* me to tell him," she said slowly.

"What would *you* like to do? What about Angela Wyatt?"

There it was. I'd like to kill her, she thought dispassionately, but I'd rather kill myself than let you know it. "Frank and I are not what you would call an item. What he does outside the office has nothing whatever to do with me. Or you, for that matter. Why did you come here, Sidney? Not to New York but here, to this restaurant?"

His jaw stopped working. His mouth opened in a smile, and she could see blood on his teeth. "To see you, of course. Truth be known, I came to ask you to have dinner with me tomorrow night."

"You must be joking."

"There's a lot more to this story, Lisa. Either you want to hear it all or you don't. Charming couple, Sheldon and Wyatt . . . room two twelve, eight o'clock? After we've talked, we'll—"

Lisa turned to Farley. "What about you?"

"Uh-uh. Besides, you're not my type."

"Oh, just when I thought my luck had changed," she murmured, getting to her feet. Once she was upright, her mouth curved in a wide, beaming smile. "Well, thank you, both of you. You can always say that the turbot was off, Farley, get a refund. Maybe they'll throw in the whole meal, you never know."

"See you tomorrow night," Sidney called as she walked away.

"Not if I see you first," she replied, loudly enough to turn every head in the restaurant.

"She loves me." Sidney grinned, unabashed.

"Yeah, I can see that. So, when do I hear from you? Have we got a deal?"

Sidney pushed his plate aside and kneaded his stomach. "Two weeks at the outside. Right now I'd say we've got a deal, but just in case I hit the jackpot, let's say two weeks."

"I don't like being used, Sidney."

"Me neither. This thing works both ways. We're going to make a great team, the Esterhuys/Niklas Agency. I'm being straight on this. Two weeks to settle some scores, OK?"

"You got it. Coffee and cognac?"

Sidney nodded. He eyed the cream-topped extravaganza on

the next table. He wasn't one to push his luck; coffee and
cognac would have to do.

The two gins on a near-empty stomach made her head whirl.
Lisa got through the rest of the afternoon somehow and went
back to the Tuscany. There were two messages and a bunch
of flowers waiting for her. One of the messages was from
Frank; the flowers were from Sidney.

Before it went out of her mind, she placed an alarm call
for six o'clock the next morning. Then she showered and
dressed again for dinner, cheered that the temperature had
dropped sufficiently for her to wear the stylishly tailored linen
dress she'd bought especially for the trip. Encouraged by her
reflection in one of the full-length mirrors, she removed her
silver-strapped digital watch and replaced it with a chain-link
gold bracelet; then she dithered over a pendant necklace that
didn't look quite right against the dusky rose of her dress and
settled for a pair of gold earrings which, once in place, were
totally obscured by the fall of her hair.

At least it was a safe meal this time. She took the flowers
with her and gave them to her hostess. Later, when it was
time to leave, she found herself apologizing for her preoccupation during the meal. It was well after midnight when
she got back to her room.

Lying in bed, listening to the hum of the air conditioner in
the window, she thought about Sidney's invitation. The fact
that she was considering it was no less surprising than her
calm reaction to the conversation during lunch. She'd *wanted*
to know what Sidney and Farley were getting at, what they
knew or thought they knew about Frank and Angela Wyatt.
It was more than curiosity. Recalling it now brought a prickle
of shame. Why had she listened? What had kept her there?
And why was she still wondering what else there was that
Sidney could tell her?

She rolled off the bed and went to turn the air conditioner
up one notch. The room would be freezing by morning. She
switched her thoughts deliberately away, to the auction. What
would happen if Farley had been right? The three offers she
had were firm but not large enough to warrant great excitement. Did Farley know something she didn't?

She fell into an uneasy sleep, anticipating the alarm call.
When at last it came, the operator got through to London
immediately. She decided at the last minute to say nothing

about Farley and Sidney, to wait until she got home. Also, not to extend her trip by another few days.

Frank said he'd called to tell her that Sidney Niklas was in New York. She laughed.

"You've seen him."

"Yesterday, with Farley. I have the feeling that between them they've gone to some trouble to scupper *Night Work*."

"Poor Lisa."

Wide-awake, she wanted to chat; she had his attention, undivided, focused solely on her. He told her to go back to sleep, that it would all wait. Distinctly comforted, she fell asleep again and slept through her breakfast appointment.

39

☐ Arion was early for his appointment with Inspector Vincent. He sat on one of the hard straight-backed chairs outside the inspector's office, hands clasped together on his knees. His mind was blanked out on memories of Cory, his breath short as they came and came and came. . . .

It had begun with "firsts," the first night without Cory, the first drops of rain, the first meal, the first Sunday, the first hour that went by without a memory. He knew what was happening and hugged the self-inflicted wounds to himself. Not even Ani shared the weight of his defeat. Cruelly, he realized, he forced her to live with her own memories. She cried in her sleep, and he lay awake, envious of her ability to weep without knowing. Her pity was for Cory, given into their keeping. She cried for him, for the children he would never know. For the loss, *his* loss. Arion, after that first day, remained dry-eyed because Cory's death was in part his. What dragged at him was more than guilt, more than simply a frightening loss; it was his own mortality, wrapped in wasted youth.

Paul was shocked by the sight of the old man waiting in the corridor. It was more than three days since he'd seen his father. Had this been a public place, he would have walked past without recognition.

"Do they know you're here?"

Arion nodded, without looking up. He did not want his son at this meeting. He could not understand Paul's sudden concern. Whatever Inspector Vincent had to say, it was for his ears only.

Paul made an impatient sound and strode back to the duty sergeant's desk. Arion shut himself off from the cross whispers and waited until Paul returned. "You did not have to come," he said mildly.

"I wouldn't have if you'd had the sense to bring a lawyer. Have you got any idea how . . . nasty all this could become?"

Arion shrugged. "How much worse?"

"Much, believe me!" Nothing seemed to be getting through to his father. He was about to tell him not to volunteer any information when the door opened. A uniformed policewoman ushered them into Vincent's office.

"Mr. Angelou." Vincent rose and crossed the room to shake Arion's hand. He looked surprised to see Paul.

"This is my son," Arion said unnecessarily.

"We've met. Sit down, please."

Despite the worn and chipped furniture, it was a pleasant room. There was a faint smell of peppermint in the air. A row of miniature cacti stood on the windowsill, and an ancient Underwood typewriter nestled between a coffee percolator and a small electric fan. Vincent himself had one of those nondescript faces, regular features that had acquired a deceptive inscrutability over the years. "Please understand, Mr. Angelou," he said, "we have not yet completed our inquiries, and you are under no obligation to answer my questions without the presence of a lawyer."

"I understand," Arion said before Paul could interrupt. "I want to know what it is that you have found out. Tell me, please."

"Very well, but there isn't much. The picture isn't a lot clearer than it was a week ago. We have, however, managed to come up with one or two new leads." Vincent saw Arion's quick frown and stopped to smile with as much reassurance as he could. He liked the old man. It was inconceivable to him that Arion had had anything to do with the fire. And yet there were mysteries that practically laid a trail to his front doorstep. "To sum up what we have so far: Corythus Angelou had accumulated two large gambling debts, one to the tune of twenty thousand pounds—"

Arion held up his hand, as though to dismiss the slur. "I have paid this money—"

"You didn't have to do that yet, Mr. Angelou."

"Did I do something wrong?"

"Not wrong, but these people are being investigated, too."

Arion waved the explanation aside. "Do not concern yourself, Mr. Vincent. It is done."

"As you wish. Now, as far as we can make out, Corythus also owed money to the second victim of the fire, a Mr. Leonard Bass—"

"Six thousand and two hundred pounds . . . I gave the money to his father," Arion said.

"For God's sake!" Paul shifted irritably.

"It would appear that this Mr. Bass, despite a stable and quite wealthy family background, was something of a thief. Not in the big time, but a thief nonetheless. He was clever, suspected on several occasions, but never caught. It's possible that he encouraged Corythus to borrow money from him, hoping to blackmail him into carrying out the warehouse robbery."

"What do you mean, blackmail?" Paul sat forward, and Vincent turned his gaze reluctantly on the younger man.

"A possibility, Mr. Angelou. Only that. We've interviewed Bass's girlfriend, and she confirms that the two men were together on the Monday night previous to the fire. In her statement she also says that young Corythus was extremely reluctant to ask for help."

"Why? Does this girl say why? How can this be?" Arion demanded.

"I'm afraid not, but quite frankly, reading between the lines, I'd say he wanted to be his own man, solve his own problems. If it's any consolation, I have no doubt that he went into the warehouse hoping to protect you. Perhaps he thought you would be disappointed in him or that you might send him back to Greece."

Paul interrupted. "The boy's motives for not asking my father for his help are hardly the issue here, Inspector. May we continue?"

"I disagree with you, but for the moment we'll let it pass. Corythus obviously gave Bass the layout of the warehouse, but the actual robbery was planned by Bass. We know that because we found various . . . items in his flat. He was a competent safecracker, and the safe in question would not have posed any real problem if it hadn't been for the fire. In any event, we've established that the two of them gained access by climbing over the perimeter fence at the front of the property. Corythus snagged his shirt as he went over. We found cloth fibers and spots of blood that matched his. They forced the night watchman to open the door, went in, and locked themselves in. Then they tied the man up, left him and went into the office that contained the safe. Corythus held a pencil light whilst Bass got to work." Vincent stopped. The blood had drained from Arion's face, and his fists clenched and unclenched spasmodically.

"Go on, please, Mr. Vincent."

"The reconstruction up to this point was relatively simple. Someone else came into the warehouse at some point, maybe earlier, maybe while they were still in there, although that's unlikely. But certainly between seven o'clock on the Wednesday night and three o'clock on the Thursday morning."

"How do you know that?" Paul demanded. "Are you saying that those two boys did *not* start the fire?"

"I'm not saying anything of the kind. I don't know. All we know at the moment is that someone else broke into the warehouse, using the rear entrance. There are unmistakable signs on the lock, and footprints. The footprints are of no help because he was wearing something over his shoes. So, what we have here is a puzzle. Not only did neither young man know anything about incendiary devices, but even if they had, would they have been careless enough to entrap themselves? The devices were sophisticated and professionally placed and timed. From what I've been able to find out about Corythus, he was capable certainly of carrying out the robbery, but he would not have placed his own and another two lives in jeopardy. Would you agree?"

Arion nodded, unable to speak.

"What about you, Mr. Angelou?" Vincent addressed Paul.

"I had rather less faith in the boy, Inspector, but I'll agree that it would have been out of character for Cory to do such a thing."

"Good. So the question remains: who planted the incendiaries and why?"

They had come to the question Paul had been dreading.

Vincent was a thorough policeman; he would dig forever to find a relevant nugget of dirt.

"Mr. Angelou"—Vincent was addressing Arion once more—"I understand that your company is under some stress—"

"Inspector, that question is—"

"Please, Paul. Yes, stress, as you say, but more than that. I have been forced to sell my shares to pay back the bank. In a few more days, I will not have a company, only Ani's and Prax."

"Your loans have been called in; is that what you're saying?"

"He's saying that he's had to sell his shares for a derisory figure, Inspector. The shares in my father's company have been falling now for some time. At the moment, because of the fire, I suppose, they stand at forty-nine pence. It's not surprising the banks got nervous. They've acquired the holding company at a fraction of its true value."

Whose side was he on? Vincent wondered idly, watching the two men with fascination. "Did your father discuss this situation with you, Mr. Angelou?"

"Which situation?"

"The state of the shares."

"No."

"Why not? You're a"—he consulted a notepad on his desk—"a commodity broker, aren't you?"

"Exactly. My father has some of the best brains in the City to advise him. To answer your question, we don't discuss business. Ever."

"What about your own shares in the Angel Holding Company? You have quite a number, I understand."

"You sound as though you expect me to deny it. For your information, I did sell two or three blocks of my shares—"

Vincent saw the shock register on the old man's face.

"*You* sold your shares, Paul? I did not think . . . why did you not say anything to me?"

"It wasn't important. I ran up against a temporary cash flow problem—"

"You sold enough of your own shares to start a run on your father's company?" Vincent asked softly.

Paul laughed. "Absolutely not, Inspector. If you check the share register—"

"Do you have any intention of taking over the company yourself?"

"If I had, it would have been mine by now."

Arion sat impassively through this exchange, lost in some private speculation. Vincent addressed him. "I'm going to ask you a question, Mr. Angelou. Don't answer it if you don't feel you should. Either of you. Would you have considered the possibility of firing your warehouse in order to collect the insurance and *not* be forced into selling your shares?"

Arion's knuckles went up to his eyes. "What?"

"Don't answer that!" Paul stood up sharply. He had begun to think that Vincent would never get around to articulating any suspicions.

"Why should I not answer? What kind of a question is it? I am not such a man, Mr. Vincent. I do not need a lawyer to tell you that I am not such a man."

"In that case, the mystery deepens even further. Our experts are convinced not only that the fuses were put in place by a professional but also that he ensured that *we knew* it was no accident. How do you explain that?"

"Obviously, we can't." Paul was now standing behind his father's chair. "Cory must have arranged for someone—"

"I don't think so," Vincent broke in. "There was no reason for him to destroy the building. None at all."

"Cory would not do such a thing. I have said so. *Enough!* What happens now, Mr. Vincent?"

Vincent liked the sound of the old man's growl. He said, "Nothing for the moment. Our inquiries will continue, and I will keep you in touch."

"If it wasn't Cory and his friend, what are the chances of finding out who *did* start the fire?" Paul demanded to know.

Vincent had long since decided that he didn't like the younger Angelou at all. Too aggressive, too . . . secretive; this whole thing smelled to high heaven. He watched Angelou carefully as he said, "Fifty-fifty, no higher than that."

Paul was stunned. Those odds were dangerous. Was there something Vincent was not telling them? "I'd rate that as pretty good, Inspector. It must be nearly impossible to find clues in that . . . devastation."

Vincent's smile came nowhere near touching his eyes. "Nearly but not quite." He took Arion's arm and led them outside. "Thank you for your time, Mr. Angelou. I'll be in touch."

He and Arion waited on the steps until Paul's Mercedes had pulled around the corner and out of sight. "Shall I get one of my men to take you home?"

"I will walk, thank you. One thing, Mr. Vincent. When can we take Cory home?"

"Home?"

"To Greece. His mother asks for him."

Vincent controlled a shudder. An indistinguishable huddle of ash. . . . "Of course. I take it you would want to accompany the body?"

"When, Mr. Vincent?"

"I'm sorry. I wish to God I could say now, but I can't. Give me a few days, a week or so, and we'll talk again."

"Thank you." Arion touched his sleeve in a gesture that said more.

The sun was shining. It was the first day the sun had come out since Cory had died.

40

☐ The invitation from Jason Corbett was addressed to her home. The handwriting was boyishly large, rounded, and looped. A dozen words filled the page. He mentioned no other guests and wasn't in when she called to accept. Angie imagined, for some reason, that he stood listening as she spoke into the Ansafone, and her suspicion kept her acceptance short. She had not expected to hear from him quite so soon after their clash in her office.

He lived in a spacious mansion flat in Kensington. A juddering, centrally located lift hauled itself up to the eighth floor, and the gates remained obstinately shut until Angie jabbed at the one button that bore no instructions. Then the steel mesh concertinaed itself threateningly, leaving just enough space for her to edge through.

"Just as well you aren't claustrophobic," Jason greeted her from the open doorway across the landing. He wore a black sweater with the sleeves pushed up to his elbows and black trousers.

"How do *you* get through? Open sesame?" She expected him to shake her hand or kiss her cheek. He did neither, standing well away from her as she entered the flat.

"I've lived here for twenty-three years. Never used it once."

"Exercise?"

"Fear."

"Claustrophobia?"

"And vertigo and muggers and starving to death in a cage."

He didn't look as though he were joking. "Liar."

Late-afternoon sun lay in shredded shafts of light over everything, touching the exquisite lithographs on the walls, deepening the shadowed colors of a batik, and slanting across a low mahogany table that held half a dozen bottles and two glasses.

No one else was coming. He saw her take in this fact and inclined his head at her nod. "All right?"

"I was going to call you."

"Let me show you where everything is, and then we can relax. Janine will serve us and then leave."

Angie slipped out of her crepe de chine jacket and placed it over the back of an armchair. She'd dressed for him, choosing quite deliberately the softest, simplest item in her wardrobe, a full-skirted tawny gold dress, and with it no accessories apart from her wedding ring. She followed Jason out of the room, dwarfed by his height, feeling oddly protected by it. She noticed again that he moved with the muscular coordination of an athlete, his limp barely noticeable. He turned now and then to examine her expression; he did this openly, peering down at her, a light flickering of lust in those blue, blue eyes.

It was a flat that had been occupied by women. Angie wondered briefly how many had been to stay, added to it, and then left. She knew that his first wife, Martin's mother, had "run off," as her father had put it. He'd divorced his second. The strangely acceptable softness in the place made her think that he was an easy man in many ways, easy to live alongside, his intolerances reserved for tangibles.

"What are you thinking?" he asked as they stood in the doorway of the fourth bedroom.

"That I like everything; it's comfortable. And that you like women."

"I wouldn't say that."

"No?"

He didn't answer. She followed him back into the living room and took the chair facing the open window.

"Whiskey?"

"With water, not much."

Two glasses in hand, he came to sit opposite her, throwing a shadow over half her body. "I'm pleased you're here."

Angie raised her glass and moved to get the light out of her eyes. "Are we going to carry on the conversation we began last time?"

Jason shrugged. "Do you want to?"

"I suppose it's something we should get sorted out, a decision made—"

"Is that why you're as nervous as a cat?"

"No."

He knew he was right. "You *are* jumpy."

"Tell me what you've decided to do," she said impatiently. They both knew he was right, but she didn't particularly want to acknowledge it. If she did, she would have had to go back over their past three meetings to find out why. Especially that first night at Calvert Hall . . .

"You knew what I would do when I was in your office. You're a clever woman, Mrs. Wyatt. Why pretend?"

"I'm wary of your reasonableness. I suspect you're a ruthless man, Jason. You don't play dead easily."

"I wasn't aware that I was doing anything like that. If that's what you think, forget it."

"You'll quote on spec like everyone else?"

"No, *not* like everyone else. I don't plan to go into competition with every other printer who'll now see an opening at Jarman's; they'll undercut each other to establish a foothold, and I won't do that. I'm prepared to scrap my standard setting prices, and you'll get individual estimates; but that's all."

"Take it or leave it?" She watched him carefully, saw his chin move down a fraction in acknowledgment. She waited. He wasn't going to make it easy for her. "I'll take it," she said.

"And you know why I'm doing it." She thought she'd misheard him, but before she could do more than raise a quizzical eyebrow, he said, "You're going to turn that place around, aren't you?"

It jarred her, coming from him. She moved again, to distract his fixed gaze. There was something of Paul Angelou's stillness about him, bringing an unnerving juxtaposition of their roles. "I'm going to do my best," she said faintly.

Jason laughed, with genuine amusement. "Modesty? I'd have thought you'd lived in New York long enough not to be embarrassed by success."

She smiled back at him. "I'm not embarrassed, just surprised. I haven't actually done that much yet."

"No? Then I'll give you a résumé of what I've heard: You've bought a lot of un-Jarman-type books and, in one or two instances, paid un-Jarman-type money for them; you've sorted out some pretty tangled and archaic lines of communication between the various departments, trimmed the waste in the trade budget, and allocated more funds to the essentials. You're visible but not over exposed, and you know what I mean by that. The people in the business are intrigued and attracted by you. I'm repeating what I've been told, you understand. It's not meant as an ego booster."

"I'm flattered nonetheless. I can understand their being intrigued by an outsider, especially a temporary one, but why should they—"

"Be attracted by you?" Jason took her glass, and while he refilled it, she lit a cigarette contemplatively. Despite his claim to the contrary, he was being extraordinarily generous; intentional or not, the facts, as he put it, were complimentary.

"You really don't know, do you?" he said, sitting down again.

"I really don't," she admitted. "I'm not particularly clever, and quite frankly I have a lot to learn about British publishing."

"The effect you have has nothing to do with your brain, Mrs. Wyatt. You *appear* not to care what others think of you; you're never quite *present*. In short, you leave 'em wanting more."

"That's a rotten . . . indictment. Are you serious?"

"Absolutely. And you *are* clever, but you're also arrogant and unconscious, which, whether you like it or not, makes you the social equivalent of a cock tease."

Angie burst out laughing. Well, yes, she thought, I can take that from you. But damned if I'll agree. She was still laughing when Janine came into the room. The cook was Spanish, a dark, untidy woman, who made no pretense at civility. She made three swift forays into the living room, inspected Angie critically, and decided that she didn't like what she saw. "Take no notice," Jason said. "She resents cooking for me. I pay her too well, and she resents that even more."

The meal was served precisely at nine o'clock and, apart from the odd token of disapproval from Janine, in silence. Raw young spinach leaves with duck livers came in chilled bowls, accompanied by a fruity white Sancerre, softened in the glass with a few drops of crème de cassis. Janine hovered somewhere behind Angie's shoulders until Jason had swallowed his first forkful. He might have been eating blotting paper for all it showed.

"Don't say anything, especially not that you enjoyed it," he ordered, just before she lifted the last piece of liver to her lips.

Janine returned with the second course, rouelle steak, perfectly round, braised, with button mushrooms and baby onions. After two glasses of rich red Rhône wine, Angie felt Jason's attention switch from the food. "I've been thinking about what you said about Martin, how you feel about his presence at Jarman's. He'll be out of your hair within a month. For the sake of . . . I want you to allow him to resign."

"Of course, but—"

"I thought that would please you. Isn't it what you wanted, Mrs. Wyatt?"

"Why do you call me that? Do you think of me as Mrs. Wyatt?"

"Certainly not as Angela."

"Angie?"

"Cute."

"Unavoidable?"

"Just so. Pass me your glass; perhaps if we had another drink, this conversation wouldn't seem so bizarre. How's Oliver? I understand you've been to see him."

Angie hesitated, the memory of that day coming back, clear and painful. "He's making progress. Physically he's at a very low ebb, but that can only get better. He's improving every day, Cissy says."

"When you see him again, tell him I want him out of there and back at Jarman's, fast."

"Back pocket hurting already?"

"I like your brother," Jason said stiffly.

"So do I," she said, and added, defensively, "Running Jarman's isn't what I came back for, Jason."

"I know that. I asked your father about you, and I didn't get a very flattering picture."

"I'm surprised you expected one."

"That aside, I know quite a lot about you, not through your father, of course."

"You're saying exactly what . . . someone else told me. *He* knows a lot about me, too."

With the infinite patience of a predator, Jason let it go. He knew she was referring to Paul Angelou. She was angry, quite suddenly, to be reminded that this, too, was a watching game. Jason was having fun, playing around with an archly seductive technique, using it to observe. He missed nothing and, like Paul Angelou, seemed to be able to read her thoughts.

Janine came in to clear the table. She lurched between the table and the kitchen, filling her hands, balancing bone china and silver condiments with the immunity of a juggler. Like well-behaved infants, they waited. A contemptuous swipe of the cloth, a crystal vase of flowers replaced, then Jason said, "I'm not allowed a sweet. We'll have coffee later."

They had used up the late sun, the dusk, the early evening. By the time Janine slammed out of the front door, a heavy darkness had fallen outside.

"What will Martin do?" Angie asked as Jason poured a second brandy into their glasses.

"I don't know how you've done it, but Jarman's is about to undergo even more drastic changes than you imagine. He speaks quite often about your arch-enemy."

Sidney. She said lightly, "I thought only Batman had arch-enemies."

"Very good, but don't underestimate your colleagues. They were on a cushy number until you turned up."

"You haven't answered my question."

"I'll find something else for Martin. And don't tell me he's old enough to do that for himself. We understand each other, he and I. There's nothing you can tell me about my son."

"I scarcely know him," Angie said. "Or you. But keep him away from Sidney if you can. Bad company."

"You say."

In the half-light Angie looked around the room again, noticing for the first time its careless order. The furniture, flawless in combination and style, just managed to miss a perfection: a low table placed erratically in front of the stereo; a photograph at navel height on the wall beside the window; objects squashed in one corner, leaving most of a shelf space empty. Small and adolescent gestures of resistance. The entire apartment suddenly had a transient feel, visible proof that after twenty-three years permanency was not in the scheme of things.

The thought startled her. She put the glass to her lips and wondered if she was drunk. And if not, why in God's name not. She had drunk enough. The brandy was good. She sniffed at it, then lit a cigarette and tipped the rest into her mouth. At the back of her mind a nagging doubt was closing in, cramping her instinct to call it a night. Jason, his obscure logic, his effortless sensual arrogance that brought Paul Angelou back to her side . . . with a reasoning prompted by a mixture of whiskey, wine, and brandy, Angie reflected that love went out to funny people—it went without reason and even without pleasure and brought with it the resentment of giving. . . .

She caught Jason's eye across the space that separated them. He looked questioning, too watchful. She saw nothing that excited her physically, and yet, as he came over to sit beside her, his hand on her bare arm caused her to straighten up, knees touching, facing away. A spurt of apprehension focused itself in a fluttering in her chest. Something was going to happen, and she wasn't sure she was ready for it.

"Is Martin your only child?"

"I have a daughter, two years younger. She lives in Brussels with her mother. We see each other three or four times a year; we get on well."

"And your wife?"

"Ah, we stay away from each other. It's strange that after all these years there should still be so much . . . antagonism. We deprived each other of a lot, even during the six years we were married, and later we each took off with a child, a division of the spoils. It didn't make sense to me, even then. I'm not sure that Claire needed a father, but Martin certainly needed a mother."

"Is that why you married again?"

He laughed. "I'd like to think so now, but no, I married for love. Martin and Audrey loathed each other at first sight; fortunately the marriage didn't last long enough to force me to make a choice between them. She set up house with one of my best typesetters; for all I know, they're still living happily together in Northampton.''

"You don't sound too upset.''

"I'm not, at least not any longer. I lead a perfectly tolerable life here. Actually Janine didn't approve of Audrey either. The only reason she stayed on after Audrey left was because I promised her that I would eat alone as often as I could. You're the first one for a long time.''

"You should have warned me.''

"You might not have come. I didn't want that.''

"You remind me very much of . . . someone else.''

"Your husband?''

"Not him. You're nothing like him.'' Again, he must have known she meant Paul Angelou. He did. And he must also have known that they hadn't been to bed together because his hand went to the back of her neck and pressed down on the muscles ridging her shoulders. She leaned into his hand. In truth, this knowing action should have been objectionable. Instead, she felt a blank, restless merging of relief and regret. Paul Angelou? Or any man?

"You're right,'' she sighed. "It would help, but it's not what I want.''

"Probably not, but it's what you need.'' Jason smiled, keeping his lips over his teeth as she leaned forward, giving him more space to knead out the gristle. "It doesn't work like that,'' he said. "Sit back.''

Bemused by the sheer size of his hands and not knowing what to do with her own, she sat back. In the shadows his eyes were like a cat's, greedy and alive, and she trembled for an instant, astonished at the agony of desire he aroused. In a voice rubbed with irony, he said, "Yes, Angie,'' using her name for the first time.

She wondered vaguely if he could see a reflection of sensation in her eyes. She closed her eyes and saw his face behind her closed lids, those incredibly knowing eyes watching her. . . .

"Enough,'' she murmured finally. "I'm as relaxed as I'm ever going to be. Thank you.''

"My pleasure,'' he said primly.

Angie laughed, yielding to a delight of exaggerated proportions. She took his hand and rubbed absently at his fingers, soothed and stimulated by the contact. The skin of his palm under her thumb was slightly rough, as though he'd recently done some manual work.

She had neither seen nor heard from Paul Angelou since that morning at Arion's house. She'd spent the time gently exploring the notion that they had been too hard on each other. And intermittently she had tried to reassemble her self-control and to put all thought of him out of her head. To that end she had begun to reestablish long-dormant friendships with people outside the world of publishing and found, unexpectedly, that she enjoyed not only the company but the feeling that London was getting to her, its impersonality diminishing. Some of it had to do with Frank and with what she'd seen that first night at Calvert Hall as a certainty: that she and Jason Corbett would come together in some way, at some point. And although it hardly seemed possible, she had to concede that mostly it had to do with how much of herself she'd left behind on her infrequent visits to the city. She had lived in London, but never for very long, yet a welcome, albeit tentative, was there. She had no idea what she'd done to deserve it or how she could preserve it. That she now wished to preserve it was what surprised her most of all.

"Oliver's not coming back to Jarman's," she said. She let go of Jason's hand and got up. He watched her circle the room once, slowly. She came back and sat at the opposite end of the couch.

"That doesn't surprise me," Jason said. "Does your father know?"

"Not yet. What do you think?"

"He won't like it, but you'll make Jarman's work in a way that Oliver never could. Is that what you're asking me?"

"I've decided to do it," she said, pulling her knees up and curling into the corner of the couch. "Take it over, but not at any cost. I don't think I could survive my father's disapproval twenty-four hours a day. You're a businessman, you know the City, what do you think my chances are of raising enough money to buy him out?"

That *did* surprise him, and the first thing he thought of was that this would keep her in London. "The chances are excellent, I'd say. *If* your father agrees, and quite honestly I can't see him doing that, not without a fight."

"We'll see," Angie murmured.

Jason swiveled his body around until he was facing her. "That sounds . . . wicked. I've known your father for a long time. What makes you think I'll stand by and allow you to do this?''

''Do what? When he accepts the fact that Oliver isn't coming back, he may welcome me with open arms.''

''That's unlikely.''

''I agree, but I have to give him that chance. If he doesn't—well, he still won't need your protection. Not from me, at any rate. If he wants to hang on to Jarman trade, that's fine; I'm not going to pressure him. But if that's his decision, what I *will* do is start a company of my own.''

Jason gave a low whistle. ''There's no such thing as a half measure with you, is there? You don't call that pressure?''

''Give me another solution,'' Angie said flatly. ''How can I do it without hurting *someone*?''

''You can't,'' he agreed. ''Why have you told me all this when you know where my loyalties lie?''

''I trust you,'' she said, making it sound self-derisory. ''You're not about to shop me. And I need your support . . . not only to raise capital.''

''That could put me in an awkward situation as far as your father is concerned. I mind about losing his trust. When will you tell him?''

''Soon.'' Within the next two weeks, whether she'd heard from Christopher Chetwynd or not. Whatever happened, she now saw with startling clarity, she was going to remake her home here, in London.

''I'll help you raise the money,'' he said suddenly. ''If necessary, I'll back you myself. Now, some coffee, I think. Then I'll take you home.''

''Do you always make decisions so quickly?'' Angie slid her legs over the edge of the couch, stretching her arms out. ''I think I understand why Janine doesn't approve of your women. Do you really think that's all I came for? To ask for help?''

''You came because there's no one else, I suspect. And you're not exactly used to seeking company or advice, are you?''

''Everyone's an analyst. . . .''

''That's entirely your own doing,'' he said crossly.

He was wrong. She'd accepted his invitation for entirely different reasons; she'd had no intention of telling him about Oliver. He intrigued her, and admitting her interest to him, however obliquely, was also a way of apologizing for the hurt she'd inflicted on him that day at her office. Maybe he realized that even now she was deliberately laying herself open to retaliation.

"You don't have to take me home," she said.

The sound that greeted this ambiguous statement was something between a hiccuped curse and a furious rush of breath. "I'll let you know when my mind heads in that direction, Mrs. Wyatt. Odd as it may sound, I'm not too thrilled about standing in for . . . whoever it is you can't get your hands on!"

Angie took a cigarette from the box on the small side table, and as he moved to light it, her eyes searched his. "I'm sorry," she said quietly. "I deserved that."

He nodded and pulled the table around so that she had easy access to the ashtray. When he glanced up again, she was still studying him with a kind of wide-eyed, penitent look.

"What!" he demanded.

"Do I disappoint you?"

Again, an impatient rush of breath that softened at the last moment. "On the contrary," he said. "I'm afraid to say you delight me. All right?"

Angie got to her feet. "Delight will do. Shall I make the coffee?"

"I was wondering when you were going to ask."

41

☐ Simon Riggs was afraid. For the first time in his life fear numbed his tongue into an uncontrollable stuttering. Reason told him he was safe; there was no earthly way the police could trace the warehouse fire to him. He went over every second of the time he had spent in the darkness, reliving his actions, probing and exploring every movement. Had he brushed against anything? Did a thread of cloth still hang somewhere, untouched in the wreckage? No. And in any case, he had long since disposed of the clothes he'd worn, including the sneakers and socks.

Dread still streaked through him. The marks of forcible entry on the lock of the back door—careless, but then he had been instructed to leave some visible evidence. Jesus, how could he have anticipated the million-to-one chance of a robbery's taking place that night? Impossible.

Harry Baird was scared, too. He had been terrified that the third body was Riggs's. Even when it had been positively identified as that of the night watchman, Baird had been scared enough to pay Riggs the balance of the money. Riggs thought about refusing it but took it anyway. He'd done the job, and he'd done it well. The fact that three people were dead was tantamount to an act of God.

He knew better than to leave the country. He also knew better than to meet again with Harry Baird. There was nothing to do except wait. Word filtered through to him that no fewer than three police departments were involved in the case. A nasty one, they all agreed, and it was a case they were going to solve, one way or another.

Sit tight, do nothing. Baird couldn't shop him; the noose was, if anything, tighter around his own neck. There was comfort in that thought. Both Baird and his principal had a lot more to lose than he did.

Riggs began to feel better. His third lunchtime vodka went down smoothly, spreading a glossy warmth. Maybe it would be all right.

42

☐ Some of them had made promises to get back to him before he left New York. None had. Sidney had spent his last afternoon waiting beside the telephone, just in case. It hadn't occurred to him that New York publishers would not open every door to him, the way Farley had. And the sound of the latches snapping shut had nothing to do with the weekend that was upon them. He'd wanted to return to London with more than expressions of interest, more than the polite let's-wait-and-see he'd got. Now he would have to accept Farley's offer . . . and pronto. If Farley were to hear that he'd been approaching others for jobs, he'd flip, fuck him.

Later, when he thought about it, Sidney realized that he'd come on too strongly about Jarman's, made his dislike too personal. Giving him a job would be like joining him in an act against Angela Wyatt. And she was very nearly an American, he reflected grudgingly, at least she'd been married to one of them. Protecting their own?

There was nothing apart from sour milk and a square of furry cheese in the fridge when he arrived back at his flat. He unpacked a few essentials from his suitcase, then shoved it, unclosed, on the top shelf of a cupboard. He called Martin and arranged to meet him at a nearby wine bar in an hour. His next call was to book a girl for the following evening. That was something else about New York: the astonishing availability of girls. He had to admit to himself that the whores there frightened him just a little, with their businesslike approach. Even the young girls displayed a standoffish sophistication which made his advances seem adolescent. Time was money, and just about everything, like vegetables on a menu, was extra. Had Farley taken him around? Like hell he had. Sidney consoled himself with the thought that there must be so few girls who'd let Farley in, that he was keeping them for himself.

Martin was wearing a rumpled corduroy suit and glowering into his wine when Sidney arrived at the Deanery. The long, narrow wine bar was crowded and noisy. A slight twitch touched Martin's lips as Sidney clapped him on the shoulder, motioning at the same time for the waitress to bring them another bottle.

"So, how did it go then?" Martin dipped a grubby finger into his wine.

"Better than it's obviously gone here. You look like you've been on a week's binge." Secretly Sidney was pleased to see the younger man looking as if he'd spent the night on a park bench. "Giving you a hard time, is she?"

"Someone will do for her," Martin replied shortly. "I quit on Friday."

"You kid me! What happened? Jesus, what did your old man say?"

''It was his idea.'' He didn't want to tell Sidney what he'd guessed: that his father wanted him out of Jarman's not because the shit was about to hit the fan but because he'd made a deal with Angela Wyatt. And he, Martin, had been part of that deal. ''In a few weeks I'll be out of there. Good, eh?''

''Jesus,'' Sidney said again. ''She moves. What's the deal?''

Martin looked askance at Sidney's use of that word. ''No deal, just good sense. How was New York?''

''Fantastic, never had a better time.'' He knew Martin was holding back; there had to have been some deal. He let himself talk, embellishing on a story someone else had told him, appropriating it for himself: a blond cabdriver offering to take his suitcase up to his room. Over the top . . . an hour later and two parking tickets. Variations on a theme, but Martin listened and was nonetheless aroused by the picture Sidney drew.

Martin's mood improved. Sidney ordered a fresh bottle of wine. Women scared the shit out of Martin. His narrow, freckled face was singularly unattractive, deterring all comers. If admiration and envy were not always so clearly mirrored in his eyes, Sidney, too, would have avoided his company.

''It's a great town.'' Sidney finished his story with a flourish. ''You don't get anything like that over here. Hey, did you hear that Lisa Barrett was in town, too?'' He liked to make New York sound like Luton.

Martin nodded. Mostly he believed Sidney's stories. He said nothing now, waiting for Sidney to fall into some bragging lie about Lisa. ''I know what you're thinking, but no, not Lisa. Freeze your balls off, that one. Point is, I gatecrashed a lunch between her and Farley.''

More like it. Martin had been wondering when Sidney would get around to Farley. Now that he was out of a job with Jarman's, this could be interesting, much more so now than it had been when Sidney had left for New York.

''Under your hat for now, but guess who's going to become an independent London literary agent with a *guaranteed* income of only twenty thousand pounds a year? How's that for openers?''

''I know that's what you went over for. How'd you swing it?'' Martin asked dully. Unless this, too, was one of Sidney's pipedreams. "Why would Farley want to leave Frank Sheldon and start up with you?"

"Because—because *he* says Frank treats him disrespectfully. Well, I don't know about that, but the lady Lisa breaks out in a sweat at the sight of him. What do you say?"

"I say bully for you, old chum."

Sidney laughed. "Play your cards right, and I might take you on at the agency."

"You said you would before you left. Don't do me any favors, all right?"

"Think your old man would like to buy you in? I'm going to do it right. No working from the front room of my flat. Decent offices, secretary, telex, the whole bit. Think he'll put up some bread?"

"Do you have to use that phony jargon?"

"What's the matter, you don't like it suddenly? I don't remember you complaining when—"

"Forget it. When will you tell her?"

"*Angie?* When I'm fucking good and ready, like probably tomorrow. What's been happening while I've been away?"

Martin tipped his head back and studied the ceiling. "She's canceled contracts, bought ten or twelve books. Apart from that, she's in the office every day and always back from lunch before two-thirty. The production people are running around in small circles, and Dunne has gone into a decline. As for Deborah and Cynthia, I've scarcely seen them, they're so busy doing her bidding. She's auctioning the paperback of *Night Work*, did you know that? *And* she's letting Cynthia handle it. It pays to tug your forelock—"

"Are any of those canceled contracts mine?" Sidney interrupted.

"Four." Martin named the books, feeling a petty pleasure at the hatred in Sidney's eyes. "Thinking dirty thoughts?"

"Not dirty. Lethal. I'll show her canceled contracts. Wait until Elliot Stone's second novel comes up. Two-book contract or no two-book contract, I'm going to make sure—"

"Stone? You've nobbled Stone for your agency?"

"Not yet, but I'm working on it, seeing him soon, putting the sweeteners on. Lisa got eighty-five thousand dollars in the States, not enough, I reckon, for our boy wonder."

"I like it." Martin giggled, sucking wine from his finger once more.

"And *that* you don't tell your father. Stone must be worth

at least ten thousand pounds a year to me, and I want him in the bag before word leaks out.''

''Wise.'' The word was drawn out; the *s*, mashed. ''I'll see what I can do, talk to my father.''

Sidney nodded. It was time to leave. Martin would soon remember nothing, too drunk now to take much in. Old Corbett's money would be useful at the outset, Sidney thought. Later he would decide to what extent he wanted to be involved with Martin. . . .

''See you tomorrow.'' Martin held up a wet finger. There was more than half a bottle of wine left. That would see him safely through the next hour.

43

☐ It was twelve-fifteen by the time they got home. On the drive back from the midmorning memorial service for Cory, Susan had spoken just once. Without apparently inviting a response, she'd said, ''Arion's going to lose just about everything he has. He knows it, and he doesn't seem to care.'' She'd spent a few minutes after the service talking to Frank Sheldon; he must have told her about the drop in the share price of Angel Holdings. She hadn't asked Paul for more information, and he hadn't volunteered any.

In recent days Paul had become sporadically conscious of Susan's silences. She had a grave, harrowed look that probably had something to do with Cory's death. But he couldn't be sure. It surprised him but did not unduly perturb him. Other things occupied his mind: Inspector Vincent's inquiries were getting nowhere. That, at least, was beginning to look good. Despite his early panic, Harry Baird, too, had settled down into a pattern of waiting; the days were passing. If he thought about it, the sequence of events could not have been more to his advantage. Not that he had wanted those men dead. Paul told himself that he had never wanted Cory's death to begin with. It was the truth only because it had not been necessary. Nonetheless, it enabled him to stand aside and view the advantages with a dispassionate eye. In a few days Angel Publications would cease to trade, and Angel House would be in the hands of others. Odd that no one had told him about Doric Video having been given back to the Barzini family all those years ago; not that it mattered any longer. Arion had managed to retain control of Ani's and Prax and the two shops Olga managed, and Paul had been able to display genuine relief at this news.

It was almost over. The success of it all was capped by a brief note from Sir Richard Jarman to tell him when and where the committee was meeting to discuss plans for Paul's official nomination. That victory was perhaps the sweetest of all. . . .

It was raining, and there was a depressing hush to this Sunday. Paul stacked several bulky Sunday newspapers neatly beside him on the floor. He could hear Susan speaking to his mother on the kitchen extension.

These would be the first uninterrupted hours he and Susan had had together since Cory had died, and now was as good a time as any to question her. Curiosity rather than unease concentrated his mind on her recent conduct. Inspector Vincent's questions had puzzled her with their seeming irrelevance, he knew. Vincent had visited the house twice, and on both occasions Susan had repeated his questions to her husband, one question in particular: what could Paul's relationship with his father have to do with Cory's death? "What did you say?" Paul asked.

"Nothing," she told him. "I didn't know what he meant. He asked me twice. What should I have said?"

"Exactly what you did—nothing." He listened to her recount the answers she'd given Vincent without trying to allay her fear that she had in some way endangered Paul by telling the truth simply.

She had also begun to spend whole days with Ani, emptying the house of more than her physical absence. He could always tell when she hadn't been there during the day or had just come in. Last week she had taken Olga's boys to the zoo, an excursion that had left her tired and preoccupied. She slept off the tiredness, but the preoccupation had remained for days. And she had begun to turn away from him at night. Paul saw this not as a rejection but as an accusation, and that touched off a remote interest. He was sure that the explanation had nothing to do with their marriage or their love for each other. Her body was as familiar to him as his own; he had to tell her that there was no mistaking its withdrawal.

Now he heard her replace the telephone receiver in the kitchen and called out, "Anything new?"

Suzy stopped in the doorway and looked at him in silence for a moment. "Ani thinks they're going back to Greece any day now, as soon as Cory's . . . remains are released. She says your father doesn't always tell her everything."

"He doesn't."

"Will you find out from him, Paul?" She waited for his nod. "Would you like a drink?"

"Please. And then I'd like to talk to you."

She hesitated. "What about?"

He turned the question lightly. "Us?"

"In that case, I'll join you in a drink." It was a feeble attempt at a joke, and he ignored it. While she was getting the ice, he put Beethoven's Fifth on very softly and gave himself that brief time to consider Angela Wyatt, not for the first time that day. It wouldn't be long now before her own investigator told her that he'd come up against a dead end, that her daughter's identity and whereabouts were impossible to find. Beaumont Gracie had done his work well, and Paul had begun to have second thoughts not only about Gracie's thoroughness in fudging the documents but also about what he might now be forced to do: tell her. He had come to accept the fact that he had misjudged Angela and underestimated the depth of his own obsession with her. It was no longer something he could set aside as a separate part of his life. Thoughts of her inhabited his mind, took him over, encroaching on his days and nights. His life was here, with Susan; nothing could ever change that. What he wanted from Angela Wyatt had little to do with what he felt for his wife. Some part of his soul that had lain untouched and pristine now glittered with the sheen of his imaginings about another woman. He hadn't seen her since the night of Cory's death. She had been making love with Frank Sheldon, and he'd wanted her to know he'd seen her like that, soft-limbed and lewd—but not that he'd wanted her, there in his father's house, with Susan in the next room. And all he'd managed to do again, was drive her away. And now what Beaumont Gracie had done so efficiently could finally put an end to everything.

Susan lowered three ice cubes into his glass and looked at

him expectantly. He'd never seen anything but a punishing
fury in Angela Wyatt's eyes. . . .

"Is there something you'd like to tell me?" he asked.

"Like what? About last night?"

He shrugged. "If you like."

"Your interest flatters me, Paul. The answer is no."

He spoke patiently, intrigued by her calm demeanor. "If it
wasn't just tiredness, perhaps we should talk about it."

"What would you like to know? Why I didn't welcome you
with open arms . . . and legs?" She said it deliberately, feeling betrayed by her assumption that he had wanted to talk
rather than interrogate.

"Must you say things like that?"

"You asked me, I'm telling you. It's no good frowning at
me, no good at all. Quite simply I didn't want you to make
love to me last night. It happens."

"It's never happened before."

"How do you know?" A siren of caution started up in her
head. How could she explain what she had seen pass between
him and Angela Wyatt?

"Are you saying I have forced you?"

"Of course not, just that you never really bothered to find
out how I felt."

He thought he understood this, even though it was the first
time in their married life they'd ever discussed sex. "How
did you feel?"

"At this precise moment I'm wondering why you're still in
the room, why you're talking about this. The subject's always
been taboo, remember?"

"Did I say that?"

"Not in so many words, but I'm wondering why you—after
so many years you want me every night."

Paul picked up his glass and went to sit beside her. He
took both her hands in one of his and turned her around to
face him. "It's either the male menopause or the fact that I'm
in love with my wife. Both maybe?"

"Neither." She eased one hand free and covered his holding hers. "Something has happened, Paul, and I think I know
what it is. Or at least, who it is." Having said it, she wanted
to retract the words immediately. A touch of fear chilled every
inch of her skin. She saw his expression change from teasing
puzzlement to blank surprise before he got to his feet.

She said, "I *saw* it. It's true, isn't it?"

He went to the window and pushed the curtains aside, letting in the sound of the rain. "You're wrong," he said, without turning.

"What is it then? You wanted to talk. Tell me."

Silence. There was a heavy whisper of exertion in his breathing. She wondered if she was killing something here by exposing it. Could she be mistaken? There was nothing for her without him, and she knew it. She would share him if it came to that and make sure he never knew the cost.

"Has it occurred to you that I, too, might be shaken up by Cory's death? That a lot has happened these last few weeks?"

"Oh, Paul." His words were like a gag in her mouth. "At least you've always been honest with me. Please don't tell me you give a damn about Cory. That's not it, and in any case, it started long before that."

"I don't know what you're thinking, but this conversation is absurd."

"Then we have nothing to talk about. May I leave?"

"I think I deserve an explanation—"

"Don't be so bloody pompous, Paul! I'm not enjoying this any more than you are, but do pay me the courtesy of not treating me like an imbecile. I care for you, *about* you, more than you do for me. That's fine. Better than that, it's wonderful. I'm not saying you don't love me because I think you do. But I see something in you now that I've wanted ever since I met you. If you're going to bring *that* to bed with you, you'd better bring it to my bed because *I'm* there, not someone else."

The shock of her words cut right through him. There it was, uttered precisely, complete, bracketed between his temples. He could think of nothing to say except "I love you."

"Perfect! Perfect. Everything has to be perfect for you. You're afraid I'll . . . break!" She was aware that this had nothing to do with his preoccupation but was now unwilling to stop. "Never, not once have you even *come* before me. You've never lost your way, never been out of control, not even in that. First things first, satisfy Susan first, then—"

"That's enough."

She sighed. "I have nothing of you, and my heart still stops when I look at you. Do you love her?"

He turned sharply, not to catch her indistinct words but to get away from them. "Are there any cigarettes in the house?"

"Over there on the bookcase. Light one for me, too, please. Do you love Angela Wyatt?"

The name conjured the face; the face brought a new yet familiar pain. "No." He gave her the cigarette.

"Have you seen her since that . . . morning?"

"No."

She didn't expect that. She watched him inhale deeply and expel the smoke in an unsteady stream. "What happened? Come here, Paul." She had to go and fetch him, tugging at his sleeve like an impatient parent. When their eyes were level, he reached out to brush the hair from her forehead, an involuntary movement that drained her anger. She asked, nonetheless, "Are you going to see her again?"

"I don't know." His hand came to rest on her shoulder. "I don't want to hurt you."

"I know that, but . . . tell me when it's over. Will you tell me when it's over? I'm not giving you permission, you understand. I just want to know."

"Nothing is going to happen."

She pulled back. "Will you tell me?"

"I'll tell you." He surprised them both by kissing her then. She surprised herself by using her tongue in his mouth. It mattered that he wasn't thinking about Angela Wyatt. She opened her eyes, loving his breath on her face. . . .

"I'm going to Greece with your parents, Paul."

"No!" It was almost a cry of pain.

"I want you to come with me. Please think about it."

"Think . . . when did you decide this?"

"Don't get angry . . . it's pointless. The way I feel now . . . it's time. You'll decide what you want to do, if you want to come with me."

"Nothing happened. I never held her hand."

"Paul . . ."

"Get it straight. I never even held her hand." The lie was necessary, he told himself. Susan must not be allowed to leave.

"I believe you."

"Then don't go."

"I must," she replied simply, the decision made then and there. He was saying no. "I'm not forcing you to do anything."

The record player clicked off with a sound like a gun shot. Pure reflex took Paul across the room. She wondered whether he would turn the record over or replace it in its sleeve. He replaced it, tapping the sleeve back into its allotted place. Their time was over.

"I'm not forcing you to do anything," she repeated.

She was. They both knew it.

44

☐ Elliot Stone was disappointed with the American sale. Lisa heard it in his slightly rebuking tone when she'd called him from New York and again on Sunday afternoon, back at her flat. He pulled her out of an exhausted sleep to query the details of the contract.

Lisa sat on the edge of her bed, hunched over the telephone. The bedside clock read four-fifteen. She'd had two hours' sleep. The hum of the plane's engines was still filling her ears with sound; her mouth and nostrils still felt clogged with stale air.

"Elliot." She broke in. "I've just got home, and I'm tired. Can we do this tomorrow?"

"Did I wake you?"

Lisa nodded.

"Lisa?"

"I'm here. I'll call you at the school tomorrow, usual time."

"How long will it take for the contract to be drawn up? I wouldn't be asking if I didn't think it was important."

"I realize it's important, but this isn't a good time for me."

"There's someone with you." His words carried resentment. He had called her at the office the day after the scene at Durrant's Hotel and conspicuously failed to make any reference to it, neither explaining nor apologizing.

Lisa bit back a retort. She shivered and hugged herself, feeling faintly ridiculous. "I'm alone, and I'm tired. I'll call you tomorrow. Good-bye, Elliot."

She replaced the receiver and swung her legs up onto the

bed. With a little groan of pleasure she pulled the duvet up to her chin just as the telephone rang again.

"No." She shook her head, burrowing deeper, a dull ache beginning in her temples. Whoever it was had no intention of giving up. Lisa sat up and eyed the telephone. Elliot again?

It was her mother. "I just wanted to know that you got home safely, darling. You sound tired. Why aren't you sleeping?"

With a promise to call her the next day as well, Lisa hung up. She sat quietly for a moment, waiting. Nothing happened. She realized that she was expecting a call from Frank. Her eyelids drooped, and she yielded to a desire to stretch out again but not to take the receiver off the hook.

The flat was unspeakably quiet. Thoughts of Sidney and Farley receded. She had not gone to the Algonquin, had not seen or heard from Sidney again. Nor from Farley. Had he by this time been in touch with Frank?

Lisa smiled drowsily as a small pulse of pleasure beat through her body. Aware of herself in a warm cocoon, she turned and slid down, letting go. . . .

There was a scribbled note from Frank when she arrived at the office the following morning. "Welcome back—see you later." Just that. "Damn," she muttered, wanting company. She left her conspicuously tidy desk and went into the outer office.

"Unless absolutely nothing happened while I was away, someone's been working very hard. My desk is too neat. What happened?"

Ruby, her slash of Mohican now a staider hue of dull yellow, looked up from her typewriter. "The boss, been working flat out. Never seems to go home anymore unless Angela Wyatt comes by to pick him up."

Lisa made herself smile. Frank and Angela. "He did all that by himself?" She gestured in the direction of her office.

"Most of it. There are some things we didn't know what to do with. They're on the shelf by the window."

"Do either of you know if Farley called? Did he call while I was over there?"

Ruby looked at Lillian, and they both shook their heads. Ruby said, "He may have called after hours, of course. Why?"

"I haven't told Frank yet, but there's trouble on that front. He thinks we don't give him his due respect—"

Ruby giggled. "He's right. Is he leaving us?"

"Possibly. No, probably. Frank isn't going to be very pleased."

"Just when Lil and I were getting into the hard-core stuff—"

Before Lillian could protest, two calls came in simultaneously. Without waiting to see if either was for her, Lisa went back into her own office. A sense of anticlimax kept her on her feet. The trip had been a success, of sorts, but she was beginning to realize that not once had she given herself over totally to the pleasure of being in New York. Some part of her had always wanted to be in London.

"Lisa, telephone," Ruby yelled, seeing Lisa pacing around through the frosted glass panel.

"Who is it?" Lisa hovered over the telephone.

"Mr. Angelou." Not Frank.

"Lisa . . ." Arion's voice, so close, made her jump. "You have not been here, Frank tells me."

"No, I—" She wanted to say something about Cory, at least acknowledge that she knew about his death, but no coherent thought came. She said instead, "How are you?"

"As good as it is possible to be, you understand. Frank is not there, I know, but it would be a good thing to see you today." Lisa didn't understand what he was saying. Was Frank with *him*? "I am at Ani's from twelve o'clock today. You will eat with me?"

Damn Frank! Had he persuaded Arion to do this? "You don't have to—"

"You can come?"

"Of course, but you . . . mustn't do this for Frank."

"For me, Lisa." She heard authority, plainly stated. "Come when you are ready. I will be here."

It was just after ten o'clock. With conscious effort Lisa took a tidy pile of papers from the shelf and began to look through them. Concentrate! She scarcely recognized herself. It was an uncomfortable feeling, a measure of the confusion she could not put a name to. Like a child's, her emotions were immediate and contradictory.

Nonetheless, she worked through the next two hours with methodical single-mindedness, dealing with each item as it came to the top of the pile. Then she read through the stack of carbon copies of Frank's correspondence and finally put a call through to Elliot Stone. He sounded guarded and subdued, as though others were listening. They must have been, she decided, because he repeated the figure of eighty-five thousand dollars over and over again with pedantic formality. He told her that he would be coming down to London the next day to check Deborah's copy editing. She hung up, relieved that he hadn't asked to see her.

Both girls had their sandwiches in front of them when Lisa went out to pick up her coat. "Lucky you." Ruby held up a corned beef on white and waved a tin of Diet Coke in the other hand. "Where will you be, just in case?"

"Ani's."

"Righto. Need a taxi?"

"I'll walk."

She walked quickly in the thin sunlight. It wasn't warm. She felt pushed, heading for a showdown. To slow herself down, she walked through Covent Garden market, heels slipping awkwardly on the cobbles. Tourists loitered in groups in the piazza, sleek and unhurried. Two jugglers waited patiently for a three-girl pop band to pack up their amplifiers and vacate the pitch. Lisa stopped. The jugglers, still waiting, went into a comedy routine of mime, meant to help the girls on their way. As she made to move on, one of the jugglers winked at her and came over to whisper, "Don't go."

Startled, she said seriously, "I must," as if the invitation *had* been serious and not part of his banter.

"Never mind, darling." His crudely made-up clown's face split in half for her. "Another time." She nodded, blinked at him in surprise, and walked on.

There was a glass of chilled white wine waiting on the table when she arrived at Ani's. Arion held her against his chest for a long moment, and she felt his hand reach up to pat her on the head.

"I've been looking forward to this," she told him, sitting down. She could see the change in him immediately, an outward gauntness, and could imagine hollows and vacant places inside him that needed filling again.

"Do not feel uncomfortable, Lisa."

"I'm sorry it happened," she said, and saddened herself further by adding futilely, "I wish I could have stopped it."

He reacted with a soft grunt that could have meant anything. "It happened. Have you ever visited my country?"

"Greece? Never."

"Then you will come and see us. Many times."

"I don't understand."

"Ani and I . . . we are going back to our village one day soon, and you will come and stay with us."

"For good? You mean, you're leaving England?"

"This is always what we were going to do. Cory . . . what happened just makes it sooner."

"Oh." Bereft already. "Does Frank know?"

"Ah, yes. He, too, will visit us. Both of you will come."

"Do you know where he is?"

"Today? No, but he did tell me it is possible that he will come here later."

Lisa looked away quickly. The joy was so unexpected she almost laughed out loud.

"You have missed Frank," Arion said.

"Oh, yes."

"Good. That's good."

"Why?" What did he mean, good?

Arion raised his hand, and Scotia was there with another two glasses of wine. "How do you do that?" she asked, though she knew that Scotia watched Arion.

"Magic, of course. Do you believe in magic?"

"I think I do."

"But magic is not always happy magic. Frank is fortunate. He has you to create this magic for him?" It sounded like a question.

She controlled her surprise. "Not me, Arion."

"Who then?"

"I don't know. Others—"

"Ach." He shook his head to stop her. "Someone else, you are saying? No, do not concern yourself, Lisa."

Lisa took a mouthful of wine and held on to the glass with both hands. "May I tell you something? Just now, at this moment, I feel a bit mad, a little crazy, and I think it's something to do with you."

"Frank is a little crazy, too."

"Tell me." A sensation akin to regret softened the demand, made it a plea. "Tell me, Arion."

He shook his head. "You know."

"I don't know. He's in love with me? *That's* crazy. No."

"No?"

"No!"

"Then we will eat." He turned her statement around. "Those who are in a state of love do not eat." He raised his hand again, and Scotia was there.

"I'm not hungry," Lisa said.

"Perhaps a little. We will have calamares and artichokes and dolmadakia and many bottles of wine. I will tell you about my people and my village. Yes?"

Speechless, she nodded. Frank? No. She could feel the blood pressing against the skin of her face, leaving it clammy. It shouldn't happen like this. The first artichoke leaf brought a surge of nausea to her throat. Then suddenly delight touched every corner of her mouth. Arion's voice wrapped itself around her, and the sweet rush of his love brought her back.

He talked until the restaurant emptied and the chill on the wine wore off. Scotia brought another bottle. Lisa began to feel the sun on her back and salt on her skin. He talked as though he wanted to leave an imprint of his life in the keeping of someone else. The fact that she was the one Arion had chosen was no less astonishing than the knowledge, firmly taken hold, that she loved Frank Sheldon. Arion spoke of groves and rocky hillsides, wells and sheep and brickmaking, newspapers, politics, and God. She shut her eyes until he took her hand, his knuckles white, without pressure. She knew then that this was not what he had intended but that it was releasing some of his own pain, relieving some of the guilt of Cory's death, unspoken until now. He was making himself believe it for the first time.

People moved around them, chairs were scraped back, and table linen was changed. The phone rang, and she saw Arion start. He blinked, and for a fraction of a second she thought she saw tears. Then his eyes lifted, going over her right shoulder. Frank. She turned to stone.

"Don't go!" she whispered urgently. Arion smiled at something she couldn't see, and then Frank's hand was on her shoulder.

"Hullo, Lisa. What have you two been up to, Ari?"

"Sit, Frank. We are, as you say, lunching."

"It's six-thirty." He sat down. "Lisa?"

"Lunch." She looked at him. He wore an open-necked shirt and blazer. She registered that she'd never seen him look quite so relaxed before. There was a hint of stubble on his chin, as though he'd shaved and dressed hurriedly.

"I'm sorry I couldn't get into the office today, but I promised Angie I'd take her around to look at some houses."

Lisa caught Arion's eye and, despite the look, said coldly, "Successful?"

"One is quite promising. So . . ." Frank paused, looking from one to the other. "Have I interrupted something?"

"No, no, I must leave soon. Ani is waiting for me."

Lisa grabbed his hand. "Don't go yet."

"I have been creating in Lisa a need to come to Greece, to Mandraki. You will bring her, Frank."

"Just say when, Ari. I think you need some strong black coffee, Lisa."

"I'll finish this wine."

"Not wise, you're probably still jet-lagged."

"I feel . . . good."

"You don't look so good."

"Thanks."

She'd lost some weight, he thought. She was wearing a narrow-cut dress and a broad leather belt that emphasized the slenderness of her build.

Arion stood up, leaving her hand stranded in the middle of the table. "You have much to talk about. And Ani is waiting for me. We will talk again, Lisa. Please stay, Scotia will fix everything."

Frank half rose, too. "You've signed the papers, Ari?"

"Today. Everything is done, my friend." He was now anxious to be away. He said again, "We will talk."

Frank asked Scotia for a pot of coffee, hoping that Lisa would have some.

"It's good to have you back, Lisa. I've missed you."

"Not enough to put in an appearance, though."

"Do I detect a moody coming on?"

"I missed you, too."

"Well"—he sat back with the unexpectedness of that—"there you are then. Do you want to tell me about your trip now or shall we leave it until tomorrow?"

"It all seems such a long time ago."

"That's Ari."

"He says he's leaving, for good."

"We won't lose him, Lisa. I promise you that."

She brightened perceptibly. "Really?"

"Really. Have you eaten anything, or have you just been drinking?"

"Calamares and artichokes—" she began.

"Not enough. A steak and french fries are what you need."

"I'm not hungry. You go ahead."

"A small steak . . ."

"Frank, stop it!" She wanted him to stop looking after her and look at her.

The vehemence startled him. He raised both his hands in mock surrender. "Sorry."

Lisa winced. He's here, I'm talking to him, and I can't say anything right. Damn Angela Wyatt, it hurt like hell. He hadn't known she'd be here with Arion; even this was a coincidence. He'd been perfectly prepared to wait until tomorrow.

"I was going to call you this evening," he said.

Lisa busied herself, rummaging around in her handbag. Her head buzzed pleasantly from all the wine. She knew there were no cigarettes in her bag, but she went on sifting through its contents. Scotia materialized with a dish of black olives, feta, and pickled green peppers. The restaurant had opened again, and the earliest customers had begun to arrive.

"What are you looking for?" Frank asked at length.

"Cigarettes. I don't have any."

He gave her a Gauloise. "Farley is probably going to leave the agency," she said, drawing the smoke in with a quick gulp. "I'm surprised he hasn't called you. Or written." She expected him to fly into a rage. She was prepared for it.

"Why is he going to leave the agency?"

Lisa held her glass out to be refilled. He was studying her with a patient frown. "Because you—we, I suppose, patronize him. That's what he says. Do you remember telling me about the strip clubs? Well, he said he insisted you go with him only because he knew how much you hated it. Everything has its price; that was apparently part of the price you had to pay for handling Farley Esterhuys's books."

"He told you that?"

"In front of Sidney. The two of them were quite . . . vicious. They hate you."

"That doesn't worry me particularly. Why now, I wonder?"

"Why aren't you angry?"

"I am, but only because I don't understand the timing. Why tell you and not me? He hardly knows you."

"I can't help feeling it's something to do with Sidney."

"Bloody hell," Frank said softly, refilling his cup and stirring in a spoonful of sugar. "Sidney resigned from Jarman's this morning. Angie told me, and I'd forgotten. That's it, must be."

"Sidney selling Farley's books over here?"

"Too convenient not to be true. Martin Corbett has resigned, too. Christ, they're probably in it together."

"I'm sorry, Frank. I'm afraid I've contributed to it. Sidney blames you for the fact that I didn't submit *Night Work* to him personally. It made him lose face, status."

"We'll hear officially soon enough. Any more good news?"

"Why aren't you angry?" she asked again, helping herself to another cigarette. "You terrified me with your predictions of doom before I left, and now it doesn't seem to matter."

"It does matter," he said quietly. "But there's nothing I can do about it."

"Right. We'll just have to work harder. I've decided to take you up on that offer of a partnership. Is it still open?"

"You have extraordinary timing, Lisa. Why should you want to do that now, when the loss of Farley's list cuts the agency's income by a good chunk?"

"It's partly my fault all this happened."

"Guilt? That's no basis for a business relationship. The offer no longer stands."

"All right. I *want* to, then."

"Better, but still not good enough. Are you going to eat anything?" He pushed the feta toward her.

"Later. Sidney did a good job of sabotaging *Night Work* in New York. I'm pretty sure he did."

"Angie and I guessed he might."

Angie. Her ears received the name, and her mind rejected the ease with which he uttered it. "That's the other thing Sidney was mouthing around, you and Angela Wyatt. He wanted to know how I—how *I* felt about it. Before you ask, I told him it was none of my business and certainly none of his."

"That was very, uh, noble of you."

"I thought so." She grinned at him quite suddenly and added, with great satisfaction, "Especially since he invited me back to his hotel for dinner and a certain amount of elaboration."

"You refused all *that*? Do you know what? I think I like you a lot better jet-lagged and drunk than rested and sober."

The instant the words left his mouth he knew he was mistaken. She wasn't drunk—happily tipsy maybe—but she didn't contradict him. To cover his confusion, he said, "You and Arion must have had a hell of a lunch."

Lisa watched him tear off a piece of pita bread and scoop up some crumbly feta cheese. A sense of the inevitable guided her next words; although she feared ridicule, at that moment the urge to define her emotions was stronger. "Arion made me think I was in love with you."

Frank choked, swiveling sideways on the chair to lower his face into the table napkin. Scotia hurried over with a glass of water, which Frank waved away and then drank from. By the time the fit of coughing eased, his face was flushed, eyes reddened and watery. "Bloody hell!" he snarled at her, wiping his eyes.

"He also suggested—no, are you going to choke again?"

Frank shook his head. "What did he suggest?"

"Before I tell you that," she said calmly, through lips gone quite dry, "how do you feel about it? I think it's true. If I were totally honest, I'd tell you it *was* true. Is. What do you think?"

"I think"—he lifted his gaze to the ceiling and took a deep, deep breath—"I think I'm . . . staggered."

"What does that mean?" She knew precisely what it meant and wanted to hear more than that. He looked stunned. She'd said too much. Impatiently she tapped the back of his hand with her fingers. He leaped as though she'd touched him with a lighted match. "What's the matter?"

He pushed back his chair. "Get up."

"Frank!"

"Come on, we're leaving." He walked away from her and held a whispered conversation with Scotia. Then he put her coat over his arm and held the door open for her.

She grabbed his arm, furious. "Where are we going?"

They walked down Wardour Street, turned left into Meard Street and across into Bateman Street. When they got to Cambridge Circus, he stopped. She was almost afraid to look up into his face.

This is ridiculous, she thought as he draped the coat across her shoulders and hailed a taxi. "This is ridiculous," she said.

"I'm going to feed you."

"Are you going to talk to me as well?"

She sat pressed into one corner of the taxi, well away from him, and began to laugh. "You think I've had too much to drink. I am hungry now, but I'm also sober. Idiot! How can you behave like this?" She slid across the seat, closer but not touching even his clothes, still laughing. Could Arion have been wrong?

She half expected him to prop her up against a wall while he paid the fare. Later she could not account for the time between that and arriving inside the flat. She had no recollection apart from the sound of the front door closing and Frank lifting her chin.

"Stand on one leg," he commanded. She did, wobbling slightly on the high heel. "OK. Take your shoes off. I'm going to kiss you, and then I'm going to feed you. Is that all right?"

"Are you really asking me?"

Up close to him Arion's words took on reality. The clean, rough texture of his skin, the heat in his still-reddened eyes, the thrumming of her entire body as her lips parted for his tongue—she felt herself sag.

"Are you drunk?" he murmured, holding her up.

Lisa shook her head without shifting her lips from his. He felt her fumble with his shirt buttons. He stood back, and suddenly it wasn't funny any longer, not for her. "I want you."

"Lisa?"

"I want to go to bed with you, Frank."

The only light in the room came from between partly drawn curtains. She remained where she was, moving only slightly away from the wall as he undressed her. Her fingers brushed ineffectually at his jacket. She shuddered, shoulders rounding as his hands removed the last of her clothing. Then his jacket came off. She held it against her bare breasts for a moment; then the tie was gone, the shirt, the shoes. She dropped the jacket.

"Are you cold?" he asked, drawing her across the room. She stood with the back of her legs against the bed and watched him straighten up, socks in hand. Her hands went to the concave hollows under his ribs, up across the mat of hair on his chest, and then around his back and down, pulling him to her, cushioning his hardness against her belly, tucked in against him.

The bedcover was smooth and chilly against her shoulder

blades. His mouth moved down to her nipples, then curved along her rib cage, each flick of his tongue pulling with invisible threads, tugging her legs apart. The pleasure of his mouth on her was almost unbearable. She inched away to bring her knees up and reached down for his ears, urging him up again to her mouth, gentle, loving, everything blacking out suddenly as he entered her, pumping the breath out of her with a great rasping cry. Shocked, she opened her eyes.

He hesitated. "Is it all right?"

"I hate it," she said, raising her hips.

She watched him, her body reverberating with his thrusts. His face, her ignorance of it, astonished her. She yelped with unexpected joy, tracing the outline of the ridges of muscle that ran down each side of his spine, the furry hollow at its base, then pushing up against the short tufts of hair that grew into the back of his neck. As she moved with him, pinned and pursued by pleasure, the sound of her own voice reached her through the clamor in her ears—a hoarse, urging, stranger's voice. Tiny, flaring pulses crept up her legs and swooped down from her neck. "Oh," she murmured politely as she felt his hands under her, lifting her up to take her more closely. She gasped once, face averted, eyes closing as all the disparate sensations suddenly converged, pitching her over the edge and into wave after wave of ecstasy.

Later, still breathless, Frank wondered how he could have imagined it any different; he had been no less thoroughly unraveled by her honest appetite than she had. She was lying damply beside him, her head in the curve of his shoulder, her own breath coming in little puffs. One hand lay protectively on him; the other was pulled up awkwardly over her eyes.

"I want to tell you that's never happened before. What you did. I loved it." She squeezed him gently, amazed at herself. "Do you mind?"

She'd accuse him of treating her like a child if he did what he wanted to do just then: cuddle her. He said, "I suppose I'll get used to it. Hungry?"

"Very."

Frank covered her with a light quilt and went into the kitchen. Dazed, he stared at the contents of the refrigerator, then padded back into the living room, drew the curtains, and turned on the light. His naked reflection in the mirror looked foolish and out of focus. He pulled his lips back from his teeth, apelike, and peered at himself. "Well, I'll be damned. Lisa."

She was lying on her back, as he'd left her, sprawled across the middle of the bed. He drew the cover down and looked at her. "Lisa?" There was no answer. In response to his touch, she turned away with a low, snuffling sound. He went around to the other side of the bed and circled his palm lightly over a distended nipple. Her lips parted.

"Are you asleep?" He did it again. "I do love you. I love you, Lisa."

"Serves you right," she murmured.

He wanted her again, but with more time. Was she really asleep? He ran his hand over her hip and back to her breast, imagining a barely audible sound that would tell him it was all right. When that didn't happen, he watched her body for any sign of invitation. Frustrated, he was considering tickling her into wakefulness when her hand came down to cover his, picking it up and placing it precisely where she wanted it.

"Where have you been?" she asked, accusing him with a yawn that disintegrated into a smile.

45

☐ Richard Jarman replaced the receiver gently, then slammed and locked the right-hand drawer of his desk. He took a moment to collect his thoughts, calm himself. Angela seemed to practice some sort of alchemy, dragging to herself, like a magnet, everything that promised pain. The last few years had been a reprieve for him and for Belinda. Angela's absence in New York had conditioned them into believing that her silence, her marriage had strengthened the matchwood exterior and softened the steely core. It wasn't so.

"Maybe that's what she came back for," Belinda had said a moment ago, annoyed to have been informed by the local parish priest that someone had been asking questions. "Maybe it was always her intention to find the child."

"Did old Bridges say when this man turned up asking questions?"

"As a matter of fact, he did. It was two days ago. You know how unreliable his memory is, Richard. I'm sure he remembered to tell me only because of that other chap a few weeks ago. That one demanded access to records, researching local history, something like that. Bridges threatened to have *him* arrested. . . ."

He went on listening to his wife with half an ear. *Two* people asking questions? The first one *might* have been a genuine historian, but somehow he doubted it. Nothing to do with Angela could ever be that straightforward.

"What is your opinion, Richard?"

"It *is* the sort of thing Angela would do without coming to us first, naturally," he said.

"Naturally. And since she's chosen to do it this way, I refuse, Richard, adamantly, to become involved a second time. I expect you to put a stop to it."

"How do you propose I do that?"

"Tell her if you have to."

"I would prefer to avoid that," he murmured in the face of his wife's impatience, adding, "Unless it becomes absolutely essential. It's quite conceivable that whoever is carrying out the investigation has not come up with anything."

Belinda let out an exasperated sigh. "Hardly feasible, Richard. It's not as though it's a particularly difficult task, in view of the circumstances. What concerns me is how Angela will interpret the decisions we had to make at the time. Unless we nip the investigation in the bud now, I can see an embarrassing situation becoming an intolerable one."

"I'll see what I can do, my dear. Knowing our daughter, I suppose it was always in the cards that something like this would happen. I'll find out what I can."

"Richard, don't leave it too long."

This on top of everything else. Damn her husband for dying, he thought savagely, punching the intercom on his desk.

"Is Mrs. Wyatt in her office, Jane?"

"Mrs. Wy—I believe so. Or she might be in the subsidiary rights department; the paperback rights of *Night Work* are being auctioned today."

"Tell her I want a few words, now, if possible. Oh, and hold my calls until we're through."

He would not have to ask Angela what she'd found out

about the child, he knew; he would be able to tell the minute she walked through the door.

She came in holding a sheaf of papers in one hand, the stub of a pencil in the other. "You rang?" she inquired, sotto voce, suppressing a temptation to salute her father's solemn features.

His muscles tightened at the familiar facetiousness. But that, with her clear, untroubled expression, meant that she had heard nothing, knew nothing. He almost smiled with relief. It must have shown because he got a grin from her that conceded some pleasure at his reaction. He had meant to have her in anyway. Outside speculation about the trade department was beginning to reach even his ears. Dispatching two of the three key editorial staff was seen as a purge, not the way Jarman's did things. What annoyed him most was that his own people on the academic side were becoming edgy.

"Jane tells me that the paperback rights of *Night Work* are being auctioned today; it all seems to have happened very quickly, from the time you bought it, I mean."

Angie put the loose papers she held on his desk and sat down. "Not really," she said. "As soon as I heard that the American rights had been sold for eighty-five thousand dollars, I asked Cynthia to submit the book over here. Eighty-five thousand is an excellent price for such an English novel; I thought we should take advantage of that enthusiasm. *Those* paperback rights could easily go for a quarter of a million dollars."

"I see. And how is the auction going?"

"It's too early to tell yet, but I think we'll clear our advance." She saw a small movement of surprise. "We're up to thirty-eight thousand pounds, and we've heard from only three publishers so far." Was he disappointed by the possibility of the book's success? She couldn't tell.

"I don't think it's a good idea to leave the auction in Cynthia's hands. She's not had much experience in this sort of thing."

"That's precisely why I'm allowing her to handle it. But don't worry, I'm keeping an eye on everything." *Night Work* wasn't what he'd called her in for. Angie crossed her legs and smoothed her skirt down over her knees. Cissy had been on the phone to her less than a half hour ago and toward the end of the conversation had said, "Oliver won't mind if *you* tell your father about his decision, Angie. It's timing, you see, it's so difficult to judge; so much easier to do face-to-face." Easier? No. Cissy was asking her to spare Oliver this last ordeal.

"I understand that young Corbett has resigned," her father said. "Would you like to tell me how that happened? Am I to expect another call from Jason?" He wondered, but would not give her the satisfaction of asking, how she'd succeeded in persuading Jason to forgo his standard setting prices for the trade division.

"Shouldn't think so," Angie said. "Martin actually leaves this Friday. Jason and I agreed that Jarman's wasn't the ideal environment for his son."

"*Jason* agreed?"

"We have an understanding."

"And Sidney?"

"Ah, that was all my own work. I went back on my promise to Oliver and more or less forced him to resign."

"How did you do that?"

"Is this what you called me in for? I stood up to him, if you must know. Like all bullies, he backed off. Would you like to see the ad for his replacement going into the *Bookseller* next week?"

"That won't be necessary. Is this the end of it, or do you envisage more resignations?"

"That rather depends on whether people work with me or against me. Dunne Morrissey might object to my definition of what he's being paid to do. At the moment he's having to relearn the difference between publicity and promotion." She stopped and lifted her shoulders. "If he doesn't have a nervous breakdown, he'll stay on. I'll let you know."

"I must say I find your cavalier attitude toward the staff reprehensible."

"Whatever else it is, cavalier it's not. Incidentally, if the right candidates turn up, I'd like to be able to offer them at least the prospect of a directorship. Do you have any objections?"

"Interesting notion, since *you* aren't a director."

"I suppose it would be tidier if you were to appoint me to the board, but it's not something I'm pushing for. As long as the bank accepts my signature on the bottom of the check, that's fine. Even our standard contract says, 'On behalf of the company.' I guess anyone, including the tea lady, could sign those.''

He dismissed her levity with a sour look. "Just as long as you don't make any absolute promises, I don't see any harm in discussing directorships. But bear in mind that the final decision will be Oliver's and that he might not be . . . fully involved for some months after his release.''

He made it sound like a prison. Angie braced herself. Should she tell him now? It was as good a time as any. . . .

"Your mother tells me you've been to see Oliver. How is he?''

That had been over a month ago. . . . She shook her head and said, "The official opinion is 'As well as can be expected.' He was weak and . . . incapacitated, but Cissy says—''

"I'll accept the official opinion. You always were overprotective of your brother.''

Angie's body curved down into the chair. How doggedly he breached her defenses. She said, trying to raise her voice from a whisper, "He's not coming back.''

"What?''

"Oliver's decided that he'd like to do something else . . . he's not coming back to Jarman's.'' The look on his face brought her to her feet. She glanced at the silver cigarette box on his desk. Then she walked out of the room into Jane's office and asked her father's secretary for a cigarette.

"What the hell's going on in there?'' Jane hissed as she watched Angie steady the lighter in both hands.

"If I live long enough, I'll tell you,'' Angie whispered back. "Come by my office sometime this afternoon.''

Jane nodded, pressed the rest of the cigarettes and the lighter into Angie's hands, and steered her back to her father's office.

"Shut the door,'' he said. He hadn't moved. "I want an explanation!''

"I don't know that I have one, Father. Do you remember that conversation we had at the Hall? There's really nothing I can add to that. Oliver's simply had enough of publishing; he wants to pursue his interest in archaeology; he's going to lecture on Greek archaeology for one of those up-market holiday firms—''

"Lecturing on holiday cruises? Are you serious?''

"He is . . . and so is Cissy.''

"You—when did you decide all this! My God, how have you managed to *disrupt* all our lives in such a short time?"

Stung, Angie tried to tell herself that the words and the tone were only to have been expected. He was shocked and pained; by his own lights, betrayed. She said, as levelly as she could, "It wasn't *my* decision. Oliver didn't discuss it with me. He made a choice; he and Cissy made a choice. Why can't you accept that?"

"Because I know you!"

Angie shook her head. "No, you don't. You know nothing about me. Or Oliver, for that matter. I was hoping we could . . . I know you're disappointed—"

"Disappointed?" She'd never seen him so angry before. Both fists, white-knuckled, rested on the blotter in front of him. He sat bolt upright, head slightly forward, as though he were going to leap up at any moment. "Oliver would never have done this, without your . . . influence. Is this why you came back?"

"No, it isn't. Please, can't we—"

"Discuss it? I have nothing to say to you, Angela. Just leave—"

"Not yet, Father. I want you to know I didn't plan this. It had nothing whatsoever to do with me except that I agreed to stand in for Oliver. But that's also changed. I'm not prepared to do that any longer, simply stand in for him under your disapproving eye. It's not much fun, for either of us. Will you consider an alternative suggestion? *Think* about it?"

"From you?" Now he did get up, turning his back on her as he went over to the window.

"This *is* from me, I haven't even discussed it with Oliver. I'd like to take over the trade division of Jarman's." She expected him to whirl around, but the only indication that he'd heard came in the sound of a slap as his hands came together behind his back. She lit another cigarette in the silence. She had no way of knowing how he'd react to her next words; perhaps the worst was over. "I mean, take it over as a wholly independent associate company. Otherwise . . ." She hesitated, recalling what Jason had said about what her father would interpret as pressure, but it was too late now to pull back. "Otherwise, if you'd prefer to shed Jarman trade, which you've described to me as an encumbrance, I'd be willing to buy you out."

He turned. "No."

"You won't even think about it?"

"No."

"Why not? Oliver's left behind a very solid base. I can build from that. I can shake it up, make it profitable again."

"Why would you want to?" he asked coldly, sitting down behind his desk once more.

Again Angie hesitated. He wasn't going to like this either. "Because I've decided to live in London and because I love publishing. I'm a publisher, as much as you are and as much as Oliver isn't. I can give you everything he tried to but couldn't, except one thing." A line from a Dory Previn song suddenly came to mind and said it all: "I ain't your son."

Did he understand what she was saying, and why? His expression told her that at least he hadn't taken it as he might have a few minutes ago: as a facetiously chiding comment.

"And if I don't agree to your . . . suggestions, if I decide to bring somebody else in to run the trade division, what will you do?"

Angie sighed and used both armrests to lift herself out of the chair. "Please think about it—"

"What will you do?" he repeated.

"I'll start up on my own here in London. It's not what I want to do, because it could reflect on Jarman's, on you. . . . I— It sounds like blackmail, but it isn't. If I could do it any other way, I would."

"Is that all?"

"Is that all I have to say? I think so." And, hoping to raise a smile, she added, "Isn't it enough?" He was looking straight through her, willing her out of the room. Before she reached the door, there was a file open in front of him, his glasses were in place, pen pointed down.

It was done. She'd done it. She grinned weakly at Jane Bullivant, tossed cigarettes and lighter onto her desk, and strode back to her own office, feeling detached, relieved, and saddened. She'd done it. She couldn't begin to imagine what was going through his mind now. What would he do? Call her mother? Or Oliver? It occurred to her to phone and warn Cissy that he would try to get Oliver to change his mind; then she decided against it. Oliver would have to face up to the old man sooner or later, and he had Cissy for support. Angie knew that this time Cissy would not be swayed, not by threats or appeals to family allegiances. Together, she and Oliver would be able to withstand the onslaught.

* * *

On her desk were four messages, none of them from Christopher Chetwynd. She swore swiftly. Did he think he was being considerate by not reporting back to her, leaving week to follow silent week? Almost daily she had the urge to call him and demand that he contact her regularly, even if he had nothing concrete to report. But that would have annoyed him, implied lack of trust, and she couldn't take the chance that he would delegate the search for her daughter to someone else and make her wait even longer.

She flicked through the messages again. Disappointment made her glance suspiciously at the telephone. Would Paul Angelou have left a message, trusted her to call him back? Yes. He knew that she had neither the strength nor the will to resist him. Far from diminishing his hold over her senses, his *absence*, since that night at his father's house, now rendered her helpless to every hitherto unacknowledged fantasy: to be taken and taken over, lulled, and absorbed. . . .

Beneath the messages lay a stack of memos from Sidney, pedantic one-line queries and atrociously detailed reports on novels, *bad* novels he'd read.

"Go now," she'd suggested when he had confronted her with his resignation, not sure why he'd chosen to hand it to her personally. "You'll be paid. Take a holiday."

She didn't want him around, subverting staff, authors, and agents. He knew that and made no pretense of considering her offer. He'd expected her to cut off his expense account. When he realized that she wasn't going to, he used the time and the money to shore up his own connections, spread the word about the new agency. Angie knew what he was doing; she said nothing, hoping that if there were enough rope, he would hang himself.

Angie slipped Sidney's memos into her bottom drawer, along with the rest, just as Cynthia Crew came into the office. The subsidiary rights manager was excited and beaming, pink, like the fluffy sweater she wore. "We're up to fifty-three thousand pounds," she said, flopping down into a chair. "I can't believe it. I'm exhausted."

Angie laughed. "Have you heard from everybody?"

"Just about, and four, at least, want the book very badly. It's fantastic. Am I supposed to be enjoying this?"

"I don't see why not. I suspect you have an instinct for tough negotiations." Cynthia was no longer the vapid, overgrown schoolgirl, eager to please; she actually *looked* as though she were doing a day's work. A month ago she would not have walked into Angie's office without calling first; these days she didn't have the time.

"Well, I'd better get back. I just came out for a breather. Will you be here for the next hour or so?"

"I'll be here for the rest of the day."

"Thanks." She almost ran out of the room.

Cynthia would do, Angie thought. And Deborah. Deborah had taken under her wing most of the new authors Angie had brought in, and although she was basking quite happily in a newfound confidence, she would need the assistance of at least one junior editor before long. But one thing at a time.

Still feeling somber and slightly at odds with the freshness of the day outside, Angie put a call through, on impulse, to Jason Corbett. He made her wait for a few minutes and then said breezily, "I'm glad you called."

"Jason?" Thrown, she didn't know what to say to him.

"You sound as though you've got through a hundred cigarettes in the last hour. What's wrong?"

"Are you busy?"

"I'm always busy."

"I mean, do you have someone with you?"

"I'm alone."

Angie flushed and swiveled her chair around until she could see the Ken Kiff picture. "I don't know why I asked you that or why I'm . . . how are you?"

He laughed. "I saw you four days ago, and my health hasn't changed. You've told your father."

"Yes, just now, but—" She hadn't called to share *that* with him.

"What can I do for you, Mrs. Wyatt? Do you want to talk or do you want to listen?"

She'd been with Jason several times since their dinner together at his flat, and she'd called him now for a touch of reality. Like Frank, he was unerring in his understanding of her needs. She found that she had begun to take her bruises to him in the same way as she had to Benn, quite openly, but not without realizing very clearly what she was doing. Jason Corbett, she knew, stood squarely between the innocent and uncomplicated love she felt for Frank Sheldon and the debilitating desire she felt for Paul Angelou.

"Listen," she said in answer to his question.

"I've spent the last two days in Piemonte, and I thought about you there. Two days in a damp, tiny villa with exploding light bulbs and built-in allergies and an unfathomably aggressive goose that attacked itself when no one else was around. The only habitable room was the kitchen, where I was invited to cook on a wood-burning stove, nice, very rustic, made excellent boiled water. When I wasn't trying not to eat the result of my endeavors, I was subjected to an intravenous drip of atrocious grappa which the local garage must have been giving away, six bottles with every gallon of petrol. I swear the petrol would have been more palatable.

"You might ask, if you're still there, what I was doing in this godforsaken place, surrounded by people—the locals, that is—who decided that I was important because I was neither weather-beaten nor fastidious about my aversion to the perpetual damp mist, mud, and stiles and Frenchmen from over the border. My hosts were Italian. This man, his wife, and their four children live in a marbled palazzo in Rome. I've been there; it makes the Vatican look like an outhouse. His color printing is exquisite; I was there to discuss some joint ventures—'in the solitude of my villa,' he said. Now, I have a liberal soul, I don't mind what people do in their own time, but I draw the line at their insistence that everyone else go gaga over a tap that spouts brown gunge, boiled milk, cockroaches and spiders so well fed and cosseted that they cast bigger shadows than I do. But—but I do as I'm told. I went, I survived, and I'm back with a price that would suggest that the grappa had a secret ingredient which destroyed brain cells. Are you smiling at my misfortune? In addition to a good price, I have been offered the further use of this villa of horror. Being a good businessman, I shall, of course, make the pleasurable noises so loved by aristocrats seeking company in their pursuit of immolation in small doses. Are you still there, Mrs. Wyatt?"

"That's a good story."

"You don't believe me?"

"Oh, yes."

"You will accompany me there one of these days."

"And we'll cook that goose, right?"

"Ah." Jason sighed. "I shall stuff it personally and bury the bones and myself die a happy man."

Angie laughed, cheered by the story. "Thank you."
"Job done?"
"All done, Jason."

46

☐ Ani was already saying good-bye. She knew, without being told, that they would not come back. Arion saw her contemplate her garden glassily, reviewing the past. She still sat
down among the flowers, weeding with the aid of an old
tablespoon and a bent barbecue fork, leaving little mounds
of garden debris in her wake. But there was a dreamlike quality to the days now, a timeless waiting. The house itself
seemed to have shrunk.

Ani was making bread this morning. She stood at the table,
her strong-wristed hands buried in the mixture. Arion watched
as she sprinkled a pinch of flour over her hands and rubbed
the dough out from between her fingers in long, curling flakes.
Soon she would round and smooth the mound and leave it to
rise under a folded square of blanket kept solely for that purpose. The regularity and precision with which she did these
things were enviable. He was beginning to see how little he
had considered Ani's life in this country. His own days had
been filled from the start. She had always been there when
his friends came uninvited; there was meze on the table, small
glasses for ouzo and an implicit welcome. What did she do
when he wasn't there?

"Ari," she called out now. "You are dreaming." Her smile
was soft and questioning. Often, when they were alone, he
would be somewhere else. She could see the past in his eyes,
a yearning for things beyond recall. "You are going to be at
home all this day?"

"Come with me," he said impulsively. "We will go to the
bank, where I must sign some papers, and then we will walk."

"Where?" She sounded faintly alarmed.

"We will see Olga and maybe the boys. I will take you to

the market, and then we will see Scotia. Maybe we will eat there.''

''You have forgotten, Ari. Susan is coming today.''

Arion passed his hand over his forehead in a gesture of impatience with himself. Was Paul coming, too? He couldn't remember.

47

☐ The man was good, Vincent finally had to concede. If the robbery and the arson were anything more than coincidence, he was bloody good. Not a trace. Not a single one of his informers had come up with a whisper. Vincent had called in favors owed, had spread the odd threat in the right direction. Nothing.

He knew that he personally would not have the option to pursue the case much longer, in any event. There were other cases piling up; pressure was being put on him to delegate the Angelou investigation. The computers would go on working, linking, analyzing, cross-referencing, but the immediate human element would be missing.

From an instinctive dislike of Paul Angelou, Vincent had developed a severe mistrust of the man. Not only did Angelou's aloofness suggest a watchful complicity, but it seemed to conceal amusement at Vincent's efforts, a catch-me-if-you-can attitude. Vincent would dearly have loved to nail him. It had become something of a personal crusade, and he didn't like himself for it. He had the uncomfortable and nagging notion that just one single, slender thread would unravel the whole mess.

Susan Angelou had made no secret of her surprise at his persistent questioning. He'd interviewed her twice, alone. On both occasions her easy politeness had slipped into confusion, as though she could not understand, let alone tolerate, the direction of his questions. No, her husband had not had much time for young Cory; everyone knew that. No, Paul was not close to his father; everyone knew that, too. She would not go so far as to say that animosity existed. "It happens," she'd conceded, lifting her chin. "Fathers and their sons."

Vincent tapped the thick buff-colored folder in front of him. At least it would not be closed. An hour later, having sent his driver back to the station, he began to walk from Ani's to Prax. Scotia, in this, his third interview, had again been of little help. Like everyone else connected with the affair, he displayed a resolute incomprehension. Vincent had by this time acknowledged the fact that he himself was looking for Arion Angelou's innocence. Over thirty years in the force, sifting facts, compiling cases with effortless patience, he found the implications here unpalatable: with his shares sinking into the mire, Arion Angelou had arranged for the warehouse to be burned down. . . .

James Bonnier was waiting for him. He opened the door of the nightclub himself. "Come in, Inspector," he said, standing aside. "Let's go into the office. I wasn't expecting to see you again."

The office was only slightly less opulent than the interior of the club itself. Vincent wrinkled his nose at the pleasant whiff of gardenias that hung in the air. Bonnier grinned at him. "My wife, no air-conditioning can get rid of the cigarette smoke."

Vincent took one of the two chairs in front of the desk. Bonnier came across as a quiet, unobtrusive man, neat and composed. Their one previous meeting had been brief and to the point. Now Vincent was looking, without much hope, for a stray detail, anything that would help make sense of the case.

"Let's begin again with the young man," he said. "What was your personal opinion of him?"

"I've known Cory ever since he came to this country, four, five years ago. He was good-looking, energetic, and very, very young."

"Young for his age, you mean?"

"Exactly that."

"From what you know of him, would it surprise you to find out that he and his friend Bass planned that fire?"

James got up and began pacing slowly from wall to wall behind his desk. "I've thought about that a lot, as it happens. I don't know what you've found out, but yes, it would surprise me. The break-in surprised me because all Cory had to do was go to Arion. He must have known that. Arion was always there. Also, Cory was in many ways too . . . innocent for that.''

''And Arion Angelou?''

James stopped pacing. There was a haughty, almost contemptuous look on his face as he said, ''No. Me, yes; Arion, never, not that.''

''Just no?''

''Inconceivable.''

''I need more than that, Mr. Bonnier.''

''It's not only inconceivable, it's stupid. Arion would no more do a thing like that than—than cook the books. Money doesn't mean that much to him. You'd be dead wrong if you went after him. For God's sake, he's given away more than he's made!''

''He's an old man. Maybe he didn't like the idea of starting again. But tell me this: would anyone destroy the warehouse *for* Angelou *without* his knowledge and in order to help him?''

James sat down abruptly. There was immediate astonishment in his whispered ''Who?''

''Oh, any number of people, if you stop to think about it. You, Scotia, Angelou's son, Mr. Sheldon—''

''You can't seriously believe that, Inspector.''

Vincent eased off suddenly. ''As it happens, I don't. Just one more thing, Mr. Bonnier. I'm curious about the relationship between Angelou and his son. Would you care to elaborate on that?''

''I suspect you've heard all there is to hear on that subject. My own views are no different. Paul Angelou is an ambitious man, probably unscrupulous. I can't say he isn't fond of his father, but for some reason he has disassociated himself from his family. One has the impression that he disapproves of Arion's . . . Greekness. It's difficult to describe, but he's moved into another world, and Arion remains, despite his wealth, what he was. Paul owns shares in Angel—''

''I know that. I also know that in the case of Angel shares the market was cleverly manipulated. Someone started a run, and the rest followed. What do you make of that?''

''I'm not a financier, Inspector. Too complicated for me.''

''I've also been told that Paul Angelou has serious political ambitions—prospects that may come to fruition in the not too distant future.''

"That's news to me. Well, at least that puts him in the clear, doesn't it? He wouldn't have risked his career by ruining his father, would he now?"

Vincent was quietly thoughtful for a moment, then got up and held out his hand. "Thank you, Mr. Bonnier. That's all for the time being. I might call on you again, but in the meantime, if you come up with a name, please call me."

"Name?"

"It's possible that we'll never know, but I think someone set out to destroy the old man's business. The fact that a robbery was taking place at the time of the fire was a coincidence. Those are my thoughts at the moment. Think about it, Mr. Bonnier. Who stood to gain by toppling Arion Angelou? That's the name I want."

It was a shot in the dark, and Vincent knew it. His gut feeling was that Paul Angelou was up to his eyes in it. But why would he take such a risk? When he and Angelou had faced each other in Angelou's office, the man had actually laughed at him; in the face of Vincent's groping questions, Angelou had called his bluff, and Vincent had come up empty.

Unless the arsonist himself was caught, and that was an increasingly remote possibility, Paul Angelou was home and dry.

48

☐ Paul had no illusions about why Sir Richard Jarman wanted to see him. He was amused by Jarman's blatant suggestion that they meet at the Groucho Club in Dean Street. Its membership was drawn specifically from people in the media; in the twenty minutes since they had been there, Sir Richard had been greeted by no fewer than six people. Not a very subtle choice by the old man. The Garrick or any one of a number of other clubs would have been more suitable. Privacy was clearly not on the agenda.

"I hope you don't mind meeting here, Paul, but I have an early dinner appointment at L'Escargot, which is—"

"A five-minute walk away. I know. As a matter of fact, this suits my plans as well."

"That's fine. I've been meaning to call you and extend my personal sympathies for the loss of your young relative in that warehouse tragedy. Rum business. Must have been quite a shock to your father, what with the police inquiries and the financial, uh, crisis."

"Quite."

They were sitting at a table near the bar. From his position Sir Richard could see everyone who entered the room. As he spoke, he glanced up at each new arrival, seemingly inviting interruption. Paul watched him, noting the confidence with which he spoke. Too confident. For such a wily old manipulator, Sir Richard was showing his hand far too early. Paul knew what was coming. He'd been looking forward to the meeting ever since he'd received Jarman's note.

Richard Jarman and his kind expected cooperation as a matter of course; gratitude and obedience were their price to an outsider. Among themselves, a nod was an understanding, a commitment. Their solidarity and mutual dependence had formed a stronghold for so long that its impregnability was something they took for granted. Their biggest mistake was to lose sight of the fact that Paul Angelou was not one of them, that his energies were fresh, his ambitions dynamically structured. He had no one to protect but himself.

A noisy commotion of friends greeting each other at the doorway drew Sir Richard's attention once more. His attitude was at once one of ease and fellowship. Paul was puzzled. He was about to skewer Sir Richard Jarman, and he felt nothing. Not even a mild satisfaction at the prospect could penetrate the fog of disquiet that had settled over him ever since he had learned of Susan's decision to accompany his parents to Greece. For the past few days he'd found himself battling his way through an unfamiliar labyrinth of emotions, at the end of which only one reality presented itself: he and Angela Wyatt had unwittingly created a cage for themselves. They were locked in by invisible bars. She represented everything he'd spent his life avoiding. Passion was weakness, control everything; she'd shattered his complacency forever.

"The police inquiries are continuing?" Sir Richard raised his dry sherry to his lips.

"Naturally," Paul replied. His whiskey lay untouched in front of him. "One can hardly expect the deaths of three men to go uninvestigated."

Sir Richard frowned. "I understand," he murmured, hoping that Angelou wouldn't make this too difficult for him. The man was an inspired money-maker, but perhaps he, Sir Richard, had been somewhat rash in putting his name forward for Cyril Kingsley's seat. Not that the others had raised any objections at the time. The constituency in question was, after all, one of the most multiethnic in London, and a name like Angelou would have been a decided bonus in their campaign. Besides, Paul Angelou was rich enough to ensure that the party's campaign coffers would be spared "petrol money," Sir Richard's private euphemism for local election expenses. The fact that Angelou's family was now involved in something of a scandal was disappointing, but on reflection it was better that the skeletons emerged now rather than later. Little as he liked admitting it, there was something about Angelou he found disturbing, an attitude he could not quite place, a feeling—absurd as it was—that *he* was being used.

That feeling surfaced now. He said carefully, "These things, unfortunate as they are, do tend to throw up complications."

Paul nodded, deliberately misunderstanding the roundabout way of telling him that "they" had come to a decision. "All problems are soluble, Richard. The police investigations are no more than routine, so much so that the newspapers are no longer interested in the story. Not that they ever were, apart from reporting the fire initially."

"I must agree with you that the media have been extremely gentlemanly, if that's the word."

Paul lifted his glass and drank for the first time. "As I said, all problems are soluble."

What the hell did he mean by that? Pressure, a bribe? It was unlikely that it was a sense of noblesse oblige; reciprocal honor was not a concept he would have associated with Paul Angelou. "Nonetheless," he said, "the incident was reported, and unfair as it may seem, your own financial success has drawn the wrong sort of speculation about Mr. Angelou, Senior."

Not even the pompous hypocrisy of that statement was enough to arouse Paul. "What sort of speculation, Richard?

That my father is involved in a conspiracy to defraud? Or that he may yet be charged with manslaughter? Perhaps both?''

Better. At least he wasn't going to have to lead Angelou by the nose. "Rumors, talk . . . one can't prevent it. It's damnable that one should even have to discuss these events in such an objective fashion.''

"You're right. But rumors die, people forget, life gets back to normal. In this instance I can see an intervening period of, say, nine months being more than adequate—"

"Nine months? You've lost me.''

"Can I get you another sherry? No? Well, I mention that time period because you will obviously want to persuade Cyril Kingsley to continue in the constituency until the time is right to announce my candidature. Am I wrong?''

Ingenuously put, wide-eyed trust—could he have underestimated Angelou? "Not wrong exactly, Paul. I don't have to tell you that the timing of a by-election in Cyril's constituency can make or break us. October, two months from now, directly in the wake of the party conference, is ideal. Not my decision, you understand.''

Decisions . . . Paul wondered if Richard Jarman had avoided responsibility for his daughter all those years ago with the same arrogant clumsiness. He took a sip of whiskey and sat back, legs crossed. "Are you telling me that your committee has decided to drop my name?''

"For the good of the party, I'm sorry to say. Given the increasing racial tensions and the possibility of more unfortunate flare-ups, the powers that be consider it imperative that we take no chances in Cyril's constituency.''

"That's odd. I was under the impression that the reason for my nomination was precisely that my name wasn't exactly English.''

Sir Richard tugged, with embarrassment, at his tie. "I can see that it might have appeared to be so, but you were, regardless of your, uh, name, the best man for the job.''

"But that has now changed, and I am no longer seen to be the best man for the job. Tell me, Richard, is it your personal belief that children are responsible for the actions of their parents?''

"I'm afraid I don't understand what you mean.''

"I mean quite simply that.''

"Well, of course, taken on a personal level—"

"It *is* personal, Richard. He *is* my father. Whatever else is in dispute here, that isn't."

"Not much point in getting het up, old man—"

"Ah, don't get me wrong. I'm curious rather than furious." Paul allowed himself a smile to add to the other's discomfort. "It is my contention that the sins of the father should very definitely not be visited upon the child. Any more than the child's should be visited upon the father. Wouldn't you agree?"

"As a principle, yes, but in practical terms we live in a world which makes principles like that a—a luxury."

"A luxury which *you* can afford and which you are telling me that I can*not* afford?"

Richard Jarman paled, and Paul felt a reluctant admiration for Angela's father. In the face of an as yet unspoken threat, Jarman's head came up, eyes deadened with a contempt which said, This is not the way to play the game; good God, where will we all be if the gutter lies so close?

"I should be grateful for an explanation, Paul."

"I don't think an explanation is called for. You're an astute man, Richard. You've led a protected life. All I'm asking is that you take into account the position of the less well . . . established."

"I resent the implication—"

"Well, then look at it in practical terms, your expression, not mine. Factually it comes down to this: you belong to a group of people who wash each other's linen in private. I see nothing wrong in that, do believe me. The only thing I object to is the exclusiveness of that group. There is a substratum, you know . . . no, perhaps you don't. It washes linen, too, but for a price. A fair price, mind you, nothing exorbitant, only money. I have come to the conclusion that money buys just about everything, including your establishment and their linen, whether they like it or not, whether they *agree* to it or not."

"You're speaking in riddles, man!"

"Am I? Maybe a book of riddles, crossword puzzles would be an appropriate gift for your son, help him pass the time during his sabbatical. That's the official line, isn't it? A sabbatical?"

There was no mistaking the genuine outrage in Jarman's voice. "Blackmail. I could construe this as blackmail!"

"Come now, not blackmail. I would not like this to be the

end of our business relationship. Nor indeed, our future political aims. We do, after all, see eye to eye on those at least.''

"I doubt if we see eye to eye on anything, Angelou.''

"That's a pity, Richard. I seem to have the same problem with your daughter.''

"Angela?'' he gasped. "What does Angela have to do with this?''

"Nothing. Nothing at all. And I shall take it greatly amiss if you mention this conversation to her. After all, she is plagued by the same dilemma—the sins of the mother being visited upon the daughter.''

Jarman's fingers laced themselves together tightly. "*She* told you that?''

Paul shook his head. "You could learn a lesson in loyalty from her, Richard,'' he said calmly.

Angela . . . Richard Jarman struggled to take it in, understand just what it was that Angelou was saying. Could Angela in some way have precipitated this, too? If she hadn't told Angelou about her daughter, how had he found out? There was only one way: he'd paid someone to dig around for Jarman skeletons, most likely the man who had posed as a local historian, the one old Bridges had sent away with a flea in his ear. But *why*? Again, the answer was simple: Angelou was threatening exposure—of Oliver's alcoholism, Angela's rape. And the child. If Angelou knew *that* much, he would also know about the rape not being reported and the adoption. It was more than enough. . . .

"How well do you know my daughter?'' he snapped.

"Well enough,'' Paul responded. Let him make what he wanted of that.

"My family seems to have evoked more than a passing interest in you. I don't know where you get this supposed information from, but—''

"Supposed?'' Paul broke in mildly.

"*Supposed!*'' Richard Jarman got to his feet and stepped away from the table. This was intolerable. His face was quite gray with fury. His right hand lay flattened over his tie; the other hung limply at his side. As he opened his mouth to speak, Paul stopped him.

"Cad,'' he said tonelessly. "Is that what you're going to say?'' And then, as Jarman drew himself up and began to walk away, called after him: "By the way, Richard, do tell your committee that I agree. October is an excellent month for a by-election.'' Several heads turned in Paul's direction, but as he'd expected, Jarman did not break his stride.

Paul gave him ten minutes, more than enough time to reach L'Escargot. Then he finished his drink quickly and walked out of the bar into Dean Street. Late workers mingled with theatergoers in the warmth of the midsummer evening. Heat threaded along his spine as he began to walk toward Shaftesbury Avenue in search of a taxi.

Jarman would persuade his committee to come to heel; Paul had no doubt about that. The man had been caught off guard, and his emotions had been clearly mirrored in the arrogant features: disgust that another man should mention such intimate family revelations, disbelief at the mere hint of using those revelations, and, finally, a white anger at the realization that Angelou had the power to control every member of the Jarman family. . . .

Paul stepped off the pavement to flag a taxi. All the exhilaration he'd expected to feel in his confrontation with Sir Richard Jarman surfaced now as he gave the taxi driver Angela's address.

Angie opened the door in response to his second ring. She swung it all the way back, as though she'd been expecting a crowd. "Paul. What are you doing here?"

"May I come in?" It was almost eight o'clock, and she looked as though she'd just come home or were about to go out again. She wore a light oatmeal gabardine suit, with a long loose jacket that hung down over her hips. A heavy gilt chain, knotted just below her breasts, lay over a finely pleated ivory silk blouse.

She hesitated fractionally. "How did you get into the building?"

"The porter let me in. He was outside, gossiping." He walked past her into the living room. A typescript lay in two neat piles on the floor beside one of the armchairs. And on the table beside it, the telephone receiver lay on its side between an empty coffee mug and a clean ashtray. He recognized Simon and Garfunkel's "Bridge over Troubled Water" coming from the stereo system. The bedroom door was shut.

Coming to a halt behind him, Angie followed the movements of his head as he glanced around the room. When he asked, "Am I interrupting anything?" with his eyes firmly fixed on the bedroom door, she laughed and moved toward the armchair.

"Why don't you take a look? Excuse me." She picked up the receiver. "Maxwell, hullo, sorry about that. Where are you calling from?"

"Thirty-fourth floor, Bennett-Poore Building, New York, New York. When are you coming back?"

Maxwell Reith—how could the accent of someone she knew so well sound so strange? He made her laugh with a waspishly sharp and funny New York publishing joke and then said, "Did you know Sidney was soliciting for jobs all over New York? He even approached us, I hear. . . . I thought you'd like to know."

"Thank you, Max. It's all right, he's leaving, resigned from Jarman's." She tried not to think about Paul in the same room, watching her intently.

"We came in on the auction for *Night Work*, did you know that? We were prepared to go up to fifty thousand dollars, even after Sidney gave us his spiel."

"Then he *was* putting it down."

"Right, but less here at Bennett-Poore than anywhere else, I think, because of you . . . and Lou. I guess he felt he couldn't entirely trust us."

Angie knew that Frank was still waiting to hear from Farley Esterhuys. Jason had discovered from Martin that Farley and Sidney were preparing to set up shop together. She wondered vaguely why it was taking Farley so long to make the break official. Jason was considering buying his son into the Esterhuys/Niklas agency, choosing to ignore Angie's reservations. She also knew that Frank stood to lose a considerable part of his income if Farley did switch his U.K. representation.

"How well do you know Farley Esterhuys?" she asked her former colleague.

"I know him." Maxwell was dismissive.

"Do a bit of politicking for me, Max?"

"Say it."

"Tell Farley what you've just told me, that Sidney was job hunting while he was over there."

"Want to fill me in on the rest?"

"There's not much else. Farley is apparently planning to leave the Sheldon Agency and work through Sidney over here. It's fairly certain that Sidney fixed all this up while he was in New York rubbishing *Night Work*. I'm just wondering how

Farley will react when he knows his generous offer was taken up only as second best."

Maxwell took it seriously because it was a surprising request coming from Angie. He didn't associate that sort of manipulativeness with her. "I think maybe England has done you some good," he said. "I'll be over in a couple of months. Save some time for me."

"Who was that?" Paul asked as she hung up.

"A friend in New York." She turned from the telephone and saw that he was removing his jacket and pulling his tie loose. She thought, objectively, that he looked relaxed and at ease with himself.

"Are you always so businesslike at home?" He held on to his jacket and surveyed her quizzically. "High heels, jewelry . . ."

Why had he come? "As a matter of fact, I was about to make one or two phone calls and take myself off to bed for an early night."

"Good idea," he said, turning in the direction of the hallway. "Why don't you make your calls now?"

Angie watched him in astonishment. She heard him go into the bathroom and immediately the sound of running water. He'd turned the shower on and left the door open. She choked back a sound that was half annoyance, half resignation and called out loudly, "Feel free."

She sat there listening to him for a while, then got up and turned up the volume of "Baby Driver." It didn't help. She picked up the typescript again, registered the page number, 178, and began to read. The words wavered and splayed themselves out into unintelligible lines and phrases and meanings that made no sense at all.

She sighed out a weary expletive. She sensed, reluctantly, that she'd willed him here tonight, and now she was afraid. She snapped a rubber band around the unread pages of the typescript before returning the whole thing to her briefcase. Then, chin held high in solitary defiance, she went to the bathroom door and pushed it all the way open with her foot. Through the steam and the greenish tint of the shower curtains, she could see only an outline of his body. He was soaping himself vigorously, reaching now and then for the shower gel. . . .

Angie leaned against the door for a moment, arms crossed, noting with an almost detached interest how swiftly and with what threatening certainty the tide of desire broke over her. It wasn't even that he was naked and no more than five feet away, she mocked herself; it was always there, a million silken threads pulling tight. . . .

Back in the living room she poured and downed two fingers of whiskey in a gulp and nearly jumped out of her skin when the telephone rang. It was Jason, inquiring politely about their lunch date the following day. "What's wrong? You sound funny."

"I've never been to Ani's," she said. "A coincidence . . . I'll tell you about it some time." She had a quick vision of Jason's strong, square hands and stirred with discomfort. Paul in her shower, Jason's exquisitely seductive voice in her ear . . . Only half-aware of what he was saying now, she picked up the phone and went to stand at the balcony doors. It wasn't yet dark; only one or two winking lights showed up in the distance. She heard herself agreeing to another arrangement for the following week and held the phone cradled between her cheek and shoulder long after he'd hung up.

"Angela."

She started, grabbing at the receiver as it fell. She wasn't quick enough to stop it from swinging painfully back into her shin. From where she stood, Paul's reflection in the glass was quite plain, but she didn't realize he was standing outside the bedroom door until she turned. There was a towel around his waist and, she noted, a sprinkling of hair was visible on his shoulders.

"Do you have a suit rack?"

"What?"

"A suit rack . . . for my clothes," he said patiently.

"What do you—" It took an enormous effort for her to remain where she was. "No, of course I haven't."

He shrugged and disappeared into the bedroom. A suit rack? What the hell was he doing in there? She followed him to the door. "What are you doing?" she asked as he leaned into her wardrobe. He looked ridiculous, holding the towel around his midriff with one hand, the other sifting through her clothes. He was looking for a hanger.

"Get dressed, Paul," she said quietly, her heart thudding erratically against her ribs.

He dropped the towel, his back toward her, and arranged his jacket and trousers neatly over a hanger. "Susan knows about this," he said.

Angie flinched. As he worked, muscles and tendons ridged the smooth skin of his back. "How? There's nothing to know."

"She says she saw it that morning, God knows how."

"It must have been me. You made my hair stand on end. I thought you were going to kill me."

"I could have," he told her, turning. "She's going to Greece with my father and mother. She wants me to go with her."

The scene was entirely preposterous. He was fully erect, waiting for her to join him, and they were discussing his wife as though she were a casual acquaintance.

"Will you?" she asked. His body was a dark beckoning shadow, immense.

"I haven't decided yet. What do you think I should do?"

"Don't . . . ask me." Like him, she was more than a little afraid, and there was a throaty sadness in her voice as she added, "You love her, you must go."

"I love you, too."

"No."

"Tell me that in bed."

"I'm not going to bed with you, Paul. Now please . . . *please* get dressed and go." He got into bed. "This isn't funny." She might have been talking to herself. He removed his wristwatch and placed it carefully on the bedside table. "Did you hear me? I'm not joking, Paul. I'll . . . call the police."

He laughed at her, sliding down against the pillows. "And what will you tell them? That I broke your door down? My clothes are in your wardrobe. I've used your towels and"— he stopped to sniff at himself—"your deodorant. You yourself are unharmed. What will you tell them?"

She had no intention of calling anyone. His hair was wet, slicked down and shiny. She said, "In that case, I'll leave. I'm going out, and I expect you to be gone when I get back." She sounded like an outraged virgin defending her honor, and even at that distance and with only the small side light on, she saw a wry humor touch his eyes when she said, "It's the same for me, you know. It's no different. Having you here is . . . difficult. So please don't be here when I get back."

Alone, Paul fixed himself a whiskey and lit one of her cigarettes. He could find nothing he wanted to read on her bookshelves and went back to bed with the *Guardian*. He didn't want to think about her reactions or the possibility that she might not come back at all. He'd read the paper thoroughly and had almost finished the quick crossword when he heard her key in the door. He shut his eyes and willed her to cross the hall quickly. . . .

Angie didn't bother to look into the bedroom. He was still there; she could sense his presence. Her ankles ached from walking all the way to Sloane Square and back via the shadowy Embankment and Cheyne Walk. All she'd achieved was tiredness. Her blouse clung damply to her shoulder blades, and even her ears and elbows felt damp.

Later the prelude to their lovemaking became a totally separate and tactile memory, for all that they'd scarcely touched each other. She came to the doorway again, outlined against the bright light of the hallway. She saw nothing clearly until he took her hand and began to remove her clothes, carefully and in silence. Skirt first, oddly. She stepped out of it and watched as he clipped it to a hanger; then her shoes, placed side by side inside the wardrobe. He found another hanger for her jacket. Before putting it away, he patted the pockets and removed her keys and two tenpence coins. Dazed, she wondered what he would do with the chain around her neck. He left it, unbuttoning her blouse and easing the material out from under its weight. She shivered as the metal swung against her bare skin. It was all she could do to stand still and not reach out to touch some part of him. Her panties he placed on a low chest of drawers, and finally the chain on top of them.

His silence was part of her growing sense of unreality. He drew the covers back, took her hand again, and, touching her only where he had to, lowered her down onto the bed. As he had done before, he began to kiss her, his hands on either side of her head. Her nipples nudged up into the springy hair on his chest, and the friction as he moved and breathed stirred her into activity. How could he be so calm?

With a fumbling, uncertain touch her hand slipped down between them and encircled him. He stopped kissing her and drew his head back to look down at her. The lamplight brought odd shades to his eyes; his mouth, softly curved, was solemn and smiling at the same time. Angie searched his face half-fearfully for any sign of triumph but saw nothing. And she could think of nothing to say except a silent ''please'' as he moved over her. His body, from what she could see and feel of it, was perfect, controlled and unhurried, even as her fingers tightened around him.

She spread her legs wider as he knelt between them, re-coiling as he brushed against her. He seemed to understand, when she jerked away convulsively, that she was already too aroused to survive his intended caress. He slipped into her, velvet-coated steel touching everywhere. Her heart stalled, twisted, and leaped as he lowered himself, covering her, his face and mouth hot in her hair. "There," he said, and began to move. That first time took her to an isolated plateau of sensation, where it had almost nothing to do with her and little to do with the identity of the man who was thrusting into her. Her cries never stopped, growing huskier, more in-tense as his rhythm became more urgent. She felt as if her skin were being speckled with hot ashes as he drove into her, felt herself attached to every fiber and muscle of his body, drowning beneath the steamy weight of him. She wrenched her head up and pressed her mouth into his shoulder to stifle a scream as her mind reeled away into splintering shards of light. Too soon . . . he held her, his hand supporting the small of her back as she reared upward, taking every inch of him, caught up in an explosion of nerve endings, curling and expanding, spiraling and cresting again and again. . . .

She came back slowly, unwilling to open her eyes, narcis-sistically aware of her pulped and heaving body, hardly sur-prised that he was still sheathed hard inside her. She brought her legs together to keep him and tried to control her breath-ing so that she could say something.

Paul lifted his head from her shoulder, kissed her slack lips, and pulled out of her. Momentarily abandoned, she raised herself on her elbows and found him sitting cross-legged beside her. His face and arms were covered with a fine moisture of sweat, but she wondered at the even rise and fall of his chest. He looked as though he'd scarcely exerted himself. It was almost with fear that she saw him reach out to run a tiny circle around her breast. Lightning jolted through to the top of her skull, with just that caress. She fell back and covered her eyes with her forearm, coming alive again, her skin jumping beneath his hands . . . kneading, soothing hands, drawing predictable, involuntary sounds from her; his face against her thigh, and then his mouth, biting, teasing, his tongue centered on the spot that snapped all the tautness

back and sent her whirling off into a new frenzy of shuddering.

Much later . . . how many times had she gone, come apart,
been shocked by her own vulnerability and Paul's tireless joy
in her? With infinite patience he tantalized and lured, releasing in her an unexpected capacity for sheer physical gratifi-
cation. Now again beneath him, filled to the aching innermost
parts of her and aroused to the point of pulling her nails
deeply across the skin of his back, she shouted into his ear.
His response was to smother her hips into stillness. He held
her there, shaking, until she fought to get away. And still he
held her, delaying her pleasure with minute calculated movements before letting himself go, his own climax indistinguishable from hers.

Finally, drained and sore, she curled away from him, drawing her knees together. The room was wrapped in colorless
shades; the world spun gently, and her eyelids seemed
weighted. She slept and woke up twice, the first time because
he was making love to her again, drawing her sweetly out of
a dream that he was making love to her. She slept with his
arm tucked under her, and when she woke up again, he was
gone.

49

☐ "I don't want to hear about Angela Wyatt," Lisa said.
She did. Frank was sitting at the kitchen table, a mug of
coffee in one hand, the other supporting the *Guardian*. His
attention was not wholly on the convoluted politics of the
Middle East. He was conscious of Lisa's moving about, opening cupboards aimlessly. Her continued presence in his flat
beguiled and engrossed him. It was as though she had just
walked in; after all this time there was not an item of her
clothing in his wardrobe, nothing left lying around. He accepted the inconvenience of her daily trips to her own flat
and her assumption that this was how he preferred to conduct

their affair. She was trying to work something out, throwing a shadow over him with the odd, baffled look that should have presaged a question. And here it was, an aloof statement that would enable him to meet her halfway.

"If you're looking for the marmalade, I keep it in the fridge," he said.

"I'm not hungry. Have you finished? We'll be late for the office."

An hour later she'd finished four slices of toast with strawberry jam, two cups of coffee, and was halfway through an apple. "Why didn't you tell me before?" she asked with her mouth full. "My brain has felt like mashed potato."

"You didn't ask me, and in any case, would you have believed me if I'd told you before you asked?"

"No. Maybe."

"Besides, I thought you had a thing about Oliver Jarman."

Lisa beamed at him. "You were jealous? It was nothing like that."

"All the same, I was jealous as hell. Not quite mashed potato," he said dryly. "More like mushy peas. Green."

His imperturbable honesty made her laugh. She could never take him unawares; he seemed to know too much. She felt not the slightest desire to shake off the possessiveness that left her emotions hopelessly tangled or the remorseless curiosity she had about the other women in his life.

When she told him about her evening with Elliot Stone, he'd injected humor into her telling of it by laughing.

"It's more than possible he'll leave the agency," she'd finished by saying, "I thought you'd be annoyed."

"About his leaving or molesting you?"

"Both."

"If he were here now, I'd beat him to a pulp for his stupidity more than anything else."

That was all. She, on the other hand, was not remotely amused by his account of his friendship with Angela Wyatt. Maybe because it meant a lot to him, much more than her indignant resentment had taken into account. She marveled at his seriousness and accepted what he told her without question. By the time he had finished telling her about Angie, she could even envisage sharing their closeness. Like Arion Angelou, Angela Wyatt was now a fact in her life.

Later, in his car, he said, "Arion has asked me to invite Angie along on Wednesday night."

"I can't believe he's really leaving. You'll miss him. *I'll* miss him."

He turned to glance at her, fearing he'd misread her mood. "I've told him we'll be over in September. Will you come?"

"Yes, please."

"And you don't mind about Angie?"

"Of course not. It took me a long time to ask you about her, and I'm not saying I'd be best pleased if you spent the night even in the same *house* with her, but that's finished."

"I'm pleased."

"Imagine how I feel."

He took his hand off the steering wheel and brushed his fingers lightly over her knee and up under the hem of her skirt. She didn't move, and he felt, rather than saw, her blush when he said, "I *know* how you feel."

Frank dropped her off before going on to park the car. She ran up the stairs, regretting it the moment she walked through the door. Ruby greeted her with "What time on a Monday morning do you call this?" and then: "Farley Esterhuys is on the phone. He's holding on *from New York!*"

Lisa's heart sank. "Frank will be here in a minute."

"Talk to him!" Ruby whispered.

"All right, my office." Still breathing heavily, Lisa dropped her handbag on the floor and eyed the telephone reluctantly before snatching it up. "Farley. Lisa."

"Hi, kid. Life so hectic over there you're out of breath this time of the morning?"

"Frank's just coming, Farley."

"OK. Listen, I want to tell you you did a great job on *Night Work.* Eighty-five thousand dollars is fifty thousand more than I thought it would go for."

"Uh, thank you." She looked up and gestured frantically at Frank, who had just walked in. Farley, being nice, complimentary. None of the customary needling was coming through. . . .

"Here's Frank."

She thought she heard him say, "Uh-huh," serenely. The sound chafed at her stunned ears. She went to stand beside the filing cabinets, well away from the desk, and listened to Frank's monosyllabic responses. Deadpan, he nodded once or twice, put in a few soft sounds of his own, and then hung up.

"Am I dreaming?" she asked.

"Not now, but maybe you were in New York. He's talking about coming over in October, not a word about Sidney, the lunch . . . nothing."

"He was even . . . pleasant."

"Steady on." He wondered why she was standing on the other side of the room. They were practically shouting at each other. "Shall we keep him?"

"What?"

"There are only two chairs in this office. There are five in mine; perhaps you'll find one more to your liking there. Come on."

Lisa followed him. When they were both seated and the door shut, he asked again, "Shall we keep him?"

The question seemed to surprise her. "Of course."

"I thought you loathed him."

"I do. What's that got to do with handling his books?"

"Not much, apparently. My head hurts—"

"I'm sorry, Frank. I know what I said about his agency, about Farley, and nothing's changed, except . . . me. The decision's yours. All I'm saying is that I won't give you a hard time if you decide to go on representing Farley."

"The decision's mine." He shook his head. "Fine. I'll let you know what I decide."

She turned to leave, and he pulled her back with "The strip clubs go with the job, you realize."

Her smile flooded across the room, and his hands went up to cover his ears. But not only did she *not* slam the door, she left it wide open. And when he took his hands away from his ears, he thought he could hear her humming on her way back to her own office.

50

☐ Cory would lie with Christos. This morning Ani had brought him the small chain and crucifix from Cory's room. The boy had worn it sometimes to please her, when she reminded him that it had been blessed by many churchmen and was a gift from his mother to wear, not to leave draped over the bedpost. The figure of the hanging Christ had been worn smooth with generations of touching, the thorns more like a blunted garland, the curled fingers rubbed into the horizontal edges, featureless. Arion ran his thumb over the sleek contours and thought of the beautiful child, also featureless, who would accompany them on the flight tomorrow. He thought of Ani's mother, crippled and cursing her God, and of Cory's mother, saying to him, "He's gone," as if Arion could call him back.

The day was nearly at an end. Arion had said his goodbyes away from the house, sparing Ani the endings. They would leave the house and everything in it, trusting Olga to bring with her, later, the things they would want, mementos they had brought with them all those years ago, photographs and some letters. She would bring Ani's aprons and the slippers Ani would leave, as she always did, inside the back door; the olivewood box with the silver clasp that held Paul's first scribblings, then Benjamin's; Arion's pocket watch, which hadn't made a sound for twenty years.

Ani was filling the kitchen table with food. There was a cautious rhythm to her movements, almost stealth, as though one false move would infect these last hours with more sadness than they could bear. Arion poured himself an early ouzo when she clucked at his efforts to help. "When do I let you pick the mint?" she asked, holding on to his hands. "You, you bring me the roots."

When Suzy arrived a few minutes later, she found Arion sitting on the back porch, a forbidden cigar clamped firmly between his teeth. "You know Ani doesn't like to see you smoking anymore," she scolded him.

Arion turned to see if Paul had arrived with her but saw only Ani in the kitchen.

"Paul will be around later," she said. "He's coming straight from the office."

"My son works too hard," he said mockingly, smiling at her. "He is not happy that you are coming with us tomorrow."

"Maybe he'll change his mind and come, too, you never know."

"He has said no definitely?"

"He's said nothing, Ari. Nothing since I told him." She

made a rueful face. "I hope he'll at least carry my suitcases out to the car tomorrow morning."

"Are you sure this is a wise thing?"

"I'm sure of nothing except that I'm getting on that plane with you whether Paul is with me or not."

"Suzy . . ."

"Shhh, it's done, Ari. It's not the easiest decision I've ever had to make, but it's one of the most clear-cut. Paul must decide for himself."

"In many ways he is not a clever man, this son of mine. His judgments are sometimes . . . strange."

"I love him, Ari. I wish I could tie him up and put him in my suitcase, but I can't. I don't own him any more than I own Benjamin. You understand that."

Her words were wistful and fierce, and he wondered if she fully realized what his son was capable of. Marrying Suzy, *loving* Suzy, was the one good thing Paul had done. Apart from Paul's business trips to New York, the two of them had not been apart for as long as Arion could remember. Why now?

Suzy's gaze went past him. "Scotia and Olga are here," she said, "and the children." She felt depleted by the knowledge that she was hurting Arion. If Paul decided not to accompany them to Greece, she would have to tell him the reason why. Until then there was a face to put on and this night to get through. "Ani has made enough food to feed an army. How many people are coming, Ari?"

"Just a few. You know them all: James Bonnier and his wife, Gina. Carlo Barzini and his family, Frank and—"

"Frank Sheldon?"

"Frank, of course, and his girl, Lisa. Also Angie."

Suzy tried, without success, to keep her voice from thickening. "Angela Wyatt. Does Paul know she's coming here?"

Arion frowned. What sort of question was that? His brain reacted sluggishly, touching on and dismissing the first obvious thought. Not Paul. Not another woman. It was too messy, too uncertain for this perfect son of his. . . .

"Ari, does he know she's coming here tonight?" Suzy asked again.

Her voice told him it *was* true. Arion bit down on his cigar, stunned. He knew it was true as surely as he knew he would not lie to her. "He knows."

Suzy got up. "Thank you," she said, pulling at the belt of

her dress. "Come inside now, Ari. Your guests are beginning to arrive."

Angie worked until the last possible moment, so that she wouldn't have to think about anything else. She read everything twice, maddened by the deathly quiet of the offices all around, itching to answer every call on the night line. When her own telephone rang, she considered not answering it. She lifted the receiver on the ninth ring. It was Jason, energetic and too friendly.

"You must tell me how you do it, Angie," he said.

"Good evening, Jason. What have I done?"

"Put the kibosh on Sidney's agency plans?"

"Is that a question? If I did, you should be pleased."

"Did you?"

"I'm not sure," she replied honestly. "What does Martin say?"

"My son could, as he puts it, 'do for you.' I'm not certain I'd do anything to stop him."

She couldn't make out whether or not he was genuinely annoyed. "Can we talk about this tomorrow?"

"What's wrong with now?"

"I have a . . . difficult evening ahead. No, not with my father. He's been remarkably controlled under the circumstances."

"Controlled." She heard the teasing irony in his voice and waited until he confirmed her suspicion. "Yes, he told me yesterday about the . . . arrangement he was going to discuss with you."

"It was hardly a discussion, but I'm not complaining. The decision he made was the one I'd hoped he'd make."

"Jarman trade as an independently run associate company, with you at its head. It was the least of all the evils as far as he was concerned."

"Oh. Did he say that?"

Jason relented. "He was furious about the ultimatum, naturally, but he's also impressed and slightly alarmed by your rapid success. I don't think it ever occurred to him that the trade side could be big business, and he wants to be associated with that, not necessarily financially but for the prestige. A thriving trade list would . . . complement his academic list. Of course, the fact that you auctioned the paperback rights of *Night Work* for eighty-seven thousand pounds helped;

before that, he had no way of knowing whether or not he could trust your judgment. With that one book, you've proved he can. I'm telling you all this because I know he didn't, and you need to be told that he's actually quite . . . excited isn't the word, but certainly intrigued by the prospect of Jarman trade as an associate company. If it works, he'll have all the kudos and none of the aggravation.''

''It'll work. Did he tell you that he wants to appoint me to the holding board as well?''

''Mmmm. Are you resisting that? Don't. Since you'll be running the trade side with total independence, he's probably decided that having you on the holding board is one way of keeping track of your activities. Give him that at least.''

Angie nodded. ''Of course.''

''Just remember, this hasn't been very easy for him either.''

''I know. Jason, thank you—''

''When will your difficult evening end? I'll pick you up.''

''Thanks again, but no.'' She grimaced at his sharp, irritated intake of breath. ''I'll call you tomorrow,'' she said, one eyebrow lifting in appreciation as he replaced the receiver without another word.

It was almost time to leave. She regretted now that she'd declined Frank's offer of a lift to Soho; she could have done with his company en route to the house she associated not with Arion Angelou or the dead boy he called his grandson but with Paul. He would be there tonight, and he would have made the decision on whether or not to accompany his wife to Greece. Angie couldn't even be sure that he would share the decision with her because she had no idea what effect their night together had had on him. It was possible that that one prolonged and varied sexual encounter had made the choice easier for him; she had joined with him not as an adversary, not as a victim of her own desire, but as a lover. Perhaps he'd come to see her willing surrender to the one demand he'd made, that she allow him to please her, as victory enough.

Outside, it had begun to rain, hard, spitting drops that splashed up and soaked her calves as she ran for a taxi. She couldn't remember now why she'd refused a lift from Frank. She enjoyed driving with him, especially these days. He was still quietly insistent that she use him as her chauffeur on her house-hunting expeditions. He had taken to driving at a snail's pace and with inordinate courtesy. When he wasn't talking about Lisa, he was smiling and touching some part of the interior of the car with his fingertips. The seat belt, lying diagonally across his chest, always came in for much petting. . . .

The driver heard her laugh and glanced back in the rearview mirror, surprised to see her smoking despite the notices on the windows.

Frank was waiting for her, standing out in the rain. "What are you doing?" she asked, taking his arm. His hair was wet; the shoulders of his jacket were sodden.

"I thought you weren't coming." He shut the front door behind them and wiped his face with a handkerchief. "Come and say hullo to Lisa."

"Why don't you take your jacket off and find a towel to dry your hair?"

He removed his jacket and hung it over the banister. "All right? Will you come downstairs now?"

There was a lot of noise in the kitchen, noise for the sake of noise, from perhaps thirty people in all. Arion blocked them all out, drawing a little "Oof" from her with his hug. Over her shoulder, he said, "Go and find something to dry your hair with, Frank," and to Angie: "You are the only person here who has been only once to Ani's, so Scotia does not know what you drink."

"I'd like ouzo, but it knocks me out."

"A *little* ouzo?"

"Why not?"

Ani was hovering beside the table; Susan Angelou was standing between two swarthy young men in tight trousers and short jackets. Paul Angelou stood with his back toward them all, alone. It took her a moment to realize that he was using the telephone.

"Mrs. Wyatt." Lisa had detached herself from another small group and was holding a glass out to Angie. "Your ouzo, not too strong, Scotia says."

"Thank you." There was a tense expression in the girl's eyes, not quite a smile on her lips. Too formal . . . Was she still not sure of Frank? Angie wondered. "I wish you'd call me Angie. Do you mind telling me if you've heard from Farley Esterhuys yet?"

Lisa didn't know what she'd been expecting, but it wasn't that. "Farley? Yes, uh, Monday. Frank has agreed to go on

handling his books. Neither of us is quite sure what happened
to change his mind.''

"Sidney fluffed it. Unfortunately I still have a few days of
him in the office. He does make my life hell.''

"I'm sorry.''

The ouzo stole through Angie's veins and pounced on her
tongue, and it didn't seem wrong to say, "I've never seen
Frank happier. I almost wish I did for him what you do.''

"Does he do for you what he does for me?''

Angie laughed, taken by the look of horror on Lisa's face
as the words came out. "No.''

Lisa groaned. "Did I say that?''

"I hope so. He's worth having the odd pang about.'' She
hesitated, then added, "But never about me.''

Out of the corner of her eye Angie saw Susan Angelou
break away from the two young men and start in her direction. She wore a pale apricot-tinted shirtwaist with pleated
satin binding around the wrists and neckline. She looked
tired, and there was almost a bravado in the way she walked,
quickly, head up, giving others a wide berth in case they
stopped her. She stopped herself, just short of joining them,
and Angie found herself holding the other woman's gaze,
immediately aware of why she'd pulled herself up so suddenly; this way would close every door. Angie shook her
head, meaning to convey "Not now. Not yet.'' Lisa frowned
in confusion beside her, and Paul was now leaning against
the refrigerator, watching them.

"I think . . . another drink,'' Angie murmured as Susan
left the kitchen, ducking out.

It went on. She picked up on other conversations and held
herself in, waiting for some signal that would tell her it was
all right to leave. Susan Angelou came back into the room,
to stand closer to Angie than to her husband. Ani went over
to her son and smoothed his tie, patting him, flat-handed,
like a child. He took a small dinner plate from her and held
it away from his body, as if it were an offensive object. Frank
wanted to talk about her immediate plans for Jarman's; Angie
found herself talking about shelves and working surfaces and
computer training for the staff, but so conscious of Paul's
physical proximity that she was scarcely aware of Frank's
attention being distracted by a softly spoken Frenchman. Two
separate convictions were forming in her mind. One was in
part a recognition of the other: that although what she felt for

Paul Angelou was not simply a compulsion that had ended with bodies in bed, he could never be enough for her, never have a true share in her life. And that she could begin to contemplate another certainty . . . that there were to be no more nights with him. . . .

She caught Arion's eye across the room and saw more than sadness reflected in the wide-eyed stare. Did he know? After three glasses of ouzo she felt she had no right to be in that room. She accepted a fourth from Scotia and took it to Arion.

He said, "You're knocked out."

"Almost. I must go."

"Yes."

Because he *did* know, he wouldn't keep her. "You're everything Frank says you are, Arion. I'm sorry there's no more time."

"*Ti na kanoume.* There will be other times." He took the glass from her, and she felt his breath expel in a sigh against her cheek as he kissed her.

When she turned, Paul had gone. He was waiting for her somewhere. A harsh urgency took her out of the room and up the short flight of stairs to the hallway. Both facing doors were shut. She opened the front door, left it open, and started down the path, eyes down in the dazzling darkness, expecting him but still jarred when he stepped out in front of her.

She couldn't see his face clearly. "No," she said, allowing him to draw her to the right, in among the shrubs against the wrought-iron boundary fence. He stopped in the dim encircling light shed by a streetlamp. There he kissed her. Her hands went up inside his jacket, around to his back, and she said again, faintly, "No."

He released her, then caught her wrist, bringing her forearm up between them. "This is going to hurt you."

The ferocious seriousness of his expression shocked her into a gasp of laughter. "Unless you're going to break my arm, this is as bad as it gets. I know what you're going to do. It's right. You knew it when you came to my flat that night. So did I."

"There's something else, Angela. Listen to me." He looked puzzled, afraid.

"I'm listening."

"Your daughter, the child you have been trying to find. I have found her."

"Let go." She jerked her arm and felt him tighten his grip.

"Let go, damn you! What do you mean, you've found her? How do you know—"

"Let me finish. I have to tell you this. At least . . . are you listening? She doesn't want to know you, Angie. . . ."

It began to rain again, quite suddenly. She lifted her face to stare at the canopy of branches above them, blinking. "Please . . . don't do this to me, Paul."

"They told her three years ago, when she was sixteen. They told her everything and asked if she wanted to know who her parents were . . . her mother. She said no. Don't look for her, Angela. You'll never find her."

She stood suspended between disbelief and outrage, quite sure that if she moved he would disappear, that this could only be a new permutation of the nightmare, one that even her tortured imagination had not come up with before. That these two utterly separate threads of her existence could be linked in any way, even by words, was at that moment obscene. Paul and her daughter—had they spoken to each other? How did he know about her? She heard herself asking, rationally, "Why are you telling me? Where is she? How did you find her?"

"It wasn't difficult. Do you believe me?"

Angie shook her head, his words starkly confusing. "No one would lie about—"

"Not even me?"

"I don't understand what you're saying." She could not look at him. "What have you done?"

"I've made sure neither you nor anyone else will find her."

The unreality of what he was telling her snatched her breath away. "Why?"

He tried to draw her closer, weakened by her unnatural calm. "To say I wanted a hold over you at the beginning would be putting it too simply."

"What do you mean?" she whispered. "You used my child to force me into . . . what?"

"I didn't think of it like that. It wasn't important then."

"Not important?" She echoed the words.

"I don't want you to look for her."

"You can't stop me. This has nothing to do with you. Where is she?" She now spoke so quietly that he could hear the sound of raindrops punctuating her words. "Please tell me."

He wondered if he had known from the beginning that

there would be no choice, that he would have to tell her, that she would never understand, and that she would never forgive him. "You can only hurt her by doing this."

"That concerns you? You're concerned about *my* daughter being hurt?"

"I am afraid for you and your daughter, Angela. Is that so difficult to believe?"

This is madness, she thought, what am I doing here? And then, incredibly, began to hear her own voice again, disembodied, *polite*: "I believe you're concerned about what you've done but only that and only for yourself."

"You're wrong."

"Then tell me where she is."

"Are you sure?"

"You have no right to ask me that!"

He shook her, suddenly afraid of what he heard in her voice. She wasn't seeing him, appeared to be hardly listening. "I have the right."

She choked on a laugh and turned her wrist, trying to break the contact between them. "Yes, I know. You love me. You've told me that."

He shook her again, needing her anger. "You don't believe me?"

"I believe you, only nobody else but you would call this loving. It isn't *love*. It's what you feel, but it isn't love. Are you going to tell me about my daughter?"

"Are you sure you want to know?" He waited. When she didn't answer, he reached awkwardly into his inside jacket pocket and drew out a bulky envelope. "It's up to you. The responsibility is yours. Here, take it. It's everything I know."

She took the envelope with her free hand, without looking at it. "Tell me where she is, Paul. I want to hear it from you."

"It's all there—"

"You did it, tell me!"

Faintly he could hear a car being revved, the sound of high-pitched laughter coming from across the road. "Do you remember that night at the Hall? Isobel Humphries . . . Lady Isobel's granddaughter? She talked about nothing else—"

"Theresa Hillier's daughter?" Slender, dark-haired. Had she seen her *once*? "That's a mistake."

"It was convenient at the time. No fuss, the family lived close by. Theresa couldn't have children of her own, and they were prepared to do anything for the sake of the child, even emigrate to France. Think about it.''

''No.''

''Think about it!''

''God damn you, Paul, let go!'' Now she had to get away. He was making it true, being there with her. She stopped struggling. It was too absurd to be taken seriously and yet . . . *''There?''* Trenton March. Angie's shock was twofold, knowing who the child was and with whom she'd grown up. Theresa and . . . she couldn't even recall the name of Theresa's husband.

''They must have decided it was the best way,'' Paul said.

He thought she was going to faint. Her wrist went limp in his grasp, and she dipped forward, her mouth opening in a silent cry. He kept her on her feet by holding her against his chest, his body shaking with her sobs, held her until his arms cramped, planted there, water splashing down from the leaves, coursing down his face into her hair. He could hear muted sounds coming from inside the house, the front door being shut and then opened again and wished now that he'd taken her farther away.

Angie heard him say, ''There's something else I must tell you, almost as difficult to say but you must listen to this, too. And believe me.'' She cringed, shuddering against him. He kept telling her to listen, as if she had a choice, and to believe him. ''I killed Cory.''

''No.'' She placed her palms against his chest and pushed herself away from him.

''I didn't kill him deliberately, but I was responsible for the fire in the warehouse.''

''Oh, God.'' Inexorably, like the rain running down her face, she was losing something.

''Are you listening? I am responsible for his death because I wanted to destroy the old man.''

''Don't tell me,'' she pleaded, even as her glance was suddenly pulled beyond him to where Arion stood, silent and white-faced, in the shadows of the porch. ''Please don't tell me.''

''I *am* telling you. Do you believe me?''

''I believe you.'' She looked around wildly, looked for Arion. But he'd melted away, left them. She blinked water out of her eyes. Had she seen him?

''Your daughter,'' Paul went on implacably, ''she is as dead to you as Cory is to the old man. I'm telling you about Cory because—''

"It won't work. You're giving me *your* life? Is that what you're doing? In exchange for what? I don't want your life. I've never wanted your life!''

"It's too late."

"Stay away from me—''

"And that's too simple." He smiled at her, a quick, disarming grin, swaying back as both her fists bunched and thudded into his chest.

"Stay away from me, Paul.''

She left him there in the pool of light and stumbled through the bushes and out of the gate. Ten o'clock in Soho—why was the street so *quiet*? She couldn't catch her breath, crouched, only shadows in the slanting rain, dead yellow lights. . . .

Theresa Hillier's daughter. The realization brought her around, facing the house, moving toward it again. She stopped at the gate, outlines suddenly filling up her clouded vision. The stooped figure of an old man was silhouetted in profile by the light spilling out from the hall, rigid as a cardboard cutout. And another, younger figure, seemingly ready to walk past him into the house.

Angie watched, a silent flickering black-and-white film rolling, the soundlessness of it drumming into her ears. She saw Arion rear up to his full height, his arm swinging up, fist blurring. In the sheeting rain she couldn't be sure, but it seemed as though Paul moved forward, inviting the blow. It never came. For a frozen moment they faced each other. Then Arion turned into the house and closed the door, throwing everything into darkness.

Angie backed away slowly, shaken by the unmistakable finality of this night. Then she began to run.

51

☐ Benn had been watching her for more than an hour. He sat, hidden by the bushy leaves of a rhododendron, on one of the three wooden benches lining the steep path from the crossroads to the cemetery. His lower back still ached from the walk, but his knees no longer felt as though they were hinged with rusty iron.

He had come to see Angie here because he needed to know that he had not misjudged her. He could not put a name to the fear that she would now turn her back on all this and simply leave. There was nothing to keep her. If she walked away, they would never see her again. . . .

Christina Isobel Hillier. Angie stood with her back to Calvert Hall. If she turned around, she could have seen the Hall beyond the trees to the right and the village, always looking threatened by greenery, on the left. A high autumnal sun glanced coldly off smooth black marbled headstones, at variance with the gnarled trees and flaked cladding on the vicarage walls. She stood facing the one place she wanted to see, Trenton March. She stood watching her daughter lead a blue roan around the perimeter of a small fenced-in field. When they had first appeared, the horse had been moving stiffly. Now it was beginning to prance. . . .

Tina. All the photographs Paul Angelou had given her with Beaumont Gracie's reports showed the girl laughing. The face held every previously imagined contour and brought a flaring recognition that this could *only* be her daughter. There was something of Belinda Jarman in the slant of the eyes, in the graceful movements caught and held by the camera.

Angie turned up the collar of her jacket and in the distance caught sight of a figure making its way slowly up the incline. At first she thought it was a child, then recognized Benn. She watched him, standing motionless. Beyond the bent figure lay a cruelly perfect landscape, glinting still with a heavy dew, green on shimmering green.

Crablike, Benn picked his way through the cemetery, head down, as though reading every name and inscription. Had he known? she wondered again.

"You should use a walking stick," she ventured, when at last he reached her. He wouldn't, of course. It would signal a defeat. "And you shouldn't have walked all the way up here."

"I needed the exercise," he replied, breathing through his nose. Angie couldn't see his face, but he managed to make the words sound capricious. "Her Ladyship would like to know if you're staying."

Staying. For lunch or overnight? "You came this far to ask me that?"

"I came to find out for myself."

"I'm staying, Benn. But not at the Hall. I'm going back to London."

He nodded, satisfied. More than that, he was relieved to see her tiredness, the bleak and openly grieving face. He said, "That's how it should be, especially as Oliver will not be returning to take up his . . . position." Angie had never before heard him use either of their names without the formal prefix.

It *was* as it should be, not only because of the girl down there. Like finding her daughter, running Jarman's was what she wanted to do, perhaps what she had always wanted to do.

Benn came to stand alongside her. "She's a very pretty girl," he said matter-of-factly. "Clever, too. She has your spirit but not your stubbornness. I'm talking about when she was younger, of course."

"I always had an idea you knew," Angie said sadly. "Would you have told me?"

"You didn't ask."

"If I had?"

"Yes. You see, I have the feeling that if I had remained that day at the clinic, if I'd stayed with you . . ."

Angie turned away. "No, it would have changed nothing." At least that man Gracie had been discreet. Unless she told her, her daughter would never know her identity. For that, and only that, was she grateful to Paul Angelou. He had left her with time, if nothing else.

Benn sighed into his shirt. "Come now. Come down with me. I've told Cook you won't be staying for lunch." Angie leaned away from him, her eyes fixed once again on Trenton March. "You can't do that. You know you can't. Come, I need your help to get down."

She couldn't control the smile that pulled at the corners of her lips. She had grown up being accosted by his brazen and invented distractions. When there was nothing else, he would send her on simple errands which he invested with almost mystical gravity. And she had fallen for the ruse each time, willingly, knowingly. He was doing it now, asking for her complicity, telling her that this, too, would end.

Isobel Humphries was being escorted across the driveway by a younger woman. Although Angie hadn't seen her for many years, she recognized Theresa Hillier. As the two women approached the fence, the girl waved her arms in delight, laughing as Isobel stopped to clap her hands with sweeping, exaggerated movements. As she watched, Theresa joined in, prompting the girl to take a bow before leading the horse over for their inspection.

To Benn's surprise, Angie laughed, too. She took his arm. Walking back down to the crossroads where Benn had left the Range Rover would bring her within five hundred yards of her daughter. He realized this, too, because he said, "We should hurry if you want to catch the twelve-fifteen back to London."

"I'm not taking the train. Someone's picking me up shortly. Don't think it, Benn. I would never do that to her."

"I didn't think you would," he replied huffily, sliding a couple of inches.

"Not as stubborn as I am, you say?"

"Not nearly. A pleasant and well-behaved young woman."

"And loved."

"Adored, as you can see."

"And good with horses. Look . . ." The girl was running easily alongside the horse, still laughing and calling out to Isobel and Theresa.

"Better than you were," Benn muttered. "Not a broken bone, all these years."

"That's good."

"There, is that the man who's picking you up?" There was nothing wrong with his eyesight. "Isn't that Mr. Corbett?"

"Jason. Will you come and spend a few days in London with me soon? I've found a house I like. We'll talk. I'll even listen."

He snorted, making her smile again. They would talk, and she *would* listen because she had nineteen blank years to fill in.

Jason came across to help them both down the last grassy slope. Benn said, "I hope you haven't been waiting long, Mr. Corbett." He'd always liked this tall man; he approved of the way Corbett was dressed, in shirtsleeves and worn corduroys. And he also approved of the fact that he drove a Bentley which was at least as old as the Range Rover.

"Is it safe for him to drive?" Jason asked as Benn disappeared in the Range Rover.

"Of course it isn't; he can hardly see over the steering wheel. But try telling him that."

"I wouldn't dare. Shall we start back and stop for lunch somewhere along the way?"

"Mmmm."

He let her be. He found the cricket summary on the radio and a half hour later pulled into the forecourt of a large country pub. "Warm enough to eat out?"

"I am. What about you?" She was wearing a pale gray pleated skirt and a roomy, wide-shouldered jacket; he'd brought neither a sweater nor a jacket with him.

He came back with two steaks and salads, French bread, and a bottle of Beaujolais. As he crossed the lawn, the wind took one of the paper napkins and deposited it near the goldfish pond.

"When did you last eat?" he asked, watching her slice into the meat.

"Last night, with you," she replied, surprised.

"Ah, you remember that. Do you remember what you ate?"

"Janine's bouzy chicken. Why?"

"I've missed you."

"What?" She picked up a chipped potato with her fingers and put it down again, confused. "I'm sorry . . . what do you mean?"

"It's been three weeks since you heard about . . . Christina. Your life has changed."

"*I* haven't changed."

"No? You've been walking around dazed."

"I'm sorry," she said again.

"Stop saying that," he said crustily. She was going through the motions once more, adjusting her response to the moment.

Angie knew what he was getting at but was at a loss to know how to reassure him; she was quite pleased to see a stain of anger darken his eyes and chose her next words deliberately. "I'm not looking over your shoulder for Paul Angelou if that's what you mean."

It wasn't good enough. "You're not tall enough to look over my shoulder."

She made a face at him, wondering at the ease with which she'd dismissed Angelou. He'd gone to Greece with his wife, as she'd known he would. Frank had been reluctant to pass on this information and had done so only at her insistence. She had had to reassure Frank, too, that the pieces of her life, scattered as they were, were for the first time, retrievable. Paul was still there, an unfathomable, lingering hurt; but it was over, and like the livid scar on her arm, that ache, too, would fade.

"Time is all I need, Jason. What I saw today, just now, is going to make everything easier."

"You don't understand, do you? *I* have to make it easier for you."

"Have to? I'm not looking for a guardian angel. You don't have to do anything."

He regarded her in silence. There was no resentment in her voice, just a quiet certainty. In her own way she was telling him that she could now stand on her own feet. She began to eat again, glancing up at him from time to time. She left some of the steak in order to finish off the salad.

"Nothing?" he asked at length.

Angie grinned at him. "Picking me up every time I fall over is no job for a grown man."

"Let me be the judge of that. I want to take you away for a few days. Will you come?" A gust of wind molded his shirt to his chest and lifted the hair away from his forehead.

"Where?" she asked suspiciously.

"We have some unfinished business, remember?"

"The goose?"

"That, too."

Jason. He was asking her to make a decision. It was easy. "Ah," she said.

"Ah, yes or ah, no?"

"What do you think?"

About the Author

Maureen Rissik was born in South Africa and has lived in England since 1960. Before turning to free-lance writing in 1985, she spent most of her working life in publishing. She now resides in Highgate (North London), where she is currently writing her second novel.

The *Choice* for Bestsellers
also offers a handsome and
sturdy book rack for your
prized novels at $9.95 each.
Write to:

The Choice for Bestsellers
120 Brighton Road
P.O. Box 5092
Clifton, NJ 07015-5092
Attn: Customer Service Group